WHITE NIGHTS, RED DREAMS

JOHN MORALES

ISBN: 978-1-7363826-2-2

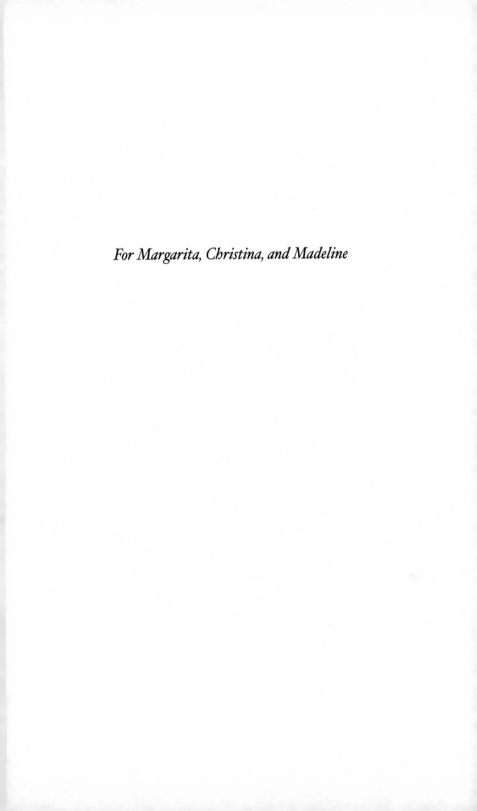

For Margarita, Christina, and Madeline

CHAPTER ONE

WHEN THE LOWER RIM OF the orange sun touched the sea, it was almost as if a signal had gone off to the senior banker. With his face toward the setting sun, he felt its warmth and basked in its momentary glow before acknowledging that there was also something poignant about the moment.

The banker turned to face the young woman that sat directly from him and tried to decide what to make of her. Her hair was thick, jet-black, and tumbled loosely around her shoulders, except for an errant strand that was hanging down one side of her face. Her blood-red nails seemed wickedly sharp. She was clearly quite confident about herself, and it was obvious that she felt smart enough to challenge anyone. She was a freaking turn-on. She was the sort of woman that would linger in his memory even if she had never spoken a word to him. The banker smiled in appreciation of her style.

"Thank you for coming on such short notice," she said.

The young woman who accompanied Yang Xu was short, thin, and wore stylish designer glasses that looked quite snazzy. Behind those glasses, her face radiated a diffidence or an impatience, which made her appear complicated and hard to please. And she had the most remarkable eyes; they were lighter in color at the top than at the bottom. She was fresh-faced and would easily attract many men, though she gave the impression that she would be tempted by few. Yang Xu and Kelly were part of today's new breed of auditors, in their twenties and thirties, with their sights set on money, very ambitious, and willing to travel.

After what seemed like an exceptionally long wait, a waiter finally appeared with a plate of grilled fish that he briefly showed to Kelly before placing it on a table beside her.

"Grilled seabass with basil, lime, black pepper, grated ginger, and olive oil," the waiter confirmed. Then, using a fork and starting at the tail end, he expertly peeled back the skin from one side of the fish and discarded it. Running a knife along the back of the fish, he separated the top and bottom fillets before plating both before her.

A second waiter quickly followed the first with two identical plates of seared tuna that he placed in front of Yang Xu and the senior banker. Their three wine glasses were then promptly refilled with more of the fine New Zealand sauvignon blanc that they had been drinking.

"Looks good, doesn't it?" the senior banker asked.

"Yes," Yang Xu agreed, looking up at him. The banker, who sat opposite her, was in his mid-forties, with salt-and-pepper hair that was carefully groomed. He had very dark, penetrating eyes that were not difficult to read. He was going to be easy to handle.

The two women had been sent by the newly formed board of the Holding Company that was headquartered in Boston. Their mission was supposedly to review the policies and procedures in place regarding operational risks in the Miami office. They claimed that they were sent to assess whether the policies were fully in line with those of the Group's and with what the Fed regulators wanted. But while what they said may have been partially true and made a lot of sense, he had also heard that the in-depth scrutiny that the two women were paying to the office implied that there must have been some other motive for their visit. The gossip in the corridors was that they were actually there to assess whether the work that was being done in Miami could easily be transferred to Boston. It was all about meeting the numbers, and if this was the real reason for their visit, then the senior banker knew that several hundred of his coworkers would probably soon be losing their jobs.

"Simplicity involves two major processes: eliminating redundant elements and integrating things to make them flow," Yang Xu explained. Then she took a sip of her wine and licked her lips.

Anxiety and unease were kicking in on the banker. Half-dreading and fully expecting the confrontation, he watched Kelly drink, seemingly in slow-motion, some of her wine after swallowing a mildly spiced morsel of her fish. The two young female executives seemed to be really relishing what they were devouring. And, like good corporate examiners, they avoided directly discussing anything related to their assignments while they were consuming their meals.

He looked at the two women and decided that he wasn't going to bring up anything that could interfere in any way with whatever it was that they were after. Perhaps it was better not to know what it was that they were going to do. He stared at Yang Xu licking her lips and imagined that those moist ruby red babies would probably taste like tart cherries.

So, after more than twenty years of service in Miami, he could soon be out of a job. The significance of the situation had finally become quite clear to him, and he had a hard time accepting that possibility. For a few moments, he sat motionless, gazing out of the window, not focusing on anything. Then the scent and smoke of the restaurant became nauseating to him. As the uncertainty and tension became gradually unbearable, he knew that it was time to leave. He always knew when his body or his mind had had enough.

He smiled at the two young women, both looking self-assured and quite determined, and pronounced how thankful he was to have been invited by them for such a sumptuous dinner. Then he signaled to the waiter, promptly paid the bill, and apologized for the abrupt ending, adding that he had a flight to catch.

"Oh, that is too bad," Yang Xu said. "We were luxuriating in your company."

"Yes, it's too bad!" Kelly chimed in.

"Well, I hope we will be talking again soon," he countered.

Would they be offering him a position in Head Office? It was very unlikely. He knew that the company's cost-cutting measures would include laying off the more senior employees of the bank.

"Definitely," the two girls simultaneously responded. "We will be in touch."

Then they watched him hightail it out of the restaurant. They couldn't help but laugh at him as he stumbled against a well-dressed woman in his haste to make a quick exit.

"Where could he be headed?" Yang Xu asked.

"Flight of fancy?" her companion volunteered, giggling.

"He certainly seemed a bit unbalanced," Yang Xu responded with peals of laughter.

CHAPTER TWO

AFTER AN OVERNIGHT LAYOVER in New York and a two-night stay in Moscow, the American senior banker finally arrived in St. Petersburg. Taking the taxi from the airport was uneventful, but when he was finally deposited in front of the Soviet-era hotel, he knew that it was going to be the beginning of a most remarkable experience. He felt like Alice going down the rabbit hole.

Built for foreign visitors—who by Soviet rules were required to stay in special locations under supervision—the hotel was a strange combination of Eastern and Western cultures meeting and influencing each other, as guests comingled looking to make deals. It was expected that each culture would experience the other in a way that permitted the development of some mutual understanding.

The hotel room that was assigned to him was large, dark, and in need of a very major facelift. When he first entered his room, he was totally disappointed. It was a genuine house of horrors! Everything in the room was black or deep crimson. Very old red velvet drapes adorned the large windows. The two dated love seats in the room were upholstered the color of faded dark red velvet, as was the matching bedspread on the king-size bed. The dressers, mica coffee table, and walls were all in black.

When he walked into the room it immediately felt strange, as though something didn't quite add up. It was like being in a dream where the things assembled didn't quite fall into place. He lay down on the bed and closed his eyes. His head was starting to ache, particularly in his temples. The only saving grace about this place was that at this period of the year when the White Nights occurred, the sun would not descend below the horizon so that the sky would never go totally dark. But one thing was certain, and that was that he needed to quickly leave the very depressing room. So, resolutely turning his back to it, he set out at once down the corridor toward the elevators, determined not to deviate in any way until he got to the bar.

. . .

THE DRAB HOTEL BAR WAS LOCATED IN THE LOBBY. There were no booths, no fine leather seating of any kind, and certainly no cocktail umbrellas adorning exotic drinks. Straight vodka and scotch ruled here, and the prices for the drinks were fair. Many of the non-Soviet bankers attending the conference were already drinking heavily. No doubt they were also trying to forget the dreary confines of their dingy rooms. How could anyone sponsor a banking conference in such a gloomy place?

From the list of attendees, he already knew that there would be three times as many male bankers as those of the fairer sex at the conference, and some of the latter were already in the lobby bar accompanying their neat scotches or wine with cigarettes.

Stimulated by the smell of scotch and cigarettes, like Proust with his madeleines, he was ironically now feeling nostalgic about his college years. To a male college student in New York City then, the American dream was drinking booze and listening to cool jazz music with a liberated woman. Even after all of those years, he could still remember tasting her sweet intoxicating breath exuding from the scotch that mingled with her Marlboro cigarettes. But that was a long time ago, he quickly realized, as he glanced at the faces of the women in the Soviet bar. What were the chances of becoming intimate with any of them in this short conference? He was never all that great at breaking the ice. He ordered a vodka martini and moved toward a cluster of bankers, the usual international mixture in suits and ties. They were all wearing their name tags. Some of these attendees were Senior Vice Presidents from major European banks. Two middle-aged men in dark suits who appeared cheerful and slightly drunk were from Den Danske Bank, which was the correspondent bank that the American's Miami office used for Danish krone transactions. The Danes had the reputation for being the happiest people on the planet.

"Hello gentlemen," the American banker began, "how do you like the lovely accommodations?"

"Very nice," responded one of the Danes sarcastically. "So, you are from Miami?" The man had taken a quick glimpse at the American's name tag.

"That's right. Have you been to Miami?"

"Yes, and I really enjoyed it."

"You know," the American responded, "we use your bank as our cash correspondent for our krone activity."

"That's great! I'm on the business development side of the bank. That's why I am here."

"It should be an interesting conference."

In the small gathering, there was also a senior banker from the Netherlands and two bankers from the Royal Bank of Scotland.

"There are not that many women at this conference,"

the American commented to the others in mild disappointment.

"No, but I suspect we will be seeing more of them tomorrow when the conference begins," replied the Dutchman optimistically. "Do you see the Oriental woman over there?" he continued. They all looked over at the only Asian woman in a cluster of female attendees.

"Yes," one of the happy Danes said encouragingly, waiting to see what the Dutchman would have to say about the very attractive woman.

"Well, I have become acquainted with her. Gentlemen," he said, "I've developed a lovesickness. A lovesickness. When I first saw her, I immediately knew that I had to have her. I wanted her, and I told her so. And, if she would just baptize me by sprinkling some of her holy water on me, I would then be saved in this godforsaken land."

In front of senior bankers from leading European banks, the Dutchman revealed, without the slightest hesitation, without any embarrassment whatsoever, that he had asked the lovely Asian banker to anoint him with her holy water. It was unbelievable! The American couldn't help but laugh out loud at the kooky man. The Danes and Brits didn't say a word. They just looked at the man in amazement. You had to wonder how the Asian woman must have reacted to the mad Dutchman when he had approached her. The American had never heard of anyone ever admitting to an audience—especially at a banking conference where everyone tended to be significantly more conservative and reserved than the general public—such a crazy thing. Balls! This guy had quite a pair. He knew what he wanted and he wasn't embarrassed to admit it. And, to everyone's amazement, the man wasn't even drunk. Balls! The guy had balls.

"What did she say? How did you ask her?" the American egged him on. They all wanted to know. They were all curious to hear how she had responded to the madman's request.

"She didn't say anything. But I will continue to press her. I really want her!"

The Dutchman was evidently a head case. The American had had enough and needed to get out for some fresh air, out into the night lights of St. Petersburg, out unto the cobbled streets. In this place, reality was becoming distorted, the characters were being driven to madness.

St. Petersburg, part of Tsarist Russia, had the great imperial schools for the performing arts. Perhaps he would discover out among the night strollers a lovely ballerina who descended directly from one of those famous dancers that had performed during the golden age of the Imperial Ballet. Maybe he would be lucky enough to find one who was a direct descendant from someone who danced in the Dying Swan with the great Anna Pavlova. He had eaten an Anna Pavlova once in New York's Russian Tea Room, with the meringue-based bottom, whipped cream, and fresh fruit!

But the American banker never quite left his hotel that first night, because two curvy killers, femme fatales that he had not previously noticed, had suddenly caught his attention. And, to be frank, he was quite fascinated by them. One of them bent down and there was a moment of discrete cleavage in the dark V of her neck-line. What the hell, he thought. He was shaking his head, then using his fingertips he began massaging his temples in gentle circles. Deadly dames and extra dry martinis, all in good fun, and the ladies made it very clear that they were interested. He was ready to enter noir heaven, ready to explore what the mean streets of St. Petersburg had dragged into the bar. They were not drop-dead-gorgeous girls by any means, but so much had happened in these last twelve hours that he was game for anything.

As they had smiled at him, he didn't hesitate to move immediately toward the red girls, the comrades. He was now feeling rather optimistic about a fantastic finish to his first St. Petersburg White Night. He liked the fact that the girls were forward because he was never any good at breaking the ice for a casual pickup, but they were forward because he was an obvious target, a foreigner, and he had no illusions. This was clearly to be a business transaction, but they also seemed genuinely friendly. There was plenty of smiling and giggling because of their awkwardness in conversing in English. He imagined that they really liked him. He was of the right age and appearance, and nothing like those despicable fat, bearded Finns that often came to St. Petersburg with nothing but negotiating terms for sex on their minds upon immediately entering the hotel lobby. They were opportunistic parasites demanding sex from the young Russian women in exchange for their filthy Finnish markka. It had been revolting to him when he first noticed it. He didn't want to pay for sex. He didn't want to be like the despicable Finns. But if the girls approached him and drank with him, and thought that they were ready to get the better of this simple American, then, he rationalized, he would be fine with it. For one thing, he really wanted to get to know the women, and they seemed to genuinely like the idea of getting it on with him. After all, America is where they really wanted to be, and here was a chance to be with one in the flesh. Yes, he thought, it would be great to have sex with them, with the red girls.

"What is your name?" the slimmer of the two girls asked. This made both girls giggle and made him smile. It was a straightforward, obvious first question to ask.

But it seemed funny to the three of them for no particular reason. What is your name? What is your name?

"James," he responded, and this made them giggle again. There was no heavy Russian deep thinking here. No baring of one's soul was required. He could have easily said "I am the Idiot," and they would have given him the same response. Who cared about Dostoevsky?

"Hello," one of them began again. "I am Anna, and this is Irina. How are you, James?"

He liked drinking the smooth Russian vodka which was made from the finest grain alcohol and crystal-clear water from Siberian springs. Was that just propaganda, he wondered?

"Happy. I am happy to be here with two beautiful Russian women." This made them happy to hear too! The thought of pouring Russian vodka on their lovely naked bodies and then licking it all up just came into his mind.

"Where are you from, James?" he heard one of them ask. He had been lost in thought, imagining that he was already licking lower down their bellies.

"America," he said and smiled as he continued to imagine himself licking the vodka off their lovely pert breasts. "Faisons l'amour," the American suddenly said to the two girls.

"What?" came from the girl named Irina.

"French is always found in the great Russian novels," the American responded.

"Ah!" said Irina, looking perplexed.

"But what does that mean?" asked Anna.

"Faisons l'amour means let's make love. There is always passionate love in those great Russian novels too. I am a blue American," he volunteered. His face was clearly red from drinking too much, and from being embarrassed by what he was imagining doing to them.

"That's quite interesting! You say that you are a blue American?" And then there was more giggling from the girls.

"And you are red girls! I love red girls!" He was now laughing again as he said this, and Anna took her cue.

"Shall we go to your room, blue sir?" she asked.

He didn't need to be asked twice. He took Anna's hand and walked with her out of the bar and into the lobby where the elevators were located. He didn't even say goodnight to the other girl. It hadn't occurred to him to do so. He also didn't notice if Anna had. But these girls knew each other, and business was business. The tall, fit American banker and the slim Russian strawberry blonde made quite a pair. He glanced at her to see if he could determine how she was feeling, and he was quite pleased to notice that she still had a smile on her face.

When he opened the door to his room he remembered again how dismal it had appeared to him when he had first seen it earlier in the day. Even after all that vodka the room still looked dreadful, like a Victorian set for a Count Dracula movie. Dreadful! But the girl wasn't at all shocked by it. The midnight light from the still lingering sun made it bright enough in the room so that the additional lighting of lamps was not required. The soft natural light in the room softened the look of the horrible décor.

He stripped and lay face-up on the bed, waiting for her to come out of the bathroom. The very slim blonde then came out in matching white panties and bra. Very nice! What he saw was very pleasing.

"So, how are you, James?" She kissed him with affection.

He responded by giving her tender little kisses on her cheek and her neck. He then took her hand and guided it to his lips. He kissed her hand, and then he had her gently slap his face.

"What would you like me to do to you?" she asked, smiling, wanting to know what turned the American on.

He was always embarrassed by his sexual feelings. In a strange way, he was actually more concerned about disappointing her.

They were randomly paired, not even acquaintances. It was not very sharp her slapping with the open hand, and it didn't even feel like a slap at one's pride. There would be no tears resulting and no pain. They were effortless, careless strikes with the front and the back of her hand. What a foolish American, he imagined her thinking.

"You really like me slapping you?"

"Yes," he nervously responded. And then when he was nice and hard she mounted him. Then she deliberately slapped him harder and gave him what appeared to be a Russian reprimand, maybe the way that he wanted. Then he started to emit a sort of chortle, intermittent at first but soon growing in frequency before developing into a full-fledged uncontrollable laughter, as he orgasmed. They were both laughing then. Nothing made sense.

"Ok, James?" she asked.

"Yes," he said. There was nothing more to be said. She carefully got off him, and then went into the bathroom. He quietly lay there waiting for her to do whatever it was that she needed to do. Then he silently watched her as she began to get dressed. When she was ready to leave, he put on his shirt and thanked her again. Anna gave him a little smile, pocketed the money that he had given her without counting it, and left.

CHAPTER THREE

Li Xiang had just had his tattoo finished in the old part of the city. Though he had left home quite early in the morning, it was already late in the afternoon by the time that he got up from the leather chair. But it didn't matter because he wasn't going to meet anyone. Li Xiang didn't have family in Shanghai and had only a handful of friends who had made the exact same journey that he had made years ago from his village in Shandong province. He turned twenty-nine on this inauspicious day, that was unusually warm for Shanghai at this time of the year.

The skyscrapers were casting their long shadows over the busy streets when he finally stepped out of the tattoo parlor after spending several painful hours with the artist. His new tattoo was of the revered jade dragon under a turbulent sky. Li Xiang needed a cigarette but hesitated before lighting one as he stared for a moment at the color of the dragon's eyes under the ultraviolet neon sign of the establishment. For the Chinese, dragons symbolized wisdom, strength, and power. It was believed that this symbol brought luck and prosperity to persons sporting it.

Li Xiang looked back into the parlor and couldn't believe the number of people that were still waiting to have their tattoos done. There were several young college students with spiky hair and facial piercings. There were also young women, scantily clad, showing-off their colorful tattoos. It was hard to imagine that in Shanghai alone there were now more than one hundred such tattoo parlors. China was rapidly changing, he admitted to himself as he started his trek along Changle Lu Street, one of Shanghai's most fashionable. Whatever he had thought about the Communist system, it was now time to reconsider it. He hoped that the changes he was now witnessing in China would lead to new freedoms and a better quality of life.

As he walked across the broad boulevard and passed the gardens, he couldn't help but notice the vast number of young professionals that resided in Shanghai today and that were now in their early thirties. They had grown up in an economy that grew faster than at any other time in the country's modern history. This had amazed him since he knew people of the previous generation had grown up during a famine. His parents and countless others like them had been forced to work as farmers in the countryside or in factories when they ventured into the big cities. But the young professionals of today weren't just a generational gap away. These young people that were born after 1980 had never experienced food rationing. They were raised after China had established new reforms after the foreign markets had been opened. This new generation was also more than just a wealth gap away from their predecessors. They had a significantly better education, differed vastly in their values, and had an informational gap that was widening exponentially every day so that they now felt that they had nothing in common with their ancestors of the previous generation. This relationship gap was a new cause for concern in modern China's society.

As Li Xiang walked along the street he passed by carts of housewares, vegetables, fish, and live chickens that were beheaded and plucked right on the spot for the local housewives. In the very late evening, the corner of Changle Lu and Fumin Lu came alive with carts of wonderful smelling street food, and among the vendors, occasional cautious offers of hashish were made to the Westerners. The foreigners had another name for Changle Lu Street: they called it the Street of Eternal Happiness.

Li Xiang continued wandering along the street that was now lined with dumpling stands and street-side noodle vendors. He stopped by one of the stands and ordered a variety of steamed dumplings. The dumplings were served in chili oil. From there he moved on to a hot-pot stall where there was an offering of succulent meats and vegetables that were ready to be dipped into cauldrons of broth of a rich deep red color. Three very pretty girls with pinned-up hair, students from the local university, were standing next to Li Xiang snacking on twice-cooked pork that was served with dry-fried green beans. Also, on their plates were chunks of tofu, accompanied by chili bean paste. The vendor at the noodle stand tried to offer the dumpling-eaters dan dan noodles that were simmered with ground meat and pickled mustard greens. But neither the girls nor Li Xiang could be tempted.

It seemed as though little time had lapsed by before Li Xiang noticed that the sun had become totally eclipsed. Everything seemed to have moved a little faster while he had been enjoying the age-old delights served on this Street of Eternal Happiness. "The pace of life is a matter of time," he remembered his father always saying.

Moving on, the Xuhui district gradually changed so that the stands gave way to trendy boutique fashion shops that sold luxury items. Western designers were flocking to open ever more expansive flagship stores in this part of the district. The best shopping could be found at the smaller boutiques that carried quirky local brands with creations by emerging local designers.

The Xuhui district boasted of having some of the most influential and affluent executives living in apartments along Changle Lu's side streets. Li Xiang had followed one of these rich executives on one recent weeknight. The man had just dropped off his girlfriend from a night out on the town. She was a sweet-looking girl with a pale dimpled face, slim white arms, and wore a striped cotton blouse over a tight-fitting black skirt. He could still hear the crisp sound of her high heels breaking over the old coble pavement. Li Xiang recognized Mei Ping immediately. He had seen her on another occasion on his way to work. They were from the same hometown. But poor boys never turned out better than expected, and he was not surprised when she failed to acknowledge his presence. He could then sense in the young woman's face a determination to fulfill the possibilities of life, and in her life, he had become insignificant in the shadow of the evening. He smiled and thought of her as a "skin-job." That was the derogatory term for the bio-robotic androids that were virtually identical to human beings in science fiction novels. These human "replicants" were detected by their lack of emotional responses.

After the executive dropped off Mei Ping, Li Xiang

expected that the young woman would soon be facing loneliness and emptiness in her finely furnished apartment. That was the best that the rich executives could offer these young girls in exchange for their relationships. Mei Ping had come to Shanghai, like many others, full of hope. But vulnerable and naive individuals morphed into a familiar type. Li Xiang had felt sorry for her.

The old executive that Li Xiang had followed that night seemed pleased enough after probably having stuffed his oversized gut at some fancy restaurant in the company of his mistress. Afterward, the man had parked his expensive foreign-made car a block away from his girlfriend's house. Li Xiang had taken an interest in the executive because of the way that he had mistreated his companion in the parking lot, with an arrogance that was meant to demean and to humiliate her. It seemed to Li Xiang that this was the type of rich executive that enjoyed wielding power over anyone who was emotionally or financially dependent upon him and most susceptible to his will. Power, money, prestige, and position in the hierarchy were all-important in the executive's domain; love and compassion counted for a lot less.

Li Xiang despised the type of man that he saw in the executive. Infuriated by the man's behavior, Li Xiang approached him silently from behind, after he had dropped off Mei Ping. It was evident that the old man had not expected to be attacked on the fashionable and well-policed street. It was more shock than fear that the man must have felt when he was taken from behind at knifepoint. Li Xiang removed the executive's Rolex watch and his fine leather wallet. Surprisingly, the executive had offered no resistance whatsoever. Li Xiang removed the money from the wallet and then gave the man his wallet back. The man's identity card showed that his name was Mo Yan.

Li Xiang had initially only intended to put fear into the executive and wasn't really after his money. But then it dawned on him that the only thing that would really hurt the man would be a financial hit because money was probably the most important thing in the executive's life. Money brought him power.

Provoked, Li Xiang slapped the executive hard on the face when the man had sneered at him with disgust. These rich pricks expected to be entitled to everything, Li Xiang thought resentfully. Then Li Xiang quickly turned his back to the man and ran off. That incident had happened several nights ago, and he didn't think much more about it, except that there was a scarred, flea-bitten, grinning tomcat that had witnessed it all. After having been spotted, the cat seemed to have spookily disappeared into thin air.

· · ·

SECURITY IN THE CITIES WAS TRANSFORMING. THERE were chengguan auxiliary parapolice roaming the streets of China's big cities day and night, helping the local police to keep order and helping to keep the nouveau riche safe. These chengguan guards were hired and organized by local governments to handle various urban problems under laws so vague and general that there was little restraint in their power. These men dispensed physical justice on the streets with brutal force on anyone that they judged to be out of compliance with how they interpreted the laws.

As Li Xiang turned the corner, he quickly glimpsed back to see if the three men dressed in chengguan guard uniforms were still following him. He had first noticed them when he had purchased the dumplings. The men had scrutinized him from a safe distance with acute suspicion. He didn't know why they should be on his tail, but he wasn't about to ask. These types of men allowed for few explanations.

Right now, he had only caught sight of a tall, broad man wearing a brown leather jacket. But he didn't have the slightest doubt that the man was one of the three that had been following him earlier. His sheer size, shaven skull, and prominent nose were unmistakable. So was his determination. He didn't appear to be walking fast, yet it was clear that he had quickened his pace to keep up with Li Xiang. His two other accomplices for now were nowhere to be seen. But that didn't mean anything.

Li Xiang turned off the busy shopping street and quickened his pace. After briskly walking for another fifteen minutes, he came into a large square that was packed with young people. This market square was full of restaurants and produce stalls that were selling fruits, vegetables, and live seafood, but also carried some of the foulest odors in all of Shanghai. Part of the stench came from the putrid food and discarded animal parts that were tossed into open bins. The noodle stalls and the other small businesses that were slinging buckets of dirty water onto the sidewalk every day didn't help. The sickly-sweet smell of the rotting garbage didn't add to the neighborhood charm.

Li Xiang moved quickly to the far end of the square where there was a hostel with a neon sign written in English and Chinese. The establishment was offering rooms to rent, inexpensive rooms with poor air conditioning. It had been promoted as a cozy hostel in a great location, near food stalls and convenient shopping. Supposedly, it was a fun place to meet people. Li Xiang considered for a moment his options: taking a room in the hostel to wait out the time in hiding or continuing his evasions through the streets. He decided that he would rather take his chances outdoors, so he moved past the hostel and turned right at the next intersection.

Light, misting rain started just as he entered the dark street. Halfway down the block he held his breath for a moment and pressed himself against the façade of an old brick factory building that had been abandoned. A chill of terror coursed through his veins. He felt drained. He didn't know if he was still being followed; all that he could hear were the dripping sounds from the rain. A white van suddenly entered the street from the far side. The van, with its high beam lights turned on, moved down the street toward Li Xiang at an unusually slow pace. There was no place for Li Xiang to advance as the van continued its approach toward him. Then, when the van was at no more than ten paces away, four men jumped out of the vehicle and began rushing after him. The big man with the leather jacket and his two other accomplices were now also approaching him from the rear side of the street. There was no way out now for Li Xiang. The notorious chengguan guards had him surrounded, and the big man with the shaved skull was the first to attack.

The big brute opened his mouth and said, "Mo Yan sends his regards." Then, as the big man began to assault him, Li Xiang realized that the executive he had robbed several nights ago was now exacting his brutal revenge. The big guard's oversized fists knocked him to the ground after two swift blows to the head. Then the two accomplices came forward to beat the defenseless man with their fists and to kick him in his ribs and back with their heavy leather boots. The badly beaten Li Xiang was bleeding profusely, but there wasn't any letup from the guards. Only the sight of some boisterous students coming around the corner made them pause in their battery of the man. The four guards then retraced their steps to the van, and quickly put their vehicle into reverse so that they could leave without having to face the students. The big man and his two henchmen also quickly took to their heels, following the van up the street. Only Li Xiang's lifeless body remained in a pool of blood for the students to find.

When the van reached the street corner, the driver signaled to an executive dressed in a dark suit who had been standing there casually smoking a cigarette. The well-dressed man had witnessed the incident from afar, and now the driver was letting him know that everything had been executed according to plan. After the driver of the van gave the executive the thumbs-up, he drove on. The executive then made his way to his Mercedes Benz, which had been parked just a little further beyond the intersection.

The guard with the shaved skull eventually reached the same intersection, and then he too made his way to the executive's car. But his two brutal accomplices didn't follow him. They just continued running on ahead.

"Mr. Yan," the ruffian began, addressing the executive through the car's open window, "there was no problem in retrieving your timepiece. Here is your Rolex. Li Xiang will no longer be keeping time!"

Mo Yan looked at the man and nodded, then gave the man an envelope filled with cash in compensation for the dirty work.

"He has repaid his debt. The slate has been wiped clean just in time before the Dragon Boat Festival," the old executive said sarcastically, almost in a whisper, as though to himself. Mo Yan then extinguished his cigarette in a sudden fit of anger. He pressed his thumb hard into the butt as though he wanted to be totally certain that the fire had been completely obliterated, just as Li Xiang's life had been snuffed out. He then closed the window to the assassin and asked his driver to move on. The tall assassin placed the envelope inside the inner pocket of his leather jacket, watched in silence as the Mercedes Benz sped off, and then slipped back into the dark street where he quickly disappeared into the shadows.

Lurking in the shadows, after spraying his territory, the pungent-smelling, muscular, stone-cold killer-and-eater tomcat settled in, and with a deft crunch decapitated his dinner.

CHAPTER FOUR

On the morning that the American banker attended his first IBC conference, it was the association's tenth in St. Petersburg. That morning the representatives were invited to a breakfast that was hosted by the IBC at the hotel's restaurant. Coffee, orange juice, and small pastries were in the offering. However, watching the babushkas pouring coffee and orange juice from buckets into well-polished tureens was not a very appetizing sight for the bankers. While the coffee turned out to be better than expected, the orange juice was far from palatable.

By 9:30 am most of the two thousand participants had moved from the dining room into the hotel's largest conference room. All of the participants were offered headphones which allowed for the simultaneous translation from Russian to English for all of the guest speakers. Based on what they were now hearing through their headphones, the agenda for this year's meeting promised to be very entertaining. The translations, however, were absolute gibberish.

"The steps taken by the regulators to improve the quality of bank supervision, consolidated supervision of bank groups and holdings: control of the bank risk management, development of the competitive environment based on greater transparency of the credit institutions and a stronger market discipline of the bank service market participants will have a substantial impact on the banking system development now and in the nearest future."

This was a very ambitious opening sentence and was probably indicative of the type of presentation and translation that the participants could expect to hear throughout the conference. "Also, on the agenda," the translator went on, "would be the committee's recommendations on mechanisms for insurance against political risks and other systemic risks in Russian transactions." This last sentence brought a warm round of applause from the audience. It was a much better translation effort. The message conveyed was that Russian President Vladimir Putin sought to reassure investors that he was committed to building a "new economy" through liberal reforms and privatization.

Wanting to first address the many complaints about business practices in Russia, the government spokesperson stated that Vladimir Putin wanted his administrators to press on with the sale of non-strategic state assets, fight corruption, reduce red tape, strengthen property rights, and cut Russia's reliance on energy exports. The conference broke at 4:00 pm. All of the participants were invited to an excursion and dinner at the Ekaterininsky Palace that night.

The Ekaterininsky Palace had been the summer residence of the Russian tsars. The sun was still shining brightly, and there was cheerfulness and lightheartedness in the air as the bankers arrived for what they hoped would be a sumptuous dinner. Everyone hoped for a new era of prosperity for the country after the expected financial reforms.

The lavish buffet dinner was laid out on tables in the most beautiful and spacious room of the palace. The impressive grand ballroom had a spectacularly painted ceiling under which the conference participants were directed to congregate.

Vladimir Putin and his wife Lyudmila were not expected to attend the dinner. So, the traditional bowing and kissing that was customarily bestowed upon the host and hostess of the traditional feast would not be taking place tonight. Perhaps after the caviar, cold meats, pickles, and sausages were consumed, and after they were all washed down with large quantities of good French Bordeaux wine, there would be plenty of kissing and something more than kowtowing between guests. At the suggestion of the President, the conference participants were treated to fish dishes that were highly valued because they were from the Volga River. They were much more expensive than the wild game that would be typically offered at these types of events.

Well, if Mr. Putin wasn't able to attend the IBC dinner, it didn't matter because Mr. Elgar from Standard & Poor's, the business intelligence corporation, proved to be very entertaining. He was a short man of average build, very young-looking. He sported a beard in order to add more weight to his presence. He was a transplant from London, residing in Moscow, and now visiting St. Petersburg for the conference. Mr. Elgar held the post of Managing Director for the Russian office. The American, like most of the other attendees, thought at first that this was probably a very cushy position. However, Mr. Elgar was quick to reassure them that it wasn't. The poor man had to tread very softly in Moscow because the rating of financial institutions in Russia was a very dangerous job.

THE SECOND DAY OF THE BANKING CONFERENCE BEGAN with a fascinating presentation by a representative of the

Federal Assembly. The representative began by stating that in the past few months Russia's president, Vladimir Putin, had been busy campaigning for foreign investments for various sectors of the Russian economy. The strategy behind the new plan for improving the investment climate in Russia was tied to easing access to strategic industries for foreign investors. However, the representative candidly admitted that no proposals had been made to increase the level of investor protection in cases where deals failed! This brought quite a chuckle from some of the participants in the audience. Many of them came from financial institutions that had recently had major financial losses related to failed investments in Russia in both the public and private sectors. The American banker from Miami represented many private banking clients that were among those unfortunates.

THAT SECOND DAY OF THE CONFERENCE, THE attendees were treated to a sumptuous dinner cruise on the Bay of Finland. The cruise had a very good western-style rock band that played well-known international tunes that kept the bankers eating, drinking, and dancing throughout the night.

There was plenty of champagne and good Russian vodka available on the magnificent yacht, and it was welcomed because the evening was rather cool for a summer night. One of the Russian bankers who had obviously been drinking quite heavily was seen whispering sweet words of affection to an equally inebriated Russian female counterpart. Curiously, as she was listening to him, she was crying, no doubt a consequence of the large quantities of vodka that she had already consumed. Notwithstanding, she was still sober enough to give an interested glance to the American banker, who sat directly across from her. The American, champagne flute in hand, was quite amused by how the Russian pair openly manifested their passion. While the Russian ardently kissed the woman, she gave the American a quizzical look that seemed to suggest, "What is to be done with such a man?" She was laughing and crying while the Russian lustily pressed kisses on her neck. But soon her partner realized that she was not responding the way that he had expected. Her tears were there alright, but she seemed to be distracted. When he turned to see what had been the cause, he was surprised to see the American amusing himself at their expense.

"Glupyii amerikanskii," the American heard him say to her. And this made her burst into laughter. They were both looking at the American now, she with amusement and he with annoyance. The American just smiled in response. He drank a little more of the champagne and then tried to ignore them. The Russian promptly began kissing the woman again, while his partner continued to stare at the American, but this time with a smile on her face. "Stupid American," he thought he heard her say. But her eyes still betrayed a keen interest in him. The American finally became bored with the scene and did the only sensible thing that he could do, he grabbed a plate full of hors d'oeuvres and stepped out onto the deck.

It was still much too light out to see any stars, even though it was getting close to midnight. Outside, the American found himself again close to the little gathering of Danish and Dutch bankers. After all the booze they had obviously been drinking, he found it amusing that they too were now discoursing on love. The happy Danes were listening again to the senior Dutch banker who was boasting about how he had still been pursuing the Asian woman. The female in question was now visible, as she was standing about twenty feet away port side. Upon closer scrutiny, she seemed to be in her early thirties. She had jet-black hair that was face-framing, wore dark-rimmed, oversized glasses, and even from where they stood she seemed quite charming with her trendy look, which came across as very sexy. The Dutch banker was six feet four inches tall and at least twenty years older than her.

Earlier in the evening, the American had been speaking to the man about classical music while they were waiting for the bus that was to transport them to the port. The Dutchman had been talking about Claudio Monteverdi. He had been explaining how Monteverdi had composed works that were regarded during his lifetime as being revolutionary, and how his compositions marked the transitional period in musical style from Renaissance to Baroque. As the Dutchman was jabbering on now, the American recalled how what the Dutchman had been most passionate about with regard to Monteverdi was the compositions known as madrigals.

"In the Madrigals of War, Monteverdi organized poetry that described the pursuits of love through the allegory of war; the hunt for love, and the battle to find love."

The Dutchman had surprised him with his very passionate feelings about the music. He was now describing to them the first book of his favorite, the eighth, madrigal, which had been written in 1638. The Danish bankers and the American were then hearing firsthand from the mad Dutchman how he had boldly "hunted" down the Asian woman earlier in the day, and what had transpired between them. No doubt, he believed in putting into practice what he had learned from the madrigals of the great Italian composer.

So, it was pretty amazing, at least to the American, to hear the senior executive from a major European bank openly reveal his predatory practices over cocktails. But the Dutchman was totally uninhibited and didn't seem to care at all about revealing anything regarding his amorous exploits. Maybe that was to be expected from someone living in a very permissive society. As the Dutchman spoke, the American would occasionally glance at the Asian woman to see if she had any sense that she was the topic of conversation. But she seemed to be totally oblivious to whatever was being discussed, consumed in conversation within her own little circle.

"So, how did it end up between the two of you?" asked one of the Danes.

"Not well," replied the Dutchman honestly. "She had no interest."

"No interest?" asked the American. "What exactly did you ask her?"

"I told her that I was fascinated by her." This provoked plenty of good laughter from the bankers hearing him admit this. Even the Dutchman began to laugh at his own comment.

"I told her that I really wanted her!" This resulted in even more uproarious laughter from the bankers who were no longer shocked by the Dutchman's unabashed comments. It was a foregone conclusion that the man had a loose screw.

"In the second half of the book, the Madrigals of Love, Monteverdi organized poetry that described the unhappiness of being in love, of unfaithfulness, and of ungrateful lovers who felt no shame." The Dutchman proudly admitted to being guilty of the very same things. The man was very entertaining.

THERE WAS A VERY FAIR POLISH WOMAN SPEAKING TO a dark Hungarian one no more than ten paces from where the American was standing. He noticed that the two women were speaking in English as they sipped slowly from their wine glasses. The Polish woman wore gold-rimmed glasses, had blonde bangs that were combed in a way that tried to diminish her somewhat large forehead, and had full lips that were painted a bright rouge. It all went along quite nicely with her full figure. She was drinking white wine. The Hungarian woman was wearing dark-rimmed glasses, had frizzy dark hair, full lips tinted in a mauve shade, and sported a very athletic body in a skimpy black dress. She was drinking red wine. The Hungarian woman was laughing at something that the Polish woman had just said, and the American thought that it was the perfect time to barge in on their conversation.

"Hello ladies," he said to them. "Even though your tags don't indicate it, are you Americans?"

"No, I'm from Poland," said Sonya.

"And I'm from Hungary, but my father was an American. He was in the army when he met my mother in Hungary." Her badge displayed her name to be Martha.

"Well, I heard you ladies speaking American English so I couldn't resist coming over to say hello," he said. "I hope I did not interrupt anything. You seemed to be having such a good time."

"You didn't interrupt anything. We were just laughing over the translation that was done for the presentation by the Standard & Poor's representative. We couldn't believe our ears when the topic all of a sudden referred to circumcisions. The representative was a Brit, and he was making his presentation in Russian. He obviously used the wrong Russian word. He turned totally red when many of the participants in the audience began laughing all of a sudden at what he had just stated." After she had explained the incident, the Hungarian girl began laughing again.

"Circumcised for circumscribed," explained Sonya, and then both women began laughing again.

By THE TIME THE BANKERS WERE FINALLY DEPOSITED in front of their hotel, it was well after midnight. Upon entering the premises, they were surprised to find several bankers that had not attended the cruise now drinking in the hotel's lobby bar. Of particular note was a confident-looking Chinese banker with heavy black-rimmed glasses who was continuously chain-smoking in one corner of the bar. The sparely built man was sitting at the same table that he had previously been sitting at on two separate occasions. Tonight, he was accompanied by the same two Russian ladies that had been sitting with the American on the night of his arrival. The Chinese banker looked rather pretentious in the way that he smiled as he drank and in the peculiar way that he pinched his cigarette between his thumb and index finger.

When the Russian girls laughed with the banker, the American noticed that even though the Chinese man was probably in his early forties, his teeth showed significant yellowing from all the nicotine, alcohol, and coffee that he had consumed over time. The man appeared to be loaded, and in St. Petersburg Russia, like everywhere else, money talked. The American had to admit to himself that he was envious of the man for having the female company.

CHAPTER FIVE

THE NEXT DAY'S conference did not hold any special surprises, but everyone was eagerly anticipating the evening's activity: an extravagant dinner and an erotic ballet performance at St. Petersburg's hottest nightclub. The Dutchman, the Danes, and the American had gathered in front of their hotel with the other participants who were patiently waiting for their transport to the venue.

"It will be a night of fox hunting," boasted the Dutchman, "and my nose is already geared up to receive the scents from the cunning vixens."

"Did you see the brochure in the hotel lobby offering fox hunting excursions in Russia?" asked one of the Danes. "It reads 'Makes an exclusive gift for business partners, top executives, CEOs, or your friends and relatives, or even yourself! Whatever you choose, we will do everything possible to make your fox hunting trip a really incredible adventure!'"

"Happy hunting, is what I'd say to the predator," the Dutchman said. "Avoid sharing time and space with as many potential predators as possible, is my advice to the prey."

"Here's the thing," the Dutchman started again. "The hunter is not wasting his time proving his manhood by going after every possible conquest. He waits for the right thing and when he finds it, he closes the deal." And that was the last word on the subject from this very entertaining man.

Forty minutes after having left their hotel, over four hundred international bankers and some government officials found themselves inside one of St. Petersburg's most luxurious dinner clubs. The candlelit circular dining tables that seated up to ten guests were covered with white linen and fine china. The tables were strategically placed around a parquet floor that could have easily served as a dancing venue for a wedding party. The American thought himself to be quite lucky at having been seated next to a very attractive Spanish banker who he had not previously noticed at the conference. She introduced herself as Paloma and said that as far as she knew she was the only representative from Spain at the conference. Paloma was a treasury analyst for Banco Bilbao Vizcaya.

The Dutchman and the Danes had also been seated at their table, along with three other Russian female bankers. They were senior representatives from Standard Chartered Bank and Deutsche Bank, and a senior Asian auditor from Price Waterhouse. As it happens, Ms. Saori Sato was the woman that the Dutchman had been lusting after. The Danes and the American were curious to see how things would develop between them throughout the night. It was surprising to see that neither had betrayed any signs of having previously spoken to each other.

Champagne, red and white wine, and vodka were the drinking options for the guests. The hors d'œuvres had already been served when the lights in the room suddenly dimmed and music from Stravinsky's Firebird slowly began to draw the attention of the audience. A beautiful ballerina in a classic pink camisole leotard appeared on the parquet floor. She seemed to be pursued by a male dancer who was wearing high-waist black Capri dance pants. What was shocking and unusual about the ballerina's attire was that her beautiful pert breasts were fully exposed! Prince Ivan, the male dancer, was expressing through beautifully choreographed moves his overwhelming desire to possess the magnificent Firebird. The pursuer and the pursued were then seen dancing in an expertly choreographed pas-de-deux that ended with the prince capturing the Firebird.

When the scene ended, there was an intermission which allowed the waitresses to replace the hors d'oeuvres with plates brimming with medallions of beef tenderloin. The guests had been very impressed with the ballet performance and could now be heard remarking on how shocking it had been when the seminude Firebird had first entered the scene. They were all very surprised that a thoroughly professional modern ballet company was willing to present their marvelous work at a restaurant club. The performance had been totally unexpected, a wonderful surprise to all of them. Within moments after the last of the plates had been placed, the lights dimmed, and there were twelve of the most ravishing classical ballerinas on stage also bearing their beautiful naked breasts to the audience, dancing to Stravinsky's bewitching music. Prince Ivan then entered the scene, again chasing after the beautiful ballerinas.

The mixture of the erotic with the artistic through the medium of dance, as performed by these beautiful classically trained ballerinas with their perfect postures and perfect youthful bodies swaying to the exotic oriental music of this ballet, was just amazing!

"Bravo," yelled many in the audience. They were ecstatic over the performance. They had never seen anything as perfectly performed as what they were now witnessing. It was inconceivable that the musical master-piece was the work of a youthful Stravinsky. It was his first project for Sergei Diaghilev's Ballets Russe Company. The work was, of course, critically received to great acclaim during its premiere at the 1910 Paris season.

LATER THAT NIGHT, THE HOTEL'S LOBBY BAR WAS ONCE again the gathering place for many of the bankers arriving from the dinner club for a nightcap. The American, the Danes, and the Dutchman didn't waste time in ordering their drinks. The Dutchman didn't say a word about his interaction with Ms. Saori Sato. Everyone had been expecting to hear what had transpired between the two, but the Dutchman was silent on the topic.

Once again, the Chinese banker was seen sitting alone at his usual corner table. He had obviously failed to attend the programmed activity with the rest of the bankers, opting instead to sit in the lobby bar where he could drink his cognac in solitude. The American had found out that what the peculiar man loved to drink was cognac, and it was always Hennessy.

As on previous nights, the two Russian ladies had also returned to the lobby bar, but they were not now keeping the man company. As the American passed the girls on his way from collecting his drink, he noticed that one of them, Anna, showed a bit of bruising on her neck. Anna was the same girl that the American had spent some time with in his room on the first night of the conference. She looked at him and smiled.

"Hello," she ventured. "How are you doing tonight, blue man?"

"Fine," he smiled back. "How are you?"

"I'm OK, too! Would you like to have a drink with us?"

He looked at them and considered it. "What happened to your neck?" he asked Anna.

"Oh, I was playing around with Irina and she was squeezing my neck. Well, I bruise easily." Irina didn't comment on Anna's explanation. She didn't confirm or deny anything, and she wasn't smiling.

"Are you sure it wasn't the Chinese banker that you were with yesterday that did that to you?" he asked. It was none of his business and he shouldn't have said anything. But he was annoyed that they had probably subjected their bodies to the man.

"No," Anna quickly protested. "What are you saying? Why would he do such a thing?"

The three of them then stole a glance at the Asian banker as he was lighting a match an inch or so away from the end of a cigarette that he had just placed in his mouth. The man brought the flame almost to the tip of the cigarette and sucked on the cigarette, waiting for the short burst. He slightly coughed as the sucking action brought the smoke into his mouth. He finally exhaled the smoke after holding it for a long time. He puckered his lips and blew a thin direct stream of smoke, and then he was ready for his cognac.

Surprisingly, the man knew how to drink his cognac. He had been holding the snifter in his palm for several minutes, warming the cognac slowly and naturally. Then he positioned his nose at the edge of the glass and gently inhaled the aroma. From having worked in a wine shop during his college years, the American knew that the first scent of a cognac was known as the montant. The girls were no longer showing any interest in the man, but the American was still observing him as he withdrew his nose from the snifter and gently swirled the cognac in the bowl. He then took in again the aroma of the cognac before finally bringing the glass to his lips, sucking in a small amount. He then let the cognac linger over his palate, enjoying every lasting moment as though it was his last.

"So, this man didn't bruise you?" the American asked Anna.

"No way," was her immediate response. Then she just looked at him and wondered what he could be thinking. Some men thought they knew everything. But Americans were not the worst in this regard, and she didn't want to get angry at him because he had been extremely nice to her the other night. Strange man, she remembered. He liked to be slapped around. No Russian man would like such a thing. But then again, in Russia, you had to scrap and claw to survive. In America, maybe things were so easy that the pleasures came from the pursuit of pain. She wouldn't mind having a few more of these easy American clients.

Unfortunately for the two girls, the American wasn't any longer in the mood for their company. The bruises on Anna's neck may or may not have been made by the Asian, but the monster had at the very least enjoyed them! I can only hope, he thought, that they have in their possession the miracle fruit synsepalum dulcificum. He smiled as he remembered the Latin name. When these berries were eaten even sour foods tasted sweeter.

Anyone observing the American's actions would wrongly think that he was biased against the Asian because of his race. But that couldn't have been further from the truth. The American's objection was solely based on the type of man that he observed him to be. He seemed to be an antisocial man of an elite class, unable or unwilling to communicate with his peers, content in his solitude, and ready to pay for the privilege of pouncing on the weaker sex when the opportunity presented itself.

At 2:00 am, the Asian decided that he needed fresh air, needed to stretch his legs, needed a break from the dreadful hotel lobby. In his customary black suit, white shirt, and red tie he proceeded to cross the street in order to walk along the embankment of the Neva River. The American also thought that he needed to take in some fresh air, but it was also true that he was curious to know where the Asian was headed. Like the detectives in the pulp fiction stories that he liked to read, the American decided to shadow the banker, but only at a safe distance. He didn't want to frighten the man; he just wanted to be able to see what he was up to. It was all a game. It was the world of secrecy, mystery, and cloak-and-dagger stuff in a foreign land.

The Asian seemed to be heading toward the bridge that would take him to the Peter and Paul Fortress. The American had been to the historical site on an earlier occasion, when he had briefly stepped out of the conference on the first day for a breath of fresh air. In St. Petersburg, everyone walked, and you were generally pretty safe on the public streets. But like in every large city, precautions had to be taken. Even during the daytime, a foreigner could all of a sudden become surrounded by gypsies and within minutes find himself relieved of all of his personal possessions. While crime and violent attacks were more likely at night, the Asian banker seemed unconcerned on this score. He proceeded at a slow pace without showing any regard for danger. On the bridge, he lingered long enough to have a smoke, and after he had finished he threw the cigarette butt into the river. Then he proceeded at a casual pace on to the island.

At this late hour, the American was no longer inclined to follow the man. The liquor that he had consumed all of a sudden caught up with him. He was now quite tired and no longer cared to know what lunacy the other man may have been up to. It was time to retire. A gypsy boy approached him on the way back to the hotel, asking him for money. Contrary to what the guide books suggested, the American gave the boy a US dollar. The American told the boy in English, "That is genuine legal tender." The boy did not understand a word of what he was saying, but he took the American's dollar bill and left. When the American finally made it back to the lobby, he noticed that all the bankers who had been drinking at the bar had already retired. The two Russian women had also disappeared. Only a handful of the local Russian clientele was still drinking. It had been a very long day, and he was now ready for a good rest.

CHAPTER SIX

LIU TANG WAS the name of the Chinese banker that the American had briefly followed on the previous night. He was 45 years old and worked as an executive for the Bank of China. With a wife and daughter, he resided in a luxurious apartment near the very exclusive former French Concession of Shanghai. Liu Tang was a member of a motorcycle gang of Chinese executives and self-made millionaires. On Friday nights the group would meet at the Coffee Bean and Tea Leaf in order to have their lattes and cappuccinos. These powerful executives would lounge about in the laidback shop to talk about the complicated politics, the explosive growth, and the upward spiraling property values in Shanghai.

Life had been quite good for Liu Tang until he found out three months earlier that one of the most powerful board members in his bank was having an affair with his wife. Liu Tang had received an anonymous note with a joke about a man who visited a doctor and requested to have blood tests performed because he suspected a calcium deficiency. When the doctor asked for his reasons for such suspicions, the patient complained that his wife was sleeping with other men, yet he still had no horns growing. The message to Liu Tang was clear enough.

It was not uncommon in China for successful businessmen who spent most of their time socializing with clients and colleagues to find that their wives had become unfaithful. Adultery existed in China like everywhere else.

Liu Tang had been a good and reliable husband and father. Apart from his Friday night meetings with the Harley-Davidson motorcycle gang, he had been a very faithful marriage partner. While it was true that he often had to travel for business, he never made it a practice to take the opportunity to cheat on his wife. Now the man found himself with a serious problem and no easy solution. The fact that his wife's lover was a high-ranking executive in his bank made the situation even more difficult to resolve.

The banking conference in St. Petersburg was a welcome change for him, but being far away from home didn't help him come any closer to resolving his problem. The fact that someone had sent him an anonymous note regarding his wife's infidelity made matters even worse for him. How many people, he wondered, were aware of what was going on? Did his immediate colleagues know? Had he become the laughing stock of the division?

His wife had never complained about any of his business trips. She never complained about his Friday night activity with the CEO motorcycle gang. In fact, she thought it quite prestigious that he was able to participate with the industry leaders in Shanghai. Other than the Friday nights and the business trips, he made it a point to always be there at home with his family. The business trips were required, and she could not very well complain about them while he was being compensated with a very generous salary.

His wife's illicit affair was a total shock to him. After being married for so many years, he thought that he knew her. She had never complained to him, never asked for anything, and he had never denied her anything. She dressed well, had her own car, and met her friends often for long lunches. She was a member of a health club and was quite fit. She seemed to be very happy with him and with her life. By having an affair with an executive in his firm she was doing something so much worse than being unfaithful: by her action, she was totally humiliating him. As he saw it, he clearly wasn't enough of a man for her. He now knew it, she knew it, her lover knew it, and only God knew how many others knew it.

Now, in St. Petersburg, every evening after the financial presentations he would go to the lobby bar for a smoke and a whiskey or cognac. Throughout the day he would attend the venues, but he didn't pay attention to any of the speakers. He didn't have any interest in the conference, but he attended because he needed to fill his day with distractions because he didn't know what else to do. The evenings were easier because he could smoke and drink for a few hours until he was ready to retire to his room in order to try to sleep. But how could he sleep?

He never sought the company of any of the other bankers at the conference because he couldn't really trust himself to be good company, and he didn't really have any interest at this time in socializing with them. He needed time to think, to try to come up with a solution to his marital problems. He had always loved his wife, but that didn't seem to matter to her. She was probably on her knees now in front of her executive boyfriend, and it must have been thrilling for her. Otherwise, why had he been important enough for her to want to jeopardize their marriage? She had come to a decision, and that was the end of it. As far as she was concerned, her husband had nothing to do with it.

Inaction was not possible for him. His lifestyle was

going to have to dramatically change. He would have to leave his firm, his family, and probably the city that he grew to love. If he were to stay, he would have to endure the daily humiliating stares from everyone who knew the circumstances, and of course, that would not be possible. The most unbearable part of his life now was having to live with her under the same roof. He couldn't begin to understand why she so recklessly continued her behavior. She knew that he would never do anything to humiliate her because even if he hadn't loved her, at least he respected her enough never to put her through such a degrading position. The fact that she didn't care about the consequences of her actions made it clear to him that he had to immediately make a dramatic change to his life.

CHAPTER SEVEN

THE BANKING CONFERENCE attendees benefited from the dismal financial condition that the Russian government was in. The government needed the banks to buy Russian bonds in order to obtain the liquidity needed to be able to function and to provide the financing for the major projects that were already underway. The conference had to be successful.

Today's conference presentations emphasized how Russia had overcome the most painful phase of its financial, economic, and banking crisis. The spokesperson from the Ministry of Finance in his presentation stated that "the challenge of the next stage of the banking sector reform is to create conditions for the long-term stable development of the banking system, including the bank regulation system based upon internationally proven methods."

During the coffee break, the American exited the conference room, took the elevator to the hotel lobby, and rapidly moved toward the concierge where he asked for instructions on how to get to the women's chess championship. The match was between a 25-year-old Chinese champion, Zhu Chen, and a 17-year-old Russian champion, Alexandra Konstantinovna Kosteniuk, for the Women's World Chess Championship title. The championship took the form of a 64-player knock-out tournament. Entering into the event, Zhu Chen had been ranked fourth in the world, and Alexandra Konstantinovna Kosteniuk had been ranked twelfth.

THE AMERICAN ALWAYS ENJOYED SEEING WOMEN compete in sports. This was not surprising since he had grown up in New York during the feminist era. During those youthful years, he would occasionally play chess with a lovely psychologist in one of the chess shops in Greenwich Village. Nancy wore the same type of over-sized glasses as Gloria Steinem, and she spoke in the same deliberate style as the feminist. The American loved more than anything else to play chess with her, especially when she wore those tight, beautifully torn denim blue jeans. When he was with Nancy he felt as if he was with a young Gloria Steinem.

Nancy was also an exceptional chess player. The few times that they played together she had beaten him soundly. One day after they had played a match, she kissed him full on the lips. This had totally surprised him because he hadn't ever dared to make an amorous move on her. He didn't want to spoil whatever time they spent together, didn't want her to end whatever time she was willing to give him. He was always on his best behavior with her, a real gentleman. So, he almost fainted when they stood up after playing a match—when she got up on her tiptoes to kiss him full on the lips. After the shock, and after several long arduous kisses, she smiled and said that she had to leave. She didn't say anything more to him, and he didn't think that he had any right to protest. Nancy, luscious lady, had left him in quite a state that day, and the resulting treasured memory was an indelible event.

Here was another surprise for the American. Mr. Liu Tang was also in attendance for the chess match! He must have been there to cheer on the lovely Ms. Zhu Chen. He was sitting in the very front row that had been set aside for special guests. The man must have arrived quite early in order to have secured his prized seat, or perhaps he may have been connected to the Chinese delegation accompanying Ms. Zhu Chen. There wasn't an empty seat to be had for the match.

During the match, most of the games began with either the Petroff Defense or the Slav Defense. The experts considered these two to be of the dullest openings. However, the games were all hard-fought down to the end. Ms. Zhu Chen was so physically exhausted after winning the match that she just walked off the stage without smiling or saying anything.

After the match, Liu Tang followed the American as he left the building. Once the American noticed that Liu Tang was trailing him, he decided that he would slow his pace to see what the man's intentions were. The American didn't know what to expect from the Asian, especially since Liu Tang had never been seen conversing with any of the other bankers at the conference. When he finally caught up with the American, he smiled at him and asked him what he thought of the match. The American was caught totally off guard. The Chinese man's English was excellent.

"Fine," the American responded. "Zhu Chen was quite good. She was a little too strong for the young Russian girl."

"Yes," Liu Tang responded. "Zhu Chen is quite good and will be an excellent champion. Would you like to have a coffee at this well-known chess café?" he asked. "I would like to give you a little insight as to why Chinese women have become so good at chess."

Well, here was another surprise that the American would have never expected. Liu Tang was inviting him to have a coffee with him. What a remarkable turn of events within less than twenty-four hours.

"Thank you for accepting my invitation. It's nice to get away from the financial atmosphere for a while. I think you would agree that there is much more to this great city of St. Petersburg than the stuffy conference."

"Yes. I totally agree with you. But, if you feel that way, then why haven't you been attending any of the evening social events? They have been quite good and have provided for an excellent change of venue from the conference."

"To be frank with you, I have not had the energy to attend these events," Liu Tang responded. "I have had some personal issues that I have been trying to work out, and I just felt that I would not have been good company for the others. I only approached you today because of your interest in this championship event, and Ms. Zhu Chen's success seemed to have changed my perspective on the weight of my concerns." The American didn't know what to say to the man's honest response. Perhaps he had totally misjudged him.

"Since the formation of the Peoples' Republic of

China in 1949," Liu Tang began, "while under Soviet influence, chess was given an official recognition designating it as a sport. Within the government's organization, it became part of the Institute of Qi, which also included Wei Qi (Go), and Xiangqi (Chinese Chess), in addition to Western chess. Because it had government support, chess began to attract a new following. Although there were some successes in the early sixties, all progress came to a halt during the Cultural Revolution."

After the waitress took their order for a cappuccino and a Wu Yi Mountain Oolong tea, Mr. Liu Tang pulled out a pack of cigarettes and offered one to the American.

"No, thank you," replied the American. "I never really picked up the habit."

"Good for you," said Liu Tang. "It is a nasty habit that I, unfortunately, picked up in my youth, and in China, it is an easy habit to acquire because everyone smokes."

"Cancer is so high in the United States," countered the American, "that now the government at the state and federal levels has begun to campaign strongly against smoking. It is now banned from many public places."

"Cancer is quite high in China as well. But the government has not taken any steps to ban it. Only athletes are discouraged from smoking. At any rate, I will refrain from smoking while we are here together."

"Please, Mr. Tang, don't concern yourself on my account. My father was a chain smoker so I am quite used to it."

"No. Please. I am glad that you do not smoke. I smoke much too much and I am certain that the effects will be manifesting themselves soon in my lungs if I don't discontinue the nasty habit. Besides, I will not be able to fully enjoy the sweet and floral aromas of the Oolong tea if I am smoking foul cigarettes."

The waitress came and put the cups in front of the two bankers. The American was fascinated by the braids that the waitress sported. The Chinese banker smiled as he glimpsed at the American admiring the girl.

When the American noticed his counterpart's reaction regarding his appreciation of the waitress, the American confessed, "Russian women are so fascinating!"

"Yes, I know what you mean," agreed the other. "Shall I briefly continue with what I was saying about our Chinese women's success on the game board?"

"Yes, by all means. But I have to tell you that I love Chinese women too!"

"Well, you do come across as an intelligent man." With this, they both laughed.

"To be brief," resumed Liu Tang, "although there were some successes in the early sixties, all progress came to a halt during the Cultural Revolution. But, thankfully, after the fall of the "Gang of Four" in 1976, chess began to be played in China again." As the Chinese banker was relating the history, the American couldn't help but observe that Liu Tang held his cup of tea with an extended pinky. Was this of British or Chinese origin, he wondered.

"Since you appear to be a chess aficionado, you may know that there are four schools of chess that have existed prior to the coming of the Chinese school of chess," Liu Tang continued. "They are the Italian School, Classical School, Hypermodern School, and the Soviet-Russian school. The Chinese School is highly critical of the principles used by these other four schools. It finds that their so-called 'theory of the center', 'theory of development', and 'theory of tempo' are all based on an inadequate understanding of chess. From the point of view of the Chinese School, there are three main principles: Strategy, Structure, and Space."

"Are you a grandmaster, Liu Tang?" the American asked.

"No. Certainly not! I am merely conveying to you the ideas that experts have expounded about how the Chinese analyze chess a little differently than the rest of the world, which could explain why our women have as of late enjoyed great success in global competition."

"Can China boast the same results with their men?"

"No. It's a bit harder with men. There are other

complications that come into play with men." The American smiled as he considered Liu Tang's explanation.

"That is the problem with life," said the American. "There is the theoretical, and then there is the reality. Whenever you think you have a handle on life, you suddenly experience something unexpected that throws whatever theory you have out the window. Personally, chaos theory seems to me to work best. Chaos theory refers to an apparent lack of order in a system that nevertheless obeys particular laws or rules. It seems to me that in order to try to find any sense in the world you might want to begin with that theory, i.e., finding the underlying order in apparently random data."

Liu Tang studied the American for a moment. He was fighting hard against a very strong urge to smoke. He was also analyzing carefully what the American had just said. Was the American just routinely dismissing all of what he had just conveyed because his theory didn't apply to the male Chinese chess players, or was the American trying to make a valid assessment of a theory that perhaps didn't seem to transfer well at all times?

"The human heart also has a chaotic pattern. The time between beats does not remain constant; it depends on how much activity a person is doing, among other things. Under certain conditions, the heartbeat can speed up. Under different conditions, the heart beats erratically. It might even be called a chaotic heartbeat."

"Precisely," the American agreed. "There are many variables that can affect an outcome, many of which we may not even be able to begin to contemplate when predicting an outcome. Can anyone even begin to understand the mind of the American chess champion Bobby Fisher? Do you know about Bobby Fisher?"

"Yes," Liu Tang replied. "He was an American genius chess player."

"That's right," said the American. "Bobby Fisher was America's great answer to the Soviet's chess challenge during the Cold War. With Bobby Fisher, we have a perfect case study of a mind in chaos."

Liu Tang no longer cared to argue with the American. He didn't even know why he had begun the conversation. It must have been because his spirits had been lifted when Zhu Chen had been declared World Chess Champion. He was proud to see his compatriot succeed. He wanted to share the experience with someone, and the American banker was the only one in the room he recognized. Liu Tang pulled out his pack of Zhonghua brand cigarettes and again considered smoking. The American was right of course. The world was in chaos. His life was in chaos. His wife's infidelity with the powerful executive was a constant pattern that disrupted his life, which created chaos. And now he had a chaotic heartbeat. The time between beats did not remain constant.

"Would you gentlemen like something else?" the waitress asked.

"Not for me," replied Liu Tang.

"I'm fine too," came from the American.

The American looked again at the young Russian waitress and fell into a reverie. The waitress smiled at him and promised that she would be right back with their check. The American watched her turn and walk away, and then he remembered the time when he was with his father at a neighborhood Greek diner. He remembered his father ordering a coffee to go from a tall, well-built fair-haired woman in a white uniform who was working behind the counter. The woman had smiled at his father when she took the order and then walked away to get his Styrofoam container of coffee.

"Make sure it's light and sweet," his father called after her, smiling. Then he looked at his young son and confided proudly to him that he was having an affair with her. Up until this day the American didn't know what to make of his father's indiscretion. What response was his father expecting him to make? Maybe back in his generation, this was something typical of their culture. But the boy had grown up differently in Brooklyn, and this didn't seem right to him, to hear his father boast that he was having an affair with the woman. What was even worse was that he had said it in front of her. The boy looked at the woman to see if she was feeling embarrassed by his remark. But he couldn't tell. She was a foreigner, recently arrived from Liverpool. The boy could see why his father was proud of his conquest. What the boy couldn't accept was his father's total disregard for his family. Between the father and son, there was a conflict of values already at an early age. Why the American would still be remembering the incident more than thirty years after it had occurred was a mystery, but that was what was running through his mind as the young Russian waitress turned to get their bill.

The American also wondered why he had bothered to enter into a conversation with the Chinese banker when as recently as yesterday he had already concluded that he didn't like the man. There was the old saying that curiosity killed the cat. The American had enjoyed the chess match between the two young women and he felt pleased to see the Asian banker expressing genuine pride over Zhu Chen's victory. He was curious to know what Liu Tang knew about Zhu Chen, and he was glad to see the man from a different perspective, other than how he had been imagining him when he showed up nightly to chain smoke and drink in the hotel's lobby bar. There clearly had to be more to the man, the American thought, especially if he had reached an executive position at an important bank.

Since Zhu Chen had won the chess match, Liu Tang had insisted upon paying the modest bill. The American accepted without much of an argument. Then they resumed their long walk toward their hotel which was an hour away, but neither of them minded because the afternoon was sunny and there was a refreshing coolness from a cold front that had descended on St. Petersburg.

"Only in utter solitude can man be safe from the doings of this vile world! By Allah, life is naught but one great wrong." Liu Tang had uttered these strange words as they set out together. The American gave him an inquisitive look but didn't comment. He waited to hear what the man meant by these strange words.

"That comes from the Burton translation of Thousand Nights and a Night," said Liu Tang. "A work that I have loved since first hearing the stories read by my father when I was a child. I think you would agree that this is one of the most magnificent works of literature that has ever been produced."

"You won't get an argument from me," assured the American. "But why do you recall that particularly gloomy quote from the great work?"

Liu Tang looked at the American and hesitated before giving any sort of explanation.

"Oh, you have every right to question me on that score since I have brought it up seemingly out of the blue," he said. "You see, I have a problem to solve and whichever decision I make will be very consequential to my life. My life will soon radically change."

The American wasn't sure how to respond, unsure of how involved he wanted to become. This was definitely a strange and complicated man. But he was curious, so he waited patiently to hear what else Liu Tang had to say.

Liu Tang then began again, "I'm sure you can guess at the theme of the problem, the eternal theme that most artists take great pains to express in their works."

"Love?" ventured the American.

"Precisely," responded Liu Tang. "O choicest love of this heart of mine! O dame of noblest line," Liu Tang quoted further Burton's translation. "Because we are strangers and because in a couple of days, we will probably never see each other again, I don't mind telling you that I have found myself in a situation that I will have to face up to rather quickly. Discussing this with someone is not what I would normally do, but since we are strangers to each other and since there can be no negative repercussions I don't mind opening up to you. I do not mind sharing my dilemma with you."

The American waited, considering carefully before responding to the man. He was right in saying that they were total strangers and that more than likely they would probably never see each other again after the conclusion of the banking conference. After all, he was from Florida and Liu Tang resided in Shanghai. So, what could be the harm in listening to what the man had to say? Liu Tang seemed to want to speak to someone about his problem, and he agreed that he didn't see a downside to hearing him out.

"You must be sure when you begin to tell me your story to be certain that you translate it well. Sometimes little nuances or subtle shades in meaning can be lost or misunderstood because of a poor translation. You will want to keep your audience interested but not confused." The American said this with a straight face.

"Yes, but I don't think you understand," interrupted Liu Tang. "I'm not about to recite to you an old Chinese tale. This is my own personal story that I will be revealing to you. So, you don't have to worry about its veracity or whether or not it has been translated well."

"What about the style in the presentation?" persisted the American. "You will want to tell your story in a style that will capture the mood of the place. Hopefully, there will be some elegance in your presentation too. But, most importantly, you will want to be faithful in your rendition. There are many fine translators of Russian novels, but I can't begin to tell you how much I truly loved reading the Constance Garnett translations."

Liu Tang looked at the American in disbelief. "Perhaps you have not totally understood me. It appears that I may have already started wrong."

"Precisely! That's what I was afraid of," came from the American.

"Please," Liu Tang interrupted. "This is my story. And, you won't have to worry about style and translation because since I am the main character in it, and since I am telling you, you are now also in the story. We will both be able to now vouchsafe for the translation and style for at least a part of my story." He said this with a smile. "You now understand me perfectly, do you not?"

"Quite so," replied the American. "But I'm not so certain that I want to be in your story."

"Well, there it is. You have no option now," came from Liu Tang. "You are now in my story."

"Well, if that is to be the case, then you must remove this part of your story to a more elegant surrounding."

"Where will you have us go then?"

"You might consider moving us to that Grand Hotel Europe that is across the way. My understanding is that the hotel has quite a good kitchen and an excellent bar. You do want to be in a ritzy atmosphere when you draw in an American banker into your story. It will make the scene more believable."

"Right, I understand what you are getting at," conceded Liu Tang, quite amused by the American.

"I thought that you might. Hopefully, there will be some fine-looking women there as well. Three or four very fashionable ladies at the bar would work well, in my humble opinion. Hopefully one of them will be wearing a ponytail."

"Let's not waste any more time here. I totally agree with your proposed setting with one minor modification. At least one of the ladies will be Asian, and she must sport a modern blunt haircut."

The two men then proceeded to cross Nevsky Prospekt, the main thoroughfare in St. Petersburg. The majority of the city's shopping and nightlife, as well as some of the most expensive apartments, were located on or right off Nevsky Prospekt, as was the Grand Hotel Europe.

CHAPTER EIGHT

AFTER THE TWO men were seated in the outdoor part of the café on the Prospekt by a lovely Russian hostess, the American was intrigued to hear what it was that Liu Tang had to say. What was the personal dilemma that he would be facing on his return home? There had been quite a few personal revelations disclosed by bankers at this conference. Perhaps it was because St. Petersburg was for the bankers a place so remote from their home-towns that they were willing to indulge in riskier behavior than they normally would have. Maybe that was why the Dutchman was so willing to boast so openly about his perversions in front of others. What happens in St. Petersburg stays in St. Petersburg!

The background music in the bar was Danza Negra by the Cuban composer Ernesto Lecuona. The musi-

cians were the Caracas Clarinet Quartet. This was a
jazzy bastardized version of what the Cuban composer
had actually written, but it was still very Cuban in style.
As the American was focusing on the sounds of the clar-
inets playing the Cuban rhythms, he found it fascinating
that they were playing the piece in a very unromantic
way. They were playing the sounds off each other, not in
unison. It was almost as though Stravinsky had rewritten
the piece. It was cool but very different than what
Lecuona had intended, and the American thought that it
made perfect sense to be hearing the piece at this time
here in Russia. But Liu Tang had not been listening to
the music at all. He was preoccupied with his weightier
issue that prevented him from being able to focus on the
hotel's background music, and he looked as though he
was anxious to begin divulging his tale.

The American was tempted to order a Cuba libre
because of the nostalgia that he was feeling for the Cuba
that he had never known, except from the stories that
he had heard from his father. So, he settled instead for a
glass of red Bordeaux wine.

Liu Tang could tell that for the moment the American's thoughts were elsewhere, but he didn't mind waiting. The waitress eyed the two businessmen. They were
high-powered executives for sure, she thought. But it
was not so exceptional to find clientele of this caliber in
this hotel, the best in St. Petersburg. Liu Tang ordered

from the young waitress a neat whiskey and waited for the American to return to the present.

"So, where were we?" Liu Tang finally asked.

"Well, don't ask me. Hell, if I know what's going on."

"My friend, sometimes one comes to a fork in the road, and a decision has to be made, perhaps a decision to regret for the rest of one's life. No doubt you've heard of the expression having "feet of clay?" That occurs when there is this innate flaw or vulnerability that prevents us from moving forward. Do you understand what I mean?"

"I'm with you," said the American.

"Have you ever heard of the Mid-Autumn Festival?" Liu Tang began again. "During the Mid-Autumn Festival in Shanghai, as soon as the moon rises, people set tables in public parks and offer each other moon cakes, melons, fruits, and so on. The celebration of the Mid-Autumn Festival has a history of over three thousand years, dating back to the moon worship in ancient times. Back then it was said that the moon belonged to yin (the female part of the yin–yang philosophy), so in the full moon celebration women worshiped the moon. During the celebration, there is a custom of having impromptu altars set up for burning incense. When the full moon celebration is done, family members stay together to drink their reunion wine, admiring the full moon and eating the moon cakes.

"Before last year's Festival," continued Liu Tang, "my firm's management team decided that it would be an excellent opportunity for many of the families to join together for the celebration. The event would help promote closer bonds between the managers of the different divisions. The team effort concept was very much in vogue at the time. The firm was able to secure a very quiet part of a park by the side of a river and proceeded to rent all of the tables, to cater all of the food, and purchase all of the beverages for everyone, for all of the participants to the event. All of the children were provided with symbolic lanterns holding candles for the nighttime celebration.

"Yin and Yang," Liu Tang continued. "Yin is female and Yang is male. They fit together as two parts of a whole. In the oracle of love, Yang leads and Yin follows. Yang also has the qualities of strength and significance necessary to implement its initiatives, while Yin is correspondingly yielding and ordinary. Yin and Yang! Yin accommodates Yang's initiatives. While Yang takes precedence over Yin, Yin has the privilege of determining both the shape and success of Yang's enterprise. I hope that you are following me, my friend."

The American was shocked and began to laugh loudly at what Liu Tang had just said.

"This is utter nonsense, Liu Tang. Yes, for now, I believe I follow you. But, you have surprised me with the topic. I expected you to be telling me something more personal in nature, and not lecturing me on Yin and Yang." The American then began laughing again.

"Yes, I can understand why you are laughing and what you must be thinking. But you haven't allowed me to get to the crux of the story. You'll see," he continued. "Indulge me a little more on this Yin-and-Yang preamble. Let me just add that desire is the signature attribute of Yang, and choice is the signature attribute of Yin. In the face of a refusal, Yang will abandon an initiative rather than impose it on an unwilling Yin."

Liu Tang then smiled before drinking a considerable amount of his whiskey. He looked at the American and considered how he would now phrase the more personal side of his story.

"Halfway through the festivities, one of the very senior executives, Mr. Mo Yan, approached each of the families at their tables in order to wish them prosperity for the rest of the year. As he approached the tables, he presented each family with delightful moon cakes that were filled with coconut cream, sweetened condensed milk, vanilla, and walnuts. He was the first to admit that they were not traditional, but they were quite delicious. He said that they were made from a recipe that had been given to his grandmother by a friend that had arrived from Malaysia."

The waitress was summoned for a second round of

drinks. It was evident that this part of the entertainment required a sufficient amount of alcohol in the system in order for the story to be properly related and understood. Everyone had a need to confess at some point, and for now, it was Liu Tang's turn. The American was anxiously waiting to see where this would lead.

"Before Mr. Mo Yan departed," Liu Tang continued, "he took a bite from one of his moon cakes to show how much he really loved them. Then his assistants began moving to the next family's table carrying the boxes of moon cakes with them. As this was happening, Mo Yan deftly passed the rest of his moon cake to Jinju, my wife. This seemed like an innocent enough operation that should not have carried any implications, except that Jinju took the bitten moon cake to her thin lips and nibbled off a piece. And while everyone was preoccupied with the boxes and with saying their farewells, Jinju returned the rest of the shared moon cake to Mo Yan who then promptly devoured it in one bite. With this naked intimate symbolic exchange, I became aware for the first time that my wife had been unfaithful."

Liu Tang was smiling as he looked at the American, and the latter didn't know what to say. They each sipped their drinks in silence. *What a dilemma*, thought the American. He didn't know how to respond. What was culturally accepted behavior in China with regard to adultery?

"Liu Tang," the American began, "is your wife aware that you know?"

"Oh, yes. She was aware that I had seen what had transpired between her and Mo Yan. Her eyes spoke volumes. Was it a decision that she had made that she would regret for the rest of her life? We had signed a contract for lifelong love, but that was now null and void. Was she worried? She was quite ingenious in structuring the smooth lies that came forth from her lips on our subsequent discussions. She said he possessed hypnotic powers, but how much nonsense can you listen to? That was what was going through this cuckold's head," Liu Tang said.

Well, what can you say to that? In this yin–yang world, Mo Yan was doing Jinju, and Liu Tang didn't know what to do. It sounded like the beginning of a comic opera, thought the American. A lovely violin-and-piano piece played in the background, taking the American out of the conversation for a brief moment.

"My good man," said Liu Tang, pulling him out of his trance.

"Y-yes?" asked the American. "Oh, I'm terribly sorry. Right! Life's an open road," ventured the American, looking somewhat somber.

"Yes. And I've come to a fork in that road. Will she be able to survive outside the gilded cage? We're venturing into unknown territory. Shanghai is a city big enough to get lost in. I can easily reinvent myself."

As time passed on, the restaurant started to fill. The clientele was an eclectic mix of artists, musicians, tourists, international businesspeople, and professionals from all over the world. The restaurant's chef was well-known for taking classic dishes of the Russian cuisine and recasting them with a lighter touch to suit modern-day diners. The evening hostess came by to greet the two bankers and to ask them if they were ready to try the extraordinary delights that were incomparably prepared in what she claimed was St. Petersburg's best kitchen.

"How are you, gentlemen?" the hostess asked.

"Excellent, thank you," replied Liu Tang.

"Yes, we are just fine, and your restaurant is quite impressive."

"Thank you! As you can see, we are the city's hot spot for meeting-and-eating. I hope that you gentlemen will be trying some of the specialty dishes that we are well-known for. When you are ready, I would like you to try the Blini Royale. Did you know that blini have been eaten by Russians around the world for over a millennium, since the time when pagan tribes worshiped the sun and honored their god during the spring solstice by eating the small golden pancakes made in his image? The great author Nikolay Gogol used to gorge on these wonderful little buckwheat pancakes. Our Blini Royale are filled with smoked salmon and red caviar, and will go wonderfully well with your drinks."

"You are quite convincing. I will try them because you have recommended them so passionately, and because you look like someone I should trust," came from the obliging American.

"Yes. You have convinced me as well," added Liu Tang.

"Excellent, gentlemen, I'm certain that you will enjoy them." And with that, the very smart looking hostess with the charming smile left them to place their orders. The young woman was perhaps in her late twenties. Underneath her lovely embroidered white blouse, the American couldn't help but notice how perfectly proportioned her breasts must have been, and her fine black wool skirt was short enough to display nicely toned calf muscles that suggested that she must spend a significant amount of time during the week working out in a health club. Why even bother to mention her beautiful, almond-shaped blue eyes and her full lips that would convince any man and many of today's modern young women to try anything on or off the menu?

It took the two comrades a couple of moments to gather their thoughts. She was quite a distraction. The last thing that these clever bankers had been considering before her arrival was ordering blini. But one look into her eyes and they were enchanted, ready for the Blini Royale with or without the salmon and caviar.

"I pray for wisdom and prudence," said Liu Tang.

"I'm very taken by her," came from the American. Then they both laughed.

"There is an old Chinese saying," said Liu Tang. "If you only have two pennies left, buy a loaf of bread with one, and a lily with the other."

"And what does that mean?"

"What do you think it means?"

"If you can only buy two things, buy something that will keep you alive, and something beautiful to love?"

"To survive you need to nourish the body, and equally important, you need to nourish the soul," explained Liu Tang. "Anyway, now you know my story."

"Yes. It's tough. It's never easy to deal with the situation where you have an unfaithful spouse."

"What is even worse, as it is in my case, is where the indiscretion has occurred with someone in the same firm where you work. Imagine that you have to see this executive in the workplace. You have to participate in meetings with him. When you see him, and when he looks at you, you can't help but think that he is sleeping with your wife. You look at each other and he is not quite sure that you are even aware of his liaison with her. You wonder if he is aware of the difficulty that he is causing you. He doesn't betray himself. He would make a fine poker player. He may not even care whether or not you know. It is your move. Are you ready to confront him, you ask yourself. Are you ready to deal with the consequences? Will you be able to face the humiliation that goes with everyone knowing that you have been made a cuckold? Your wife prefers to sleep with another man!

"In this situation, I cannot possibly win. If I were to decide to confront him, I may be asked to resign because of his power within the institution. I can decide to ignore the situation, but that would require me to be a more dispassionate person than I am. I don't think that I could live with that situation. My other option would be to resign from the firm and take my chances elsewhere.

"Of course, there is one other option. I could confront the man privately. There is no denying that I would like to inflict as much pain on him as possible. But because of his power, I may end up spending many years in jail. Would it be worth it? Remember that my wife has already decided that she prefers him to me?

"No. The last argument is not really an option because I would like to consider myself a civilized man. If my wife prefers some other man, then she has every right to make the decision to be with that man. I must accept her decision and move on. The only issue here is that it has happened in my place of work. This will require me to have to leave the firm."

"Gentlemen, how did you enjoy the blini?" asked the hostess.

"Vkusna! Is that the right word in Russian?" asked the American.

"Yes. That is the word for delicious."

"Chudesnaya, prelesnaya," continued the American.

"So, you found them to be wonderful and cute?" enquired the smiling hostess.

"Nezhnaya, privlekatel'naya!"

"Oh, and tender and pretty as well?" asked the blushing woman. She then really began to laugh before adding, "I can see that you are very passionate about your food."

Not wanting to be left out of the repartee, Liu Tang added "Da, ti ochen krasivaya."

"Having we been discussing the Blini Royale, or did you mean to add that you found the blini to be beautiful?" She then smiled at Liu Tang before adding, "The chef did make a wonderful presentation. The blini with the Eggs Brouilles on top, with another blini on top of that, and the smoked salmon julienne on top of that was quite amazing. And, in gilding the lily, the last of the blinis was placed on top with a dollop of sour cream that was capped by the luscious red caviar. Yes, quite lovely! I whole heartily agree with your assessment, gentlemen."

Red luscious lips, like the caviar. She is beautiful and therefore to be wooed. She is a woman and therefore may be won.

The combination of the booze and the babe triggered the quotes in his brain. The American was glad to have met Liu Tang.

"And now, gentlemen, are you ready for the modern classics? There are several dishes here that are exquisitely prepared that you may choose from, such as the Beef a la Stroganoff, or our magnificent Chicken Kiev. Perhaps our Luli Kebab with potato cabbage cakes tempts you, or maybe even our famous Salmon Kulebiaka. Anton Chekhov called the Kulebiaka 'a temptation to sin.' Are you gentlemen ready to sin?" she asked in a very seductive manner. She was quite a tease. Who could resist this temptress?

Liu Tang didn't waste time in ordering the Luli Kebab.

"Excellent choice," she said. "The grilled lamb patties, or Luli Kebab, have been traditionally paired with the potato cabbage cakes since the eighteenth-century. And for you, sir?" She was now looking at the American.

"I'll have the Beef Stroganoff."

"Excellent choice! If you have not tired yet of my little historical asides, I will tell you that our Stroganoff follows the 1909 recipe, which includes onions and tomato sauce, and is served with crisp potato straws, which are considered the traditional side dish. You will definitely enjoy it."

The delectable hostess then left them to what she was imagining would be a continuation of their conversation on a very complex financial transaction. She was aware that there was currently a major banking conference taking place in St. Petersburg and, from their conference tags, she knew that the Chinese and American men were part of that contingent. That was why she had decided that she would personally attend these power bankers, as she assumed them to be. They should certainly have immediately discerned that she was not a waitress, but rather the managing hostess of the ritziest establishment in the city. These were seasoned salt-and-pepper haired financial experts from opposing parts of the globe. They had been very receptive to all of her recommendations, and she could tell that they were also quite appreciative of her other excellent attributes. But how could they not be? The American was practically drooling. The Chinese man's eyes were less revealing, but still clearly appreciative.

When the hostess left them, Liu Tang looked at the American and said, "I have taken a great deal of your time talking about myself, and you have been most kind to indulge me. Clearly, you are a very patient man. I know that you are an American and obviously a banker, but not much else."

Their waitress, and not the hostess, then came over to take their next order for drinks from the bar. Liu

Tang did not hesitate in ordering another neat whiskey. He was now also lighting his first cigarette of the evening. The American noted that it was a Chinese brand he was smoking.

"Liu Tang, there is nothing quite as interesting happening in my life. I take it as a great honor that you have taken me into your confidence. I must be honest and say that it is not too clear to me what options you may have if you decide to leave your employer. Will it really be that simple for you to find another job?"

Liu Tang took a long drag from his cigarette before responding to the question. He was evaluating how much more personal information he was willing to divulge to his new American friend. He took a sip of his whiskey and gave the American a hard stare. Then he took another drag of his cigarette, looked at the end as it burned, and finally responded in a careful, measured way to the question. "Well, to be perfectly frank, I do have a secondary business that has been quite profitable. I have entered into a private association that engages in the business of imports and exports. Some of these transactions have a very high-risk component to them, but with the high risks come high returns."

In vino veritas, thought the American. Now we may be getting to what Liu Tang may have really wanted to discuss. Was everything that he had said up to now been nothing more than a subterfuge? He always felt that when someone referred to their line of work as "import–export" there always seemed to be an illegal component associated with it. That was because in his side of the world the Colombians and Mexicans were notorious for the "import–export" business that related to the smuggling of drugs. Was Liu Tang involved in some sort of smuggling operation? What high risk was the Chinese man referring to?

It was no secret that heroin smugglers were running rampant across Asia, and from all indications, it seemed that the problem was getting worse. As opium was getting farmed, processed, and shipped—primarily out of Afghanistan and Myanmar—the exportation of the drug was creating a series of grave problems, especially for Russia and increasingly for China. The problems ranged from the enormous profiteering by crime syndicates, to the spreading of drugs that exacerbated the epidemic of HIV/AIDS.

The post-Taliban boom in the Afghanistan opium crop was resulting in higher volumes in the overall global heroin trade. And, while Afghanistan and Myanmar were the principal sources of the opium crop, central Asia was becoming one of the key transit routes for the heroin runners who were taking it to Russia, Eastern Europe, and also increasingly into China. A Vietnamese newspaper recently reported that five people had been arrested in Hanoi after police found them with more than ten kilograms of opium stuffed in watermelons that they were transporting into China. There was also another recent report of arrests where smugglers had stuffed heroin into packages of noodles that were also destined for China. Could Liu Tang have been involved in drug smuggling into China?

"Apparatchik," he suddenly remembered that word. He couldn't remember where he had read it, perhaps in novels, but now it was forefront in his mind, and he had a strong desire to hear it in the flesh so to speak.

"My beautiful Snegurochka," began the American, tenderly addressing the hostess.

"What are you saying?" asked the laughing hostess. She knew that the bankers had been drinking quite a bit, so she was not surprised at all by what the silly American was saying.

"Snegurochka was a beautiful snow maiden," replied the American. "And you are our beautiful snow maiden. We were wondering if you are able to love, or if your heart is cold?"

"No, I have a very loving heart. I'd hoped that you would have been able to see the very special attention that I have been giving you gentlemen. I want your experience here to be totally pleasurable. Have you not been properly attended to?" she asked in a very tender loving manner.

"Yes, we most certainly have," the American was quick to answer.

"Absolutely," also quickly chimed in Liu Tang, not wanting to appear insensitive to her charms.

"So," she continued. "What can I do for you? Why have you called me over?"

"Well, I remembered a word that I had read somewhere," began the American. "And I was hoping that you would clarify it for me. Do you see that table over there with the Russian gentlemen?"

She looked over to the table with the six businessmen that he was referring to. "Yes, I see them. What would you like to know?"

"Are they apparatchiki?"

"Are they apparatchiki?" she looked at him and laughed. "What are you asking?"

"The word 'apparatchik,' I have read it in books, but have never heard it pronounced by a Russian, nor am I sure that I have ever seen an apparatchik in the flesh. Now here is the perfect time to identify one or several at a time. Are those gentlemen apparatchiki?"

She couldn't stop laughing at his silliness. "Yes, those men may well be apparatchiki. But I won't be the one asking them. You do know what an apparatchik is?" She then began laughing again and walked away shaking her head.

"What is an apparatchik?" asked Liu Tang.

"It comes from the Russian word apparat for "party machine." In the Soviet Union, the political machine referred to the Communist Party. The chik suffix implied an agent. So, apparatchik became a Soviet colloquialism for a full-time professional agent of the Communist Party. Nowadays an apparatchik is a derogatory word for a blindly devoted official of an organization. She is quite attractive, don't you think?"

"Yes, she is."

The American hadn't yet come to terms with how much more he wanted to know of Liu Tang's business. If the business was illegal in nature, would he be willing to divulge it to a perfect stranger? Perhaps there was nothing illegal about his business activities. It certainly would be nice to come up with a get-rich-quick scheme. His eyes were roaming from table to table searching for no one in particular. They were all travelers on the same bus heading toward different directions. A young Jewish woman in her late twenties was sitting alone to dinner nearby. Her table was not too far from Liu Tang and the American. She had frizzled light-brown hair that cascaded down freely to just below her shoulders, juxtaposing against a very light complexion, and piercing blue eyes. Her aristocratic nose was not too pronounced. She was wearing a white jacket that ran down to her waist, and beneath it, a very dark rich purple dress that was full in length. When she had first arrived, the American had noticed that her hips were a little wide. All in all, she was quite an interesting looking woman.

But why was she dining alone? When the American first fixed his eyes on hers, he sensed that there was an immediate critical assessment on her part. She also seemed to be bitter about something. She was attractive and appeared to be self-assured, but at the same time, there was something about her that showed that she was disappointed about something or someone. His glance had been quick, and it was just as well because on a second look her eyes conveyed the sense that they didn't want to be looked at. She was wearing dark brown leather sandals, and so he was able to see that her toes were not painted. Her alert eyes noticed how he had even been perceptive enough to take that in.

Not wanting to show how much he enjoyed looking at her, he dissembled by periodically feigning to be looking for someone else. But he sensed that his frequent casual glances in her direction betrayed his true intentions, and her alert eyes were not fooled. With her elbow resting on her table and her hand resting against her cheek with the index finger near her ear, she was now displaying the classic thinking pose, and he was considering that if he kept up his accidental stares in her direction she was liable to get pissed off quite soon. She was a force.

"So, Liu Tang," he began. "Please tell me what it is that you are importing and exporting."

Liu Tang studied the American and seemed to be reflecting on how to best breach the subject.

"Sure," he agreed. "I can tell you, but how is it that they say in America? If I tell you then I will have to kill you." They both looked at each other and, after a moment of silence, both began to laugh.

"You know," began Liu Tang, "the illicit trafficking of tobacco is a multibillion-dollar business today. The trade is so profitable that tobacco is the world's most widely smuggled legal substance. It is believed that almost one-third of the world's cigarette exports simply vanish. Billions of cigarettes, once exported, mysteriously get lost in transit. I'm sure you will not be surprised to learn that things really changed in the late 1990s when the Chinese obtained the technology to reproduce the protective holograms on packs of top Western cigarette brands. At that point, a tobacco-counterfeiting giant was born. Today, China has become by far the world's largest supplier of counterfeit cigarettes. Ships loaded with Chinese fakes of Marlboro, Camel, and other brands are now smuggled into ports worldwide."

Liu Tang paused a moment to take another sip of his whiskey. He seemed to be organizing his thoughts, probably weighing how he was going to phrase the next part of his story for the American.

"You probably will be shocked to hear that some leading tobacco companies have been colluding with criminal networks to divert cigarettes to the world's black markets. The big tobacco companies are obviously doing it for profit. With the underground networks, they are able to circumvent the harsh new regulations that had been implemented in certain markets and avoid billions of dollars in taxes. They are also increasing their market share while recruiting growing numbers of smokers around the globe. The tobacco industry is not merely turning a blind eye to the smuggling; they are managing the trade at the highest corporate levels."

The American had been taken totally off guard by Liu Tang's arguments. This certainly was big business, and the product that Liu Tang was working with was not the one that he had been expecting to hear about. Officially, the big tobacco companies were on record committing publicly to help fight the illegal trafficking of tobacco. But the way that Liu Tang explained it, with profits rivaling those of narcotics, and with relatively light penalties, the business was fast reinventing itself. The smuggling business had previously been dominated by Western multinational companies, but cigarette smuggling had significantly expanded with new players, new routes, and new techniques. According to Liu Tang's sources, today's underground industry ranged from the Chinese counterfeiters that mimic Marlboro holograms to perfection, to Russian-owned factories that mass-produced the brands made exclusively to be smuggled into Western Europe.

"The illicit trade business has become very complex," continued Liu Tang, "and the expert intermediary that can discretely handle the import and export details related to this activity stands to make a tidy profit. Tankers loaded with Chinese fakes of Marlboro, Camel, Lucky Strike, and other brands of cigarettes are found in shipments disguised as chinaware, toys, and furniture, and these are delivered into ports worldwide. The intermediary helps to facilitate the international trade between the importer and the exporter. The services offered are of help to the exporter who may encounter considerable difficulties in estimating the risks involved when dealing with certain countries or buyers. Of course, in keeping with a cautious and farsighted policy, we as intermediaries have to be careful when called upon to assume risks for transactions with which we are not familiar, where the extent risks are difficult to assess."

"Let me see if I understand you correctly, Liu Tang. Are you saying that you are providing documentary credit services?"

"Let me just say that I provide consulting services where my expertise in the field is required. As you well know, an international banker has connections all over the world. I would be pleased to provide someone needing my assistance with information and expertise for the particular country that may be of interest to the seller. I offer services that will assist in the decision-making, considering the economic and political climate in the buyer's country. I facilitate the procurement of licenses for the jurisdiction. I clarify how the flow of funds will occur, and explain how they may be safeguarded through letters of credit. These are the services that I offer to clients."

"To be frank, Liu Tang, I am very impressed. It sounds as though you have set yourself up quite nicely. No wonder you may not be too concerned about leaving your bank. In your shoes, I could see how easy it would be to rid yourself of an unfaithful wife and of an uncomfortable situation at the firm. Congratulations, my friend. We should be drinking champagne!"

But Liu Tang did not look as though he was ready to start celebrating any time soon. However, he finished off the last of his whiskey and signaled to the hostess to come over. When the lovely hostess arrived, Liu Tang asked the American if he really wanted champagne.

"Yes, most certainly," was his reply. Why shouldn't they switch to a nice bottle of the bubbly?

"Great," replied the hostess, who had promptly arrived at their signal. "What did you have in mind, or would you like me to make a recommendation?"

"What would you recommend? Something that is not too extravagant," said the American.

"We have a lovely bottle of Champagne Perrier-Jouet. You can't go wrong with the brut. It will go great with the Strawberries Romanoff." When they started to protest about how much they had already eaten, she immediately held up her hand to stop them. "Gentlemen, you know that no Russian meal would be complete without a 'sweet.' And as for the Romanoff, there are some who believe that Catherine the Great caused the assassination of her husband, Peter III, over an argument as to who should have the last bite of the Strawberries Romanoff at a state dinner. I will have you know that ours is exceptional."

"If I'm to be totally honest, there is nothing that I can refuse you," replied the American. "No, really, please don't laugh! How can anyone say no to you? I can see why all of the male clientele here pine after you. All of these artists and musicians, tourists, international businesspeople, and professionals fall quickly under your spell. You bewitch us all. You have such an effect on me that you can't even begin to guess at. Every time you approach our table, I begin to tremble. I'm surprised that I have even had the courage to tell you. No, really. Please don't laugh. We will be gaining fifty pounds before we leave here tonight because we can't say no to you. Ask Liu Tang here if you don't believe me."

"Yes, he is quite right. I have never eaten so much in my life," replied Liu Tang. "You are hazardous to our health!" He had said this as though he really meant it. He was quite a dissembler. The hostess, laughing, left them to get the bottle of bubbly.

"Before we start celebrating too much you should know that there are real risks from being associated with this business. While the product is legal, there have been plenty of studies showing that tobacco smuggling has had a significant impact on the public global health crisis. Worldwide, one out of ten adults dies prematurely from tobacco-related diseases such as lung cancer, emphysema, cardiovascular disease, and stroke. It is believed that if current trends hold, tobacco-related deaths will result in some eight million people dying each year by 2030. And with cigarettes being heavily marketed in poorer countries, eighty percent of those deaths will be in the developing world. As you can see, I have done the homework. What kind of a man with any kind of conscience commits himself to such an enterprise?" asked Liu Tang.

"Here you are, gentlemen," interrupted the hostess. "A glorious ending to an aristocratic Russian meal. Count Pavel Stroganoff could not have had it any better from his Parisian chef. So, you now have in front of you a magnificent dessert from Imperial Russia and an excellent bottle of champagne from one of the finest producers in France. Gentlemen, I will tell you a little-known fact. As you may already know, a cuvée de prestige is proprietary blended champagne that is considered to be the top of a producer's range. What you may not know is that Louis Roederer's Cristal cuvée de prestige was the first one ever produced in France back in 1876, and this was strictly for the private consumption of the Russian Tsar Nicholas II. This was the same Nicholas II whose wife, son, four daughters, the family's medical doctor, the Emperor's footman, the Empress' maidservant, and the family's cook, were killed by the Bolsheviks on the night of July 16, 1918. I thought you might find that fact interesting."

"How can you remember all these facts," came from Liu Tang. "It's amazing."

"Even if you were making these facts up, I would believe you. Even if you were to admit that you were lying about everything, I would still believe you. Do you know why? Because I could not possibly believe that anything from your lips could possibly be false. I look at your lips and I immediately know that nothing wrong could ever come from them. If those lips can say something wrong, then the opposite couldn't possibly be right. It would be like finding a false note in a Beethoven composition, or a sloppy brush stroke in a Vermeer painting. It's just not possible. And because they are so perfect, I love those lips, your magnificently imperial lips! They were made to be perfectly kissed! Nothing else will do them justice."

"And let me guess," she began, with cheeks beginning to flush. "You are the only one that will be able to provide this perfect service?"

"Klimt, Rodin, Brâncuși, and countless other masters have tried to capture this perfect expression of love. But I hope to show you that, should you consent to meet thy hopeful lover's lips, you can expect to receive from me that most perfect kiss."

"I feel as though we are in a Woody Allen movie," was her response. "Everything you say is so funny, so comical. I have never met anyone like you. Maybe it's because I don't often have the opportunity to speak to Americans. Do all Americans speak like actors in Woody Allen movies? This is so funny. You must be a New Yorker."

"How could you guess that?" came from the astonished American.

"Are you also Jewish, because from the Woody Allen movies it is clear that Jewish New Yorkers tend to appear to be quite neurotic, apparently from all of the guilt that they seem to have. But why the guilt is not clear to me. So, are you Jewish?"

"I confess to being circumcised, but I'm not Jewish. Truthfully, I am a Catholic. I was baptized and have thoroughly confessed so that I have rid myself of all guilt. And I now stand before you as naked and as honest as I can possibly be, and as crazy for you as any neurotic character that has ever played at being in love in a Woody Allen movie!"

"Well, I feel as though Woody Allen will be coming out of hiding at any moment," said the young hostess.

But, at this point, Liu Tang interrupted their little repartee by saying, "I assure you that that won't be the case. And do you know why?" He waited a moment before responding, "Because there are no Chinese characters in any Woody Allen movies."

With that, the hostess and the American burst into peals of laughter. Woody Allen had indeed left Orientals out of his crazy world.

"Gentlemen, it has been a real pleasure chatting with you. Forgive me while I go to attend some of the apparatchiki at the other tables." She winked at them as she said this, and then moved on still laughing. Critically looking at her again, as she was leaving, he could honestly say that she didn't have any bad parts. He smiled as he considered the descriptions for such a dame in the great pulp fiction novels. His imagination went on as he watched her hips swaying as she approached the table with the Russian businessmen.

She was partly the reason that he had been spending so much time talking to this Liu Tang. What the hell did he care about this man after all? He had nothing better to do this afternoon, and that was why he accepted the invitation to have a drink. But that was quite a while ago. This hostess was exceptional, and she had a way of keeping him enthralled. A hostess like this Russian woman could put a great deal of pressure on a man. She would be quite difficult to refuse. Men go crazy over women like her. They become obsessed. They stalk them if they are refused. And if the woman accepts them, they become quite possessive and jealous. What a woman! Some men would give up everything for a woman like that. While they are in heat, they will do anything that they are asked. They permit themselves to be used, financially, physically, emotionally. They can't get enough of the torment from the woman. With her, pain becomes pleasure. They are slaves to their passions, and they can't get enough of the woman. There was a story that he had once heard when he visited a Caribbean Island. It was about a man that had just carved up his wife and her friend with a machete because he was so jealous and feared that she was planning to leave him. But you didn't have to go to the Caribbean to hear horror stories about jealous lovers. Everyone had heard about the football great in the United States who killed his wife and her male friend because of his insane jealousy.

"Liu Tang," began the American, "that woman will conquer us all. She is the female equivalent of the great

Genghis Khan. Do you remember what the great Khan is known to have said? 'The greatest joy a man can know is to conquer his enemies and drive them before him, to ride their horses and take away their possessions, to see the faces of those who were dear to them bedewed with tears and to clasp their wives and daughters in his arms.' I fear that this woman will be able to do whatever she wants with me."

Liu Tang looked at the American and laughed. "I think she knows it too. Yes, she is a terrible distraction. They should not allow her to work here. She is detrimental to your health. Your face was quite red when she was here. Your blood pressure must have gone up quite a bit." Liu Tang looked at the American with concern and then began to laugh out loud again.

"Why is it that she doesn't have the same effect on you?"

"I have so many worries and issues troubling me right now that there is very little room left for anything else. To be perfectly frank, I'm feeling quite nervous. The money that I am making is quite good, but I can't help but remember that there are plenty of negative consequences related to my personal business. I hate knowing that smuggled cigarettes are getting into the hands of those most vulnerable, the young people and the poor. The suppliers are also pushing cut-rate cigarettes into the black market, selling products often of dubious quality. Also, the illicit tobacco trade feeds an underground economy that supports many of the most violent gangs in the world. Organized crime syndicates and terrorist groups such as the Taliban and Hezbollah facilitate global distribution and use the profits to finance their activities. When you are involved in a business, you do a great deal of reading on the subject and you can't help but see all of the negatives associated with the venture. All in all, you will agree that this is a difficult business to be in. With all of these issues constantly jumping at me, do you now see why the lovely Russian hostess does not have quite the same impact on me as she does on you?"

"Yes, I do. Your little chat just now has given me a reality check. If the political and human consequences are of such an impact, are you not worried about being caught and of having to face what could be a very stiff jail sentence? I would imagine that receiving a sentence in China could be very tough. The Russians are also notorious for harshly sentencing people. I hope the rewards are worth the risks."

"They are for me, in my particular situation. The current circumstances in my life force my course of action."

"Well Liu Tang, you may be right in what you say. You need to have a good pair of balls to get along in this world. You only have to look at the current leader of the

Russian people, Vladimir Putin, as an example that bears this out."

Liu Tang was smiling as he was listening to the American talk about the Russian leader. He didn't really know what to make of it.

"So, you see Vladimir Putin as quite a good leader. You are, no doubt, impressed by the way that he has fought white-collar corruption and also by the way that he has handled the infamous Russian mob. It appears that Putin has made Russia safer at least for the Russians. Also, by his implementation of strict economic reform and tax codes, Putin has stabilized the previously plummeting Russian economy. In nationalizing the Russian oil industry, Putin has also seen massive amounts of money flowing back into the Russian government coffers. Finally, it appears to everyone that Chechnya is no longer an issue. Yes, Putin has been good for Russia. But my balls are not so big."

"Well, you also can't believe everything that you read. I don't know about you, Liu Tang. But I'm ready to clear out."

"Yes. I have had enough of this very fine establishment. Something now more vulgar would be a welcome change."

At the other table, the so-called apparatchiki were now on their third bottle of champagne. The hostess was explaining to them that besides Beluga, they also had Osetra and Sevruga caviar. "The Imperial Osetra caviar is unique golden Iranian caviar. It is produced by the rarest and most mature Osetra sturgeon. It is known for its gorgeous nutty flavor, big size grains, firm texture, and golden-brownish color."

As the American and Liu Tang passed by their table, the hostess excused herself for a moment in order to thank the two gentlemen for their patronage. "Gentlemen, I hope that you found everything to your liking."

"Oh, yes," responded the American. "Everything was definitely to our liking."

"Quite so," agreed Liu Tang. "You have been an excellent hostess."

"Yes. We were quite impressed by your expertise. You are impossible to resist."

"Thank you, gentlemen," was her response. "I hope that you will visit us again soon." She had the most brilliant teeth and didn't fail to show them off with her radiant smile. She winked at them before returning to the Russians.

"Now, gentlemen," she immediately began explaining again to the smiling comrades. "The Sevruga caviar is the choice for those who like their eggs full of taste and flavor. Among connoisseurs, they are the most highly appreciated for their unique taste. What you may not believe is that Sevruga caviar is also the least expensive, mainly because Sevruga sturgeon is to be found in the greatest number." Besides being extremely knowledge-able about her subject, her voice was incredibly seduc-tive. The American and Liu Tang smiled at the open-mouth apparatchiki who were clearly mesmerized by the hostess. Both men then began laughing, wondering how much caviar she would be able to sell to this group.

Outside, the two new comrades continued laughing, marveling at how talented the hostess had been. "She is worth a fortune," said Liu Tang.

"Absolutely," agreed the American. "She will be selling everything tonight to those poor, unsuspecting Russians. Did you see how they were drooling after her?"

"I saw you drooling at her too!"

"She is extremely dangerous, like the Sirens in Greek mythology. She is quite impossible to resist."

"Thank goodness we left when we did. I don't think that I could have eaten another morsel. You seemed to be prepared to keep ordering everything that she suggested."

"Yes. I'm sorry, Liu Tang. But I did confess to you that I was powerless in front of her. In America, women are fond of always saying that some men always seem to be thinking with their pricks and not with their heads. I think you will agree that there is definitely some truth to that."

"In China, we have a saying, 'A rat who gnaws at a cat's tail invites destruction.'"

"Nice. I think some American women would love that saying. There was also a saying from a famous American actor (I can't recall who it was) that said, 'God gave men both a penis and a brain, but unfortunately not enough blood supply to run both at the same time.' So, at least that implies that we men are clearly not to blame for our shortcomings. God is at fault in the manufacture."

"Well, it's important to be able to pass on the blame for our shortcomings, especially when we don't have the right size balls to own up."

"Amen, brother."

THE TWO MEN WERE GLAD FOR THE LONG WALK THAT had finally brought them to their hotel.

"I wonder what new nightmare will be with me tonight in that dreary hotel room. This is definitely the most depressing room that I have ever stayed in. Even the rooms in the haunted houses at American amusement parks are not as gloomy as the rooms in this hotel."

"The rooms in this hotel are quite gloomy," agreed Liu Tang.

"That probably also explains why there are a good number of flirts in the hotel bar. The Western businessmen need their company to relieve themselves of the horror of the place. How could anyone possibly fall asleep in such gloomy accommodations? I could easily believe it if someone were to tell me that Dostoyevsky had stayed once at this hotel. The room would be the perfect horror setting for the character Raskolnikov. One night in my gloomy hotel room is enough to fill anyone with anguish and make them want to commit murder. A nice Russian girl is what is required in order to put out of focus the reality of the place. But the place is so depressing that it is difficult to believe that anyone could ever even get an erection. As you are lying there with the girl, you can't help but imagine that Count Dracula will be emerging at any moment from some dark corner. What the hell was the designer thinking when he came up with his plans for the rooms? Maybe Stalin designed the place. Keeping any foreign dignitary in this hotel would be like keeping him in a sort of prison. Shall we have another drink before retiring, or are you ready for your slumber?"

"I, unfortunately, have to go out again. I have some unsettled business to attend to. Perhaps I may join you for a drink later if you are still around. Thanks again for the company today."

"Thank you, too. Take care."

· · ·

AFTER THE AMERICAN WATCHED LIU TANG STEP OUT again, he proceeded to the lobby bar, not because he needed to drink but rather because he was looking for company. It was only 9:00 pm and it was still quite bright out. He felt like taking a shower, but then he remembered how foul the water was in his hotel room and decided against it. The water pipes in St. Petersburg were notoriously old and were known to disperse water of various colors, ranging from dingy yellow to rusty brown. The water was so bad that tourists coming to St. Petersburg were advised to drink only bottled water. Many tourists were even instructed to brush their teeth with bottled water to avoid exposure to giardia. The parasite was known to live in St. Petersburg's tap water, and it could produce disastrous effects on the stomach. Besides causing diarrhea, it could also cause severe vomiting and other very unpleasant side effects. And, as if that were not bad enough, parasites were not the only problem with the water. Chemicals and metals were also issues that raised concern.

All the gloom and doom reminded the American that tomorrow he was hoping to visit the Alexander Nevsky Monastery complex. The Trinity Cathedral in the Monastery complex was one of the few churches that had remained open during the Soviet era. The Tikhvin Cemetery on the grounds of the monastery was quite interesting. There, he would be able to visit the graves of Borodin, Glinka, Tchaikovsky, Mussorgsky, Rimsky-Korsakov, and Dostoevsky. That was the plan for tomorrow, after the morning's conference. For tonight he had to improvise on some other option.

She was quite young, maybe twenty. There was a sweet and gentle smile on her lips. Her friend, a little older, a bit paler, and more serious, stood beside her.

"You talk a lot of nonsense," he heard the younger girl telling her friend.

"So, you don't believe it?" was what the taller girl responded.

"No, I can't say that I do."

When they noticed that they were being stared at by the American, they burst out laughing. He had been distracted by their conversation and had absentmindedly looked in their direction. He was momentarily amused by their laughter, and it showed on his confused face. For the past half-hour, he had been quietly reflecting on everything that Liu Tang had told him. The Asian was tangled in a web of complex issues, and he now felt sorry for him. His thoughts about the man were no longer the same as what he had imagined on the previous night.

The girls nodded to him and raised their wine glasses in salutation, and before long they were by his side.

"God, it's wonderful to see such beautiful Russian women in excellent health." He put his arms around their waists and kissed them gently on their cheeks.

They were quite pleased with him because he appeared to be the successful banker that they were hoping to catch. They could also sense that he was not going to be any trouble as he already seemed to be a bit tipsy. This was going to be a definite deal. What was not decided yet was which of the two girls was going to have him. Another drink was required in order to have this sort itself out. They sensed that he had not yet committed to either of them.

"I've had a long day," he suddenly said.

"Yes?" the taller one was first to respond. "Perhaps you need a massage." As she said this she started rubbing him firmly around his neck. She was taking the initiative, she was the more assertive, and before anyone knew how it happened, it had been decided that she would be the one.

"I'm sorry, babe. Jet lag disorder," he explained. "My internal clock has signaled that it's time to sleep," he gently confessed.

"Don't worry about it, honey. I perfectly understand. Sweet dreams," the girl said, winking at him.

CHAPTER NINE

"THE GOVERNMENT of the Russian Federation, in cooperation with The Central Bank of Russia, has worked hard on developing measures aimed at improving complex issues in the banking sector. Specifically, they have worked with the Banking Congress on addressing serious defects in law enforcement practice and on the overall low general level of transparency in the financial sectors." This was how a Division Head of The Central Bank of Russia began his address to the members of the International Banking Congress.

"We must take the necessary measures," he continued, "to improve the overall system of corporate management and internal controls using the best international banking practices, including the recommendations of the Basle committee on banking supervision. Access to the information must be made available to all interested parties (shareholders, participants, customers, and auditors), and the activity of credit organizations must be disclosed within the framework of the current legislation."

The audience gave a resounding ovation to the Central banker's recommendations. Everyone was to now be aware that business under Russia's Vladimir Putin would not be conducted as it had been in the past. Russia was destined to become an economic force in the near future, and this required all of the participants in the financial sector to adapt to the newly proposed recommendations. After those closing remarks, the American began to plan his cultural excursions for the day.

The first order of business was to take a peek at the Propaganda Café, which was situated just off the Nevsky Prospect. A decade had passed since the fall of the Soviet Union, but the theme of this fast-food establishment was a retro look at the post-Revolutionary epoch. The restaurant was decorated according to the aesthetics of the 1920s, the era that denied the bourgeois way of life. The interior of the place was designed with the geometric styling of Soviet propaganda posters. The walls were decorated with unique original-time posters of the constructive style of the Soviet 1920s. There was even an electric chair where you could sit to have your meal. A small statue of Lenin sat on the windowsill. The place was designed with tourists in mind, but Russians also frequented the establishment. It was a nice place to take in a break, and in keeping with the theme of the era, the service was appropriately slow which was to be expected in the eating establishments of that time. This was the era, the proprietor noted, where "romantic dreams were tightly connected with the most destructive ideas." The proprietor noted that in his restaurant today the proletariat and bourgeoisie were served Japanese Kamchatka steak, Mexican fiesta salad, Arabic dumplings, and American hamburgers.

Having had his lunch, the American was now eager to resume his walk along the Nevsky Prospect. Nikolai Gogol had once said that there was nothing better than Nevsky Prospect. The Russian muzhik arguing with his wife on the street corner about his coppers, the old women in their tattered dresses rushing on their way to the churches, indecently overweight shop owners and their salesclerks every morning getting their shops ready, decent men with thick velvety whiskers in long frock coats and ladies in colorful riding coats and hats, these were all of the colorful characters that Gogol painted in his wonderful short stories set in St. Petersburg. When the romantic American strolled along the boulevard, he wanted to look at the locals through Gogol's eyes. "But strangest of all are the events that take place on Nevsky

Prospect!" cautiously whispered one of the characters in a Gogol story. "I always wrap myself tighter in my cloak and try not to look at the objects I meet at all. Everything is deception, everything is a dream, and everything is not what it seems to be!" It had been said that on Nevsky Prospect, people of various guises appeared, disappeared, and reappeared in other likenesses. There was a deceptive nature about the place, changing constantly without reasonable explanations.

The American arrived at the Hermitage at two in the afternoon, and he soon realized that his limited time before closing would not be nearly enough to take in many of the great paintings. But before proceeding to any of them, he wanted to first take in Antonio Canova's remarkable statue known as The Three Graces. The Three Graces were the daughters of Zeus, and they were the companions of the muses that bestowed their gifts upon humanity. Canova depicted them from left to right as Euphrosyne (mirth), Aglaia (elegance), and Thalia (youth and beauty). The three goddesses were sculpted as beautiful young women, artless in their nudity, and touching in their intricate embrace. They are united by their linked hands, and also by the scarf which lies loosely against their naked bodies. Critics had stated that the unity of the Graces was one of the piece's main themes.

"So, here you are, at the feet of Canova's women." It

was the hostess from the previous night's restaurant. "What's so extraordinary about the work?" She was wearing a fine white cotton shirt stitched with blue silk and embroidered with little red flowers. Her pants were of blue denim, closely fitting. Her hair was beautifully braided into a single plait. "I've been standing here watching you. So, what do you really feel about these women? Tell me."

He was quite surprised to find her at the Hermitage. "Wow! I can't believe that you are here. That was an excellent meal that you recommended to us last night. Thank you for the excellent suggestions. But what are you doing here?" She could tell that he was extremely delighted to see her. She smiled at him.

"I'm a student at St. Petersburg State University. I'm currently taking courses there in languages and art. I often come to the Hermitage for research. It's a wonderful place." She stopped for a moment and smiled. "You know, on my off hours, I am not in the habit of lecturing. So, you have been staring enough at Canova's women. Now you must confess to me what you really think about this work of art."

"What do I think of these beautiful women? I'm jealous of their intimacy, of their freedom in the way that they openly display their admiration for each other. They are oblivious to the outside world. They are graceful women, tender in the way that they touch each other, in an eternal embrace. I'm jealous of the way that they can display so much honest affection for each other. This is an intimate moment, eternally captured. The onlooker is left longing to participate in their embrace, but he is left alone, and he can't help but admire their beauty. That is what I think."

"I can see that you are a very passionate man," the hostess said. She seemed very impressed by his assessment of the work. "You have really considered the work, and have intimately responded to it. I know that you are a banker, but are you also an artist?"

"No, but Antonio Canova has really moved me with his creation. It is absolutely beautiful, and unquestionably a masterpiece. Now, I have a question for you. How is it that I do not know your name? We spent a great deal of time yesterday evening talking to each other, but I never quite learned your name."

"So, you spent a great deal of time talking to me, and you don't even know my name. Perhaps you weren't too keen on knowing it, or maybe you were really concentrating on what your Chinese friend was saying to you. It is not important," she concluded.

"I'm kidding," he quickly interjected. "Of course, I know your name."

"Do you?"

"Yes. It is quite obvious."

"What is my name, then? How is it obvious? What do you mean? You've got me intrigued."

"Your name is Snegurochka, the Snow Maiden," he said, laughing.

"Snegurochka?" she repeated, smiling. "What are you talking about? Who told you that is my name? Now I remember that you said something to that effect last night."

"Ha! I have been studying you too, you know. In pan-Slavonic mythology, Snegurochka is the daughter of Frost and Spring, and she is drawn to the warmth of mortal love."

"I was right, you know. You are a romantic!" She laughed at him.

"The Snow Maiden," he continued, "whose heart is at first as cold as snow, but later is filled with unrestrained passion! The Snow Maiden finds herself in the world of mortals. But being a supernatural creature, she can live only as long as her heart is not warmed by mortal love. If she falls in love, the rays of the sun will melt her!"

"So, you don't think Snegurochka is capable of love?" she very sweetly asked, pouting her lovely red lips as she was doing so.

"Are you?" he asked. "Are you capable of loving? First, your beautiful eyes lure one's soul out. Then your poor victim finds himself confused and disappointed when he realizes that your tender love will not be forthcoming."

She was really laughing at him now as he was saying all of this nonsense to her.

"I didn't realize last night at the restaurant that you were so crazy. Where do you get all this stuff from?"

"Don't worry," he said in a way that he sincerely hoped would be reassuring to her. "I fully understand your predicament. It is quite clear from your beauty that you are not of this world, and I know what will happen to you if you fall in love."

"You are really amazing. And you figured all this out by yourself? Well, of course. Who else could have possibly helped you to come to this crazy idea, unless it was that Chinese man that you were with last night."

"Liu Tang? No, he was preoccupied with something else."

"Another woman, no doubt?"

"You don't want to know."

"I want to take you somewhere. Come!"

CHAPTER TEN

THE FIRST THING that he noticed when he entered the café was that Bach's Italian Concerto was playing in the background. He had reluctantly accepted her invitation to go to the Singer House, a historical landmark building located at the intersection of Nevsky Prospect with Griboyedov Canal. Reluctantly he went, not because he did not want to be with her, but because there was still a great deal that he had not seen at the Hermitage. But how could he possibly pass up on her offer? She was herself a masterpiece!

"Originally the Singer Sewing Machine Company had commissioned the architect Pavel Syusor to design a skyscraper building that would be similar to the one that was being constructed for their headquarters in New York," she began like a tour guide. "However, the building code of St. Petersburg did not permit the building of a structure taller than the Winter Palace. The architect's elegant solution to the restriction was the construction of a seven-story building with a tower on the top that was crowned with a glass globe. The globe symbolized the worldwide reach of Singer's activities. The famous art nouveau building, now also known as the House of Books, was given to the Petrograd State Publishing House after the October revolution. The building is an important part of the city's architectural heritage and is much visited by citizens and tourists alike."

After an initial appreciative look at the outside of the building, they had moved on to the second story where they found the delightful Café Singer. The place was elegant and comfortable, and with the palm trees surrounding the wooden tables, there was an old-world charm about the place. The patrons sat on cozy chairs upholstered in dark green leather. The lunches and desserts were served on fine white porcelain. It was the perfect place to take a break between museums and sightseeing.

She ordered for herself an amazingly thick hot chocolate that could have been consumed with a spoon, along with a very tart cherry pie. He settled for the blueberry-blackberry tart topped with meringue, and a cup of coffee. The tart was very good and had a generous portion of berries.

"This is absolutely my favorite café in St. Petersburg. I hope that you like it."

"The old historical building is fabulous, the pastry is excellent, the coffee is good, and the company is exceptional. I couldn't be happier!"

"That is good," she said. "You know, hearing about all of those bankers attending the conference makes you wonder how a person chooses a career path. How and when did you know that you would become a banker? I would really like to know how you went about making that decision."

"Yes, citizen, have you been wondering how a capitalist comes into being." He was grinning as he said this, raising an eyebrow. "Well, I can't speak for anyone else, and I'm probably the poorest example of the lot. Sometimes decisions come into being after a sequence of events that, to the uninformed, may appear to be illogical."

He took a sip of his coffee and gave a pensive gesture, while he was thinking about the series of events that led him to the career path that he had chosen. She watched him, patiently waiting to see what he was going to say. And it didn't take him long to respond to the question that he had never been asked before.

"When I was in my first year of college, I was taking

chemistry, biology, and calculus courses that I hoped would lead me to a medical career. The most challenging one of the three was the chemistry class. I can still remember that lab class for the chemistry course as if it was only yesterday."

She noticed that, for the first time, he had taken a very serious tone in the way that he was expressing himself, forming his hands into a steeple. To her, he seemed quite an interesting man. He appeared to be free and easy in his approach to life. He didn't seem to be the alpha dog that she had seen in other banker types. Those, to her, were the rather boring types. In a very superficial analysis, they seemed to measure everything by results.

"In the chemistry lab, we worked independently," he continued. "We had to go through a series of tests on an unknown compound. The task was to correctly identify the compound. A partial grade for the course would be determined from the results of the lab study." He paused here for a moment, painfully recalling the experience. "Would you believe that after weeks of testing I came up with the solution?"

"Wonderful! And that is why you became a banker. You're right! It doesn't seem to make sense. This cherry pie is quite good!"

He looked at her and didn't doubt for a minute that

there was no way that she could possibly understand what he had meant from his illogical answer.

"Yes, I'm sure that your cherry pie is quite delicious. And your lips look sweet and deliciously red too because of your pie. God, I would love to see what they taste like."

"Yes, I'm sure you would. But it is not possible. We cannot fraternize with the patrons."

"But I am not your patron," he quickly interjected in protest.

"Yes, but you have been, and you may well be again," was her retort, avoiding eye contact.

"Hmm! If that is to be the case, then please make a note that I will no longer be a patron. I will most willingly relinquish that role. So, do not wipe your lips because I'm quite ready for my taste."

"I'm sorry but I can't. You see, your reasoning doesn't make any sense to me. It doesn't make sense to me how you became a banker from that little episode that you have just told me. And, you just can't say now that you will no longer be a patron. It just doesn't add up, any of it."

He looked disappointed, but he didn't push it. There was still something that he had left out of his story, and she knew it.

"Let me see. What could I have possibly forgotten to

tell you about my story? Yes, there is one additional detail. My results were confirmed later when I received a grade C for my efforts. You would have expected me to receive an A for an accurate finding. But what you don't know is that I was swayed by discussions with others in the class into submitting a result that was different from that which I had found in my experiments, and this left me with a disastrous outcome. Medical school is very competitive in the United States, and a C will not get you in. Sure, it was only one course. But I had learned a lesson about myself that was difficult to accept, and I no longer cared about entering into the medical profession. That was one of those turning points in my life that I can't seem to ever put behind me. All of these years have passed by and I still can't get over it."

"That is quite a good story. It is very revelatory. I really like it."

"I thought you might. And now, will you be telling me your name or will you be denying me that as well?"

"Ah! I thought you were content with knowing me as Snegurochka. I sort of liked that. You were quite convincing in your argument. Anyway, my name is Nadya, Nadya Ivanovna." She said this as she was leaning back on her chair, totally at ease and in control.

"Nadya Ivanovna. Nadya Ivanovna," he repeated. He seemed to be searching for something as he said it. It sounded like one of those lovely names that he had once read somewhere in a Russian novel. "Very nice," he said.

"Thank you. I'm glad that you like it. But, even if you didn't, it's the only one I have."

"It has been very nice of you to take out some of your personal time to bring me here. I really appreciate it."

"Oh, it has been my pleasure. I love coming to the Singer Café whenever I can. It's a real treat for me as well. I was also curious to know what kind of a capitalist banker you were," she added, narrowing her eyes to feign skepticism. "But now I will remember you as the plodding chemist that came up with the right answer and then made the wrong decision. You sound as though you could be a Russian. We always have all the right answers and still manage to make the wrong decisions."

CHAPTER ELEVEN

WHEN HE RETURNED to the hotel lobby bar later that evening, he managed to find a copy of a British newspaper lying on a small table. The folded newspaper had been left open to a small article that had been quoted from a Reuter's story. The article stated that in Beijing a court had convicted a Mr. Hao Lu on smuggling and bribery charges. Mr. Hao Lu had been sentenced to life imprisonment. The conviction, the article continued, effectively ended the career of a man who had been running a vast smuggling ring that was part of a network that operated in Hong Kong and Shanghai. The network was involved with the importation of cigarettes, cars, oil products, and industrial materials and textiles. The news agency reported that Hao Lu had been successful over the years because he had been able to bribe fifty-five officials through gifts of cash, real estate, and vehicles.

The American ordered a glass of wine and looked toward the corner of the room where Liu Tang normally sat. It was still relatively early, so he was not surprised that the Asian was not there yet. Russian girls were already sitting together at the bar, no doubt waiting to see what bankers they would be enticing later that evening. The three Danes and the Dutchman were also already sitting together at their customary table. The Polish and the Hungarian girls were seated at the table adjacent to them. The female Japanese banker that the Dutchman had lusted after was sitting with two British bankers from Barclays bank. They were all creatures of habit, thought the American, miles away from home and already adapting to comfortable routines. Like clockwork, the bankers had arrived for their last drinks before retiring to their rooms. It was the last chance to socialize, to network, to maybe get lucky with a new partner. But there wasn't much time left for this to happen. And soon, before they even knew how it happened, they would all come to an agreement that it was time to give up, at least for that day.

But where was Liu Tang? Would the fallout in China affect him in any way? Did he participate in any of the activity that was tied to Hao Lu's business? It had been reported that several Chinese businessmen in Canada were being deported to face charges related to Hao Lu's trial. China had conceded that it would not execute any of the businessmen in the event that they would be found guilty. This concession was important to Canada because it was well-known that anyone facing corruption charges in China would undoubtedly be found guilty.

Liu Tang had stated that he was sufficiently distanced from the actual smuggling operations so that he would be reasonably safe in the event of a crackdown. He insisted that he was only an intermediary agent that facilitated the transfer of funds between buyers and sellers which transpired when the delivery of goods occurred. If there was some smuggling that occurred in the delivery process, then how could he be implicated? His participation, he reasoned, was a legitimate one tied to the world of trade financing. Invoices were presented for payment after bureaucrats signed off on transferred merchandise and again after the goods had been received at the ports. This was how the commercial world operated globally, legitimately. This was how he viewed his part in the transactions, and this was what he had relayed to the American.

The American didn't feel like socializing with any of the bankers. He had had a pleasant afternoon at the Hermitage, and couldn't believe his good luck in having run into Nadya Ivanovna. He loved the brief time that he was able to spend with her at the Singer Café. Nadya

Ivanovna, the name sounded familiar but he couldn't quite place it. When would he be able to see her again? There weren't many days left to the conference.

The Polish and Hungarian girls spotted him and waved. He decided that perhaps he would say hello to them, so he moved to their table with his glass of wine. Martha was the Hungarian one, but for the life of him, he couldn't remember the Polish girl's name.

"Lyubov!" he said to them, as he raised his glass in a toast.

"Lyubov?" the girls simultaneously asked.

"Lyubov!" he responded. "I think it means 'To love.'"

"Lyubov!" they then repeated in unison, lifting their glasses and displaying wide grins as they said it.

"Quite a useful toast," he remarked. Then his eyes widened as he suddenly remembered that the Polish girl's name was Sonia.

"Yes," Martha agreed. "Do you have any other useful toasts that you would like to share with us?" She had a mischievous smile on her face as she said this.

"Let me see," he seemed to be trying to remember. "Yes, there is Passashok!"

"Passashok?" They looked at him with mouths opened in wonder.

"Passashok! It means one last drink for the road."

The two girls burst out laughing when he said this.

"Yes," Martha said. "That is quite a handy one to know."

"Yes," agreed Sonia. "It's very important to be able to get one last one in before leaving." With this, they all burst out laughing again.

"I can see that you are making good use of your time here in Russia. You are learning all of the important things," Martha said.

"We noticed that you weren't at the conference this afternoon. Is that when you were fine-tuning your expertise in Russian?"

"You've caught me. I spent the afternoon at the Hermitage, and then a lovely native volunteered to take me to her favorite café. What could I do?"

"You poor baby," said Sonia.

The two girls looked at him with amusement. The Russian girls were also glancing at him and smiling from their table. They raised their glasses to him in salutation as well.

"More new friends?" inquired Sonia.

"Well, St. Petersburg is a great deal friendlier than I would have ever imagined," he said. Then he noticed that Liu Tang had just entered the lobby, so he thought it was the best time to introduce a new topic. He asked them if they had heard the news about the arrest of the major Chinese smuggler. They had not heard anything.

Liu Tang spotted him, and after the American signaled, he made his move to join them.

"Hello ladies, and my good friend. I hope you don't mind if I have a nightcap with you?" said the Asian.

"By all means, Liu Tang," responded the American.

"Yes, join us," chimed in the two girls. The Russian girls raised their glasses to Liu Tang too when he looked in their direction.

"A whiskey, then, neat," he said to the waitress. "I did not see you today in the conference room, my friend," said Liu Tang to the American. "I hope you have not been ill."

"Nope," Martha volunteered. "He has just informed us that he spent the day at the Hermitage, and then took private Russian lessons at a café with a native beauty."

"Excuse me! I don't recall ever having said with a native beauty."

Martha blushed after having been corrected.

"Nope, you're quite right. I hope that I have not compromised you in any way. He is quite right," addressing Liu Tang now. "He did not say anything with regard to a native beauty. I stand corrected. In fact, she was an old hag." Then, addressing the American again, he said, "There now, I hope I have not gotten you into any trouble." Martha tried to look quite contrite.

"Yes, you should be sorry" the American began

chastising her. "And you will have to make it up to me," he added, displaying a mischievous smile.

"Yes, I agree," Sonia said. "She should make it up to you. You shouldn't let her get away with it." Then both girls started laughing again. Shortly afterward, they excused themselves from the men, saying that they had a previously agreed-to dinner engagement.

"Oh, what a pity. At another time then," came from the American.

"I hope that we will see you at tomorrow's conference presentations," said Sonia.

"Yes, if you can break away for a little while from your private Russian lessons," added Martha with a snicker.

As soon as the two women had left, the American began speaking to Liu Tang about what he had read in the newspaper. But Liu Tang immediately raised his hand to stop him from commenting further. Liu Tang took a slow sip of his whiskey and smiled at the Russian ladies. They, in turn, raised their wine glasses to him. The American didn't say another word. He was feeling rather foolish. He didn't know why he had bothered to even mention the article. It was none of his affairs. He wasn't engaged in any way to the enterprise or the man. There was no reason why he should concern himself with the other man's business. Fuck him, the American thought.

Liu Tang swirled the whiskey in his glass, then closed his eyes and inhaled deeply the scent of the liquor. It was clear that he was enjoying this little exercise, this very precious moment. His face then took on a very tranquil demeanor. The American followed suit. He took the wine goblet to his nose and took a moment to inhale the scent from the wine. Then he proceeded to take a sip of the wine and swirl it in his mouth as wine connoisseurs always did when they were trying to judge the characteristics of the vintner's product. Then he finally closed his eyes too before finally taking a sip. Strangely enough, the little exercise gave him a better appreciation of the wine that he had been drinking. It wasn't at all that bad, he conceded. Meanwhile, the Russian girls stared at the two men, waiting to see if they were going to be interested in their company. They didn't know what to expect from these two idiots, and the two men didn't know what to say to each other. Neither of them was ready to break the silence, so they continued drinking in silence. It was really quite relaxing.

"Do you have a preference for either of the Russian ladies?"

"No, not tonight, Liu Tang."

"Then I hope you will forgive me if I go and have a necessary chat with them."

A necessary chat is what the Asian said.

"Go ahead. Please do," replied the American.

CHAPTER TWELVE

"DESPITE YEARS OF ECONOMIC POLICY FAILURES," the expert began, "we are now seeing that a bright Russian future is still possible. The economic collapse of 1998, while devastating, has given way to a new strong effort to dig out from beneath the rubble and start afresh. There are strong indicators that the slow economic progress that began recently has gained some momentum." Mikhail Lobov, Russia's leading economist, was given the unenviable task of trying to convince the foreign investors that Russia had made recent significant changes in its economic strategies and was well underway to a remarkable recovery. The energetic, thin-faced man with bushy eyebrows and rimless glasses paused to take a drink of water before mapping out his reasons why Russia was well situated to show significant economic growth in the very near future.

The American had been scanning the room of participants and was not surprised to find that attendance for this morning's presentation was high. He smiled when he noticed that the Dutch banker was sitting next to the female Japanese banker that he had been lusting after. He wondered if they had finally come to an understanding. He doubted it.

"Importantly," Mr. Lobov went on, "the Russian government is using the breathing space created by the high oil prices to implement the much-needed tax simplification and government spending reductions. As you may know," the speaker took another slight pause for a drink of water, "Russia's Center for Strategic Research prepared an economic reform program which emphasized reducing government spending, balancing the central government's budget, eliminating many state subsidies, and implementing a 13% flat income tax rate. With regard to the last item, we are happy to report that President Putin has just signed the flat tax into law, calling it the most important event in the country's life." The speaker was then briefly interrupted by a warm round of applause for this latest breakthrough. "Amidst these signs of slow economic recovery," he then began again, "foreign investment is tentatively trending toward pre-August 1998 levels. More than fifty billion dollars in foreign capital has entered Russia during the first five months of this year, which is twice as much as during all of last year."

Try as he might, the American could not find Liu Tang in the audience. Could he still be entertaining in his room? That was not very likely. But perhaps he had been unnerved about the news regarding the smuggling crackdown in China. That had to be disquieting even if he had not been implicated at this time. The American was then distracted as he noticed the Dutchman surreptitiously passing a little note to his neighbor. She briefly glanced at it but displayed no reaction. The Dutchman reminded him now of school-age kids that slyly passed silly notes to their classmates that were always a distraction to the other members of the class. Was the Dutchman professing his lust for her? The man was a lunatic!

As if on cue, just as the Dutchman got up to leave the room, the bushy-browed speaker moved on to explain why he thought Russia was now poised to move forward.

"Perhaps most important for Russia's future is the fact that young Russians are now significantly more supportive of democracy and free enterprise than their older compatriots. The younger generation in Russia, which seems less influenced by the legacy of Soviet Communism than their parents, displays an entrepreneurial spirit that was largely unknown in Soviet days. Remarkably, three-fourths of the 18 to 29-year old group believe that it is important to achieve success with a business of their own. This energy and vigor can transform Russian society and Russia's economic future if it is not indefinitely stifled by current government impediments to the market." This last argument brought on an even stronger round of applause from the audience. "Tough times don't last, but tough people do," he concluded.

It was strange for him to be having those bleak thoughts now. To be perfectly frank, the American was fed up with being a banker. He loved the perks but hated the culture. He loved attending the conferences because it allowed him to travel business class and to stay at first-class hotels in many exciting cities. He loved being catered to and being looked after when he traveled, but the demands that the job made on him throughout the years were grueling. There were the long hours and the tight deadlines that were continuous, year in and year out. There were the monthly goals that had to be met, and the bullshit that he had to take from people that didn't even know where they were standing. He had to take it all in and not complain. Tough times don't last, but tough people do. That resonated with him now. Then he looked in the mirror, raised an eyebrow, stared at his squinting eyes, lit now with an inner glow or twinkle of mischief, and left with a rush of adrenaline. He was ready for action.

The American had seen an advertisement on the internet for what was termed the complete Vodka Experience. This was being offered in the same hotel where he had dined with Liu Tang and where the beautiful hostess Nadya Ivanovna worked. The ad stated that guests registering for the Vodka Experience would learn how to pair the Russian spirit with food, participate in a cocktail master class, and indulge in specially created vodka spa treatments. This seemed to the American to be the most perfect ending that he could hope for that evening.

In business casual attire he showed up at the hotel at 8 pm, which was the earliest session offered. Much to his disappointment, there were only three women and five men showing up for the event. The unexpectedly small turnout was probably because the 10 pm session would be the more popular one. The Vodka Experience began with a food pairing of Astrakhan Beluga Caviar with Beluga Vodka, marinated salmon with Tsarskaya Gold Vodka, and for dessert, strawberries dusted with icing sugar served with Russian Standard vodka. The servings of vodka were extremely generous so that by the time that this part of the event was over the guests were feeling very satisfied.

The cocktail master class was given at one of the

hotel's smaller bars. The session began with the Wake-Up Call, which was the first cocktail that was taught. The ingredients included a mixture of ginger, honey, lemon, and Standard Platinum Russian Vodka. Following this heady mixture were Dirty Martinis, Bloody Marys, Moscow Mules, and White Russians. By the end, the American was feeling a bit intoxicated and he was glad for it.

After the master class, the lovely spa hostess gathered the guests and confirmed to them what they already knew, that they were now ready for the excellent services of the spa.

"Based on the circulatory boosting elements of vodka," explained the hostess, "you have the choice between two vodka-based treatments designed to rid the body of unwanted toxins. These are the Welcome to Russia Vodka Scrub or the Vodka Massage."

The therapist explained to the guests that the Welcome to Russia Scrub started with the therapist pouring premium vodka into a shot glass and then adding lemon and caviar to create a nourishing mixture which was then gently smoothed onto the stomach. A scrub was then applied to the back and left to soak in before it was showered off.

The Vodka Massage, on the other hand, lasted sixty minutes and began with a ritual washing of the feet using a hot vodka compress. This was to be followed by a full body massage, using a delicate mixture of vodka and the oil of Arctic birch.

After deciding on the Vodka Massage, the American was escorted by a lovely oriental therapist to one of the modern spa rooms for his treatment. Before asking him to disrobe, she surprised him by commenting on the loveliness of his Polo shirt. It was just a simple white buttoned-down shirt with the dark blue Polo insignia over the left side. He looked very neat and well-manicured. His mustache was very precisely trimmed and expertly cut so that it coincided with where his upper lip ended, and his salt-and-pepper hair was cut shorter this time than he was normally accustomed to having it cut. He was in his late forties, but the years didn't really show because he was tall, elegant, and polished. But he wasn't what they referred to in south Florida as a metrosexual. He didn't go for manicures and pedicures, or the shaving of his chest hairs. In his mind, he was the rough-and-tumble James Bond that Ian Fleming portrayed in his novels. These were the novels that he couldn't put down in his early high school years and that still largely resonated in his fantasy world. Polished and cultured yes, but he could be rough at times too. He imagined that what the Asian masseuse saw in him was this mixture of the two types of men, though in all likelihood what she probably saw was an inebriated successful American businessman looking for a sensuous massage.

They locked in a momentary glance and then simultaneously smiled at each other. There was an undefined understanding between them; they were compatible.

She asked him to disrobe and to lie face down on the table, and before leaving him, she dimmed the lights of the room and turned on the soothing music that was normally associated with yoga, Reiki, and massage relaxation. Soon he could expect her to release the accumulated tensions of the day with this blend of ocean waves and soft music, which would perfectly complement her blissful massage.

Several minutes later she entered the room and found him lying naked, face down on the table. He had decided to ignore placing the towel over his posterior. He wondered how she would react. He soon found that she had decided to ignore the towel as well. She positioned herself in front of his faced down head, poured oil into her hands, and rubbed them together to make sure that they were warm before beginning to massage his upper back.

"Hi. Are you ok?" she asked.

"Fine," he responded.

"My name is Xixi," she said. "Do you like it hard or medium?"

He raised his head to look at her and smiled as he said, "Medium, I think."

"What is your name?" she asked him a few moments

later. She had lovely oriental features and a very athletic body with surprisingly strong hands. The hotel had to be very careful in selecting their female therapists. The girls had to be very appealing to attract the wealthy male patrons, but they also had to be careful. After all, the hotel's reputation was on the line.

"James," he responded to her.

"Are you American?" was her next question.

"Yes." He kept his answers brief.

"I really liked your shirt," she admitted when the session had ended. And then, after thinking about it, she added, "I hope that you are making the most of your visit to St. Petersburg." When he questioned her about her ancestry, she showed him several photos of herself from where she lived in a town just south of Shanghai. One of the photos showed her in a very formal red dress sporting a very sexy pose. The photo had been taken at the wedding of her best friend.

Though he felt physically relieved, he still had that tired feeling that was probably the result of his inability to sleep. During their brief exchange, as he dressed, and just to make conversation, he had mentioned to her that it was the Chinese year of the snake. To which she responded that she had been born in the year of the snake. The snake, he remembered from reading the paper placemats back home in his favorite Chinese restaurant, represented an intelligent personality that was full of grace. Known to possess a spirit of material-ism, the snake had a personality that was sharp at deci-sion-making. Chinese mythology held that a half-human snake was the father of the Chinese emperors. Chinese women born during the year of the snake were suppos-edly endowed with beauty and wisdom, esoteric knowl-edge, and spiritual discovery. This brief discussion about Chinese culture with the girl had made him feel hungry and made him long for his favorite Chinese restaurant back in New York. Before leaving, she made a comment that surprised him.

"Nobody's ever really happy or happy at the appro-priate time, since happiness is always referencing to a time that recalls a past," she had said.

"Is this one of those wise sayings from Confucius?" he asked her.

"No. That is what I see," she said.

He thought about it and considered that perhaps she had misread something from his facial expression, as he had been recalling that delicious Yang chow style rice and the tasty Tsing Tsao shrimp that he often ate at the Tang Pavilion. But he didn't say anything.

"Thanks again," he said as he was leaving. She then courteously bowed to him with folded hands and said goodbye.

CHAPTER THIRTEEN

On his way back to his hotel he passed by a bar where musicians were playing American jazz. The band was apparently from the Czech Republic. There was a tenor sax, a trumpet, a trombone, a clarinet, a bass, and a drummer. When the American walked in, the saxophonist was playing fancy little flourishes in the middle range, while the trumpet player came out with his rough, dirty, sobbing tones that sounded like they came from another world. The clarinet player wailed shrilly in the highest register of his instrument while the bass player played so softly that it was almost too low to be heard. Then the trombone player sank to the explosive depths of his instrument to build up the bass as the alto sax began again with his little flourishes. Incredibly, they all came together like magic to produce a beautiful sound. It was a Miles Davis tune that they were playing.

The place was small but had a pretty good crowd that seemed to be quite appreciative of the music. The music made the American have a deep and awful longing for something, but what the longing was for he couldn't possibly say. He suddenly felt alone and seemed to be suffering from a depressive melancholy. He had read once that there was a Russian word for this feeling, a word that in English did not exist or that did not exactly capture the feeling that he had. Vladimir Nabokov had referred to it as something like a soul-ache. Tocka was the word, the very sad Russian word that defined the feeling and that was very popular in Russia for quite a long time. It was the word used to express the great spiritual anguish that occurred without any specific cause. The soul ached because there was a longing, but what that longing was for was not self-evident. It was also the feeling of missing something or someone that you never had in the first place. It was a word that was deeply embedded in Russian culture, and it was contagious. Now, what was that magic potion that could bring him back to life? The locals called it Slavyanskaya.

"Slavyanskaya, please," he said to the barmaid. Slavyanskaya was what was recommended by the locals when you were in a rut when you were having that tocka feeling. Slavyanskaya would help you cope, and if you drank enough of it, it would help you forget that you had ever been longing for anything.

When the band had started again with Riverside Blues, he decided that it was time to move on. But as he scanned the room he noticed that there were two girls sitting together speaking in English by the bar. One seemed to be Chinese, but the other clearly wasn't. This second girl had her back to him, so he couldn't make out her face. But her hair was braided in the same manner that Nadya Ivanovna, the hostess from the Grand Europe Hotel, braided hers. What a wonderful surprise, he thought as he decided to approach the two girls. As he approached Nadya from the back, he covered her eyes with his hands so that she could not see who it was, and then he kissed her gently on her cheek. The Chinese girl looked at him and smiled as she waited to see what the reaction of her friend would be. When he removed his hands from her eyes she quickly turned to see who the lover boy was, and then they were both shocked when they realized that they didn't know each other. She was not Nadya, and she did not know him.

"Oh my God! I'm so sorry." He immediately apologized. "I thought that you were someone else. Your hair is combed just as my friend combs hers, and from behind you look just like her." The Chinese girl was really enjoying herself watching the two of them reacting to the incident.

"Oh, don't worry. I perfectly understand."

"Well, may I at least buy you ladies a drink? Let me at least recompense for the intrusion." He was hopeful for their company.

"Well, what are you drinking?" came from the girl that he had kissed.

"Slavyanskaya vodka. A local favorite, I have been told," he said.

"Slavyanskaya?" the girl repeated. "Well, that probably explains why you were so confused," said the girl, smiling. "Did you have many of them?"

"Not as many as I should have had, or as many as I want to have," he responded.

"In the mood, then?" she countered.

"Yes, definitely in the mood. And you?" he asked.

"Oh no," she said. "I have no sorrows to drown out." The Chinese girl had been silent throughout their exchange.

"What about you?" he then said to her.

"Ok, that will be nice," the Chinese girl agreed.

"Great," he said. "What will it be? A cosmopolitan, a martini, or perhaps a black Russian?" he suggested.

"Oh, I'd like to try the Slavyanskaya vodka martini. I want to try what the locals drink, too."

"So, you want to drown your sorrows?" he asked the Chinese girl.

"No. I just want to go local."

"Well then," he said. "Will it be three?" he inquired of the Russian girl.

"Ok, I'll go along," the Russian girl agreed. "But I can assure you that I have no sorrows to drown."

"That's obvious. You are clearly too young for that."

The Chinese girl was called Pei Ling Wu, and she was a visiting student from the London College of Arts. The Russian girl was Katia Zhelinskaya, a student at St. Petersburg State University. The two girls had met by chance at a fashion show, immediately decided that they liked each other's company, and agreed to go for a drink at the nearby popular jazz bar. They didn't really know each other.

"College girls, then," he remarked. "Great."

"And you are?" Katia asked.

"A capitalist banker from America," he said. "Here for a conference."

"Is that why you are in sorrow?" Pei Ling asked.

"No," he responded. "I actually like it here. Are you ready to have a good laugh?"

"Yes, please make me laugh," Katia said. "I'm ready for a good laugh." The American noticed for the first time that she had the most spectacular green eyes.

"Well, I will," he said. "For some strange reason," he began, "all of a sudden, I felt a strange longing for something and yet I didn't know for what. Isn't that rather idiotic? I have been told that there is a Russian word that perfectly describes my symptoms. Tocka is the word for it."

"Interesting," said Pei Ling. "And you say that you don't know the source for the feeling?"

"Yes, that's right. Strangely enough, I just had an excellent massage. But rather than feeling relaxed after the massage, I suddenly felt quite sad."

"Maybe the massage wasn't any good," suggested Katia. "A bad massage can leave you quite dissatisfied."

"No, the massage was excellent," he reassured her.

"Are you sure it wasn't that the masseuse was excellent, but the massage was mediocre? These masseuses in St. Petersburg can be quite pretty, but they often have poor technique. They are extremely popular with the tourists."

"I can assure you," he added smiling, "that her technique was quite good."

"Well, maybe the Slavyanskaya will help," volunteered Pei Ling.

"Yes," Katia agreed. "And don't be too concerned about your emotions. That type of feeling is very common here in Russia. It is more so in the winter in Moscow, but not at all that common in the summer in St. Petersburg. Since you are a foreigner you may have been more susceptible to the rare summer virus. But Pei Ling is quite right. The Slavyanskaya should help." Then the two girls began giggling. "But if you are not careful with the Slavyanskaya," Katia added, looking quite concerned now, "you could end up crying like a baby. That is what I have noticed follows this type of treatment." Then the two girls began laughing again.

Without noticing it, the three of them were now halfway through their second Slavyanskaya martini.

"Well, to be perfectly frank," he said, "I have been thinking about visiting Dostoyevsky's grave."

"What? Right now?" Katia asked. This made the two girls begin tittering again.

"Well, you can't do that now even if you wanted to," Pei Ling said. "The Tikhvin cemetery has already closed for the night."

"That is too bad. I would have really liked to have said a prayer tonight at Dostoyevsky's grave." This last comment made the two burst out laughing again.

"Don't worry," Katia said. "Dostoyevsky will keep where he is until tomorrow, and I'm sure he won't mind the fact that you couldn't make it today." Then there was more giggling from the girls.

"I'm curious to know why you have that tocka feeling," said Pei Ling. "By a strange coincidence, I have been doing research for my doctorate on emotions across cultures, and the inability of languages to precisely capture the essence of the emotions expressed. Strictly from an academic perspective, I wonder if you wouldn't mind explaining precisely what it is that you are feeling. I would really love to hear what you have to say."

"Yes, I would also be quite interested to know as well," chimed in Katia. "I'm currently working on my master's in psychology, and, also strictly from an academic perspective, I would love to know what would make a successful capitalist have that feeling known in our country as tocka. So, if you wouldn't mind, we would love to hear you elaborate on your feelings."

"So, you would love to hear me spill my guts out so that you may both satisfy your academic curiosities."

"Precisely," said Pei Ling. "We are really curious to know what you have to say, from a clinical perspective. We do not wish to pry into your life for any personal reasons. This is strictly from an academic perspective."

"I see. Yes, I am to be a case study for you," he said.

"Exactly," said Katia. "We will, of course, keep you anonymous. No one will ever know that you are the source of our study. But you must be totally honest with us because it is important for us to know that we can rely on the data that you are providing for our study."

"Let me think about this a moment," he said. "Do you mind if we order another round of Zhelinskaya before proceeding? It would allow me to disclose my information to you without inhibitions. If we are to proceed, I don't want to withhold anything from you for the sake of the accuracy of the study."

"Yes, we can agree to that," said Katia. "But I think you mean to order Slavyanskaya and not Zhelinskaya. Zhelinskaya is my last name." Both girls chuckled over his error.

"Now remember," Pei Ling added, "don't hold back. There are added benefits in disclosing fully. You may experience catharsis, a release of emotional tensions that will help pull you out of that tocka that you say you are feeling. So, for your benefit as well as ours, don't hold back."

"Yes, don't worry. I agree," he said.

"So, if you are ready, you may begin," said Pei Ling.

"First let's make a toast to the success of our journey, wherever it leads us," he said. "Now, let me see how I can best describe the emotions that I feel in terms that will make sense to you."

"Yes," interrupted Katia, "but don't make it too elaborate. Let's keep it as pure as possible."

"I understand," he said. "Let me say it as best as I can, and then you can take from it whatever you want."

"Ok, I'm sorry I interrupted you. You are right to proceed in whatever way you want," said Katia.

"Well, then," he began. "In my most recent dream, I find myself in the middle of a train terminal with hundreds of people on the move. They are dodging one another as they head very quickly to their destinations. I can identify the place. It is New York's Grand Central

Terminal, the epicenter of Manhattan. The terminal is the largest train station in the world by number of platforms. There are forty-four platforms with sixty-seven tracks on two levels, that are below ground. And in the middle of the terminal, there is a beautiful concourse that thousands of commuters use as a thruway on their way to their destinations.

"As I have said, I am there, in that concourse, in the middle of all that mayhem looking for the train that will take me to where I need to go. My destination is the Street of Eternal Happiness. I am extremely anxious as I look at the famous clock in the middle of the concourse to check the time. The time that is displayed by the clock doesn't logically register with me. My anxiety increases as I sense that time is running out, and if I don't hurry, I will miss the train. Logically, I can't move because I don't know which way to go. To which platform or to what track should I go? None of the destination display boards show Shanghai as a destination, and I am realizing that all will be lost if I can't keep my appointment.

"Grand Central Terminal is filled with secret passageways, underground private tracks, and secret staircases, and directly below the circular information booth where the magnificent clock is found, there is one of those secret staircases. The staircase is spiral-style and it is hidden by a secret door that leads directly to the information area on the lower level. As I glance at the door, a woman emerges. She is rather tall and very slim, and she is attired in a navy-blue suit and a white blouse. Her attire fits rather closely on her so that it is quite apparent that she has a very splendid body. Her hair is chestnut colored and is tied into a ponytail that reaches down over her left shoulder. She is an enigmatic creature with long, slim legs and mysterious eyes. They are big, dark eyes and look as though they don't have any irises at all. I quickly move toward her to ask her about the trains, but I stop when I realize that she is crying.

"Are you alright," I ask her. In response, she winces in obvious pain. She whispers to me in a confiding manner that she has recently had a tattoo pierced on the left side of her chest, which is exactly where her ponytail rests.

"Really," I said. "I hope that it was worth the pain." But she doesn't respond. "What type of a tattoo is it," I ask. She replies that it is an inscription. "Someone's name, perhaps?" I ask. She then lowers her blouse so that I can take a peek at what is there. The name that has been tattooed on her chest is Baba Yaga!

"That's it, that's the dream," he told the girls.

"That's it?" they simultaneously asked him.

"That's it," he repeated to them.

"The witch Baba Yaga?" they both asked, laughing. He nodded in confirmation.

On the podium, the saxophonist was now playing solo a strange, raw, forlorn version of a song that the American had heard before, but that he couldn't quite identify. The American glanced over at the musician and then drank the last of his vodka. The girls didn't appear all that willing now to attempt to decipher his dream. They weren't volunteering any comments. They followed his lead in swallowing down the last of their vodka, and then they waited to see if there was anything else that he wanted to say.

"Now then, ladies," he said. "Just in case you are wondering, the Street of Eternal Happiness has nothing to do with sex. It is a very real location in Shanghai, and I even know a banker that resides there."

"Good to know," said Katia.

"I knew that already," said Pei Ling. "It is a very affluent area in the new Shanghai. Many executives live in that area. Have you been invited to visit there?"

"Not exactly," he said. "But the banker that I know there has invited me to join him in a business venture."

"Ah," came from Pei Ling. "Well, that seems to now clarify the dream a little. You have to get to your appointment at the Street of Eternal Happiness, but you are not certain how to get there."

"Yes, I've thought about that. There is definitely something of that in what you say," he said. "To be perfectly honest, I'm not certain that I want to be a part of the business deal that has been proposed to me. But I was hoping that you would identify for me the woman with the tight-fitting outfit. She, on the other hand, looks worth going after."

"No doubt," said Katia. "Long legs, tight-fitting outfit highlighting the curves, and sporting a tattoo with the name of a Russian witch. She's quite an interesting woman. She's a scholar with curves and a bit of grit. What a dream! Pretty straightforward, then, your dream. Not much of a puzzle after all. Are you sure this was your dream or did you just make this up for us?"

"Hey, come on. That was my dream all right. And now I also recall that there were also plenty of KGB agents hidden within the many secret recesses of the Grand Central Terminal concourse that were in constant surveillance, waiting for the right moment to capture me."

"Right, the KGB agents at the New York Terminal," said Katia.

"Yes," he confirmed. "Agents with bad taste, poorly dressed, ready to pounce on their prey. Just thinking about them gives me the shivers. These were real animals without a conscience, totally uncompromising. I'm still trembling as I recall the nightmare. Ladies, please, let's have another Slavyanskaya now that you have forced me to relive the horror. How did I ever survive that nightmare?" He knew that it wouldn't be difficult to convince the girls to have another round of drinks. The band seemed to be taking a prolonged rest, but the saxophonist kept playing a slow melody, deep, hoarse.

"Maybe you can explain for us the girl with the tattoo," said Katia.

"No, I have to admit that that one confuses me as well. Who would want to be her lover? Every time you make love to her you have that damn Baba Yaga staring at you. That can be very unsettling," he said.

"Baba Yaga," repeated Pei Ling. "I don't really know about her. But what was her role there?"

"Good question," he replied. "It seemed that she was there to reveal to me a way out. But why the tattoo, and why did I have to see it? It seemed to have a meaning. That Baba Yaga is an enigmatic creature, many-faceted. Sometimes in the tales, she helps those that she encounters, but she is just as likely to hinder those that seek her out as well. The terrifying and ferocious-looking old hag is an all-knowing and all-seeing creature that will reveal the truth to those who would dare to seek it from her. But keep in mind that Baba Yaga has iron teeth and a ferocious appetite."

"So, was she there to warn you against the proposed business dealings or to warn you about the Nazis?" asked Pei Ling.

"Well, they were actually KGB agents," he said.

"Maybe they were the descendants of the Nazis that settled in Russia, and that later became KGB agents," said Katia.

"That's not getting us anywhere. Why was she there to meet me with that tattooed message? That was more startling to me than the KGB agents. Notice how it was after that that I woke up."

"Yes. She seems to have stopped you cold, just as you had begun to admire her curves and her mysterious eyes," said Katia.

"Yes. I remember her clearly with that skin as white as cream and those eyes that were sparkling like candles. I looked into the depths of her eyes, but they were so black that it was scarcely possible to read anything about her in them. When I read her tattoo, I almost instantaneously remembered comrade Stalin's most infamous words, 'I trust no one, not even myself.' You're quite right, Katia, when I read that tattoo, I became a tongue-tied idiot, incapable of uttering a word. For some unknown reason, thinking of the character Baba Yaga kept me preoccupied and kept me from thinking clearly. Comrade Stalin may have known himself and therefore had concluded that he couldn't trust himself. The other side of the coin was that comrade Stalin didn't really know himself, and therefore couldn't trust himself. Either way, they were two opposite premises leading to the same conclusion. So, instead of hurrying to find the platform that would have led me to my appointment at the Street of Eternal Happiness, and instead of moving quickly to avoid the KGB agents, I just came to a screeching halt trying to work out the arguments that immediately sprang to mind when I glanced at her tattoo."

"Well," Katia began, "I think it's quite funny that you should have thought about Stalin right then. No doubt the next thought that must have come to you, thinking as a capitalist, was what Stalin had said about them. 'When we hang the capitalists, they will sell us the rope we use.' It's no wonder that you couldn't move. You were obviously quite afraid. Something in your future business plans must be making you uneasy. You must be having doubts."

"Yes," Pei Ling chimed in, "Comrade Stalin had another witticism that is well-known in China. 'Death is the solution to all problems. If you eliminate the man, you eliminate the problem.' Very direct, don't you think? After all, 'You cannot make a revolution with silk gloves.' Now, you must tell us, comrade," Pei Ling continued mischievously. "What are your plans?" She then paused to present to him her most charming coquettish eyes, before continuing with her logic. "Only when we have all the facts will we be able to intelligently advise you on whether or not you should proceed with your tentative plans."

The American looked at the two inquisitive ladies and smiled. He then took another sip of his freshly delivered vodka as they waited to see what he would say. They seemed to think that he was seriously considering whether or not to tell them of his plans, but he was only trying to think of one final Stalin quote to feed them. He smiled at them when he was finally able to deliver.

"Ladies, please drink up," he began. He was genuinely enjoying their company. "I have very good news for you, or at least for me." They were now at the edge of their seats waiting to see what he had to say. "First of all, I have to thank you. You have helped me rid myself of whatever it was that I was feeling. That horrid tocka feeling is gone, and I know it is because of you. You, the club, the wonderful jazz music, and the Slavyanskaya have helped me work my way out of my rut. Ladies, a toast to the good times," he said as he lifted his glass of vodka to them. They clanked their glasses together in a toast, and then each took a sip of their vodka. But there was some disappointment showing in the girls' faces as that was clearly not what they had been expecting to hear.

"Are you not going to confide in us about your business?" asked Katia.

"Well," he began, "just to have one last quote from comrade Stalin. He once famously said, 'Education is a weapon whose effects depend on who holds it in his hands and at whom it is aimed.' That thought is in perfect alignment with his comment about trust. In order not to get into any trouble, I try to follow the example of those three wise little monkeys that have their hands covering their eyes, ears, and mouth, so that they can't hear anything, see anything, or say anything."

"Perhaps, but that sounds cowardly. We didn't expect you to be like that."

"Well, I don't really know you all that well to be able to trust you. But that doesn't mean that we can't get to know ourselves better," he quickly added with a rakish grin. Both girls thought that the American was very likable.

"Well, we will have to see," said Katia, seemingly analyzing the possibility.

"It's all a matter of trust," said Pei Ling.

"Which is in short supply," came from Katia.

"What shall we do?" they simultaneously sang.

"You sound like the witches in Macbeth putting together a spell. If you start chanting "Fire burn and cauldron bubble," you will be amazed to see how quickly I can disappear."

"Oh, is that how you see it?" asked Katia. "We thought this was about a foreign capitalist wanting to exploit the local comrade female students," she said with a smirk.

"I see now that I was right to be careful," he said.

"Next I will be accused of politically agitating the comrades. Are the gulags still operational? Is that where the re-education occurs? I think it's time for me to leave you, ladies."

"Oh, come on," said Katia. "I was only kidding."

"Yes, of course," said Pei Ling. "Don't make us feel guilty now."

"No, ladies, I'm leaving because I am exhausted. It was wonderful coming into this little bar and finding the two of you here. It was exactly what I needed, and you girls have been wonderful. Thank you for the company, really."

"Ok," Katia said, "but I don't want you to leave disappointed for anything that I may have said. You were very good company for us as well. You never know what you are going to find in these bars, and you were a nice change of pace, for me at least."

"Yes," Pei Ling agreed. "Absolutely. It was great meeting you. When we first met you earlier you said that you were in a rut, that you were having that tocka feeling. You now seem to have gotten rid of it. I just hope that you are now not getting that same feeling again, and certainly not because of anything that we may have said."

"Oh, I could not have asked for better company, really," he said. "You were exactly what the doctor ordered. But now I need to get out because I really need to rest."

"Well, good night then," they both said. Then he promptly left into the cool night that was still eerily showing plenty of daylight. He wasn't used to this world.

Saint Petersburg during the White Nights was an enchanted city. During this period, the sun dispersed an amazing light, which shined on the spectacular cathedrals and majestic palaces, making them gleam and sparkle. It was no wonder then that the phenomenon would also wreak havoc on a man's biological clock, making him confused because of the lack of darkness.

At that late hour, he breathed in the sweet night air deeply and tried to focus his senses and his wits, stumbling along, trying to look like a respectable businessman.

CHAPTER FOURTEEN

As he entered the hotel lobby, he noticed Liu Tang waving at him from the bar. The man lifted a glass and indicated a comfortable chair across from his own. The American felt a dry, harsh taste in his mouth and felt some sticky sweat under his arms. Liu Tang stood up, and for a moment both men stared at each other.

One of the benefits of attending conferences like these was the possibility of establishing new contacts. Connections could lead to new business opportunities. Now, for the first time in his career, he managed to successfully come upon something that could lead to a significant payday. Liu Tang had stated that he had decided to move into this new type of business after he had been made a cuckold. His wife and the disrespectful executive at his firm had forced his hand, and when the opportunity presented itself, he immediately made his move. The gamble had so far paid off, and he was now becoming financially sound. It was only a matter of time, he had said. Once he had enough money, he would make a clean break from everything and everyone that he knew. He was now working hard to reach that day.

But the American was not in Liu Tang's shoes. His decision would not be driven by the same circumstances, and that was probably why he had not yet committed. Liu Tang was motivated by a smoldering and all-consuming anger. He had been betrayed and humiliated at home and at his workplace. But what was the motivating factor for the American? Well, he could be losing his job in Miami, but nothing had been decided yet.

"The interested parties in Shanghai," began Liu Tang, "have come together to create a collective investment scheme that is similar to those that are created in Europe, the so-called SICAVs. This collective group of investors, the 'Corporation' from Shanghai, wants to establish an account with your Geneva office." Here, Liu Tang paused to give the American a moment to digest the information before continuing. "The Corporation would be depositing a significant amount of money into your affiliate bank with the understanding that their funds would be invested in very liquid high-grade bonds or preferably in United States Treasury Bonds. Against these investments, a Standby Letter of Credit would be issued in favor of a Russian corporation that will be exporting goods to China. The Russian entity will expect to drawdown funds from the Letter of Credit after their goods are successfully delivered to the Corporation's agents in China. Pretty straightforward, I think. Do you have any questions so far?"

"The due diligence that will be performed by our Geneva affiliate will require full disclosure of the goods being purchased. For regulatory reasons, they will have to verify that the goods being delivered have a value that is in line with what is being paid. This requirement was implemented in order to establish that what is not taking place with the transaction is money laundering. As long as we can establish that there is a semblance of value between the goods and the proceeds from the transactions, we should have no problems. Will your Corporation be able to comply with this requirement, Liu Tang?" asked the American.

"Most certainly," answered the Asian. "We will make that our top priority with the transactions. We understand that the Swiss financial institutions are heavily regulated, and this is the very reason that the Corporation wishes for the account to be established in Geneva. The investors want to have their capital in a market that provides maximum privacy but that is also quite safe. They are willing to pay premium fees for that privilege."

"Liu Tang, I don't have to tell you that every investor

that is part of the Chinese Corporation will be carefully scrutinized. You can expect there to be due diligence to establish individual credentials. Our affiliate bank will not compromise on anything that may damage its reputation." The American wanted Liu Tang to acknowledge the implication of what he had just said.

"Understood," was his immediate response. "All of the investors will measure up to whatever checks are made. You won't have to worry on that score. These investors are upstanding businessmen in China. Their credentials will not be questioned."

"Excellent. I will leave it up to you to later provide me with the details of the goods that are being negotiated for the proposed transactions. Again, please ensure that the value for which they are assessed is in line with the proposed proceeds. Because this Corporation will be a new client, we need to be certain that there is nothing unusual with the initial transaction."

"Of course," agreed Liu Tang. "We all want this to be successful. Leave it to me. I will keep you apprised of everything before anything is submitted to your affiliate. As our agent, you will be in complete control of the transaction. After all, that is why you will be earning your fee. You will be held responsible for the financial side of the transaction. Nothing must go wrong. We are dealing with large sums of money, and these are extremely powerful men. They don't expect to lose any of their capital through the financial side. There must be no freezing of accounts, delays in payments, or any possible errors related to this account. This is private wealth, and investors get very nervous when strange things happen to their money. Let's be certain that everything is in perfect order every step of the way. Remember, you will also have something to gain here."

Liu Tang looked at the American and felt something was not quite right with the man. Fortunately, specific details had not yet been revealed. Up to now, the American had been given general information. Liu Tang smiled at the American, but made no additional comment. He was going to wait and see what the American had to say.

For his part, the American no longer felt like having any more of Liu Tang's company. He was feeling rather tired from all of the vodka that he had consumed earlier in the evening, and he couldn't care less whether the two would come to an agreement about the proposed venture. Yes, it was true that this was an opportunity to make a great deal of money. But he would be dealing with many unknowns. At this moment, his fear of transacting with high net worth Russians and Chinese businessmen that didn't trust each other outweighed his temptation for the big payday. He told Liu Tang that he was feeling very tired, and apologized for having to call it an early night.

Liu Tang smiled at him but didn't say a word. Truly a strange man, he thought. He had never experienced anything like this before. It was all nonsense! The man must have been drunk. How could he have been such a poor judge of character?

The American moved on, passed the smiling cocottes in the lobby bar, and headed straight to the elevators. He was now feeling extremely tired. Tonight, he didn't care what the room looked like. Nothing was going to be able to keep him up tonight.

CHAPTER FIFTEEN

THE SIMULTANEOUS TRANSLATION of the presentation from Russian to English the next morning was often quite poor so that the participants were left with the arduous task of trying to reconstruct the words that were being said into something that made sense.

"With the purposes of counteraction to penetration into the banking sector of the criminal capitals to ensure fulfillment of requests of the Federal law about counteraction of legalization (laundering) of the incomes received in a criminal way, were guided in the actions on the best international practice." There was audience applause after that statement. As far as the American was concerned, the applause must have been to congratulate the translator for his manner of translating something that probably made complete sense in Russian into an English phrase that was completely incomprehensible.

The American couldn't imagine what the Asians and Europeans who didn't understand Russian and who spoke English as a second language could have managed to understand from that morning's presentation. But they were probably the ones that applauded loudest and that would, of course, make sense where nothing else did. The good news was that the theater of the absurd was now over and the bankers were now free to explore St. Petersburg for the rest of the day.

After changing into more casual attire, the American began his trek on foot toward the Alexander Nevsky Monastery. The weather was absolutely wonderful, and he was really looking forward to spending the day strolling through the lawns of the famous Necropolis, visiting the final resting places of many of Russia's most famous artists.

On his way to the monastery, he ran into Nadya again. Now she looked even lovelier than the last time that they had met. People passing her on the street turned their heads to quickly look at her as if they suddenly realized that they had almost missed something special. He remembered that she had hinted at how she was temporarily tired of Russian men, letting him gather from that that there had been some sort of unfortunate love affair.

"Well, hello," she said to him with that radiant smile of hers that he was sure would revive even the gloomiest of spirits that went about the streets of St. Petersburg. Nadya was twenty-three years old. The American looked at her and imagined what it would be like to be in a permanent relationship with her. There was no one like her, at least not right now in his life.

"Wow, you look amazing," he finally managed to say. She smiled and took him by the arm.

"Well, where are you off to now?" she asked. "What part of our lovely city are you planning to visit?"

"The Alexander Nevsky Monastery," he replied. "But I'm open to any other suggestion that you may have," he quickly added.

"Come with me," she said. "I think you may have some real fun where I'm headed. Afterward, you can continue to the Monastery," she added.

"I'll go wherever you want," he responded, smiling at her. And with that, they walked arm in arm to her secret destination.

"It's great that you have the time to take in some culture while you are here. St. Petersburg is a great city, and there are things that you will see here that you will not find anywhere else. It just so happens that I spend quite a few hours a week working where we are now headed, and I must admit that even if I were not getting paid I would be happy to spend hours there working for free. But please don't tell anyone what I have just said because I can always use the extra income."

"Nadya, you seem to have quite a few jobs. You work as a hostess at a restaurant in a hotel, and you also work at the museum. And now you are saying that you have a third job, besides being a university student. How do you manage it all?"

"The Hermitage and this other one, I am passionate about. The hotel job pays quite well, so that is why I continue there. Well, we are here." Nadya had brought him to the Demmeni Marionette Theater.

"Nadya, are you a puppeteer?"

"No," she said. "I assist with the creation of the window frames, which are based on theatrical subjects. The Demmeni Marionette Theater is the oldest professional puppet theater in Russia. It was created in 1918, and they staged their first performance the following year. The first production was *The Tale of Tsar Saltan*, which was based on Pushkin's work. This building that we are in now was given to the troupe in the mid-1930s." As usual, Nadya had a treasure trove of historical information, this time about the theater and about the current landmark building where the performances took place.

"About 250 plays have been performed on the theater's stage," she continued, "and among them were the first Russian puppet productions of works by Shake-

speare, Pushkin, Gogol, and Chekhov. Today the reper-
tory consists of fifteen various styles and genres, which
draw upon Russian and foreign authors. If you accompany me, I will be able to show you the handcrafted
marionettes."

"I can't believe how lucky I am to have run into you
again. The government should also place you on their
payroll for the marvelous way that you advocate for this
magnificent city."

"It's my absolute pleasure! Now, if you are not in a
rush, there will be a performance of Petrushka in a little
while. And, if you stay, I promise to get you the best seat
in the house!"

"Of course, I will stay. Will it be performed to the
music of Stravinsky?" he asked.

"What else?"

"Marvelous!" he said. "You have totally captivated
me," he added. "You are impossible to resist. Will you
have dinner with me afterward?"

"We will see," she said, with a wink.

When the American was seated he was given a
program about the production. While reading it he was
reminded that Stravinsky's orchestration for Petrushka
was considered one of the most magical scores in all of
classical music literature. Stravinsky originally composed
the score in 1911 for Sergei Diaghilev, the ballet impresario and founder of the Ballets Russes. The ballet

company at the time had the best young Russian dancers, and Vaslav Nijinsky and Anna Pavlova were among them. Nijinsky danced the role of Petrushka in the work's premiere in Paris.

More specific to the Demmeni Marionette Theater production, Petrushka was described as a character of Russian folk puppetry with origins going back to the seventeenth century. Traditionally, Petrushka was a kind of jester who was either a marionette or hand puppet that stood out with his red clothes and his red pointed hat. Petrushka's body was made of straw. But in the story, he comes to life full of emotions.

The American was a little disappointed that Nadya was not going to be sitting next to him during the performance. However, he was not alone as the small theater was now packed with children and adults. When the lights dimmed, the audience became silent as they waited to see what the Charlatan would look like. It was wonderful to see the anticipation showing in the children's faces when the flute playing finally began.

As the curtain lifted, the audience finally glimpsed the Charlatan playing his flute. With his instrument, the Charlatan was able to cast a magic spell that brought the puppet figures of Petrushka, the Ballerina, and the Moor to life. The beautifully painted scenery depicted the puppets in a square during a Russian carnival. As the Charlatan played his flute, the three puppets came to life, performing a vigorous Russian dance. And then when the music finally faded and as the lights dimmed, the curtain closed, bringing an end to the fabulous first act.

Suffice it to say that for the rest of the story poor Petrushka is given a tough life with a tragic end. He is imprisoned, falls in love with the Ballerina that spurns him for the Moor, who later kills him with his sword. Petrushka, madly in love, had attempted to disrupt the Moor's seduction of the Ballerina, but being small and weak, is soundly beaten by the antagonist. All in all, this was a very sad tale for the children to witness. At the end of the tale, the Charlatan returns to the stage carrying the limp body of Petrushka. He does so to remind the audience that they should not take the story of Petrushka to heart because, after all, he is but a straw-filled puppet. But the captive audience wasn't so convinced that the Charlatan didn't deserve imprisonment for having put forth such a sad tale.

"Well? Did you like it?" Nadya had run up to him as soon as the curtain had closed in order to get his immediate reaction. He smiled at her, marveling at her abundant enthusiasm before they walked out of the theater together.

"Beautiful production," he finally admitted. "You were absolutely right to bring me here, and I'm extremely grateful. It would never have occurred to me to come to a puppet theater." He looked at her for a moment before saying "That was absolutely lovely. How could anyone fail to fall in love with Petrushka?"

Nadya looked at him in anticipation, sensing that he had something more to say.

"I'm leaving soon," he finally said. Nadya was about to say something but then held back. "Everything in St. Petersburg has been so wonderful," he added. Nadya looked at him without commenting.

"Have you ever drunk kumis?" he quickly asked, changing the subject.

"What? What are you asking me? Are you referring to the alcoholic beverage that was made from fermented mare's milk, that was made originally by the nomads of Central Asia? Is that what you are referring to?" she asked in disbelief.

"Yes," he said. "That is exactly what I'm referring to."

"And where do you expect that I would have drunk that?" she asked the foolish American in disbelief. "Have you seen any kumis anywhere in St. Petersburg?"

"No, I haven't. But I read about it in a Chekov story, and I was hoping that I would be able to try it here."

"That was over a hundred years ago, silly man," she said with an amused look on her face. "It was at another time, in another world. I think that you will be hard-pressed to find any kumis in our St. Petersburg. Vodka, my dear, is the drink of choice today."

"Ah, I'm very disappointed!"

"Better not think," she said. "Better not think about it." And with that, she took his arm, and they walked into the Zulu Café located within the same building that housed the theater. After the waitress took their coffee orders, the American began seriously considering again the Petrushka production.

"Well, I suppose it's inevitable to identify with Petrushka's role," he began. "The Charlatan places the poor character on the stage, brings him to life, and then poor Petrushka doesn't understand the limitations of his role, which results in a tragedy for him. Petrushka imagines that he can beat the Moor, but he is too weak and frail for that combat. He also imagines that he can win the Ballerina's love, but she is not interested. So, he is doomed from the start."

"Are you blaming the Charlatan?" Nadya asked him.

"Am I blaming the Charlatan? That is a very good question." He looked at her and seemed to be considering it. "Nadya," he began, "my Catholic upbringing tells me that the Charlatan equivalent breeds life into us, but that we ultimately have a free will to act in whatever way we want. So, from that perspective, the Charlatan is blameless."

"That is quite interesting," said Nadya. "You have now brought your personal thoughts about your religion to defend the Charlatan." She looked at him, somewhat astonished. "You have thought about your God's role with regard to your life. So, are you a Petrushka?"

"No, I insist that you cast me as the Moor," he said. "I want the Ballerina."

"But you are not Oriental! You cannot be the Moor," she protested.

"What I'm really beginning to see is that you want to give me the shaft," he shot back.

"The shaft?" she asked. "What do you mean by that?"

"The shaft!" he repeated. "That means that you want me to end up just like poor Petrushka," he said, pouting his lips, looking for sympathy from her.

At that moment, the waitress interrupted their discussion by placing two espresso coffees before them. The aroma from the cups suggested that the coffee bean used was quite good. They both looked pleased with what they were tasting.

"Well," she began again. "Petrushka must know his limitations, and you are not Oriental so you can't be the Moor."

"Fine," he responded, giving her a very disappointed look. "But then I will change my mind and blame the Charlatan for the lot that he assigned me because clearly, you seem to think that there is no way out for me. According to you, everything has been predetermined."

"I don't know anything about that," she countered.

"All I know is that if you are a Petrushka, then you can't be a Moor."

"And then I can't have the Ballerina?"

"Not if you have been given the role of Petrushka," she confirmed.

"You are depressing me. Remember, I'm not Petrushka and I want the Ballerina."

"Americans always think that they can get whatever they want," Nadya countered.

"Only those entitled get what they want."

"Are you entitled?"

"Yes. So, if I want you I can have you."

"That's only in America, comrade. We have a separate set of rules in Russia." She winked and smiled.

"Yes," he agreed. "You have your own Charlatan at work here. He is not as beneficent to his puppets as the one that we have in America." They both laughed at the idea of the distinct Charlatans at work in their respective countries. He really liked her, but he knew that he was substantially older than she was.

In a short time, he would be returning to his country which was a world away. He would more than likely never return, unless, unless he agreed to go into partnership with Liu Tang. But, despite whatever the Asian said, there was always a risk element when you entered into agreements with syndicates that transacted in contraband goods. Perhaps they were, as Liu Tang stated, all executives residing on that Changle Road, that Street of Eternal Happiness. But they were still criminals. They were smugglers and they were operating outside of the law. These were powerful men, and certainly well connected. And, more than likely, these men were ruthless and used to getting everything they wanted. Were these the types of men that he wanted to be associated with?

Petrushka had gambled and lost his life because he tangled with someone bigger and stronger than he was. Chasing after the Ballerina had been his downfall. All of a sudden he laughed, as he remembered the words of wisdom that his running buddy had once told him at a bar. "James, remember that you will always lose money by chasing pussy, but you'll never lose pussy by chasing money." As he started to remember this stupid one-liner, he couldn't help but chuckle as he reminisced about his old friend. Nadya gave him a puzzled look, curious to know what he had been thinking.

"I'm sorry, Nadya. I was just remembering something that a friend once told me. It's silly and wouldn't make any sense to you."

"Please try," she said, "I'd like to know American humor."

"But American humor can be rather distasteful to foreigners. Anyway, it's funny how the mind works. I was initially thinking just moments ago about a serious proposition that had been offered to me. But I can't seem to decide which way to go. Then all of a sudden I start recalling a joke that a friend of mine had once told me years ago in a bar. My Charlatan has me quite confused."

"You're back to blaming the Charlatan?"

"You're right. He's always there in the forefront of my mind. I can't seem to get away from him. I make him responsible for everything. He sets the stages and brings me to life. Then he watches to see how I will perform. He doesn't judge me, but I can't seem to forget that he is always there watching me. He must find me delightful, otherwise, he would put an end to my life. He is a voyeur. I can't escape from him. And the worst thing of all is that I'm still trying to work out the meaning of it all. Do I exist just to please him? How could I possibly ignore him, knowing that he is always there?"

"So, you literally believe in the Charlatan?" asked Nadya. "Or is this just more of the American humor?"

"Don't ask me. Like Petrushka, I just want the Ballerina."

"Well, you can't have her."

"Then I should be exploring alternatives. It's a question of mind over matter. In order not to get hurt, smart investors know that they need to remove emotion from the equation to achieve their goals. Perhaps I should now move on to the Alexander Nevsky Monastery because otherwise, I will become certifiably mad."

"Wow, I didn't realize how much of a capitalist you are at heart. It almost seems as though it's an escape mechanism for you, a way of redefining perspective. I think that you would make an excellent case study for someone in the field of psychology."

"Thank you, but not today. Poor Yorick beckons me to the Necropolis. Memento mori, he reminds me. It means that we too shall die. A sobering thought, don't you think?"

"What are you on about?" she asked. She looked at him and didn't know what else to say. "Shall we go together to the Alexander Nevsky Monastery?" she finally asked. "You can introduce me to Yorick." Then she took him by the arm and steered him in the direction that would eventually take them there.

When they finally reached the grounds of the Monastery, Nadya immediately headed to one of the benches.

"Well, crazy man, you are now in our beautiful complex of churches dating back to the time of the city's founding, and you are by the prestigious cemeteries that include the graves of some of Russia's cultural giants. But the very long walk on the way here has made me so exhausted that I doubt that I can take another step anytime soon."

"Oh, you surprise me. I thought that Russian women were supposed to be real fighters and some of the most extremely energetic women in the world," he remarked.

"Well, so now you are an expert on Russian women too? I'm glad to hear it. Go on then, describe to me what you think is the character of the typical young Russian woman. I'd love to hear it, as stupid as the generalizations may sound."

"Nadya, I'm sorry. You misunderstood me. I never intended to give you that impression. I freely admit that I understand very little about women, and least of all about Russian women. You see, that is one of the reasons for my trip. I want to learn as much as I can about Russian women, and I hope that you will let me study you in greater detail. I want to learn as much as I can."

She gave him a playful nudge, offering a bemused smile. "Well, to begin with, you must know that a typical Russian woman seems like she knows what she is doing and affirms herself." Nadya stopped for a moment to reflect, it seemed to him, on how best to deliberate on the subject. He was all ears.

"Russian women," she proceeded, "especially young women, are quite pushy in their daily lives. You see, to really know a Russian woman you must know the subculture that she comes from. You referred to them as fighters, and that at least would make sense because you have to be a fighter in Russia to succeed. This is a trait that is embedded in the makeup of their character. But this should not be misinterpreted to mean that they are always straightforward and independent in their relationships. The traditional morals are still in play with regard to relationships. If you have a Russian girlfriend, she will expect you to nurture her, to accompany her everywhere, to open a door for her, to pay her bills, in short, to be very courteous and to act like a real gentleman."

"Go on," he urged her on. "I find this fascinating."

"On the other hand, she will be happy to help you push through a long queue, help you win an argument with a policeman about your outdated visa registration card, drink more vodka in one night than you ever did during the previous three months, and slug you hard if you behave badly. Is this making sense to you too?"

"I have to admit that it is becoming more complicated," he answered, shaking his head emphatically.

"Why is it so complicated," she sounded a little frustrated now. "Russian girls want to succeed in life, but they are very romantic. They will plunge into a relationship without having a second thought if they feel like it. They will spend all day walking around aimlessly holding your hand even if they have an important exam to take the next morning. They will go to the end of the world to be with their lover. They will expect much of you, but they will also give even more in return."

"Well, that sounds logical and healthy," he said, narrowing his eyes.

"Logical and healthy?" she repeated. "You shouldn't expect the practicality that you may find in the West," she continued with a bit more passion. "According to recent government figures, only one in four Russian women use contraceptives. In this day and age, it is hard to believe that the most common way to avoid pregnancy is through abortion. Aids and sexually transmitted diseases have been on the rise. Russian girls, in general, are very lax about protection when having sex, so you must really think about it unless you want to plunge into the dangerous zone together."

"Well, you're certainly convincing me not to go after the Ballerina. Maybe Petrushka was getting off easy."

She looked at him, taking a deep breath before answering. "Some people wonder why so many Russian girls are looking to meet a man from the West. Ten years ago, when the economic conditions were really bad, some women saw it as a way out of poverty and out of their daily struggle. But nowadays life is better and people want to stay in their own country. There are indeed some women who have this belief that Western men are much more gentle, attentive, and amiable with women than Russian men. So, if you manage to demonstrate these qualities, you may have a chance. Don't give up so quickly on the Ballerina."

"Nadya," he said, "have you met many oligarchs in your restaurant? I know very little about you."

She seemed quite taken aback by his sudden change of direction. "Why do you ask that?" she answered after considering the question for a moment. "Is there something in particular that you wish to know? I obviously meet many businessmen in the hotel restaurant. Remember, that is where I met you and Mr. Liu Tang. The hotel is one of the best in Russia, and the restaurant, as you can appreciate, is set to meet the standards of the most demanding clientele, which is what we get. You can also expect that since I work there I will undoubtedly meet very many prominent businessmen. So, why do you ask?"

"I have been imagining you as a perfect spy. You have access to all of the prominent players in the financial and political world, and you would logically make the most perfect intermediary to assist in facilitating the most clandestine business arrangements."

She shrewdly began assessing him again before saying anything. "To begin with, I will confess that I have learned that when an opportunity presents itself you take it, whether it presents itself by chance or not. One of those so-called oligarchs that you referred to once told me that the business world's alpha and omega demands that you do not hesitate or consider fairness when the moment arises. You just go for it if you want to be very successful."

"Ruthless, then?" he baited her.

"Yes, with weapons sharpened and at the ready." She wasn't smiling as she said this. She was all business. "But why did you interrupt me? So, you no longer want to hear about our devushkas?" asked Nadya. "Maybe you are more interested in the more mature middle-aged women, our zhenshchiny. As you have alluded to the recent shifts in economic conditions in our country, you should know that with the abrupt changes in the 90s, the people that were born in the 60s and 70s have had to face the biggest challenges of all in Russia. Previously, they were used to having one kind of life, and suddenly the world changed for them. Our middle-aged women who are working in the cities will be quite stressed trying to adapt to the new economic climate. Many of these women continue to work with their Soviet-era mentality, not caring about being polite or about how much they must sell to make profits for their firm. But this behavior is quite understandable given that for all of their previous lives they have been used to working in places where everyone received the same pay regardless of their efforts."

"It sounds like the zhenshchiny are a work in

progress," he said. "I will stick to the devushkas if you don't mind."

"But if you are really adventurous, you might want to try our babushkas," she then added. "These are our toughest women. They will not shy away from telling you off on the metro, fighting their way to get a seat on a bus, or pushing anyone out of their way to get to the head of a queue at the bank. These women grew up during very hard times, and never miss the opportunity to remind everyone about it. Sadly, their monthly state pensions amount to about fifty US dollars a month, so many of them will look for whatever jobs they can get to make additional money."

"Now you are beginning to depress me again," he said. "And we were doing so fine."

"Well, I shall have to see how I can cheer you up."

"Why?" He looked at her quite seriously when he asked her.

"Why?" she asked him.

"Yes, why do you want to cheer me up? Tell me about your rich businessmen friends. Did you introduce them to Liu Tang?"

"What are you talking about?" she asked, quite startled. "Why are you so interested?"

"Liu Tang has made me a business proposition, but I don't seem to have it all that clear. I was wondering if your friends were in on it as well. Have you been asked to speak to me?" He tried to discern something from her, but she wasn't very revealing.

"In our conversations, Liu Tang has also brought up the recent major economic changes that have taken place in his country and of the way that people have had to adjust so as not to be left behind. One of the debates that is taking place back in his city of Shanghai centers around the question of whether the modern Chinese society should develop with unique Chinese characteristics, or if it should continue to embrace Western culture. Many Chinese have forgotten what it means to be Chinese, and they are suffering from cultural amnesia. Others seem to be in a constant state of anxiety. Many of them are reverting to the traditional philosophies in an attempt to hypnotize themselves as a way of coping, rather than proactively working toward changing the circumstances that caused their anxieties in the first place. It is not easy to figure out which way to go when you are lost and unsure."

"Well, if you are lost and unsure then you have a problem," she said. "But don't expect to get to the Street of Eternal Happiness if you are on a train that doesn't take you to Changshu Lu station, because it won't get you there. It's as simple as that. Know your destination and take the appropriate steps to get there. Don't keep asking questions and frustrating yourself and everyone else if you are not prepared to act."

"Nadya, you have been holding out on me." In the garden, there were lilac bushes, heavy with bloom, drowsy and languid in the cool evening air. But to him, the garden now looked somber and unfriendly, and he had a desire to get away.

"Where do you want to go?" She gazed at him with wide-open eyes, as if fascinated, waiting for him to come out of his indecisiveness with something significant. She looked at him full of expectation, ready for something. "You will never regret it, never repent it, I'm sure!" She was very convincing. He tried to say something to her, but could not. A couple of bearded old men walked by, smoking cigars, and the fumes of the tobacco permeated the air for a good while after they had passed. They sat silently for a while, and then they moved on to a nearby coffee shop where he treated her to tea and biscuits. There was hardly anyone about. He thought that Nadya had seated herself as the guilty do, timidly, giving him cautious glances.

"In one of Chekhov's works one of the characters states that one should look at life through a sort of prism," she began. "In other words, you must divide life in your consciousness into its simplest elements, as if into the seven primary colors, and each element must be studied separately. And as this life stretches out before us, drawing us onward in a vague and mysterious way, it leads us to places that we never would have imagined."

"Yes," he agreed, "like to the Street of Eternal Happiness, I daresay." It was a very romantic notion. But he wasn't in the mood. They had talked themselves out, and now he was ready to walk her to the train station.

"Right now, I have an easy carefree existence," he said. "But that can all quickly change. I can easily become like one of those Chekhov characters that goes to bed at peace with his family. Then suddenly one night the police are rapping at the door to his house because it has been discovered that he has committed embezzlement or a forgery. Then it is farewell forever to the easy, carefree life!"

He could tell that she wasn't buying any of his spiel. She could see right through him. "What are you thinking?" he asked her.

"That you lack courage," she replied honestly. "You couldn't be more perfectly placed for the job. But you lack confidence and have no backbone. It's rather unfortunate. The circumstances couldn't be more perfect, and all at a minimum risk to you. Remember, you are only the intermediary agent. There are major players here, and no one expects any problems. This is legitimate import–export trade. How could you possibly be held responsible for anything going wrong with the shipment of goods? You are the agent banker, responsible for processing documents, making sure that they are all in order, and in compliance with what the buyer and seller have already agreed to. You might want to reconsider before making your decision. It may not be as risky as you seem to think it is."

"I'll have you know that I haven't made my decision yet. We haven't even discussed my compensation yet."

"Yes, I almost forgot to mention that an escrow account would be set up for you and that the funds would be made available once the payment was made from your bank after the buyer approves and accepts delivery of the goods. I've been told that it would be the typical procedure for a Letter of Credit transaction, except that your personal commission would be placed in escrow at another bank. The participants assume that you would not want to receive your commission at your affiliate bank for obvious reasons. You would of course have to agree on the selected bank for the escrow. That should not be an issue."

"As usual, you are well informed," he said. "Have they also mentioned the terms for the commission?"

"One-half of one percent of the total paid per transaction. On a fifty-million-dollar deal, you will get a tidy two hundred and fifty thousand. That is tax-free undeclared income, as long as the escrow remains offshore."

"Truly one of hell's belles," the American responded. "Where exactly is your niche in this world of high-flying entrepreneurs and international bankers? For whom are you acting as agent? You have left me doubting everything." He paused a moment, realizing how he had been totally hoodwinked by her.

"It's mind-boggling to think that just a few days ago, when we first met, you were recommending to me, as hostess at one of the St. Petersburg's finest restaurants, the specialty dishes to be had with all of their historical significance. And now, just days later, I find you dictating the terms that I can expect to receive in an offshore escrow account if I agree to provide banking services to the high-flying Chinese entrepreneurs and the Russian oligarchs whom I have yet to meet. Compared to you, I definitely don't know where I stand. Who are you? What is this all about? Who do you represent?"

"Why, I thought that we had already clarified that point," Nadya responded, with a coquettish look on her face. "I represent the devushkas, of course. I am a totally free agent, available for the right price." She waited a moment to allow him to digest this first bit of information. "Because others believed that there seemed to be an affinity between us—rightly, so I thought—I was approached and propositioned for a modest fee to undertake the task of recruiting you for what was termed a very lucrative enterprise. My employers seem to think that you are the right man with the right bank for the proposed business. And I have been assured that everything concerning you will be completely kosher."

"No downside for me, then. It sounds quite tempting. And you? What about you? Do I get to have you as well as part of the arrangement?"

"Oh, no," she said, smiling. "My role here is quite limited. I'm merely the messenger."

"So, you don't get entangled in any of it?" he asked. "You are strictly the messenger, a free agent?"

"Correct. I am unimpeded and unencumbered. Free to move about willy-nilly, as you Americans say." She held his stare for a moment. "You see, I can be willing, or unwilling."

"So, with you, it will be hitty-missy and totally unpredictable," he responded.

She laughed at him when he said it. "Hitty-missy, I like that," she said. "Hitty-missy and willy-nilly, it sounds like the beginning of one of those children's books by your famous Dr. Seuss."

"Yes," he agreed. "It's all mumbo-jumbo and gobbledygook. It's all a lot of colorful language that sounds like gibberish. But there is real meaning behind it in disguise. Do you like hanky-panky too?"

What he wanted to tell her was that he wanted all of her, because she was a perfectly cooked dish. But he didn't want to appear gross, and Nadya was the most exquisite woman that he had ever met, even though he had to admit that he did not understand her.

"Better not think," she whispered. "Better not think

about it." Was she referring to the hanky-panky or the business proposition?

"Dostoevsky, Dostoevsky, Dostoevsky," she said. It was just out of the blue, not related in any way to what he had just said. But he didn't interrupt her. He just watched her and waited to see what else she would say.

"Someone once told me that Dostoevsky is pure soul," she began. "It is a soul steeped in shame and humiliation." She stopped then, as though reconsidering her friend's comment. "But that soul is found in the other extreme as well, in love, compassion, and happiness. Dostoevsky had great compassion for the poor, the oppressed and tormented. Many people don't know that the young Dostoevsky used to spend time wandering in the hospital garden where his father worked, listening to the suffering patients tell their stories. His father was a military surgeon and a violent alcoholic who served at the Mari-insky Hospital for the poor in Moscow. The hospital was situated in one of the worst neighborhoods. Dostoevsky once said, 'We sometimes encounter people, even perfect strangers, who begin to interest us at first sight, somehow suddenly, all at once, before a word has been spoken.' You know, you fell right into that category for me."

He looked at her, trying to decide if this now was just another clever tactic on her part to win his confidence. He wasn't ever sure of his footing with regard to this very complex woman. Moments ago, she was criticizing him for not having the courage to commit to the proposed arrangement. Now she was seducing him, saying how she really liked him.

"Dostoevsky was also credited for having once said that the cleverest of all, in his opinion, is the man who calls himself a fool at least once a month. It's important to be able to face up to your shortcomings." He could sense that she was sizing him up again, still without a verdict.

"I hope that I can measure up to your expectations," he quickly said. There was no point in closing the door to anything yet. "Don't give up on me."

"You will at least die hard trying, right?" she added, laughing. She then left him with the excuse that she had a previous commitment. However, she agreed to meet him later that evening.

CHAPTER SIXTEEN

AFTER NADYA'S DEPARTURE, he continued alone down the path that led him toward the Tikhvin Cemetery, which was to the right of the Alexander Nevsky Monastery. Because it was getting late, he didn't stop by the monastery but rather moved on with a few other tourists to the Necropolis. The place was an oasis of peace and tranquility. He was particularly impressed by the beautiful and artistic monuments and busts that marked the final resting places of the very famous artists. Moving in an anti-clockwise direction, he quickly came to Dostoevsky's grave, which was surrounded by low railings and prominently featured his bearded bust. Dostoevsky had years that were marked by personal and professional misfortunes, including the forced closing of his journals by the authorities in St. Petersburg, the deaths of his wife and his brother, and a financially destructive addiction to gambling. Dostoevsky's troubled life had enabled him to portray sympathetically characters that were emotionally and spiritually beaten and who in many cases epitomized the traditional Christian conflict between the body and the spirit.

Before moving on to Tchaikovsky's grave, out of the corner of his eye he noticed a beautiful young Russian woman approaching. She had the classic features that were considered very beautiful in the West. This Russian woman exhibited the high cheekbones, small nose, and plump luscious lips that would always score very high points in Western beauty standards. And then there was also her long blond hair that was beautifully braided. Within this woman, he sensed the final result of the wild mixture that had taken place in Russia over the last two thousand years. An in-depth analysis of her DNA would surely reveal an amalgamation of genes derived from the Early East Slavs, Finno-Ugric peoples, Mongols, Germans, and all the others that had invaded Russia and that had created a melting pot over the centuries that finally resulted in the exotic mixtures of Eastern and Western features found in the true Russian beauty, with her soft, fair skin and her exquisite blue-gray almond-shaped eyes. It was also clear by the way that she dressed that she had a real passion for colorful clothes and exquisite jewels. Gold and precious stones in earrings, bracelets, and rings adorned her beautiful features.

Russian women were known for being strong in bearing things, in forgiving, in struggling for survival, and in keeping themselves beautiful despite the worst living conditions. But this woman was not part of that subcategory. She was all style and sophistication. Every detail of her stature exuded wealth and status.

"Я верю, что ты банкир, что я ищу," she said to him. But then she smiled and said it in English when she realized that he didn't understand.

"I believe that you are the banker that I am looking for."

"I really hope that I am," he responded, with a gleam in his eyes. He looked at her lips, trying to anticipate how they would move in response to what he had just said. He was totally fascinated by her and wanted to experience her in every way possible every moment that she remained in his presence.

"I have been asked to invite you to supper this evening if you are available."

"You want to have supper with me?" he asked, incredulously.

"Well, to be precise, there is a group of friends with shared interests that will be getting together for supper this evening at a dacha about an hour away from St. Petersburg. They thought that you may find the reunion quite interesting and very entertaining. Nadya Ivanovna has asked me to inform you that she will also be attending the soirée this evening. She hopes that you will be able to attend."

"I still have one wish left," was his response.

"Sorry, I don't understand."

"Thank you for inviting me," he said. "But I don't even know your name."

"Ah! My name is Vera."

THE AMERICAN ENTERED THE DACHA NOT KNOWING what to expect. The invitation that he had been given had been deliberately vague, but he had nothing better planned for the evening. He also knew that at least two of the women that were to be in attendance were incredibly beautiful, and they would more than likely not be attending the soirée unless they thought it would be entertaining.

He first noticed Nadya lounging on a divan by the window. She had a silver filigree butterfly in her hair. She was wearing a cotton blouse that was in color like the reddish orange of sunset. It was offset by a sleeveless jacket of black crinkled crepe that was decorated with the same reddish orange satin piping. Her black, crinkled, crepe trousers were loosely fitting and completed the image that she wished to convey of the high-class

Chinese courtesan of the famous sing-song houses of Shanghai from the late 19th century. Nadya appeared to the American as the very essence of a magnificent work of art in every sense. He was entranced, and she must have felt his intense glare because she suddenly turned her gaze toward him and was not at all surprised to find him there. She waved to him from the divan, beckoning him to approach the little group that had assembled there.

Sitting next to Nadya was a rather attractive Chinese woman that appeared to be in her mid-thirties. She was wearing a simple smooth-woven cotton blouse under a satin-trimmed padded silk jacket that had a pale turquoise background and piping with a woven pattern of gold potted orchids. This attire was also perfectly in keeping with the period costume that Nadya wore. In her hair, the woman had a pair of green jade hairpins in the shape of lotus pods. Her radiant complexion and limpid eyes completed the picture of a woman that was at once stylish and graceful.

On a plush chair next to the divan sat Liu Tang. He was wearing a cotton white shirt and blue denim jeans. He was holding a half-smoked cigarette in one hand, and unmistakably, a neat scotch whiskey in the other. Liu Tang had not yet noticed that the American, his prospective business associate, had arrived.

Opposite the divan, there was a worn leather sofa

where a young Russian couple sat. They had their backs to the American, so he couldn't quite tell whether or not he had previously met them. But the chances were rather unlikely since they didn't appear to be bankers and therefore probably not attending the conference.

As the American approached the little gathering, Nadya got up to greet him. When Liu Tang realized who it was that was kissing Nadya, he also got up to firmly shake his hand. Eva and Alexander were introduced as coworkers of Nadya. They worked with her at the puppet theater. Eileen Li was introduced as the resident Chinese historian and faculty member on Asian studies at the University of St. Petersburg. There were at least thirty other guests scattered throughout the impressively furnished dacha. The host for the soirée had apparently not yet arrived.

"My first visit to a dacha," said the American.

"Well, you have certainly come to a very special one," Nadya responded. "But you must find yourself a drink so that you can participate with us in what Professor Li has painstakingly prepared for our entertainment. I think you will find it most interesting."

"Even I, being Chinese, find myself privileged in being able to participate in this divination session that is being presented to us by such a learned scholar as Professor Li," chimed in Liu Tang.

As the American went about looking for his glass of

wine, Ms. Li pulled out a tube-like container that was filled with long, thin, wooden bamboo sticks that she referred to as the Sticks of Fate.

Now, with his wine glass in hand, the American seated himself to the left of Ms. Li. He didn't know how the evening would pan out, but he was game for anything. Ms. Li took a moment from her presentation to look at her new neighbor, and then she asked him if he was familiar with the Chinese deity Kuan Yin.

"No," he said. "I must admit that I have never heard of her."

"Well, Kuan Yin is revered by millions of Chinese around the world. She ranks among the most beloved of all sacred beings. She is adored by Buddhists and Taoists alike. She is the female manifestation of the Buddha of Compassion. You know, shrines and temples dedicated to Kuan Yin can be found throughout East Asia and wherever Chinese people have traveled or settled."

"I have noticed that you have brought out a canister filled with bamboo sticks. These Sticks of Fate, are they tied in some way to this story of the Goddess Kuan Yin?" asked Nadya.

"Right. These Chien Tung, as you can see, are tipped with red on one end and are numbered on the other. A full set of one hundred of them is required for the Kuan Yin Oracle."

"Where can you find these Sticks of Fate?" asked

Alex. "Are they something easily found in Oriental shops?"

"Complete one hundred sets are normally sold outside Buddhist or Taoist shrines. Packs containing approximately sixty or seventy sticks are more commonly found in stores. These may be suitable for games or other systems of divination, but one hundred sticks are required for full utilization of the Kuan Yin Oracle."

"And these Sticks of Fate, how are they tied to the Goddess Kuan Yin?" asked the American.

"Well, if everyone will allow me," began Ms. Li. "To begin with, you should know that each of the sticks has a poem associated with it. The number on the stick refers to the number associated with a specific poem. The one hundred poems have been associated with the Goddess Kuan Yin for centuries. Versions of these poems can be found in Buddhist temples and shrines around the world. Usually, there is a small pot or bamboo tube placed in front of a statue of the Goddess Kuan Yin with the one hundred sticks inside of it."

Ms. Li paused her explanation to allow the waiter to take away the empty glasses and to ask if anyone wished for a refill. Liu Tang happily put in his request for a second neat whiskey. "That was quite nice," he commented. "Do you know what brand of whiskey it is?" he asked the waiter.

"Macallan scotch," was the waiter's prompt reply. "It is the 18-year-old single malt."

"Lovely! I've never had it before," added Liu Tang.

"I wouldn't mind another glass of this red wine. It is rather good."

"Yes? That's the 1992 Banfi Brunello di Montalcino."

"I'll have a glass of that as well," said Nadya. Alex and Eva decided that they would also try the red Italian wine, and Ms. Li confirmed to the waiter that she wasn't having anything.

The American was able to give Nadya a quick glance while they were all handing their empty glasses to the waiter. He wondered where they were headed with Ms. Li's deliberation on divination. At least the wine was very good. There was also a very promising barbeque in the works.

"By the way, Nadya, what can you tell me about that lovely woman that brought my invitation? She led me to understand that you knew each other. Is she also with your puppet theater?" asked the American.

"Vera? No, I only recently met her through Liu Tang."

"Vera is friends with one of my business associates. He is the one hosting this party. He has unfortunately been delayed. But we can expect to see him and Vera quite soon. Vera is his personal assistant."

"Mr. Tang, thank you for also inviting me to this

soirée. The dacha is quite lovely, and your friends seem very nice. I must say that I was extremely surprised to hear that your friends had an interest in the topic of the Goddess Kuan Yin. I thought that perhaps this was a gathering of people interested in discussing comparative religions. But I no longer feel that is the case. I hope that I have not bored all of you with my ramblings on the topic of Kuan Yin," said Ms. Li.

"Not at all," everyone protested.

"Ms. Li," Liu Tang interrupted, "I was hoping that you would be able to give your perspectives and interpretations on some of the results that we will be getting as we draw the Sticks of Fate from your container. I think we all agree that you have provided us so far with an excellent orientation on the history and cultural importance of the Goddess Kuan Yin. I believe that I speak for all of us when I say how truly grateful we are that you have taken the time to enlighten us with your expertise on this very interesting topic. But I hope that you will not abandon us now when we will need you most, as we plunge ourselves into the task of looking for answers from the deity to the questions that we may have. Please indulge us for a few more moments, Ms. Li."

"Yes, Ms. Li, now that you have transported us to the threshold, we all hope that you will guide us in interpreting whatever answers we receive from the Sticks of Fate. Without you, it will all be a sort of hieroglyphics for us. You are the key to our understanding any of it," Alex pleaded. He was in total earnest in his plea as he really did want to have a complete picture of this different world in order to make any sense of it, especially if he should later decide to incorporate it into the little theater.

"Yes, of course we can continue since I can see that there is genuine interest in the topic. Certainly, by all means, let us proceed." After saying this, Ms. Li picked up the container with the Sticks of Fate and continued with her explanations.

"Let us imagine that we are in a temple and that you wish to ask the Goddess for advice," she began. "Having made your obeisance and offerings, you tilt the container and begin shaking it until the Sticks begin to move out." As she said this she demonstrated the motion with the container that she was holding. "You will then select the Stick that is furthest out and refer to the numbered poem for guidance. So, who will be the first to select the Stick of Fate? Who has had a question in mind that they have been thinking about and that they are not certain on how to move forward? Who will be the first volunteer?" After having said this, Ms. Li glanced around at her audience wondering who would initiate the process.

"I would like to be the first to propose a question to the deity," said Liu Tang. "But I hope that I will not need to reveal the issue that has been troubling me. It is rather personal in nature." Everyone looked at Liu Tang as he said this. The American wondered if this was perhaps related to the issue of his wife.

"Yes, Mr. Tang, don't worry," Ms. Li explained. "Your question remains between you and the deity, and no one will need to know what it is. Even though we will all see the deity's response, only you will be able to know how it applies to your particular question. So, please select the Stick of Fate if you are now ready to proceed."

Everyone watched as Liu Tang pulled out his Stick of Fate. The selected number was sixty-six.

"So, now Mr. Tang, let us see what number sixty-six has in store for you." Ms. Li proceeded to read the poem aloud. 'The ship is broken down in the rushing shoal.' So, Mr. Tang, you have now received your answer from the deity."

As Ms. Li said this, everyone looked at Liu Tang and began to laugh. Liu Tang then began to laugh as well, as it was quite apparent that the response was not easily discernible to anyone.

"Well, Ms. Li, you have left me more confused now than when I first began with my question. I have no possible idea what the deity could mean by this," said Liu Tang. Everyone was still laughing at Liu Tang and at the resulting answer from the Stick of Fate.

"You must be patient, Mr. Tang," Ms. Li began. She was also laughing at the group's response. "I think I should be able to assist you a little in helping to decipher this poem. I have seen some expert commentaries over the years on some of these poems, so I don't want to take full credit here." They were all still smiling, waiting to see what the expert had to say, and seeing if Liu Tang would be able to apply it to his particular case.

"Let's see," she began. "Your ship has gotten stranded on the sandbank or shoal. Negotiations regarding something have perhaps come to a deadlock. You are forced to let go of something. Keep in mind that it is life's obstacles that help you grow. And it is growth that helps you reach your goals. That is how the experts begin their interpretation of the number sixty-six." They were very impressed with Ms. Li's initial comments. Liu Tang was now looking at her shrewdly, waiting for the rest.

"Mr. Tang, pulling up roots can be a sad occasion for those who are especially close to home and loved ones. Turn whatever crisis there may be into an opportunity for growth in a new direction. Something that was broken should perhaps not be mended. You are resilient enough to bounce back. That is all that I can remember about this. Only you will know if this has addressed your question in any sense."

Liu Tang appeared to be astonished by her thorough response. Everyone looked at Liu Tang, waiting to see what he had to say. The American had recalled Liu Tang's personal story regarding his situation at home with his wife, and knowing this, he couldn't believe how appropriate the Stick of Fate had responded to that question. From the look on his face, everyone sensed that Mr. Tang had been given a response that seemed to be quite appropriate.

"Well, Mr. Tang?" Nadya asked. "Please don't keep us in suspense. Have you been given an appropriate response from the deity Kuan Yin?" She asked this in a teasing manner.

"Ms. Li, you have left me speechless," he responded. "How is it possible to receive such a response?" In total earnestness, he said, "You have converted me." And, as he said this, his audience began laughing again. "Yes, I believe in the deity Kuan Yin!" His audience continued to laugh uncontrollably as they stared at his comical facial expression. "You are truly a medium if I can say so, Ms. Li. Thank you."

"Not at all," Ms. Li responded.

The waiter came by again, looking to see if anyone needed anything. Liu Tang made most of the opportunity by finishing his whiskey quickly. He handed the waiter his glass and promptly requested another. Nadya and the American also asked for refills. Now that Ms. Li proved to be successful with her presentation, she decided that she would try the red wine as well.

"Oh, Ms. Li," said Nadya, "I was afraid that you were perhaps a teetotaler."

"I'm sorry to have given you that impression," responded Ms. Li, smiling. "I thought that I should initially refrain from the alcohol until at least one communication with the deity," she added, all giggles. She then looked at the American for a moment without saying anything. She seemed to be studying him.

"Perhaps you would like to take a turn with the deity next," she asked him.

"Sure," he responded. "I'm always ready for a turn with a goddess." He took a moment to study her as well. She chuckled at his remark.

"Are you ready then?" she asked.

"Yes, I'm always ready for a good time."

"Well, I should warn you that the results are not always in line with the expectations."

"I'll take my chances with you."

"You mean with the deity Kuan Yin," she corrected.

"Her too," he was quick to agree.

Ms. Li picked up her container holding the Sticks of Fate and began to slowly shake them again until one of them seemed to slide slightly further out than the others. Everyone watched as the American leaned forward to pull the stick out. Ms. Li watched him as he drew the stick close to his breast, keeping the number hidden from view, as though it were a poker hand.

"You seem to be uncertain as to whether or not you want to go forward with this," Ms. Li teased. She gave him a rather surprised look, and then said, "It's good to approach the deity with respect."

"I wholeheartedly agree. I just don't want to display my stick to the deity without being ready," he said grinning. "I think it would be rather disrespectful. It might provoke her into doing something that could be really painful for me. You now can understand why I have been reluctant to reveal myself. You must all forgive me if I seem a little coy."

"Very good," Ms. Li agreed. "You definitely want to be ready as you approach her. That is a common mistake that many people make. Only approach your deity when you are ready, because then she may show compassion."

At this point, Liu Tang interrupted their little dialogue by asking the American if he was now ready to proceed, and if he didn't have the nerve, then perhaps he should postpone his turn until another occasion. "It is never wise to proceed," he added, "if you are not confident about yourself."

The comment Liu Tang made could be construed as a challenge that referred back to the other pending business that the two men had previously discussed. The American had not yet given Liu Tang his commitment with regard to the opening of the company account with his affiliate bank in Geneva. Liu Tang had been disappointed with his indecision. The conference was soon drawing to an end, and he had hoped that they would have come to terms by now. But the American had been reluctant to commit. Neither of them understood the reason for the hesitation. The American wondered if this evening's invitation had been initiated by Liu Tang in an attempt to get him to commit.

"Here you are, Ms. Li. I submit to whatever the deity has in store for me."

"Oh, let's see what you have. Right, number eighty-seven. 'Washing the sand for gold, and you get the gold!' I like that one." Everyone waited to see what Ms. Li had to say about the American's fate.

"You will receive what you are searching for," she began. "You have the opportunity to make your dreams come true. Keep a big smile on your face and see what happens, as things seem to be running quite smoothly. A lucky break could come your way now. It's up to you to make the most of it. I think that is all. Most promising, I would say."

"It sounds as though you are ready to move into your Street of Eternal Happiness," volunteered Liu Tang. "The stars are aligned in your favor, and even the Goddess Kuan Yin seems to agree that the timing is right. All it takes now is courage and commitment. I congratulate you." Liu Tang was smiling as he said this.

"Thank you, Ms. Li," said the American.

"Not at all," she replied. "I hope that at the very least you have all been entertained."

"Absolutely," replied Alex. "You have been invaluable in opening up another fascinating world to me." He was already deep in his thoughts as to the type of theatrical programming that could be possibly developed from what he had seen this night.

"I love what you and Nadya are wearing," said Eva. "Can you tell me a little about the costumes?"

"Sure," Ms. Li said. "Nadya came into my office at the university when I was unpacking costumes that I recently received from Shanghai that dated back to the late 19th century. They are part of an exhibit that the Asian society is putting together next month. We thought that it might be fun to wear them tonight. They are typical of the clothing that the courtesans wore in the pleasure quarters of Shanghai. The leading courtesans in Shanghai at the time were considered minor celebrities and trendsetters in fashion. Besides exquisite clothes and shoes, leading courtesans were adorned with expensive jewelry. I'm glad to hear that you like them."

"They are gorgeous," Eva said.

"I hope that all of you will be able to attend the exhibit. On opening night we will have an all-female cast presenting three plays from the same time period. The works are titled The Green Screen Mountain, A House Full of High Officials, and Beating the Princess. It should be quite an entertaining evening."

As the American was watching Ms. Li speak, he

suddenly remembered some of the funny things that his Jewish buddy used to tell him back in Brooklyn when they used to jog around Greenwood Cemetery on weekends. They were silly sayings that were always attributed to Confucius. 'Confucius says,' he remembered hearing, 'that the man who has his head up the ass has a shitty outlook on life.' And then there was the one 'When wife complains too much about no magic in marriage, husband will disappear.' Liu Tang interrupted his musings when he suddenly tapped him on the shoulder.

"Our host has arrived and would like to say hello to us privately," Liu Tang told him.

The American followed Liu Tang across the room and down a corridor that led to a door at the extreme end of the dacha. Liu Tang knocked on the door, and then both men entered a room that appeared to be like a financial library. There were framed stock certificates on the walls, and there was a running ticker tape flashing stock prices across a wall behind an elegant cherry wood desk. On the desk, there was a computer terminal that was connected to Bloomberg. Also on the desk, there were porcelain figurines of a bull and bear and a paperweight of a US hundred-dollar bill. Seated on a leather chair behind the desk was the host of the party.

"Gentlemen, how are you? I am Mikhail Potanin." The man was wearing a light blue silk shirt with tennis-themed cufflinks, and dark blue pants with a thin leather belt. He had been smoking a Puro Cuban cigar. As he greeted the two men, he quickly stood up to shake their hands. He was extremely tall, maybe six feet four inches, and quite fit with broad shoulders. It was evident that he made time for daily workouts at the gym. He appeared to be in his mid-forties, and his smile revealed perfect pearly white teeth.

"I must apologize for not having met you earlier. I've been held captive here longer than I expected on a long-distance call with a business associate. But now that the business has been settled, we can move on to the dinner party. I hope that you have been able to get your drinks."

"Yes, thank you," said Liu Tang.

"What a lovely dacha you have here," said the American.

"I'm glad that you like it. It has been in our family for many years." He looked at Liu Tang for a moment and then said, "Mr. Tang, we have met before. I also know for a fact that we have been silent participants for opposing sides on several transactions, and I would like to add that it has been a pleasure to work with you."

"Oh?" replied Liu Tang, rather puzzled. "I can't seem to recall where we could have transacted before."

"Well, you're partially right. You did not deal with me directly, but rather with one of my firms. Onexa Ltd.," he added.

"Yes, of course," said Liu Tang. "Let me see, that was

several months ago. That was all perfectly settled within ninety days, as specified."

"Precisely," said the Russian. "I think we all made rather well on that transaction. You should know that we are planning on a new transaction that is to take place within the next two months. It will be similar in nature to that last transaction."

"Excellent," Liu Tang said. "That is precisely the type of transaction that works best for us. Uncomplicated and profitable, what more can one ask for?" Liu Tang added.

"Yes, but what we want is to be able to do larger transactions. And in order to mitigate any settlement risks, we would like to have additional banks participate in this import–export program." Then, addressing the American, he said, "Is it your bank in Geneva that we will be transacting with?"

"Nothing has been settled yet," Liu Tang interceded. "We are still in discussions on the possibility of using his affiliate bank in Geneva."

"Ah, I see," said Mikhail. "But you know that we would like to have the matter settled as soon as possible. Time is money, Mr. Tang."

"Quite so," Liu Tang responded. "But I believe that my friend is looking for additional reassurances."

"Is that so?" Mikhail responded. "Perhaps I can be of

assistance to you on that score. What are your concerns?" he asked the American.

"We know very little about your business. What exactly are you planning to import and export? We need to know what it is that we are getting ourselves into."

"Can we speak freely here?" he looked at the American as he asked this. "We are looking to help our friends in Cuba unload their addictive white crystals." He was expecting a reaction from the American, but the latter was not going to make any comments until he heard everything that the Russian had to say.

"We are dealing with a contraband trail of white crystals along China's southeast borders. This is the area known as the Golden Triangle, the area that borders Vietnam and Thailand. But the substance that is crossing the borders is not what you think. The product that we are dealing with is sugar."

"Sugar?" asked the American in disbelief.

"Sugar!" responded Mikhail. "The motivation for the trade is the same as it was for Golden Triangle's narcotic traffic: hefty profits for smugglers. That is the product that we offer, that the Chinese want and that the Cubans have plenty of in surplus quantities."

"Mr. Potanin, importing sugar is not illegal in China," Liu Tang said.

"Sugar itself isn't illegal in China, of course, Mr. Tang. But the legitimate imports of the commodity have to obey market forces, and global sugar prices haven't been very profitable lately. They have hit a twenty-month low as a large production surplus has weighed heavily on the market. A ton of imported sugar will sell for about 5,300 Yuan portside in China. But the government sets a higher floor price of 6,550 Yuan for its stockpile of domestic product, which it does so in order to protect the incomes of more than thirty-seven million sugar farmers in the poor southern areas of China which include Guangxi, Yunnan, and Guangdong provinces. Within the twenty-five percent mark-up is the smuggler's commission.

"The sugar trade is immense. The Guangdong Sugar Association last month estimated that contraband imports in the first quarter this year have already reached 500,000 tons, slightly more than the volume of legitimate sugar imports tracked by Chinese customs. China is the world's top sugar importer. The expectations of tight supplies in China are also underpinning prices, as official economic planners say that the Chinese sugar market is likely to face a consumption deficit of two million tons this year, largely because of poor weather during the crucial growing periods earlier in the season. In the longer term, Chinese sugar consumption looks set to keep rising over the next ten years. We believe that for our enterprise, things can only get sweeter." Having given this explanation, Mikhail didn't see the need to provide any further details about the operation.

"I'm very impressed," said Liu Tang. "I feel quite comfortable with what you have said and look forward to being able to provide my services."

The American also liked what he heard and professed an eagerness to participate in the venture. Since the product was legitimate, he didn't have any qualms about being a participant in the process. For the first time in his life, he felt the real possibility of making significant money, and he knew that this was probably the only opportunity that he would ever have. He was determined now to go along with what had been proposed. Even the divination from the Sticks of Fate had been encouraging.

"That is great news, gentlemen," said Mikhail. "Let us now join the party and drink to our success. I am quite confident that we will all make money on this transaction. The Cubans will be especially happy to hear that we will be moving forward with their product. They are quite desperate for money."

"You know that we cannot make payments directly to Cuba," said the American.

"Of course, I know that. I also know that you cannot have any letters of credit made in favor of any Cubans. You should not even know anything about Cuba. Your role in the transaction comes into play between my firm and our Asian counterparts. We will deal directly and separately with our Cuban friends. Don't you worry about that," said Mikhail reassuringly. But the American needed reassurances because he still felt uncomfortable transacting with smugglers and with people that had no qualms about circumventing the law. He hoped that the party would distract him from thinking any further on the matter.

When he was out with the others at the party, Mikhail appeared as a man of warmth and generosity, choosing his words carefully, giving a half-shrug or a grin that conveyed secret knowledge. There was also a definite mischievous twinkle in his eyes. Like many Russians, he had a fondness for vodka, and soon he and his intimate friends were drinking to the jazz music that was playing, to the wonderful white night, and to the incomparable beauties that were found in this magical land of the firebird.

The dacha was a handsome nineteenth-century farmhouse, a large white clapboard house with green trim and shutters, shaded and decorated on three sides by mature blue spruce, Norway spruce, and sugar maple trees. At the back of the house, there was a wooden deck, and across an expanse of lawn, there was a swimming pool that was a sparkling invitation on this warm July night.

On the back deck, in the enclosed Veranda, Mikhail

was a solid presence as he sat at the head of the dining room table. Choosing his words wisely, Mikhail began addressing his guests by saying, "Friends, this is where we eat, drink, talk, argue, discuss politics, as the lovely eau de vie flows into us on this festive occasion. Liu Tang, I opened a Chinese fortune cookie this week that said this was to be my lucky week. I thought that it had to do with the fact that I was about to embark on a new business venture with you. However, it seems that it had to do with something entirely different. Friends, my Vera Zvonareva has consented to be my wife."

Everyone stood to congratulate Mikhail on his choice of wife and to offer their best wishes. After that, Mikhail signaled to one of the waiters that they were now ready to begin their dinner.

Two long tables had been simply drawn together and then set with white linen Russian table cloth that was embroidered with red cross-stitching. The silverware and china were very simple. Vases with mimosas had been placed in the middle of the table along with bowls of oranges and tangerines. The hors d'oeuvres were set on the table, and the guests passed them to each other while Mikhail poured the vodka. There was caviar, marinated herring, pickles, and a macedoine of vegetables. The meal progressed slowly. Kvass, a homemade fermented drink usually drunk in the country, was then offered to the guests. After the hors d'oeuvres, the cook served a succulent stew made of game.

The conversation throughout dinner was very general. The American had the good fortune to find a seat between Ms. Li and Nadya, and Liu Tang had managed to place himself directly opposite them.

"Ms. Li," the American began. "You have left me quite curious about the establishments where the sing-gong girls worked in Shanghai. Were they legal in China at the time?"

"Oh, yes," Ms. Li answered. "But please call me Eileen. Prostitution establishments, like the opium shops, were perfectly legal in the foreign concessions. The brothels were subject to license fees and taxes, and they were monitored under various police regulations. The fees for the sing-song houses varied depending on the quality of the house and the number of girls working there. Because of these regulations, we have very good statistics as to the number of prostitutes that worked there during the 1870s. Health officials recorded that there were about 1,650 prostitutes in the International Settlement sector, and another 2,600 in the French." After providing her statistics, Ms. Li finished the last of her vodka and requested a refill. "It seems to me," she then said, "that this is the right occasion and the right group of people to drink with."

"Absolutely," Liu Tang said encouragingly, while

Nadya chuckled at seeing the professor wanting to really drink.

"You know," Ms. Li began again, "the sing-song houses were an important meeting place for friends and business associates at the time. They were places where social networks were extended, where businesses were conducted, and where advice was sought and given among friends and colleagues. They played a very special role in society."

"Ms. Li, you seem to be painting a wonderful picture of these establishments. I wonder if the women that worked in them found them to be as wonderful as you picture them?" asked Eva.

"To begin with," Ms. Li began, "one factor that featured prominently in the supply of prostitutes to these houses was poverty. The sale of female children was a frequent occurrence among desperately poor families. During the years of flood and famine, little girls were sold openly on the streets, and most of them ended up as servant girls or prostitutes. There are plenty of documented horror stories. And while some girls were sold by their relatives, others were kidnapped by gangs that specialized in human trafficking. That should give you a clearer picture as to the type of women that worked in these houses and about my acute awareness with regard to their human condition. Unfortunately, as a historian, I must also admit to the beneficial role that these establishments played in society."

"Eileen," Alex began, "I am extremely excited about the possibility of creating a new play for our puppet theater based on everything that you have told us tonight. The deity Kuan Yin, the Sticks of Fate, Sing-song houses, the human angle on the girls, and the wonderful period costumes all lead me to believe that we have a treasure trove of material that can be used to create a magnificent work for the theater. You have even alluded to the period plays that were staged and the music that was played at these establishments. I hope that you will agree to collaborate with us in the creation of a new work. I have to confess that I probably won't be able to sleep tonight just thinking about all of the possibilities."

Coffee, cognac, and a German Eiswein were offered at the end of the meal. It was then that Mikhail's fiancée finally made her first appearance. Vera Zvonareva was very good-looking, tall, slender, and meticulously well-dressed as she walked up to Mikhail. Her long blonde hair was still in a single plait. She gazed at Mikhail with wide-open eyes, full of love, as if fascinated, waiting for him to say something.

"You're late," he finally said, smiling. "And now there is no room for you," he added.

"All right! Goodbye, then!" she responded, feigning a pout.

"Quick, take a last glimpse, everyone," countered Mikhail. Everyone started laughing then at the silly exchange of the lovesick couple. It was then that Vera informed them that she was going to be registering for a course on assertiveness training.

Someone at the table spoke up and said, "Vera, what more could you possibly want?"

"People don't always succeed at what they try to do; at the things they want most to do," Vera tried to explain. "I want my actions to count for something. I want to be able to succeed at whatever I try to do." She then concluded by saying, "You know, there are things in one's life that are waiting to happen."

"You know, you are now getting much too philosophical for us," Mikhail protested. "And it's quite unfair because you haven't been drinking as much as we have."

"Yes," someone else shouted, siding with Mikhail. "What are you trying to pull on us now? You shouldn't be permitted to speak to us in your condition. You need to have at least five more glasses of vodka in order to make any sense to us. What has come over you? How can you speak to us like that?"

"Assertiveness training?" someone else asked. "What does that even mean? Mikhail, you need to watch yourself. Look at all the mischief that Pussy Riot has created.

This is all part of the new world order?" This last remark elicited a riotous outburst of protest from more than half of the guests.

"Hey, we love Pussy Riot," someone yelled out.

"Ok guys, let's not get crazy now," Mikhail pleaded. Then he turned toward Vera and said, "You see where your assertiveness training will lead to? Chaos! Pussy Riot! I hope that you will not register for this course, please."

Vera couldn't help but laugh at his hopelessly pleading look. "Ok, Mikhail," she said. "I will think about it." And with that, they kissed like hungry lovers. Everyone then realized that the party had come to an end.

The American and Liu Tang knew they weren't going to be getting any love tonight, not unless they were going to pay for it back at their hotel. Nadya and Eileen were getting a ride back toward the university, near where they resided. Liu Tang and the American were getting a private chauffeur ride to their hotel. As a parting gift, Mikhail gave them each a box of Havana Diplomaticos cigars. During the presentation of the cigar boxes, the three men agreed to get together soon in order to put together a plan of action.

· · ·

WHEN LIU TANG AND THE AMERICAN REACHED THEIR hotel lobby, there were quite a few high heels about the place. The American and Liu Tang were glad to see the young women. They improved upon the overall atmosphere of disenchantment that permeated throughout the hotel. The women were also a welcome break in the scheme of things and helped to diffuse any tensions that may have been accumulating throughout the conference. The time seemed ripe for a romantic interlude, but during these time fragments, you never knew how things would work out.

When Liu Tang noticed that his regular corner table in the lobby bar was vacant, he quickly headed for it and extended an invitation to the American to join him for a nightcap. But the American declined because he said that he had to meet with one of the Danish bankers that he just noticed was sitting by the bar with a group of other conference attendees. The American's pretext was that he intended to discuss with the Dane the recent notifications that his bank had received regarding changes to their intraday credit lines.

"The interbank credit lines are tightening up, Liu Tang," said the American.

"That's right," Liu Tang agreed. "See you later, my friend."

"Right," the tired American responded.

But the American never followed through with his

intention. He headed straight to the elevators that would take him to his room. He was no longer feeling in any mood for company. In fact, he was really looking forward to entering his miserable room, stripping off his clothes, and quickly getting into bed. It was amazing that he hadn't realized until then how tired he had become. Mercifully, he was also feeling very sleepy. Nothing was going to keep him up that night, or so he hoped. The digital clock on the night table showed that it was only 9:00 pm, and it was still quite bright out.

Liu Tang was left wondering what the American was up to. Why would he say that he was going to have a chat with the Danish banker when he clearly wasn't? Why the sudden change of plans? It was true that they had now in principle come to an agreement. They were to be business associates. But there was still something unsettling about the American, something that made Liu Tang feel doubt about the American's commitment. He didn't see in the American a hunger for the business or a desire for wanting to make more money. He didn't seem to be engaged at all but rather appeared as someone that was just going through the motions, going along for the ride for the lack of something better. What a strange man, and even stranger capitalist.

CHAPTER SEVENTEEN

IT WAS LESS than two hours into his sleep when the fantasies began. The pedestrians on the streets were all heading in the same direction, toward the square by the cathedral. There were hundreds of people already gathered for what they were saying was a punk prayer meeting. Many were reciting in unison, "Christ has risen."

"This is God's shit," someone shouted.

"No believer should say this doesn't concern them," someone else cried out. And this was followed by another person shouting, "Mother of God, rid us of Putin."

A woman dressed in a very colorful shift that went down to her ankles got up on top of a car with a megaphone and stared at the assembled crowd. It was strange that the American recognized the outfit that she wore, but he couldn't remember where he had seen it. Her shift was bunched up at the waist with a thin leather belt. The shift had very vibrant colorful inserts that were characteristic of a primitive costume. The asymmetrical geometric patterns of the inserts on the shift were squares and circles, and these had inserts of symmetrical crosses, dots, and diamonds. The pretty young woman lifted the megaphone to her lips and began addressing the crowd.

"Our goal is to change humanity," she began, "to be the voice for the voiceless. Talk and compromise will get you nowhere. We want to transform consciousness, to free society from prejudices. Putin is a demon with a brain. We mustn't be complicit participants in this horrific theater that is led by the totalitarian demon. We need to riot! Mother of God, rid us of Putin," she then shouted. And with that many in the crowd went into a frenzy shouting in unison, "Down with Putin."

The young woman then raised her hand, imploring the crowd to stop.

"Please remember that we bear no ill will to anyone," she began again. "We are not against religion. What we cannot tolerate is the relationship between church and state! We need a Russia without Putin."

The crowd was then treated to harsh, loud music that was being piped in from an unknown source. The young woman threw down the megaphone and began to dance on the car. There was no rhythm to the music that was being played or to her dance movements. Some in the crowd started to scream as she danced frenetically. Some started to protest that it was a blasphemous dance. Others began shouting that Putin had been hiding behind a bush. Mayhem finally broke out when smoke bombs were thrown into the crowd. Out of nowhere, the police had suddenly appeared wearing riot gear, and then the crowd quickly dispersed. No arrests were made. The young female leader seemed to have vanished into thin air. The police were quite at a loss as to how this could have happened. She had been their target. Someone remarked that God must have been watching out for her.

The American didn't want to wait to see what was going to happen next. He quickly left, turning into one of the streets that he knew would take him back to the hotel. But along the way, he sensed that he was being followed. He turned left at the corner and quickened his pace in an attempt to lose whomever it was that may have been following. At the end of the next corner, he turned again, continuing at the same pace, because he could still hear the footsteps trailing behind him.

During the protest in the square, he had noticed that there had been two men wearing black suits and black shirts that he thought were staring at him, but he didn't give it much thought because he didn't think that there should be any reason for them to be doing so. He sure as hell didn't look like a protestor, so why should there be any interest in him?

None of this made any sense. He felt like a character in a Kafka novel. He was running through the streets like a madman looking for an escape. And he didn't understand the reason for the threat. Why was he now in danger? God damn Pussy Riot, he thought. And just like in a Kafka novel, he couldn't find anyone to help him. The fucking street names were all in Cyrillic, which he didn't understand.

Finally, glancing back, he could see that the two men in black were still on his tail. These were two big burly men, heavily built, and from that quick glance, he knew that they would only ask questions after first beating the shit out of him. "Fuck," he said out loud. There was nothing to do but to continue with the pace, and hope that he could outlast them. His nerves were on edge. "Fuck," he said out loud again.

At the end of the street, he turned right into a winding alley that had a small theater at the center of it. Seeing lights within the theater, the American decided to enter, hoping that his pursuers would be reluctant to try anything in front of an audience. The front door to the theater was locked, but he noticed that a side door leading in had been left open. After entering, he tried locking the door behind him. The aisle that faced him was dark, but there was sufficient light coming in from the windows for him to see that he could either work his way forward toward the audience seating or turn left toward the stage. He decided that he didn't want to attract any attention, so he crawled forward away from the stage and toward the audience seating. But there was no audience tonight.

As he moved toward the back of the theater, he could see that there were dancers on stage. The group was in the process of stretching while they were discussing choreography. He couldn't understand what they were saying because they were speaking in Russian, but it was evident that they were about to begin the rehearsal of a work.

The choreographer signaled to the pianist to begin playing, and when he heard the opening chords, it was clear to the American what the ballet was going to be. Yes, the unmistakable 1-2-3-4, 2-2-3-4, etc. The chords were systematically proceeding in their rhythmic groups of four, followed by an asymmetrical loud one. The radical composer at the time understood that the human ear found it aurally pleasant to hear the rhythms in groups of four. But then he unsettled the listeners by using asymmetrical rhythms following the groupings. In addition to the incongruous use of rhythms, the composer also failed to adhere to the traditional rules of tonality. By using dissonance and by creating tension throughout his work, the composer was able to keep the listeners unsettled. And, as if that wasn't enough, the original choreographer for the ballet wanted his dancers to appear to be twisted into unnatural postures and contortions within the body-shocking routines. The choreographer intended to display something so primal that it would shatter preconceived notions of ballet as it was known up until then, where movements were always exquisitely performed with a perfect delicacy and in graceful refinement.

The radical nature of the music and the unorthodox choreography provoked a riot at the ballet's premiere back in Paris. The ballet intended to tell the story about the annual springtime pagan ritual that was to have occurred somewhere in Russia. During the ritual, a virgin was required to perform a sacrificial dance to satisfy the god of spring. In the final scene of the ballet, there is the solemn pagan ritual where the repulsive sage elders are found seated in a circle watching the young girl dance herself to death!

As the American watched from the back of the theater, he soon realized that the ballerina who was going to perform the sacrificial dance in the current production was the same young woman that had appeared earlier in the evening with the megaphone at the square. As he was studying her, he suddenly recognized the costume that the young woman was wearing, that she had been wearing throughout the evening. It was a copy of the costume that the principal ballerina wore at the ballet's premiere in 1911. As he sat there watching the young woman dancing from the back of the theater, he suddenly began feeling quite tense. This young woman was wanted by the police, and he was fearful that he may have inadvertently led them to the theater where they were now pursuing him.

The American just sat there, unable to take more evasive action, fascinated by her dance, 1-2-3-4, 2-2-3-4, etc.... The music was creating the tension, and the ugly repulsive elders were seated in a circle watching the prima ballerina begin her sacrificial dance. As he watched her get to her feet in her colorful primitive costume, he noticed that the men in black who had been pursuing him earlier had now entered the theater and were moving along the aisles searching for him. There were more of them now, perhaps as many as eight, and they were accompanied by the police. But he still didn't take any evasive action. He couldn't take any action because he was too fascinated by the ballerina. His concern for her in her role was greater than any fear that he may have had of the men. And, as the ballerina danced on frenetically toward her fatal end, the men were now closing in on him as they approached the row where he had been hiding. When the men had finally spotted him, they inexplicably began laughing. But he ignored them and continued watching the ballerina. He was sweating profusely and they could tell that he had become quite agitated by what he was seeing on stage. It didn't make any sense to them, and that was why they had been laughing. It was so absurd!

"Get up," one of them yelled. But he continued to ignore them and continued to watch the ballerina.

"Get up, now!" The man in black closest to him repeated the order. But the American continued to ignore them. And then there was the loud blast, quite suddenly, unexpectedly. But he knew that it wasn't part of the original score. After the blast, the young dancer collapsed on the stage well before the choreography called for it. Suddenly bells started ringing, and they became louder and louder. They became so loud that he no longer could hear the voices of the men shouting orders at him. Nor could he hear the sound of the Stravinsky score being played on the piano, though he could see that the pianist still pounced on the keys despite the loud intrusive sound that had come from the blast, from the gunshot. The pianist continued to play, just as the ugly, repulsive elders remained seated, watching the young woman collapse right in front of their eyes. It was all so scandalous. The pagans were sacrificing the maiden to satisfy the Putin god!

There were no boos and catcalls during this performance. There was no outraged audience. The house lights went on and off for a while, and the ringing of the bells continued. They were growing louder and more insistent every minute. He couldn't hear the music, loud as it was, because of the din, and this made him furious. And then he bolted out of the theater and landed on his bed before the police were able to nab him.

Pussy Riot in my dreams, he thought, and then he began laughing and laughing. The phone in his hotel room had stopped ringing.

IT WAS STILL LIGHT OUT WHEN HE WOKE UP A LITTLE after 11 pm. The two-hour power nap had left him invigorated. He couldn't reconcile himself with sleeping while there was still light out, so he decided to dress and go down to the hotel lobby bar.

The American found Liu Tang still sitting in his favorite corner drinking his preferred neat whiskey in the company of the two Russian habitués that were always promising fun to the visiting businessmen. These cheerful girls served as goodwill ambassadors to the foreigners, and they performed an invaluable service in making the businessmen feel welcomed. The hotel managers were quite clever in turning a blind eye to whatever business transactions these girls turned in accommodating their affluent guests.

"Sing-song girls, Liu Tang?" the American asked, smiling.

"Hardly," Liu Tang responded, after taking a long drag from his cigarette. "But I believe that you are already acquainted with the lovely ladies. Won't you have a drink with us?" he asked. "Where did you run off to, when we first arrived? I thought that you were going to chat with the Danish banker."

"Liu Tang, I think my sugar levels must have dropped because I felt all of a sudden extremely exhausted. So, I went straight to bed."

"Oh, I'm sorry to hear that. Are you feeling OK now?"

"Fine," the American responded. "I slept for two hours, and now I feel totally refreshed."

"Excellent. Then you must have a drink with us."

"Yes, you must have a drink with us," chimed in the two girls.

"Don't worry. I definitely will," he responded. "And what shall we make a toast to?"

"That's easy," Liu Tang responded. "To wealth, strength, and honor!"

"Wealth, strength, and honor, is that what they are toasting to back in China?"

"Exactly, my friend," Liu Tang answered. "The New Culture Movement has been calling for a wholesale reassessment of China's past and is now embracing a systematic plan that includes a more extensive borrowing from foreign sources. The thinking is that if one course leads to ignorance, poverty, and weakness, then this should be cast aside. If an alternate course proves to be effective in overcoming those things, then we must adopt it, even if it proceeds from barbarians. The new reformers encourage us to repudiate or demolish the ancient ways of thinking in order to save our nation. We must forge a modern China. We must restore it to its global preeminence."

"Wow, you seem to be convinced with whatever your leaders are selling in China," one of the girls said. Then both girls started laughing at how silly it all sounded.

"Money is changing our neighbors," the other girl said. "Before, under the communists, everyone belonged to the work units, and that was what determined your work and life. The state decided where everybody lived. Now with prosperity, everything is changing, everything is being reevaluated."

After hearing her friend, the other girl proposed a toast. "Now, then, to wealth, strength, and honor, as Mr. Liu Tang had previously proposed. And to the new world order!" she quickly added.

"May we all prosper," her friend then said. As they all lifted their glasses, the American felt the hand of one of the girls squeezing his thigh under the table. This was the girl that he had taken into his room just a couple of nights earlier. It was up to him now to make the next move.

"To customized Harley-Davidsons and fading traditions," Liu Tang put in.

So here we are, the American thought, quite an unusual quartet. He couldn't decide what it was that he really wanted right then. He couldn't think of what to say. Life was in a million pieces. Drinking made it easier to act like somebody else, made it easier to change gears without having to think too much about it. And what was the point of it all? Does anyone really get what they want, he wondered?

This was like participating in a Russian drama about musicians. The leading ladies were seated opposite the two men. The quartet was remarkably free, natural, an unbound collaboration of four very different, but like-minded players. They were an ensemble of four performers with four voices, and sometimes good things did come from their playing. There didn't have to be any special significance assigned to what they did, nor was there any expectation that some significant result would come from their efforts. The quartet was going to play whatever they were in the mood to play. The two violas would play their parts as best as they could, and they would hope that the violin and the cello would closely follow. As the American was daydreaming about all of this silliness, he suddenly recalled that he didn't go to

Alexander Borodin's gravesite earlier today at the Tikhvin Cemetery when he was visiting the Alexander Nevsky Monastery. He regretted not having paid his respects to the great musician. Borodin's String Quartet Number 2 was one of the greatest in the classical repertoire. Sigmund Freud had perhaps been right when he stated in his psychodynamic theory that when patients speak out for themselves, worked through their own material and free associated, they could recover and comprehend crucial memories while being fully conscious. The American had been free-associating ideas with himself about the four of them at the bar, and from there he came to the notion about the musical quartet, which eventually led him to his regretted failure at not having gone to the great man's grave earlier that day.

"Well, I'm afraid I have to be running." They were all astonished when the American said this. The girl that still had her hand on his thigh couldn't believe what he had just said.

"But why are you leaving us?" she asked, squeezing his thigh a little harder.

"I have been served a fillet of soul," he answered.

"You have been served a fillet of sole?" the same girl asked in bewilderment. "Where, when have you been served the fillet?" None of them could make any sense of what he was saying.

"I'm afraid I haven't expressed myself correctly," he began. "When I say that I have been served a fillet of s-o-u-l and not s-o-l-e, I mean to say that I'm feeling quite guilty right now for not having visited Alexander Borodin's grave this afternoon when I was at the cemetery. You see, Liu Tang and I were invited to a dinner at a dacha earlier this evening, and I had to leave the Alexander Nevsky Monastery earlier than I would have liked in order to be on time. I now realize that I may not have another opportunity to visit Borodin's grave if I don't go now, as I will more than likely not be returning to St. Petersburg in the foreseeable future."

"But the Tikhvin Cemetery is closed," the other girl said. "I'm afraid that you will not be able to see Borodin's grave tonight!"

"Well, then, that settles that," Liu Tang said.

"Maybe if I speak to someone in the cathedral, they may let me in," he persisted.

"No, they will not let you in," the girl who still had her hand on his thigh countered. But seeing him take it so badly made her want to take it back. "Perhaps there may be a way," she said. The three of them then turned to her, wondering what she had to offer. "I know someone there who may be able to help."

The American looked at her and didn't doubt for a moment that she would be able to get him in. There was something quite intelligent about her.

"I will not be going to the cemetery," the other Russian girl protested. "I'm sorry, but I just prefer not to go if I don't have to go. There are just too many unpleasant memories that I have with cemeteries, and I don't have any desire to bring them back."

"Don't concern yourself," Liu Tang reassured her. "I'm not one for cemeteries either," he confided. "We will stay here together, keeping each other company."

"That is just fine," the girl next to the American said. "Because I didn't think that I would be able to get everyone in." After saying that, she took the American by the hand and proceeded to lead him out of the hotel lobby.

ONCE THEY HAD REACHED THE CEMETERY GROUNDS, the young Russian woman admitted to the American that she didn't have a specific plan to get in.

"Why would you say that you could if you couldn't?" the bewildered American asked her.

"You were planning to come anyway, and I needed a change of scenery and a change in company. So, that is why I came up with the idea."

"But you had my hopes up, and now this is a bit of a letdown."

"Well, let's not give up yet. After all, we are already

here. You may still get to see your old friend in the cemetery," she said, laughing.

"Yes," he responded, with a sigh. "It's one of the few places where you can feel the past. I think of it as a jewel box of a theater, a magical place. It is a provocative theater, a surreal place that envelopes everyone who enters."

"I can see that you will be having a great deal of fun once you find a way of getting inside." She was quite amused by the American's enthusiasm.

"You are laughing because you don't know any better. But I will have you know that in some cities in America there are nighttime ghost tours that are very popular. In America, expert raconteurs put on their seventeenth-century costumes in Williamsburg and in Boston to lead their adventure seekers on informative nighttime tours through the burial grounds of the historic final resting places of the most famous personalities from the Colonial period. These tours are extremely popular and quite important in that they help generate income for the preservation of the historical sites. I'm certain that the monks here would benefit immensely if they were to implement a similar program."

"It doesn't surprise me that some clever capitalist came up with this idea in America. People are always ready to listen to ghost stories. We have a rich tradition of that in our literature. And, as you say, there is something quite magical about the cemetery. A nighttime tour through the grounds could be quite entertaining if the right person were giving it. I, however, would not feel comfortable being alone in the cemetery at night. It's just so scary being there among all those dead souls. But I suppose that with a fun crowd, and hearing the stories adorned so that they would be very entertaining, I see how it could possibly be fun."

"Exactly!" was his response. "And you never know," he added, "you might find someone quite interesting on the tour."

"So, you are now making it into a love tour as well?"

"No, that is not what I meant. But you may find someone interesting on the tour that may want to continue the discussion over a drink at a bar. That would be just one additional byproduct from the experience."

"Yes, I see what you mean. It would be an additional place to meet interesting people," she mused, "at the cemetery. I can see all sorts of possibilities. I like your idea." She then started laughing out loud. "It is an extremely funny idea."

"Why don't we continue walking around to see if we can find a place to enter," he suggested. As they began walking along the metal rail fence surrounding the cemetery, he couldn't help but wonder why she was still willing to indulge his requests. She was a lovely girl with elongated gray eyes like a cat's, a straight nose, and perfect teeth. She also had an extremely desirable lithe body. He was feeling quite aroused by her now, as though a biological force had suddenly and inexplicably seized him.

"I am superstitious, you know," she suddenly volunteered. "We Russians, in general, are a superstitious people."

"How so?" he asked.

"Well, for example, if a person accidentally steps on another person's foot, it is common for the person who was stepped on to lightly step on the foot of the person who stepped first. This is so as to avoid a future conflict between them."

"Good to know while I'm in Russia."

"Another very important one is talking about future success, especially boasting about it. It is considered bad luck. It is far better to be silent until the success has been achieved or to even sound pessimistic."

"That one is common in America as well," he said.

"Well then, one last one for you. It is often considered taboo to step over people, or parts of their body, especially those who are on the ground. It is often said that it will prevent the person from growing if they are not fully grown already. It is better to politely ask the person to move or to find a way around them. If one accidentally steps over a person, it is sometimes necessary to step backward over them."

"Now that last part would not go over very well in America," he said, smirking. "I don't think that retracing your footsteps over someone you have just stepped over would be acceptable even if you were doing it for their benefit." He smiled at the thought of it. "I know you must be kidding me on that one."

"Not at all," she protested. "I am being quite honest about these superstitions. They are deeply rooted in our culture. Have you never heard that if your right eye itches, you're going to be happy soon, and if your left eye itches, then you'll be sad?"

"No," he began laughing again. "I can't say that I have." He considered her a moment before asking her a follow-up question. "What if your lips are itching, what meaning does that have?" he asked.

"That means that you will be kissing someone soon," she explained, and then she started laughing. "And if your right-hand itches, you're going to get money soon. But if your left-hand itches, you're going to give someone money."

"It always ends up being about money, doesn't it?"

"You are the banker. You certainly are in a better position to know that," she quipped back, fluttering her eyelashes at him coquettishly.

"Yes, I suppose I do." He seemed to be all of a sudden distracted by something. She followed his gaze to see what it was that he was looking at. It was then that she noticed that a door leading into the cemetery had been left open.

"Now all we need is a lantern that will help us see a little better the names on the gravestones," he said.

"Maybe it is better that we don't have a lantern since we shouldn't even be here. I don't even want to think what the monks will say if they should find us here."

"Yes, I suppose you're right."

There was still enough light filtering through the old trees for them to be able to make their way, as long as they kept to the path. The cemetery was not very big and the filtered light made it look quite fantastic, like a strange and imaginary place. It was not unreasonable to believe that a supernatural event could take place in the graveyard. This could be a place where the laws of reality may have to be changed in order to be able to explain an event. This was the realm where dreams, drugs, illusions of the senses, and madness sometimes took you. In literature, this was the place where you had to decide whether the woman who you were with and who you loved was really a woman or the devil.

"So, are you ready to be sacrificed?" he asked her.

"What? What do you mean?"

"Don't you feel the primitive tendrils by your feet urging you back in time to a raw, savage, and mysterious era where the peasants prayed to their pagan gods in an ancient Russia? Surely you can sense their spirits. The mood here is so emotional and intimate. Imagine them wearing their primitive clothes, which make them appear bizarre and strange. They are earth's abstract figures moving in a hypnotic ritual, leading their chosen maiden. She is to be sacrificed. They are chanting a melody in gratification of the chosen one. It is easy to imagine how they are locked into an ecstatic mood, a groove. With each moment their chanting intensifies into an almost violent scream that leads into a joyous intonation, a prayer. As they chant, they are also performing a sacrificial dance. Their dancing is not rhythmically connected to that of their chants. They are certainly driven, and their chanting and dancing grow louder and faster. There is an incredible exhilaration in what they are feeling, their adoration of the earth. There is an excitement that is generated from the energy that is being transmitted, and it is all leading to a sensory overload. The great sacrificial ritual is now ending. The only thing that remains is their rhythmic urges. It all leads up to the maiden's death, to the snapping of her neck."

"Wow, you are an imaginative storyteller. How did you come up with that so quickly?"

"Are you ready to be sacrificed?" he asked her again. It was obvious that she didn't know Stravinsky's Rite of Spring.

"Here and now?" she responded.

The transitional moment had arrived. As she came toward him, he saw a smile pulling at her face, and when they lightly kissed on the lips, she sighed. The American dropped to his knees and unfastened the bottom-most buttons of her blouse exposing her bare midriff. Her umbilical dip was significantly depressed and vertically oriented, and he found this to be extremely sexy. He stared at her in admiration for a few moments before proceeding to touch her with the tip of his tongue in the area just below her navel. He then began to gently press his lips to give her very tender loving kisses. There, in front of the gravesites of Russia's greatest composers, he instinctively knew that he was going to make love to this lovely Russian woman. He sensed the erotic sensations that she was feeling as he was kissing her, and she was surprised that his kisses were now producing for her a tingling feeling.

He wondered if it was insane to be thinking this way as he proceeded with his lovemaking. But it felt wonderful. She was now lying flat near one of the nondescript graves, totally naked below the waist. And, as she lay there, she marveled at how much pleasure he seemed to be getting in kissing her on the hallowed ground. The American was unpredictable and totally unconventional. There was something fresh and wonderful and easy-going about this blue man, whatever that was. And then she wanted to please him too.

CHAPTER EIGHTEEN

THE NEXT DAY, after the morning's conference, the American ran into Liu Tang in the hotel lobby.

"Well, my friend," the Asian began, "I have news for you."

"Oh," the American responded, "and what news is that?"

"It seems that Mikhail Potanin was quite pleased with our meeting at his dacha yesterday, and he has already initiated steps with our Corporation in Shanghai requesting that they firm up your commission for your commitment to the business. He has also informed me that we should move quickly with regard to the opening of the Shanghai corporate account in your Geneva office because there is already a very large shipment of sugar that is ready to be moved out of Havana. The buyers in

China have already agreed to the proposed terms, and the only pending issue is the issuance of the letters of credit from your bank on behalf of his company for the transport of the goods to take place. Time is of the essence."

"Liu Tang, I did not think that everything would be happening so fast. Due diligence on the Corporation in Shanghai will have to be made by our Geneva compliance team before anything can happen. As you can appreciate, Geneva is an extremely regulated financial center."

"Yes, Mr. Potanin and the board members of the Corporation in Shanghai are well aware of that, and they have no problem with having all of your firm's regulatory issues promptly and completely answered."

"What I could do is call someone in our office so that they can schedule a meeting with Shanghai. The Corporation in Shanghai can expect to have a visit from the Geneva banker that will be assigned to the account. If they can begin having everything ready, then the account-opening process should proceed quickly."

"I will certainly relay everything to the board members. You should know that Mr. Potanin is extremely confident about your capabilities, and he wants you to know that he is very happy that you will be acting as agent. He has suggested to the Corporation that they should give you something equivalent to a sign-on bonus since you have now become an important team member in this process. Everyone has unanimously agreed and has already executed a numbered account for you with Union Banque Privée in Zurich. I would like you to now please write down the details with regard to accessing your personal account."

"I can see that Mr. Potanin is a man of quick action. It is rather impressive that all of this has been managed in one day."

"When you visit the bank in Zurich," Liu Tang continued, "you will be required to provide an account number and a reference name. The account number that has been assigned to your account is 04302007. The referenced name for the account is Citizen T. A signature will not be required for you to access the account, as long as you provide the correct number and name. The funds will be payable to you on demand in Swiss francs or American dollars. The Corporation has placed an initial deposit of fifty thousand dollars in the account for you, which should be considered as your sign-on bonus for joining the team. After every successful transaction that you participate in, you will receive a deposit into this account at the terms that we have previously negotiated. Lastly, you will, of course, understand that all of the transactions going through this account will be completely confidential. There will not be any reporting to any tax authorities or any other government agencies anywhere. Do you have any questions?"

"No," the American replied. "Please let the board members know that I will be calling our Geneva office immediately to begin the account-opening process."

"I'll let them know at once," Liu Tang replied.

"Liu Tang, I want you to know that I'm now extremely pleased and committed to working with you. Thank you for providing me with the opportunity."

"Not at all, my friend," Liu Tang replied. "I think that we are helping each other. It is a great opportunity for both of us."

"Yes, I can see that." Then, as an afterthought, he added, "Who knows, maybe one day soon I will be visiting you at that Street of Eternal Happiness in Shanghai that you are always talking about. Well, should we have a drink now to celebrate?"

"Later, my friend," Liu Tang replied. "Right now, I have another issue that I will have to address. But we can meet later in the lobby if you are free." And with that, the two bankers shook hands and went their separate ways.

LATER IN THE AFTERNOON, THE AMERICAN SPOTTED A European newspaper in the hotel lobby with a headline that had a disturbing effect on him. The lead article in the newspaper stated that Chinese merchants had accused the Russian government of allegedly turning an initial blind eye to goods being imported from China only to then have them confiscated because they were found to have been smuggled illegally into the country. The Russian government, in its defense, claimed that it had only recently stepped up its efforts to curb the illegal smuggling business coming in from China because of the impact it was having on the local economy.

It was believed that more than two billion worth of Chinese goods had been confiscated by the Russian government. Many Chinese merchants in Moscow protested that if the Russian government really intended to curb smuggling, then why were the merchants permitted to bring in their goods in the first place? The Sing Tao Global network news reported that as a result of the confiscation, tens of thousands of Chinese businessmen were going to be bankrupt overnight. It also reported that, as a consequence of their losses, many Chinese merchants had committed suicide.

The Russian General Prosecutor's Office addressed the smuggling matter by simply stating that they would be destroying all of the imported shoddy Chinese merchandise at some date in the very near future. However, many of the very angry Chinese merchants were skeptical. They believed that their stolen goods were actually already being marketed by the Russian government.

This was not what the American wanted to hear as he was approaching his new business interest which involved trading activity between the two countries. He hoped that the major players that he would be dealing with were well-connected businessmen that knew how to circumnavigate these complicated issues. Money from deep pockets always solved the thorniest of issues.

LATER THAT SAME EVENING THE AMERICAN SPOTTED Liu Tang in the hotel lobby bar. Sitting with him was a bald, heavy-set man who the American had previously recognized at the conference. When Liu Tang noticed the American, he signaled him to come over. Liu Tang introduced the man as Victor Yeltsin.

"Victor here has been telling me how much has changed in Russia, with regard to business opportunities, since the collapse of the Soviet Union," Liu Tang said.

"Yes," Victor quickly agreed. "I think that no one will deny that the collapse of the Soviet Union ended one of the cruelest and most violent and viciously ideological regimes in the history of the world. The Soviet Union collapsed, crushed by the material and spiritual burdens of its collectivist ideology." Victor took a sip of his whiskey before continuing to elaborate on his understanding of how everything had been evolving so rapidly in his country. "The collapse of Communism in Russia," he continued, "ended not only the Soviet police state but also the Soviet-era centrally planned economy. In January 1992, there was for the first time in the experience of most living Russians a genuine opportunity to build the foundation of a free enterprise system. The necessary bricks for that foundation were clear enough. The question now was where and how to begin."

"Gentlemen," the American interrupted, "this all sounds quite fascinating. But what do you say if we were to move our discussion to the restaurant at the Grand Hotel Europe? To be perfectly frank, I am famished."

"You sly devil," Liu Tang said. "You want to see that lovely young hostess that works there."

"She must be quite special if she is working at the Grand Hotel Europe," Victor said.

"Yes, she is quite special," the American agreed. "But I'll have you know that the food is exceptional there as well. I only have a couple of days left in St. Petersburg, and I would love to have another meal there. So, what do you say?"

"Well, why not," said Victor.

"Why not, indeed," Liu Tang also agreed. And with that, the three of them left the hotel lobby and hailed a taxi that would take them to the restaurant.

Once they were settled in the cab, Victor Yeltsin

asked the American if he remembered the name of the hostess.

"How could I possibly forget her name?" the American responded. "She is the most impressive woman in all of St. Petersburg!"

"No!" Victor exclaimed. "You say that she is the most impressive woman that you have met in St. Petersburg? She must be really something then because St. Petersburg has some of the most beautiful women in the country. I can't wait to meet her."

"You will see, Victor. The young woman is quite impressive," Liu Tang agreed.

"Nadya Ivanovna," said the American. "That is her name. She is a student at the University of St. Petersburg, but can also be found on some days at the Hermitage, where she is involved in some project. She is also a member of the art department at your famous puppet theater."

"The Demmeni Marionette Theater?" Victor asked.

"Yes, that is it," said the American.

"Yes, she is a remarkable young woman indeed," Victor agreed. "I have met her. And quite lovely too," he added.

"The complete package," confirmed the American.

"Yes, quite nice," agreed Liu Tang, "and quite charming."

Within moments the taxi pulled up to the entrance

of the hotel, and as the men stepped out of the cab, they were greeted by the doorman, who opened the door for them that led to the luxuriously decorated lobby. From there the three men made their way to the sounds of the piano, which they knew would be found under the beautiful stained-glass window at the back of the elegant restaurant. The tables were already impeccably dressed with their lovely white linens, fine bone china and well-polished silver-plate cutlery. In the center of the tables, there were lovely single-stem lilies in beautifully polished sterling flower holders.

As soon as the three men approached the entrance to the restaurant, Nadya Ivanovna approached them with a surprised looked on her face. She was quite happy to see them and said so.

"Gentlemen," she began, "I'm so happy to see you again."

"You are quite right," Victor said rather loudly to the American. She is quite lovely." Having heard this, the young hostess smiled at the Russian and then turned and winked at the American.

"It's a pleasure to see you gentlemen here again," she then said to them.

"You already know Victor," Liu Tang said, indicating the Russian to the lovely hostess.

"Hello, Victor," she responded, extending her cheeks to the Russian. "I will make sure that you gentlemen have the most wonderful culinary experience tonight." After saying that, she led the three bankers to their table.

"Yes, quite lovely," confirmed Victor to the two bankers after the hostess had left them.

"So, Victor," Liu Tang began, "you were about to expound on how the new Russia had to move if it were going to succeed at building a free enterprise system. Please, would you be so kind as to continue? This is a critical topic that also concerns us in China. I would very much like to hear how Russia is moving forward on this. So, my friend, please proceed if you don't mind."

"Certainly," Victor responded. "You can imagine the enormous challenges that must be faced in order to move from the Soviet Union's state-controlled economy to a free enterprise system based on private property, markets, and individual choice."

"To begin with," he continued, "Soviet-era laws and regulations governing commerce would have to be repealed. Then, you will need to establish new legal protections for private property, and private contracts would have to be enacted. The courts will have to try to establish public confidence in a system so that it will be accepted that private contracts going forward will be enforceable. Not surprisingly, we have seen significant changes taking place on this front recently in Russia.

Many well-placed politicians have profited immensely from the first initial changes to the law."

"Yes," Liu Tang concurred, "we have seen changes taking place in China right along those lines, and we have also had our share of commissioners that have benefited financially from the changes to the law." Liu Tang then turned to the American, almost as an afterthought, and said, "By the way, I failed to mention to you that Victor is Mikhail Potanin's private banker. Your bank in Geneva will be dealing with Victor directly as funds get transferred from the Corporation in Shanghai to Mikhail Potanin's corporation, which has an account with Victor's bank. Victor will be coordinating the transactions on behalf of Mikhail Potanin."

"Yes, that is correct," Victor confirmed.

"Well, it's nice to meet you, Victor," said the American. "It's important to know who is behind the transactions. I'm certain that you must feel the same way."

"Absolutely," replied Victor. "Though sometimes you can meet people and never really understand them. Opportunists are popping up everywhere these days. But you do really have to be careful and know who it is that you are dealing with. And, if the law isn't really clear, or enforceable, you can stand to lose a great deal of money. That is what I was trying to explain to Mr. Tang. Now, let me also tell you something." Victor was now directing his words explicitly to the American. "Russia today is more corrupt, more lawless, poorer, and more unstable than it was when President Clinton was in office. But perhaps what is most important for Russia's future is that young Russians today are significantly more supportive of democracy and free enterprise than their older countrymen. The younger generation in Russia, which is less influenced by the legacy of Soviet Communism than its predecessors, displays an entrepreneurial spirit that was unknown in Soviet days. Remarkably, three-quarters of the young entrepreneurs believe that it is important to achieve success with a business of their own. This energy and vigor can transform Russian society and Russia's economic future if it is not stifled by current government impediments to the market."

After they had been given their drinks, the waitress came over to ask them if they had any questions regarding any of the items on the menu. She was a tall, slim, Slavic-looking girl in her early twenties, with high cheekbones and lips that were painted in a shocking deep purple. Her large blue eyes were tinted with a dark gray-purple shade, and her blonde streaked light-brown hair was held together in a very traditional ponytail. She was wearing designer blue jeans and a white blouse.

"What do you suggest?" asked Victor.

"I was advised by Nadya that the traditional Beef Wellington is today's special. It is beef tenderloin that is covered with pâté de foie grass and mushroom duxelles, wrapped in puff pastry and baked. This is something that we only have occasionally, and today is one of those days."

"Victor, you see," said the American. "This is the best place to eat in St. Petersburg!"

"Yes, you won't get an argument from me. This is an exceptional place."

"You know," the American was now addressing the waitress. "I would like to change my drink if you don't mind."

"Certainly, sir," responded the waitress. "What would you like?"

"In one Ian Fleming thriller, James Bond ordered a double gin and tonic with the juice of one entire lime. I think that is what I would like. Please add the squeezed halves of an entire lime, and plenty of ice."

"Very good, sir," the waitress responded.

"Oh, and make it with the Bombay Blue Sapphire gin, if you have it."

"Of course, sir," responded the lovely waitress.

"Bond seemed to like his gin and tonic tart," the American said to his two friends after the waitress made her exit.

"And you are feeling like James Bond now?" asked Liu Tang.

"Shaken and not stirred, if I remember right," said Victor laughing.

"And in which of the James Bond adventures was this drink described?" asked Liu Tang.

"Doctor No," responded the American.

"Of course," came from Liu Tang. "That is the one with the sinister Asian!" The three of them found that to be quite amusing.

The waitress came with the gin and tonic and set it in front of the American. She and the two bankers then watched as he stirred his drink, and as he took his first sip of what should have been a rather tart concoction. The three of them then simultaneously grimaced, imagining the taste of the sour mixture. But he surprised them when he didn't react in the way that they had anticipated.

"This drink is incredibly refreshing," said the American. "And it's not hard to imagine why James Bond ordered one of these as he sat in his hot tropical hotel balcony overlooking Kingston Harbor."

At this point Nadya joined them, curious to see why the waitress and the others had taken such an interest in what the American was drinking.

"So, you've piqued my interest," the hostess said. "What is it that you are drinking?"

"A Bombay Blue Sapphire double gin and tonic with the juice of an entire lime," responded the American.

"And are you enjoying your drink?" asked Nadya.

"Very much so."

"And it's not too tart?"

"Here, have a taste and tell me what you think." Nadya smiled and considered his offer. She then decided to take his glass and have a try at it. They were all watching her to see what she had to say.

"The high proportion of the lime juice, which according to your specifications is equivalent to about half the amount of gin, appears on the palate of this drink before the familiar flavors of gin and tonic, making it deliciously tart and refreshing. Before I tried this, I imagined that the lime juice would overpower the drink. But I am surprised by how well balanced the drink is." She then took another sip. "Yes, it's quite nice."

"That is Ian Fleming's original recipe, though the Bombay Blue Sapphire was not the gin that he would have used since it did not exist at the time. He would have probably used Gordon's or Beefeater," the American explained.

"This drink has a lot of ice in it, which chills the drink thoroughly. It makes for an ideal cooler in those very sexy and steamy hot Caribbean locations where those James Bond films often take place. And you would expect that there would be excessive ice melt that would dilute the drink. But the drink is so cold and so tasty that the ice wouldn't be given much of a chance to melt.

Bravo, Mr. Bond," was what Nadya then said, lifting the glass. Then, turning to the waitress, she added, "Please bring our Mr. Bond here another drink since I have just about shamelessly finished his."

"We wish you would finish that one and another one with us," said the Russian banker. "I was told by my two friends that you are quite exceptional, and now I can see that they did not exaggerate one bit."

Nadya laughed and then agreed to stay a few moments to finish the drink with them.

"I hope that I am not intruding. You gentlemen seemed to be having a serious business discussion until the waitress appeared with the now-famous gin concoction. Seeing how you were all commenting on it, I couldn't help but come to see what all of the fuss was about. Curiosity got the better of me."

For a brief moment, the American got the impression that Victor and Nadya had something more intimate than a casual acquaintance between them. There was something very subtle that he sensed for one brief instant. But he couldn't quite pinpoint what it was that he saw or heard that had given him that impression. Liu Tang appeared to be very neutral during all of this and seemed quite content with just being able to enjoy the good company and his neat whiskey.

"After dinner, and if it is not too late, I was wondering if you would like to accompany me to our

little theater? I wanted to show you what we are planning to put into production next month."

The American was caught off guard by Nadya's
proposal.

"It all depends," he finally said. And after he said
this, she looked at him with surprised eyes. She even
seemed a little embarrassed now at having suggested it.

"Well, of course, I don't know what made me assume
that you didn't have any other plans for tonight when
you are clearly engaged with your friends. I just thought
that since you were leaving us so soon and since you did
show great interest in our little theater, that you might
want to take a peek at what we were currently working
on for our next production."

"Nadya, I think you misunderstood me," the American replied. "I didn't mean to imply that I would be
busy with my friends later tonight. I meant that it all
depended on how the Beef Wellington turned out." He
was now flirting with her. "You see, should it disappoint
us, we may have to find another place to eat. So, please
make certain that the Beef Wellington measures up
because I would rather leave with you than be dragged
around the city by these two comrades."

"And in order to have an impartial assessment, Liu
Tang and I will be the ones pronouncing judgment,"
volunteered Victor. Liu Tang smiled and nodded in
agreement.

"Fine," said Nadya. "In that case, I will have to leave you gentlemen in order to see how our chef is progressing."

Victor and Liu Tang refrained from making any comments with regard to Nadya's invitation. The American didn't say anything either as he wasn't quite sure what to make of her. She was the perfect woman in every sense of the word, and that was rather intimidating because it meant that you had to really measure up to meet her expectations, or to what you thought should be her expectations. And once expectations entered into an equation, all bets were off.

The three bankers remained unusually silent for the brief moments while they waited for their entrées to be served. During this interval, the waitress stopped by to see if they needed refills or if they would be interested in ordering wine. Liu Tang and Victor were content to keep drinking their neat whiskies, but the American declined another gin drink and opted instead for a glass of red wine.

"The virtue of reliability is too often discounted in the otherwise admirable pursuit of the new."

The two bankers were startled at hearing the American blurt out such a lofty thought out of the blue.

"While we have been sitting here drinking our fine whiskey, fantasizing about the two girls attending our table, you have the nerve to bring up for discussion this concept without giving us any warning. I don't really know how Liu Tang has remained your friend."

Liu Tang and Victor then began laughing out loud. It all seemed so ludicrous, nonsensical. "The virtue of reliability what?" began Victor again laughing. Liu Tang began laughing loudly too. "What could you possibly be thinking?" Victor continued. And then the two bankers began laughing again.

"Yes, you are right," agreed the now red-faced American. "I don't know what came over me. Sometimes the mind pursues things on its own terms, totally out of control. When you are thinking of pussy, is that with the left side of the brain or the right?" The two bankers looked at the American in disbelief and started laughing again.

"I think the right side of the brain is supposed to be for creativity," continued the American, seeming quite serious and ignoring them as they continued laughing. "And I believe that the left side of the brain is what is used for math. So then, explain to me which side of the brain you are using while you are fantasizing about pussy?"

This brought on more laughter from the other two.

"Stop, please stop before I pee on myself," the Russian said. Liu Tang looked at the Russian and the American and continued laughing uncontrollably.

"My friend, you need both sides of the brain when

you are thinking about pussy," Liu Tang finally said. "You will need to be creative and calculating if you are to be successful with anything related to pussy. Otherwise, you will be lost." And then there was more boisterous laughter from the two bankers.

"Look at what has happened to our Mr. Putin if you don't believe me," said Victor. "He has had pussy rioting all over the place. We have almost had a state of emergency because of it." The three bankers could not contain themselves any longer. Only the arrival of the Beef Wellington restored seriousness to their table.

"Well, it looks like you will be going with that Nadya to the puppet theater because this looks like a culinary masterpiece," said Victor.

"Yes, you are quite right, Victor. This looks exceptional!" said Liu Tang.

Nadya had now come to their table to receive the bankers' assessment of their meals. She had a smile on her face as she watched them savoring their entrées. She didn't say anything, not wanting to interrupt them as they made their funny gestures in appreciation of the heavenly morsels. Finally, the American cleansed his palate with his red wine and then closed his eyes for a moment as he turned to her. It was as though he was processing the experience like a professional connoisseur, translating the results into the appropriate words that would best confirm his judgment.

"The bottom line is this: We are obligated, I devoutly believe, to be absolutely open-minded in recognizing and embracing that greatness is not the sole prerogative of a handful of venerable, recognized establishments. You know that you are seeing a true professional at work when you see the chef being able to produce that great experience again and again, and when you know that the constant is the passion for the flavors and techniques that produce such exquisite results. Nadya, your chef is a true artist! This is a remarkable meal," said the American.

"I could not have said it better myself," said the Russian, smirking!

"Wonderful meal," added Liu Tang, not wanting to be left out.

"I was fairly certain that you would be pleased. Our chef is extremely talented." And, having said that, she left them so that they could enjoy the rest of their meal.

"Ah, Nadya," cried out the American. "Shall we leave directly, right after we finish our dinner, or should I come back to pick you up later?"

"I'm through for the evening, so we can leave after you have finished."

CHAPTER NINETEEN

"So, Nadya, you are a student at St. Petersburg State University?"

"Hic tuta perennat," Nadya quoted. The American gave her an inquisitive look. He obviously didn't know what she was saying.

"That is our school motto," she explained. "The Latin loosely translates into 'Here we stay in peace.'"

"Hic tuta perennat," the American repeated. "'Here we stay in peace.' It has a rather calming effect, doesn't it?"

"Yes," she responded. "It is a refuge where the scholar should feel safe in challenging old ideas, and in looking for new solutions to old problems. Our university was founded in 1724 under an edict by Peter the Great. He was the one responsible for leading a cultural revolution that replaced the traditionalist and medieval social and political system in our country with a modern, scientific, European-oriented and rationalist system."

"How well do you know Victor Yeltsin?" he asked her.

She raised her head and looked straight at him; her eyes had the blank, veiled look that he had seen before, a questioning look that seemed to imply that she didn't understand what it was that he was searching for.

"Not much," she finally answered. "He eats at the restaurant and seems to be quite successful at whatever it is that he does. I don't know much more than that."

"What about Liu Tang?" it suddenly dawned on him to ask. "Have you seen him here at other times, in other months?"

She studied him again, momentarily, and smiled before responding. "Yes. I have seen him here occasionally with other business associates. But, I have never spoken to him until his visit with you. Why do you ask? What do you want to know?"

"Just curious."

"Is that important?" she asked him.

"Not particularly, Nadya. It's just that I'm entering into business with these gentlemen, but I don't know much about them."

"Well, I can't offer you much more than that."

"That's fine. I didn't expect much more. It's really

not important." Then he smiled at her and abruptly changed the topic of conversation again.

"I really would like to know what you are planning for your little theater."

She seemed pleased that he had steered the conversation away from the businessmen and toward the new production. "Well, we are planning on doing another short Stravinsky piece. It's the Pulcinella ballet. Do you know it?"

"I know the music. It's wonderful! I love Stravinsky."

"I thought you did. We will, of course, be presenting an abbreviated version for our little theater."

"When will it be in production?" he asked.

"Oh, in six weeks or so, I think. I know that you won't be around, but we already have some of the scenery finished and the figure of Pulcinella has been completed. I thought you might want to see it."

"Thank you," he said. "I feel privileged." She could tell that he was being sincere.

"Do you know the story?" she asked him.

"No, not really," he answered.

"The story of Pulcinella," she began, "comes from an Italian manuscript that dates from around 1700. The character originates from the Commedia dell'arte, which you may know was a form of Italian theater that began in the sixteenth century. The Commedia dell'arte was characterized by the masked character types that appeared on the stage that usually represented stock figures such as foolish old men, devious servants, plotting maids, etc. The plots of the Commedia dell'arte were mostly about disgraceful love intrigues, clever tricks to get money, mistaken identities, or disingenuous plots designed to outwit simpletons."

"As you are describing this world," the American interrupted, "I can imagine Stravinsky's mind at work, scheming on how he would use the instruments of the orchestra to represent these characters. He would be recreating the psychological world of the past through the use of the woodwinds, strings, and trumpets. Teams of instruments would form and reform generating sounds and an exciting rhythmic energy." He stopped then to look at her and he wondered how anyone would not want to squeeze this intellectual beauty. If he didn't have the feelings that he was having for her now, he would have to be classified as abnormal.

"I'm sorry that I interrupted you," he said, "but I couldn't help but wonder how Stravinsky must have felt when he was offered the commission. He is said to have stated that through Pulcinella, he experienced an epiphany through which the whole of his late work became possible."

"Well, I didn't know that," she said. "We seem to perfectly complement each other on this, you with the music and me with the theatrical side."

"In this world, either you are virtuous or you enjoy yourself," he said. "Not both, Nadya, not both."

"What do you mean by that?" she asked him, quite surprised.

"Nothing, I meant nothing by it. I was just thinking of something that I had read long ago," he lied, "and suddenly I reacted to it. It has nothing to do with anything that we have been talking about."

"Well, that is pretty amazing, that you should remember something from the past, and now you suddenly react to it."

"Yes, a very delayed reaction," he admitted. "I'm sure that something similar may have happened to you at some point. You sense that there is something that you should know, but you can't quite put your finger on it. Then, much later, you suddenly have an epiphany or that eureka moment where it all comes together, where the solution becomes evident. That is what that moment was for me just now."

"'In this world, you are either virtuous or you enjoy yourself.' That is what you said. That is quite an interesting statement. I would love to hear more about that eureka moment."

"It was a direct quote from a character in a book that I read years ago, a book by Ayn Rand. Do you know her?"

"No, I've never heard of her."

"This will surprise you. She studied at your university, here in St. Petersburg. Her Russian name is Alisa Zinov'yevna Rosenbaum. Russian born but moved to the United States in 1926. The conservative Republicans in America absolutely love her because of the philosophy called Objectivism which she expounds in her book *Atlas Shrugged*. Anyway, it was a character in her book that had that line which I quoted, and which you have found so interesting." He looked at her with reassuring eyes, hopeful that she would not want much more of an explanation on what he had meant by what he had said.

"I've never heard of the author, and since I've never read the book I won't ask anything else about it. I will have to accept your explanation, and that is that." But by the look that she gave him, it was clear that she was not satisfied with his explanation at all.

"Good," he said. "And now I hope you will continue giving me the storyline for Pulcinella. I really would like to know what your play with the marionettes will be about."

They were crossing the street to the little theater as she began describing the story to him. Even though it was 10 pm, he was still amazed at how the sun was still shining quite radiantly. It was still bright enough for children—if there had been any around—to play an outdoor ballgame. Strangely, he had yet to see children playing anywhere in St. Petersburg.

"It sounds like a wonderful story. The audience will love the characters displaying all those raw emotions onstage. They will laugh at seeing the old father chasing the young suitors away, and at the jealous Pimpinella getting angry at her unfaithful Pulcinella. I only wish that I could be here to see it. And Stravinsky's music is so ravishing. The production is a great idea," he concluded.

"I thought that you would appreciate it. Let me now show you how we have recreated the original costume for our little Pulcinella." She then led him backstage to where the marionette was found hanging by his strings in full costume. He was dressed in black shoes, red stockings, and a long white, pleated blouse that draped down the marionette's knees over his baggy white pants. The girth of the overweight Pulcinella sported a black belt that matched his shoes.

"What a wonderful costume," said the American. "The children will love the colorful character."

"Yes, we think so too!"

"Now you have your bookends! The Petrushka and Pulcinella characters are steeped in tradition, and you have the marvelous Stravinsky music to carry the ballet stories along. In one sense your productions are not traditional, as the original productions were full of dialogue and that was what moved the action along. In your production, you have opted to follow the ballet stories as commissioned by the famous impresario of the Ballet Russe."

"Yes, that's it exactly. We felt that by using the ballet productions we would be able to present a theater that would be universally accessible to all. We didn't want the language to become a barrier."

"I find the way that you have decided to juxtapose the two leading characters to be quite fascinating. In each of the productions, you have a principal male suitor vying for the affection of a woman. On the one hand, you have the faithful Petrushka in love with the Ballerina. In the other ballet, you have the unfaithful Pulcinella vying for the affections of Pimpinella. Petrushka's honesty fails to win over the Ballerina, who has decided to reject his advances, falling instead for the seductions of the exotic Moor. In the other production, you have a Pulcinella who proves to be quite successful when he uses his guile and deceit to trick Pimpinella into falling in love with him. Petrushka's passionate love leads to his tragic end. He is slain by the Moor. The crafty Pulcinella is not passionately in love but in the end, he gets his way. There seems to be a lesson in there somewhere."

"Aha," protested Nadya, "that is your religious background influencing your perspective on the productions. A different perspective would be to consider the types of women involved and the alternative lifestyles that are being offered to them. The Ballerina is perhaps seeing Petrushka as a simpleton. The Moor offers her an exotic alternative world, much more exciting than what Petrushka can offer. In Pimpinella, we have an artless, trusting, open-hearted woman who can't help but fall for the deceitful man. I think that there are probably other perspectives on this as well. That is what makes the stories so wonderful."

"Nadya," the American responded, "you are so clever. You're going to make someone very happy someday."

"And who may that be?" she asked him, with a big smile on her face.

"Happily, we still do not know who that will be. At this point, we are all in the running."

She just giggled in response. "Come, it's getting late. I have to lock the place up."

"Great! I was hoping for a change in scenery."

"I'm not redoing my makeup," she answered firmly but with a mischievous look in her eye.

"I think we are ready as we are for a little magic. Do you have a special place that you would like to go to, somewhere to have a nice drink? I want to take in more genuine Russian vodka before leaving. Where do you suggest?"

"There is an elegant little nightclub that is not too far from here."

After twenty minutes of walking, Nadya and the

banker finally reached the Taleon Club. The Club was situated in what was the former private residence of a wealthy merchant named Stepan Eliseyev. The mansion was opulently decorated with renaissance art and exquisite antiques. But club members were able to enjoy themselves in the modern comforts that were found throughout the mansion. The great salon room had plush blue-leather sofas and chairs off the main bar lounge. There was also a cigar lounge where the clientele, high net worth Russians and millionaire ex-pats, all connoisseurs of the very fine Cohibas or Monte Christo cigars, smoked over their pricey well-aged cognacs.

Nadya excused herself momentarily from the American and made her way to the corner where a businesswoman was speaking to two club members. The businesswoman and Nadya exchanged a few words, and then both made their way back to the American.

"I would like to introduce you to Anya," said Nadya to the American. "She is the Executive Director of the Foreign Business Club, which happens to be having a social meeting here today. The Taleon Club is opened today only to members of the Foreign Business Club, but Anya has graciously consented to allow us to remain as her personal guests."

"Oh, that is really quite nice of you," said the American. "Are you sure that we are not putting you out? I would hate to be interfering in any way with the Club, and I'm certain that we can easily find some other place for drinks."

"Not at all. This is a social gathering, and we have other invited guests here tonight as well. Enjoy yourselves! It will be my pleasure to have you both here tonight. But you must excuse me, as I have left an unresolved matter with the other two gentlemen that I was just speaking to. Please, enjoy yourselves."

"Thank you, we will," responded the American.

"Thank you, Anya," said Nadya.

Anya then left them in order to return to the two gentlemen.

"My God," said the American. "You are extremely well connected!"

"I met Anya at one of the social functions in the museum," Nadya explained. "She is quite a lady."

"Yes, she looks it. Did you know that the Club would be meeting here tonight?"

"I wasn't totally sure, but I thought that they might."

"And you still came knowing that?" he asked her.

"Well, I wasn't only looking out for you," she smiled with a wink. "But, with you being a foreign banker, I thought I could easily justify my being invited in. It is a rare opportunity for me, and I didn't think you would mind."

"No, it's wonderful! I'm glad you thought of it. What exactly is the Club, and who are its members?"

"The Foreign Business Club is open to foreigners only. Members usually hold senior managerial positions in business, diplomacy, education, and other related fields. The Club was established to create an international forum for cultural and social exchange, where members could share their working and living experiences in Russia. It is also a place designed to assist foreigners in adapting to Russia. Foreigners, especially newcomers, can obtain information about their communities and receive advice on legal services. It is hoped that the Club will help to develop constructive dialogue between its members and the state structures, and non-governmental organizations. So, there you have it, as Anya explained it once to me."

"Yes, quite nicely done! And now I am ready for a genuine Russian vodka martini, extra dry, shaken, not stirred, with three large olives. How do you think that we can go about finding one?" No sooner had the American said this than a waiter appeared to take their orders. Surprisingly, Nadya opted for the vodka martini too.

At the adjacent table to where they were sitting, the American overheard a man speaking English with a thick German accent, and then occasionally slipping into his native tongue, furiously complaining how he didn't understand why Russia had declared him to be a threat to national security. The German businessman, whose firm sold small electric engines, speculated that he was being targeted because a local bureaucrat didn't want to return to his firm one million Euros in value-added taxes. "The other possibility is that maybe it was because a business enemy of mine paid someone off. Any successful businessman has enemies in Russia, but these are only conjectures," the man went on, protesting his innocence to his associates.

"Earlier in the day," replied one of his associates, "I read in the Moscow Times that at least twelve business people have been denied entry over the past two years, apparently for national security reasons. As you would imagine, the circumstances around the twelve cases are steeped in mystery. Russia, like other countries, is under no obligation to explain its decision for refusing or revoking visas, and the Foreign Ministry and Federal Security Service routinely decline to comment on the cases."

"Some foreign business leaders," the other associate remarked "believed that the expulsions were isolated instances. But a review of explanatory documents obtained by several sources suggests that the cases may be the tip of the iceberg. The expulsions appear to be linked to business dealings, and several people have stated they believed their Russian rivals had bribed officials to blacklist them. If that is the case, foreign investors could have a new reason to exercise caution when doing business in Russia."

The American was quite amazed to hear the foreign members openly criticize the state of affairs in Russia. But maybe they had reached a point where they were so fed up with the system that they no longer cared about the consequences if somebody should overhear them griping.

Nadya didn't make any comments with regard to what they had just overheard. She merely smiled at the American and fidgeted with her hair while she waited for the martinis to arrive. The American was amused.

At another table sat three other businessmen discussing politics. The three of them were Asian, but they were conversing in English. The youngest of them was drinking red wine, while the other two middle-aged men were drinking whiskey. The youngest was confiding to them what had been told to him by a friend.

"My buddy began his story by telling me that he had taken an active part in the elections that were held in his home town municipality of Novosibirsk in Western Siberia. He was saying how the elections there offered a clear example of the dysfunctional political and economic system that has developed during President Vladimir Putin's rule. The political system that is in place in Novosibirsk and the other surrounding remote districts is what is mockingly referred to as a "businessocracy." In Novosibirsk, as in the other municipalities, career businessmen hold office and use their authority to enrich themselves, their families, and their close friends."

As the American overheard this discussion, he began to laugh. He looked at Nadya, shrugged his shoulders, and laughed again.

"Nadya, is this a setup?"

"What do you mean?" she asked him, with a surprised look.

"I mean that this seems to be a perfect setup for some sort of entrapment!"

"What entrapment? What do you mean?"

The waiter just then appeared at their table with two generous sized martini glasses. Both had opted for the olives.

"Is there anything else that I can get for you?" the waiter asked.

"No, thank you," responded the American. "But I wonder if you could tell me what type of vodka you used to make these drinks?" he asked.

"Tsarskaya Zolotaya!" responded the waiter.

That translated into English as the Golden Vodka of the Tsar. This grain vodka was referred to as the high-water mark for elite vodkas. Supposedly, only natural, raw materials and pure Ladoga Lake water were used for its production. Also incorporated in the blend were lime-tree honey and lime blossoms, which contributed a mild flavor to its taste.

"Na Zdorovie!" said the American.

"Na Zdorovie!" responded Nadya. Then the two clanked their glasses before trying their martinis.

"That's very nice! It makes me feel like Bond again, James Bond. I wonder if you will be sending me a postcard from Russia."

"A postcard? What kind of postcard do you want me to send you?"

"One that says, 'From Russia, with love,'" he said laughing.

"Oh, you are so funny."

"How do you like the martini?"

"Delicious," she responded, and then she took another sip to confirm her verdict. "Yes, that is very nice. I wonder how Peter the Great would have felt about having his face plastered on every bottle."

"Well, for the record, let everyone know that I have been having a splendid time in Russia and that everything has been just perfect!" The American said this rather loudly to attract the attention of the neighboring tables. "Yes, I have had a most wonderful time, and I am grateful for having had the experience," he continued on the loud note.

"What are you doing," asked Nadya, quite shocked by his boisterous remarks.

"I just want everyone to know that I have been quite happy here, and have no complaints whatsoever." He then finished off his martini and signaled to the waiter to bring him another.

"That was all rather strange," she said. "Is it this particular vodka that is making you behave like this?"

"No. I just want to make sure that should there be any apparatchiki present in this Club, that I am not mistaken for one of those that the government has labeled as a threat to national security. Because, you see, I would very much like to be able to come back to see one of your wonderful productions!"

"Thank you," she said, and then squeezed his hand. "But you mustn't worry," she tried to reassure him. "I promise that no one is trying to entrap you. And, as far as I know, no one will be declaring you a threat to national security." She continued, "As a matter of fact, you are the exact type of businessman that Russia needs: a banker that will assist with international trade financing."

"How much do you know about my involvement, Nadya?"

"I hope that I have not been out of order. If so, please accept my apology and count on my discretion. I'm sorry for having brought it up again," she finally said.

He looked at her but didn't respond. Then, in their momentary silence, they overheard one of the Asians at the adjacent table speaking again.

"It has become quite obvious that the commercial

interests of the people in power have distorted their priorities beyond recognition. The general welfare of the people has been eclipsed by the vested interests of the ruling cliques. Their only concern is to suppress competition, to form regional and local monopolies, and to create murky structures for embezzling state funds. They have created a system of propaganda and repression designed to keep the beneficiaries of the "businessocracy" in power."

The American looked away. The slight, slumping movement of his shoulders gave the impression of release and disappointment.

"Trust is the assured reliance on another's integrity. Trust is given when there is a belief that someone or something is reliable, good, and honest. The level of trust in government officials and business executives has remained dramatically low in Russia, according to the local news authorities."

Someone had once told him that the man who is proudly certain of his own value, will want the highest type of woman that he can find, the woman he admires, the strongest, the hardest to conquer. This is because only the possession of a heroine will give him a sense of achievement and not the possession of a brainless slut. What a stupid notion, he thought. The mind creates a desire and makes the choice for you. A man's sexual choice is impervious to reason.

"The Russian Museum currently has a new exhibition on nude photography," he began on a different vein with Nadya.

"I have seen it," she replied. "During the Soviet Era, nude photography was declared harmful to the masses and was therefore suppressed. But nude photography in Russia has now become more freely developed and explored. The exhibit has been titled *Beauty without Glamour*."

"Yes, that is exactly the exhibit that I was referring to. Do you know why it was titled that way?" he asked her.

"Let me see if I can define it for you by recalling one of the photographs in the exhibit." She paused a moment before continuing, in order to nibble on one of the olives in her glass. Then she took a swig of her martini, placed the glass back on the table, and smiled at him before beginning to explain what *Beauty without Glamour* was all about. "Tatyana Cherkeyzyan," she began again, "has on display a self-portrait from her 2011 *Deep Inside* series. In it, she depicts the artist lying on a bed with the string of a tampon visible between her legs. Inevitably, questions should arise to the appreciative viewer. Should the work be considered only for its aesthetic qualities, without taking into consideration that it is an intimate self-portrait? Should the viewer recognize the self-revealing nature of the photograph, and should the photographer be admired for her courage? Finally, if one does consider the photograph to be beautiful, is there not also a certain objectification in its vulnerable portrayal of a female subject? What more is there that is implicit or hidden? Is there glamor in the work like that found in many of the other photographs?" And after that explanation, she finished the rest of her second martini.

He stared at her, made no comment, and thought again about how impressed he was by her. He ate all three of his olives, and, like her, finished the rest of his martini. Afterward, the American was feeling a little tipsy.

"Belye nochi is a Russian term that refers to the loveliness of these Russian nights," said Nadya. "You may not be acquainted with this expression, but that is what we Russians say when we refer to the beautiful White Nights."

"No, I didn't know that," said the American. "But why don't we order some more martinis so that you can tell me more about it." Nadya looked at him and without hesitation consented to another round of martinis.

"I should warn you first, however," said Nadya, "that I can really hold my vodka. So, if you are not a very good drinker, please don't try to keep up with me. I don't want you to feel miserable tomorrow because of me."

"Don't you worry, Nadya. I know when to stop."

Here Nadya paused to remark on the American's eyes. They were no longer milky white because more of the small red veins were beginning to show.

"I'm fine," he replied, with a silly grin on his face. "Please, go on with your story."

"Fine," she said, not wanting to argue with him. At least she knew where he was staying, and it would be easy enough to call a taxi. She had to admit that she really liked the American.

"Please go on," he urged her. "I love hearing all about this."

"OK, OK," she said and then began telling a story. "Well, on one of these beautiful summer nights, there was a particular St. Petersburg lady that was very taken with Johan Strauss during one of his musical concert series visits."

"Russian women are so beautiful," he interrupted, giving her a seductive look as he said it. She paused to laugh, then took a sip of her martini before continuing with her story.

"Olga Smirnitskaya, who was the daughter of a Russian bureaucrat, was known to have been a very sensitive young lady and to have had some talent for the piano. After she met Strauss, she fell in love and the feeling was mutual. The young lovers tried to keep their relationship a secret by using all sorts of strategies. Like young adolescents, they wrote notes to each other on candy wrappers and delivered them through mutual friends. The nearly one hundred letters written between them that exist today are wonderfully romantic and are a testament to their feelings for one another.

"When Strauss was forced to leave Russia, his letters of the period were filled with despair. In them, he stated that he would have preferred to die rather than to endure the torment of departure. In St. Petersburg, women of that era did not marry outside of their social rank, even to composers as great as Strauss. Sadly, their affair ended when her parents refused to agree to their marriage. It is amazing when you consider that Strauss was admitted to the highest levels of St. Petersburg society and was considered a friend of the Romanovs. Years later, Strauss gave many concerts in Pavlovsk, and the residents there affectionately referred to him as Ivan Straus."

"Ivan Strauss," he quoted her and contemplated. "That was quite a romantic story. Thank you for enlightening me. I had no idea." He looked down at the table, avoiding her eyes, and wondered why this beautiful, young and extremely intelligent woman was spending so much of her time with him.

He called over the waiter to order a fourth round of martinis.

"Are you sure you want another?" Nadya asked.

"Don't you think that we have had enough? I don't want you to feel sick later."

"Nadya," he replied. "Truly happy people seem to have an intuitive grasp of the fact that sustained happiness is not just about doing things that you like. It also requires growth and adventuring beyond the boundaries of your comfort zone. I have never had the four-martini experience, and today I would like very much to have that experience with you."

Nadya studied him for a moment and then started to laugh and laugh and laugh. "So, you are doing this out of curiosity, in order to see where it will lead you?" she asked. Then she started laughing uncontrollably again. Tears started coming out of her eyes from all of her hard laughter.

"Yes, it must seem very funny to you. I'm glad that you are enjoying yourself. Please, go ahead, by all means." He ended by saying, "I want you to have fun with me," and she knew that he meant it.

"Don't worry," she reassured him. "I am having fun." Then she smiled at him and reluctantly went along with his suggestion for another round of martinis.

"You know, Nadya, from time to time it's worth seeking out an experience that is novel, complicated, uncertain, or even upsetting. And, of course, by opening yourself up to a stranger you always run the risk of becoming susceptible to their lies and deceit. But there

JOHN MORALES

is also real excitement in not knowing where it will lead you."

"What are you suggesting?" replied Nadya. "And here I was in the belief that you were too far gone with drink to be able to have any coherent thoughts. Now I am wondering whether you are setting me up for something." She laughed halfheartedly and looked at his eyes again, hoping to obtain a firmer confirmation of his status. "You know," she said, "you drink like a Russian!"

"Nadya, can any of us ever correctly predict who our lovers, our friends, our business partners, and even what we, ourselves, will become, especially when we find ourselves in a new set of circumstances? Learning relies in large part on recognizing our mistakes. Catching lucky breaks gets much harder as we get older. This is not because our opportunities change, but because we do. Over time we develop a pattern. Some of us will have trouble ignoring our incessantly chattering minds, which might tell us we're not qualified enough to do that job, or not attractive enough to succeed with that beautiful woman. But our reasoning will not always lead us to the truth."

"What's the worst that can happen?" he then blurted out. Then he began laughing as he realized what he had just said.

She looked at him with questioning eyes. What was

he referring to? "What do you mean by that?" she asked him. "What are you referring to?"

"Please ignore what I have just said. My mind starts to ramble on, and even I don't know what the hell I'm saying." Then he took another sip of his martini and followed up on that with some nibbling on an olive.

"I think it's getting rather late, and I still have some work to do at home," she said.

"Sure, no problem," was his only response. Then he drowned the last of his martini and made ready to leave with her.

"Some say that maturity can give us the courage to do the things that we were too afraid to do in our youth," he started rambling again. "And others say that it's the month that you are born in that will determine the kind of luck that you will have. Scientists have established that certain conditions, such as schizophrenia, and even some personality traits are linked to the month that we are born in. No, it's not the planets at work per se. The scientists argue that the subtle influences on fetal brain development are due to the external factors that differ from season to season. Summer babies grow up to be more open-minded and less neurotic than those born during the winter months. Those born in May were found to be luckiest of all. So, the scientists concluded, if you want to have fortunate offspring, then you need to procreate in August!

"I was born in August," he blurted out. She looked at him in disbelief and started laughing.

"You are funnier than what I would have imagined," she said, smiling.

"You know," he began talking again, "from the pulpit you hear things from early on in childhood that can't help but make an impact on you, on the way that you think. That was all just gibberish."

"Interesting," she said. "Why did you decide to tell me that?" He looked at her and thought for a moment about how he should respond to her.

"It's just gibberish that comes out from the subconscious," he said, before trying to come out with another explanation.

"Yes, I think I know that," she said, "but why that particular comment?"

"Well, if you want to know that, then that is going to require another vodka martini," he said. "You see, that particular observation insists upon the avoidance of two particular vices, immodesty and covetousness. Now," he continued slurping, "covetousness is defined as an unreasonable desire for that which we do not possess. Mixed in there in the statement is the clear reference of the sensuous appetite rebelliously demanding its gratification against reason, which is demanding its own spiritual interests and trying to assert its control."

"No," she stopped him before he could continue.

"No more martinis. I have to get going, and I think we have had enough." She then waved to her friend Anya, who happened to look in their direction just then.

"Anya, thank you for allowing us to participate in your little gathering," she said.

"Not at all," Anya responded. "I'm only sorry that I was not able to spend any time with you. These members are always looking to see how they can best utilize this meeting to help solve some of their issues, and my position here is to help guide them through the processes that will hopefully bring them closer to what they want."

"We perfectly understand, Anya," Nadya responded. "Anyway, we want to thank you for opening this venue to us. My good friend has been sampling the local Russian vodkas, and I was certain that we would find some real quality vodka in your beautiful establishment. Please accept our thanks. We are truly grateful!"

"Of course. It was my pleasure."

"Could we ask you to find our waiter so that we can settle the account, and if you could also call a taxi for us?"

"Certainly," Anya responded.

"Yes, Anya, thank you for allowing us to visit your club tonight," the American said. "It has been a wonderful evening."

"It was our pleasure," she said, warmly taking his hand. "And now let me see about your taxi."

The waiter then came by to attend them. But when they asked him for the bill, he responded that as Anya's guests, there was to be no charge.

When the taxi arrived, Nadya gave the driver the address of the American's hotel. She had flatly refused to accept a ride home because she said that she lived quite close to where they now were and would prefer to walk in order to take in a little air. She then quickly kissed the American goodbye on both cheeks and wrote down her email address for him in case he should ever decide to visit St. Petersburg again.

This was not the way that he had wanted to say goodbye to her. He had hoped to be able to get her a little gift in appreciation for the very generous way that she had treated him. At least he knew that he could always send her the gift to her place of work at the hotel. But this did little to satisfy his disappointment in not having planned better.

"Can you travel?" he quickly asked her.

"Yes," she answered. "I have connections that can help me with a visa. But I rarely do any traveling." She moved away from the taxi as she said, "Please enjoy your flight tomorrow." It surprised him momentarily that she knew that he would be traveling tomorrow morning. He didn't remember mentioning that to her.

Nadya was going to be very high maintenance. All of her contacts seemed to be very high rollers. She was well connected with the business elite and clearly had access to their clubs, private dachas, and only God knew what else.

CHAPTER TWENTY

WHEN HE ARRIVED at the Miami office, he immediately called the division head of Private Wealth in Geneva in order to see how the account-opening process was going for the Chinese conglomerate that Liu Tang represented. Mr. Prado, the division head, was extremely ecstatic about the possibility of developing relations in Asian markets and expressed his gratitude for the lead. Mr. Prado confirmed that the group of Chinese financiers behind the corporate account was indeed made up of very prosperous businessmen from Shanghai, which was in line with what Liu Tang had asserted. The rising number of new wealthy Asians in China represented more than a third of the growth in global high net worth over the past decade, and Head Office had not been able until now to make any penetration into this very lucrative region. With this new lead, the Private Wealth division in Geneva was now making fundamental changes to their business and operating models in order to convince Asia's wealthiest that they could expect to receive exceptional services in Corporate and Investment Banking. In closing, Mr. Prado made it clear to the American that he could expect to receive a special compensation bonus for having referred the account to their office.

When the conversation ended, the American sat back and looked out of his office window for a few moments. He was daydreaming now, and the dream was taking him to another world. What had happened to him at the conference had never happened to him before. He couldn't believe his good fortune in having met Liu Tang. Why Liu Tang had decided to approach him for the business venture was still unclear, but he was grateful for it. The favorable accident in the finished dream appeared strange, but dreams in most cases lack sense and order.

It was also hard to believe that there was such a place as the Street of Eternal Happiness, but Google had confirmed that it was real enough. Everything was moving along better than could have been expected and, as luck would have it, everyone had an interest in having the account succeed.

The Russians were going to be pleased. The sugar

shipment from Havana was already on its way, and there was still plenty of time to establish the Letter of Credit in their favor once the Chinese deposited their funds in the newly established account. They would be paid once the shipment passed through customs in Shanghai. The American had accomplished what he had been instructed to do, and now everyone just had to wait until the transaction ran its course.

The less said about any of this, the better. The American was not going to talk about any of this to anyone. The best thing about having an account in Switzerland was that Swiss law forbade bankers from disclosing the existence of an account or any other information related to it without the client's consent. If that privacy were to be violated in Switzerland, then immediate prosecution would be executed by the Swiss public attorney's office. Bankers found guilty could face up to six months in prison and be fined up to fifty thousand Swiss francs. The violated clients also had the option of suing the bank for damages. Understandably, then, Swiss banks were very careful about safeguarding all information regarding their clients. The only exceptions to the Swiss banking privacy law were for criminal activities such as drug trafficking, insider trading, and anything related to organized crime.

These were the arguments that Liu Tang had given the American as to why the Chinese partners had wanted to open an account in Geneva. Liu Tang had also explained how forty miles west of Hong Kong was Macau, which for centuries had served as a center for trading and piracy in the South China Sea, a base for vice, gold smuggling, and espionage. In the last ten years, Macau had become a major conduit for cash on the lip of the world's fastest-growing economy. The casinos in Macau were doing phenomenally well because of the affluent Chinese patrons. But Macau's success was not totally due to the Chinese love of gambling. It was also because many of the visiting wealthy Chinese were very nervous about the corruption and the uncertain political climate back home. Macau had become the world's gambling capital, being four times bigger than Las Vegas, but it was also the perfect place to launder money. Mainland China offered its citizens very little protection by way of private property. The wealthy knew that they were at risk of losing all of their money quite suddenly. Many were always fearful of losing their political patrons every time that the Communist Party elected a new generation of leaders. So, it was no wonder that those with accumulated wealth sought havens for their money. In Macau, it was well-known that many of the wealthy Chinese were shopping for currency and not for jewelry.

"Mr. Tang," the American spoke into the receiver, "are you back on your Street of Eternal Happiness?"

"Hello, my friend," replied the mild-mannered man. "Yes, I'm back in Shanghai. How are you doing?"

"Great. I have just finished a call with the Geneva office. They were quite impressed by the owners of the Corporation."

"Yes," replied Liu Tang. "I was certain that they would be. But between you and me, we will need to be extremely cautious with everything regarding this business. These men do not want to lose money, and they can be unforgiving if they feel that they have been wronged in any way." There was a momentary silence on the line after Liu Tang said this. He wanted to be sure that the warning that he had just passed on registered. And the American had no doubt as to what had been implied.

"I understand perfectly," the American responded.

"But I also don't foresee any problems."

"Neither do I."

"My only concern, to be perfectly frank with you, is what is transpiring between Russia and China related to the import–export business."

"Yes," Liu Tang cautiously reflected, "that is of concern for me too. We will have to be extremely cautious should any issues arise." A significant moment of silence then followed Liu Tang's remark. It was like that moment of silence that occurs out of respect when something bad has happened, when people bow their heads, remove their hats, and do not speak or move.

"We will all do our best, Liu Tang," said the American, laughing. But it was nervous laughter evoked after the awkward silence. It was a laughter related to the stress and anxiety that resulted from knowing that you were transacting with powerful men in a risky business.

"I'm certain of that," Liu Tang responded.

"The Letter of Credit drawn in favor of the Russians will, of course, require the Corporation to deposit funds in order to cover the future drawdowns. What size of a deposit will be transferred to the account in our Geneva office?"

"The Russians have advised me that they expect to be paid twenty million USD for this first shipment. The Corporation will be transferring fifty million in US Treasury bonds to be held in your custody as collateral for the drawdown payments."

"That's fine. I believe that we give a lending value of 95% on US Treasuries. So, there should be no problem on that score. Our Mr. Prado will be personally supervising the account. He will be glad to hear that fifty million in US Treasuries will be headed in his direction."

"Good. Let's keep in touch."

"Of course," said the American.

CHAPTER TWENTY-ONE

AT FIRST, Liu Tang didn't notice the apple seller on the street below. He had been too preoccupied thinking about what he intended to discuss with the banker before dialing the long-distance telephone number that was on the American's business card. But then he noticed that a white truck sporting a painted shield had suddenly pulled up behind the vendor with his loaded tricycle. Four men jumped out of the truck and rushed at the poor man in a flash. The men overturned the old vendor's cart and then proceeded to roughly knock the man about until he fell to the ground. His apples had rolled everywhere, scattering all over the street. The men then yelled menacing threats at the vendor before getting back into their truck and driving away. The entire incident had lasted under two minutes.

That encounter had been Liu Tang's first exposure to Shanghai's chengguan guards or parapolice, which were referred to as the urban management enforcement team. Liu Tang had heard about the controversial actions of these thuggish squads in cities across China many times over the preceding couple of years, but he had never seen them in action. Even though they were unarmed, they were often quick to intimidate and to use violence. The chengguan guards were charged with the responsibility of patrolling the city streets. They were the enforcers of the laws pertaining to sanitation, construction, environmental protection, and vending, but they also had a reputation for being thugs. Street hawkers were the easiest targets for the chengguan. Many of the unlicensed vendors were rural migrants who sat at the bottom of the urban social ladder and were often looked down upon by locals. Because they were generally engaged in illegal occupations, they were unlikely to go to the police for assistance when they were treated harshly by a chengguan unit.

In the past few weeks, new stories of chengguan brutality had surfaced again, calling the country's attention to the unruliness of these law enforcers, and several cases had sparked an outcry against the blatantly abusive actions of the chengguan. Chengguan violations generated widespread disgust and denunciation when they occurred, but Liu Tang noted that the public outcry often subsided quickly. This was because most people in China, including many of the urban migrants, still felt that their lives were on an upward mobility course, and the Chinese Communist Party worked hard to remind the country's citizens that it deserved credit for the recent decades of economic growth and improvements in their living standards. But the unapologetic violence that the police demonstrated left Liu Tang stunned. The apple vendor who had been knocked to the ground said nothing in protest and had made no attempt to defend himself against them. After the officers drove away, the man straightened his tricycle cart and rode off, leaving the Street of Eternal Happiness littered with apples, which was ironic because this was one of the most important avenues that the chengguan were responsible for keeping clean.

This episode left Liu Tang feeling unsettled, and he didn't think that he was in the right frame of mind to begin a discussion with the American banker. He decided that what he needed now was a good scotch whiskey to calm his nerves and a relaxing place to eat. With a twelve-hour difference between Miami and Shanghai, he knew that if he waited a couple of hours, it would be a better time to place his call.

At 333 Changle Road, Liu Tang entered a restaurant that was called the Secret Garden. The establishment promised fine dining in a converted villa that had been decorated in the classic oriental style. The hostess led him through a series of darkened anterooms with flickering candles that created an atmosphere of old Shanghai. When he was finally seated, he noted that the large room was decorated with wood panels and screen doors, and the seats were adorned with lavish satin pillows. He couldn't help but appreciate the incredible attention to detail that the owner had lavished on the place.

He first ordered a Macallan twelve-year-old whiskey before allowing the waitress to order whatever she recommended from the menu. He was still unsettled from witnessing what the chengguan had done to the old vendor. China was supposed to be the cradle of civilization. The written history of China was traced back to the Shang Dynasty from around 1700 BC. That chengguan guards could get away with severely abusing poor vendors trying to eke out a living in modern-day Shanghai was hard to take.

Liu Tang finished his first whiskey just as the waitress brought out the house special salad, which was made up of juicy cubes of melon and curls of lettuce that were glistening from the soy sauce dressing. Tomato and dried grapefruit were tossed above the salad so that the combination of the different textures and flavors made for an unusual and flavorful dining experience. Happily, the second whiskey arrived just as Liu Tang had finished his salad, and it was beginning to work its magic on him.

The next dish placed in front of Liu Tang was the salmon sashimi, which was composed of four miniature volcanoes of fish that surrounded a little tower of cucumber that was topped with orange roe. The salmon laid atop white radish shavings and nettle leaves, which were perfect for cleansing the palate between bites. The Japanese-style wasabi had just the right punch. Liu Tang took time to admire the way the chef had made his presentation. The expertise in presentation, the combination of flavors, and the whiskey were beginning to have a dramatic effect on him. It all worked to relax him and to make him forget the thugs. The meal reminded him of the excellent dining experiences that he had had in St. Petersburg with the other bankers. He was now in a proper frame of mind to call the American.

There was still time for one last whiskey to accompany the braised Australian scallops in soybean sauce with petite squares of diced pumpkin. This was an unusual combination for an oriental dish, but it proved to be extremely tasty. The scallops were meaty and dense, and the accompanying sauce made for the perfect authentic oriental flavor. Liu Tang wished that his recently made friends could have been here to experience a truly exquisite oriental meal. There was obviously no way that he could finish all of these dishes, so when the waitress offered to pack some of them for him he didn't refuse. *Well, at least our cuisine has progressed over the years*, he said to himself, *more so than the way that we sometimes treat our good comrade citizens*. The last of the whiskey finally brought him to the cheerful mood that he so much wanted to be in before contacting his overseas partner.

AFTER HIS DINNER AND FIVE WHISKIES, LIU TANG decided to take a cab ride to Shanghai's Yangshan deepwater port in order to see the cargo freighter that had recently docked there. He had been advised by his business associates earlier that day that the 500,000 sacks of Cuban brown sugar had successfully arrived in the ship's containers and were now ready to be transported to the warehouses. The Bill of Lading and all of the other documents had already been formalized and were on their way to the American's bank in Geneva for processing. If everything was found to be in order, the Russians could expect to be paid in less than seventy-two hours. That had been the reason for wanting to call the American, to let him know that everything was in order and that the only remaining item pending was the transfer of funds to Mikhail Potanin's company. At the conclusion of the financial transaction, a commission would be paid to the American at his newly established account in Zurich.

At the port, Liu Tang took a moment to marvel at

the magnificent skyscrapers that formed the Shanghai skyline. He took an empty crate to the water's edge, pulled out his pack of Zhongnanhai cigarettes, and sat down to smoke one of Chairman Mao's favorites. From where he was sitting, he could appreciate the view of Jin Mao Tower, which was the third tallest building in the world and the tallest one in China. He remembered reading how the architect of the skyscraper had ingeniously combined the elements of traditional Chinese culture with the newest architectural styles of the time, which made the Jin Mao Tower one of the best-constructed buildings in the country. The building included modern offices, a deluxe five-star hotel (the Grand Hyatt Shanghai), an observation deck, and entertainment facilities. As he smoked his cigarette and looked at the tower, he considered how fast things had been evolving in his life.

When Liu Tang finished smoking his cigarette, he tossed the butt into the Yangtze River and watched it flow toward the sea. He then painfully admitted to himself that the forlorn feeling that he had was because his wife was cheating on him. "I wear the green hat," he whispered to no one. Perhaps women in China didn't always make the decision to marry in their own best interest. They made decisions based on what was better for the whole, meaning for the parents, for relatives, for friends. So, the person a young woman eventually married might not necessarily be the one that she really wanted to be with. *I suppose that I was just the appropriate match at the time. I then wouldn't think it much of a stretch,* he continued with his painful logic, *to assume that having affairs is atypical for this reason. And, assuming that divorce is not in the best interest of the whole, especially if children are involved, it seems only natural that one eventually grows tired and anxious in a loveless marriage. A spouse may then decide not to get divorced but to just simply have an affair. And both the man and the woman will adapt to the change in order to prevent making waves in the marriage, in the family, for the good of the whole. Well then,* he disgustedly concluded, *when we Chinese talk to our friends about how much we value our traditions, our family, our culture, it should all be taken with a grain of salt.*

As Liu Tang watched the cigarette butt being taken out by the tide to the open sea, he thought that perhaps it was high time that he headed home to his family, to his Chinese women, to his wife and daughter. China was a unique country and one of the few that achieved a semblance of equality of the sexes without a women's liberation movement. He had learned that in a history class in college. Feminism, many did not realize, found its beginnings in the class theories of Marxist ideology. "Women, as a class of people," he remembered his professor lecturing, "have historically been exploited by men. China's past has been no different. Our country has had a history with one of the most extreme forms of sexism against women where they were not considered people but merely property by men and society as a whole." "But," the professor went on emphasizing the greatness of the Party, "as our country underwent Communist revolution, women instantaneously achieved parity with men overnight."

Walking along Qibao Street, Liu Tang was in better spirits as he was reminiscing on his college days. As he walked along, he passed by some old women street vendors who were selling clothes from racks, and shoes and socks. Near them was a man selling sweet potatoes, and further along, there was another man selling nuts. As Liu Tang passed them, he mused that here was a great opportunity to shop for a complete wardrobe and dinner all in one spot. Just then, the woman with the clothes rack was trying to jump over a planter to get to where Liu Tang was standing. All of the other vendors suddenly started running as the police seemed to appear out of nowhere. They were now grabbing the poor old women who had been selling the shoes and socks. "Chengguan," he heard a passerby say.

The male vendors managed to get away, but the two old women selling clothes were caught by the uniformed police officers. People were quickly scattering, trying to avoid getting mixed up in the conflict that was unfolding. One vendor had made out all right by quickly handing her profits to the police. They left her clothes rack overturned on the ground and proceeded to surround the other woman, who had been clutching to her cash box for dear life. The woman struggled against the officers, but she was eventually overpowered and thrown to the ground. Several of the chengguan officers then grabbed all of her belongings and the cash box while she was being forcibly kept down by several of the men. Liu Tang had stood by at a distance in utter shock, unable to believe how brutally the old grannies had been attacked by the government thugs. The most frustrating thing was to be a witness to the incident and to know that there was nothing that he could do to help these victims of police brutality.

With good reason, Liu Tang was fast becoming a nervous wreck and an alcoholic. As soon as he made it to his home that night he poured himself a large whiskey. When he finally settled into his western-style leather sofa, he was glad to find that his wife and daughter had already retired for the night. He was extremely exhausted and in no mood to have a conversation. Mercifully, the whiskey had again quickly worked its magic, and before he had even finished his drink, he had fallen asleep and had dropped his glass onto the carpet.

. . .

By the time Liu Tang woke up the next morning, his wife and daughter had already left the apartment. Liu Tang looked at the empty glass at his feet and couldn't help but laugh as he imagined what his wife must have thought when she saw him this morning. After showering and shaving, he was quite surprised to find that his wife had bothered to make a pot of coffee. She may have ignored the whiskey glass at his feet, but she continued to perform all of her other domestic duties. We must keep everything in harmony, he remembered with disgust.

At his office, he carefully went over all of the copies of documents that had been submitted to the American's Geneva office just to be sure that everything was in order. He didn't want the bank in Geneva to delay payment to the Russians because of some minor clerical error. As he looked at the documents signed by the Corporate Secretary he noticed that among the list of silent shareholders was the name of Mo Yan. Furthermore, the document stated that this same Mo Yan was owner of 47% of the Corporation.

Liu Tang was left devastated by the shocking news. How was it that no one had ever mentioned Mo Yan's name at any of the meetings that he had attended? Mo Yan had never even participated in any of the events nor was referred to in any way by anyone. Liu Tang looked at the document again in disbelief, hoping that he had been mistaken on his initial reading. But there was his name staring at him, the silent partner. This was the very man that was having an affair with his wife, and that had made him a cuckold. Evidently, Mo Yan was to be a primary beneficiary in the transaction with the Russians. There was no doubt too that Mo Yan had a list of all of the members of the Corporation. So, he must have known that Liu Tang was also a partner in the business. Mo Yan must have had a private chuckle when he had read his name in the Corporation's directory. To Liu Tang, it now seemed as though there was no escaping his adversary. This was the most devastating thing that he could have imagined.

Was it possible that Mo Yan had informed his wife of this second business that he had been so secretive about? He now realized that all the plans that he had been working on toward his independence would probably not come to fruition because of an unfortunate stroke of luck. What were the odds that Mo Yan would be a silent partner in the Corporation that he had placed all of his hopes on and that had offered him an escape from the one man that had humiliated him at his home and his job?

The Corporation had sent fifty million in US Treasury securities as collateral for the trade-financing activity related to the Russians. The initial Letter of Credit had been issued in favor of the Russians for twenty-five million dollars. This left about twenty-two million dollars that could be drawn against the balance of US Treasuries left in the account, and that was because the lending value on the securities had been set at 95%.

Now, Liu Tang was not a violent man so any action that he was going to take would not be along those lines. In his fit of rage, Liu Tang immediately knew how he would want to exact his revenge against the executive that had made his life miserable. He had had enough of Mo Yan. Fortunately for him, all the elements for exacting a financial blow to Mo Yan were under his control. Liu Tang also knew that by executing his plan he could financially secure his future and for once sever all of his ties with his unfaithful wife. Mo Yan was going to pay dearly for the green hat that Liu Tang had been forced to wear.

Now that he was determined to move forward, there was not a moment to lose. His first order of business was to execute a payment instruction from the Bank of China—where the Corporation had their primary account—to the bank in Geneva where the fifty million in US Treasuries were being held in custody. Liu Tang knew that the operations area in the Bank of China would not question the issuance of his payment instruction because he was a trusted executive and an authorized signature for the Corporation.

The authenticated payment instruction would request the bank in Geneva to wire twenty-two million in USD funds to a private account at a bank in Zurich. No one would know that the account was the same one that had been recently established by Liu Tang for the American. It was the account that Liu Tang had been instructed to establish in order to compensate the American for his services. The account currently had fifty thousand USD, which was the sign-on bonus that had been paid to the American for joining the team. The American would also be receiving his commission of two basis points on the new twenty-five-million sugar transaction that was already in progress with the Russians, which would amount to another fifty thousand USD. Only Liu Tang was privy to the name of the bank in Zurich and its account number since no one else had been made responsible for this menial task. By executing the funds transfer instruction immediately, Liu Tang knew that the funds would be transferred at the first hour of business the following morning in Geneva. After executing the payment, Liu Tang would destroy all of the paperwork related to the American's account.

The payment would be executed by Geneva against the line of credit that had been established against the US Treasuries. Liu Tang suspected that anyone from China later making any inquiries about asset positions for the account in Geneva would receive confirmation of the securities held in their custody. But it was highly unlikely that it would occur to anyone in the Corporation to question anything regarding lines of credit because it was not something that they had been made aware of. Liu Tang issued the payment instructions for twenty-two million USD because he knew that the bank in Geneva would reject any wire transfer instruction exceeding that because it would jeopardize the letter of credit commitment for the twenty-five million USD that had to be paid to the Russians. Liu Tang knew that once the payment order had been executed, there was no going back.

The next order of business would be to advise the authorities anonymously that there had been a commodity smuggled into the country, but Liu Tang could not do this until the Russians were paid their funds, so not for another seventy-two hours. If he were to advise the authorities before then, there was always the possibility that the payment to the Russians could be stopped because of the illegal aspect of the transaction. Liu Tang had no desire to upset the Russians; he just wanted to hurt Mo Yan. He had no desire to create additional enemies. Once the funds were paid to the Russians and the Corporation had been debited for the additional amount in favor of the American, then the real damage to the Corporation would take place. If the cargo were to be confiscated, then the Corporation would lose the funds and the cargo. More than likely, the top executives of the Corporation could also face jail time for their participation in the illegal activity. As a silent partner, Mo Yan would probably escape prosecution since his lawyers would argue that he had no say in the transactions that the Corporation executed. His lawyers would contend that his sole role was that of investor. He would however feel the significant financial loss that the Corporation stood to have as a major shareholder.

For the next seventy-two hours, Liu Tang was at risk of being discovered if someone from the bank in Geneva were to call the Corporation questioning the funds transfer. This could occur if the manager in Geneva assigned to the Corporation's account was concerned that the assets under his management were being transferred out of the account. More than likely, Liu Tang reasoned, nothing would happen until the payments were executed. By then Liu Tang hoped that he would be long gone. His biggest concern now was how to break the news to the American.

CHAPTER TWENTY-TWO

THE AMERICAN WAS STARTLED out of his daydream just before noon by a long-distance phone call.

"Hello," came from a woman's voice with a very pronounced foreign accent. "Is this James?"

"It is," responded the American.

"Hello, James," the woman responded. "This is Nadya Ivanovna from St. Petersburg. How are you?"

"Nadya, this is a wonderful surprise! I can't believe that you are calling. How are you?"

"Fine," she said, "just fine. Mikhail Potanin and Viktor Yeltsin are having dinner here at the hotel, and they suggested that I call you."

"Great. I'm thrilled that you called." the American said. "I didn't really get a chance to properly thank you on that last night for all of the time that you spent with me, for making my trip so special. I don't think that I can ever thank you enough!" As he said this he felt extremely disappointed with himself for not having given her a gift in appreciation for that last night. Nadya was the most remarkable woman that he had ever known.

"Oh, it was a pleasure for me as well. I didn't think that bankers had such a passion for the arts! I could see that you had a real appreciation for our Russian artists. Anyway, I really enjoyed the time we spent together." Then she abruptly changed the topic of conversation to pose a question on something that Mikhail had asked her in Russian.

"Mikhail sends his greetings to you. He also asks if you are aware that the cargo has been successfully delivered to Shanghai."

"No, I was not advised," the American responded. "But tell him that I believe that the agreed terms between the buyer and Mikhail were for payment to be made within seventy-two hours after the documents were submitted."

"Hello, James," Mikhail had taken the telephone from Nadya. "How are you doing?"

"Hello, Mikhail, I'm fine. Nadya was just telling me that the shipment finally arrived in Shanghai, and that is excellent news."

"That is correct, my friend, excellent news for me and you. Now we just need to get paid."

"Mikhail," the American said. "Let me call Geneva right away to see what is going on. But it might already be too late to call tonight. It's already 6 pm in Geneva. Let me try, and I'll get right back to you."

"Very good, James. I'll be right here having my dinner at the hotel. Please call me back if you find out anything. You know," Mikhail added, "this is a twenty-five-million-dollar deal and sometimes these Chinese can be a little tricky. But I don't anticipate any problems."

"Don't worry, Mikhail. The Letter of Credit cannot be altered. As long as everything was complied with from your end, and as long as the documents that were presented are in order, there can be no reason for you not to be paid. Remember, the Chinese Corporation had the funds in their account in Geneva, and that they cannot touch. So, your funds are secure."

"That is correct, my friend. So, I should be seeing my money quite soon."

"Let me make the call, and I will get right back to you."

"Go ahead; I will be right here waiting."

. . .

AFTER THE CONVERSATION HAD ENDED, THE American put down the telephone and just stared at it for a moment. Mikhail had been cordial during the conversation, but there was an unmistakable undertone in his manner that suggested a threat. The Russian had made it clear to the American that he wanted to get paid his twenty-five million dollars soon, very soon. The man was a heavy!

The American sat at his desk stupefied. This reminded him of the very dangerous situation when his bank had to close several accounts that they had inherited when they had acquired a Venezuelan bank. The accounts were for clients that were residents of a small town at Venezuela's border with Colombia. This was during the time at the height of the cocaine activity in Colombia. The small border town had huge amounts of transactions related to tourism, the Venezuelan clients claimed. But the bank knew that tourism in that part of the country was almost nonexistent and downright dangerous because of the internal guerrilla warfare taking place at the time. When the accounts were subsequently closed, representatives of the clients showed up at the Miami office questioning the bank's decision. They also requested the names of the bank officers who had authorized the account closures. Those very dangerous men didn't want to see their money-laundering activity through the bank coming to an end.

The Russians were promptly paid the following morning. There were no issues with regard to the shipment of goods, and all documents had been properly and promptly submitted. There was therefore no reason to withhold or to delay the twenty-five-million-dollar payment. This time it was Viktor Yeltsin's turn to call the American to confirm receipt of payment and to thank him for his help. No reference had been made to Nadya Ivanovna. The American was glad to have this end of the business behind him. He wondered if Liu Tang had been made aware of it.

ON HIS WAY HOME THAT SAME EVENING, LIU TANG spotted the hated uniformed chengguan parapolice with their red armbands, armed with nightsticks, parked close by the entrance to his apartment building. He waited a few moments at an intersection that was about 100 feet away to see if he could determine what had made them stop there. He took out one of his Zhongnanhai cigarettes from his breast pocket and studied it for a moment before lighting it. There didn't seem to be any unlicensed vendors in sight, so why were they stationed there? Liu Tang considered his options as he lit his cigarette. He had to be careful. Nothing unusual had occurred at the bank today with regard to the wire transfer, but that didn't mean anything. Any matter related to the Corporation would probably be handled outside of the bank, on the quiet.

According to sources, some chengguan officials had connections to organized crime. That was not very surprising since China never really paid its civil servants enough money for them to be totally honest. No wonder then that hardly a week went by without a new controversy involving the thuggish municipal officers. There were plenty of beatings taking place at the hands of these ruthless men throughout the provinces, and they wouldn't be expensive to contract. As of late, the chengguan had even been implicated in several deaths.

"No overdrafts allowed," Liu Tang said to himself partly in remorse, and then he immediately moved on, wanting to steer clear of the hated officers. First, he headed straight for the crowded Fake market on Nanjing Road, which was one of the favorite tourist shopping stops in Shanghai. The Fake market offered both tourists and locals the opportunity to shop for many types of famous brand knock-off products at bargain prices. This market had a sprawling collection of stalls filled with counterfeit, defective, and smuggled merchandise from the world's biggest brands. Liu Tang nervously strolled through these streets, smoking his cigarettes, and not noticing anyone. As he made his way, he listened to the vendors shouting to the tourists "Cheap watch!" and "I make you good deal!" The options were limitless for seemingly any item of clothing desired. The foreigner had his pick of fabrics, styles, and colors. The Fake market was very crowded, but the only danger there was that of the occasional pickpocket.

Liu Tang moved on next to what was referred to as the Wet market. The place was packed mostly with locals, perusing everything from live chickens, fish, to many types of fruits and vegetables. In this market, the fresh fish were killed, scaled, and chopped up right in front of the buyers. The meat was always butchered early in the morning, and whatever was not immediately sold had only the fan or occasional wave of the vendors to keep the flies at bay. The chickens were kept in small cages, but there were a few that had been lucky enough to have escaped, and these were wandering freely behind the counters. Liu Tang knew that to Westerners the Wet market did not look very clean, but the locals weren't so picky and, despite his problems, he found comfort in watching the shoppers jostle for bargains.

At the intersection of Hua Hai Central Road and Shanxi South Road, Liu Tang took a taxi to the Grand Hyatt Hotel in the Jin Mao Tower, which was located in the center of Pudong in the Lujiazui business district. He did this despite knowing that it made no sense because he could run into some of his colleagues from the Bank of China there, or worse still, associates from the Corporation. Upon entering the lobby, he took the elevator to the eighty-seventh floor, which was where the Cloud 9 bar was situated. The panoramic nighttime views of the city from the bar were spectacular. The intimate and mysterious ambiance of the Shanghai bar was heightened by its interesting architecture and by the warm and cool materials that shaped the interior. The décor featured a maze of vertical columns and polished chrome that were set against a dark mahogany background.

Cloud 9 created a venue that attracted a great mix of locals and ex-pats. If you combined this with the well-made drinks and the backdrop of Shanghai at night, you could understand why this had become one of Shanghai's most popular destination in the after-hours scene. On occasions, Liu Tang would bring foreign clients to Cloud 9. Sure, it was touristy and expensive, but the male clients liked the place because there were lots of ex-pat groupies, local girls looking for older foreign guys, or local girls already with older foreign guys. Very often there were the very good-looking local girls looking to make new friends, but for these, it was exclusively a pay-for-play arrangement.

Earlier that day, Liu Tang had anonymously informed the authorities about the contraband white crystals that had been smuggled into the country by the Corporation. There would be serious consequences for all Board members if they were found to be guilty. The charges of corruption could easily be trumped up to include many other charges that were normally associated with the smuggling. Embezzlement of government money was one that was routinely included in the charges through indirect association. The Board members could also be charged with oppressing the farmers of the sugar-producing province because of the illegal importation of the commodity. Additionally, the passing of the foreign sugar as a local product was another very serious offense. Sugar was being smuggled in for hefty profits, but it was notoriously difficult to catch the culprits because there were many entry points, and the guards were easily bribed. The state-backed China Sugar Association offered rewards for tipsters who helped to expose the criminal sugar smugglers.

The sugar trade in China was huge. The Guangdong Sugar Association estimated that contraband imports in the first quarter that year had already reached 600,000 tons, which was slightly more than the volume of legitimate sugar imports. China was the world's top sugar importer. Expectations of tight supplies in China had been underpinning prices. The official economic planners stated that the Chinese sugar market was likely to face a consumption deficit of two million tons this year, largely because of poor weather conditions during the crucial growing periods. Forecasters were also predicting that Chinese sugar consumption would be rising significantly over the next ten years.

Liu Tang had informed on the Board members and had embezzled twenty-two million dollars from their foreign account. In the late edition of a newspaper that someone had left at the bar, Liu Tang read that several Board members of the Corporation were being held in custody pending further investigations. The reporters alleged that there had been an ongoing investigation on the Corporation for several months and that the crimes had involved massive sums of money, which had also been tied to a money-laundering ring.

The Beijing government strictly controlled cross-border capital movements as part of its ongoing effort to preserve savings at home and in order to protect its banking system from sudden external financial shocks. The Corporation's alleged underground banking network, which extended to the coastal metropolis of Shanghai, illustrated an increasingly popular channel through which the wealthy Chinese were able to get around the country's tight capital controls. Chinese authorities in recent months had stepped up their crackdown on these types of networks while pledging to take more action to stem the illegal cross-border capital flows. As part of its stricter measures, it had prohibited citizens from taking more than fifty thousand dollars out of the country in a year. The money-smuggling ring in

Shanghai showed the difficulty in enforcing these restrictions. Government sources alleged that the criminal ring had illegally transferred more than one billion dollars for its clients within the past two years. The Board members of the Corporation were charged with engaging in illegal business activities, which included the use of fake electronic companies and bank accounts to help clients evade China's capital controls, the prosecutors alleged.

Sources familiar with the investigations said that the Corporation would take Yuan funds from clients and deposit the money in accounts on the mainland. The Corporation would then arrange to have an equivalent amount of funds in foreign currency deposited in the clients' offshore accounts. Prosecutors stated that the clients of the Corporation included an unspecified number of businesses from across the country.

The case came just as Chinese officials had become increasingly focused on government corruption, an area where the nation's leaders had acknowledged persistent problems. Funds sent overseas illegally by Chinese officials had become part of the problem. Just last month, a senior anti-corruption official had told the state-run news agency that China was strengthening its measures to recover the illicit assets that were transferred abroad. The government would be asking the countries where the funds had been deposited to freeze the assets. This kind of capital flight was what was helping to create the widening income gap between the haves and the have-nots, analysts said, threatening the social stability of the country. The ruling Communist Party was determined to fight this type of corruption, and all those involved with this case could expect to serve life sentences.

Liu Tang was shocked to learn that the Corporation had already been under investigation. His anonymous call must have triggered the immediate action from the investigators, who must have decided to act once it was clear that others were beginning to suspect that there was something wrong with the Corporation. Liu Tang wondered if he could expect to be picked up soon by the authorities because he was a member of the Corporation and an officer of the Bank of China. He could potentially be implicated with the rest of the Board members, especially since he had an authorized signature for the Corporation which allowed him to move funds.

Liu Tang had wanted to get his passport earlier in the evening, but the chengguan had been parked by his house and he was not going to take any chances with them. He suspected that they may have been sent there under explicit instructions by suspicious Board members. If the government had issued orders for his arrest, they would have sent the normal police agents to pick him up and not the chengguan thugs. Now, instead of urgently finding a way out of the country, he was drinking whiskies in Cloud 9.

As he sat by the bar drinking his scotch, smoking his Zhongnanhai cigarettes, he remembered that he had not yet advised the American about the twenty-two million dollars that he had instructed to be transferred to his Swiss account. In hindsight, that may have proven to be a lucky break because he was pretty sure that the American would not want to be implicated with anything related to the Corporation. The American would certainly be in total shock once his Geneva colleagues advised him of the scandal that was breaking out in China with regard to the Corporation. The American's affiliate Swiss bank had shown a great interest in opening the account. They had high expectations that this initial corporate account would lead to other potential accounts from China. Now the bank would be associated with a corporation that was implicated by the Chinese government for criminal activity. The American had referred the Corporation to the Geneva office. He would not be happy to hear from Liu Tang that embezzled funds had been transferred to his newly established personal account at a private bank in Switzerland. There was no way that Liu Tang could inform the American, at least not yet.

Preoccupied with all of the taxing issues revolving around his life right now, Liu Tang had not taken notice of the two high-priced escort girls who had taken a seat next to him at the bar. But knowing how to communicate and connect on a physical and emotional level was their expertise, and they soon had his attention. Xin Yu, he had overheard one called, was a real stunner. She had a perfect body with a matching pretty face and shoulder-length jet-black hair. Xiu Mei, the one accompanying her, was the sexier of the two, with a slim body, long legs, and tight C-cup breasts. Her skin was creamy and smooth, neither pale nor dark. Her hair was long, thick, and black, and it flowed luxuriously down her back. Both girls were knockouts, cool and classy, erotic and tantalizing, dark and mysterious. People were not born equal, nor were they meant to be. Either of the two lovelies could help to cheer him up. They were young but experienced, and he had no doubt that they could easily strip most men of their personalities, turning them into their objects of entertainment.

Liu Tang knew that not all escort girls in Shanghai were prostitutes. In high-scale clubs, escort girls merely engaged in conversation with you or sang with you, maybe even letting you plant a kiss on their cheeks. But sex would be out of the question. Their job was to make you feel comfortable by providing companionship, not by satisfying your lust. If the companionship proved to be fun, it was expected that the gentleman would tip the girls accordingly.

On other occasions, if you made a very favorable impression and if there was a real monetary incentive, a girl of a different sort could negotiate with you. This happened more often with the older, wealthier businessmen. Some women found these types of men to be irresistible.

"Sure," Liu Tang overheard one of the two businessmen sitting by the bar on his other side say. "Some people say that Shanghai women are bad, materialistic, gold-diggers. But come on, if Shanghai women are materialistic, it is because the men are ready to pay. And if the men are ready to pay, it means that the women are something special. Let me conclude then by logically saying that there is something irresistible and special about Shanghai women that drive men crazy."

"I don't know," the other businessman said in response. "Maybe it's nothing. Maybe it's a coincidence that a lot of men have crushes on Shanghai girls. Although, according to *China Hush*, Shanghai women are the seventh most beautiful girls in all of China. These girls are found to be exquisite and very fashionable. Would you believe that Chongqing girls were ranked second, behind the Dalian and are supposedly as hot as fire? I personally think that they deserve the top spot." The two businessmen men then raised their whiskey glasses in admiration of the women from Chongqing.

Liu Tang couldn't help but smile as he overheard the

comments that the two drunks had been making on the topic regarding the beauty of Chinese women.

The businessman who had first opened his mouth began deliberating again. "Women's beauty should not be intimidating, but beautiful women make men lose self-control. Beautiful women demonstrating their intractable personality is not passive beauty but charm that can destroy men's rationality." Liu Tang couldn't stop himself from laughing when he heard that. He couldn't make any sense of what he had just overheard. But the two drunken businessmen understood each other perfectly, and in confirmation, proceeded to lift their glasses to toast on the wisdom of what had just been pronounced.

Cloud 9 games, thought Liu Tang. The light and color of the spot were meant to transport you to another place. The ambitious businessmen in their full combat gear were eyeing the two tiger lilies. Bad behavior, shameful behavior was to be expected for their results-oriented strategy. The two businessmen were momentarily silent as they schemed on how to pounce on their prey. Harsh professional action, based partly on necessity and partly on indulgence, was required. Cloud 9 was the place where they came to have fun, but maybe out of despair, searching for their dreams. Underneath their costumes, there were human beings. The two lovely tiger lilies could sense the scent of money around them.

Liu Tang looked out of the window while he absent-mindedly used the swizzle stick to stir the ice cubes in his whiskey. The trick was to escape. The bartender prepared the magic potions, the chemical weapons that helped everyone to make the decisions that they wanted to make, that they needed to make.

"Speak to your neighbors," the barmaid smilingly whispered encouragement.

Liu Tang looked out of the window into the dark night and didn't want to consider anything.

"I have lived in Shanghai since 1995," one of the businessmen began again. "I have had one or two Shanghai girlfriends during this time. For the most part, they are OK, but kind of lazy and incapable of doing simple tasks that might be expected of the average human being. They are spoiled, not so much in a princess-like way, but more in a way of never wanting to do anything by themselves. This inability to do things, like making tea, cooking, or buying things for the house, transcends into all of the other areas of their lives where they expect everything to be done for them. They expect everyone to jump to attention when they ask for stuff."

When he had finished saying this, the businessman took a sip of the drink that the barmaid had just placed in front of him and waited to see what his friend had to say to that.

"Apart from their behavior," the other began, "which

is like that of an eight-year-old child most times, they are not more beautiful than the girls from any other province in China. It's just ridiculous to suggest that they are. Shanghai is the Hollywood of China, and so a lot of good-looking girls live here. Walk down Nanjing Road and you can see hot girls everywhere. To assume that they are all Shanghainese is just laughable. Unfortunately, many Shanghai girls have bought into the ideology of the Shanghai Princess and have adopted it into their own style of living. I can only think that they regard their behavior as being cool or smart, when in fact many of them are now wondering what the fuck is happening to their lives."

"Maybe," his buddy began again, "it's because Chongqing is a city in the mountains, and Chongqing girls have been climbing the hills ever since they were young." *Nice continuity in thought*, thought Liu Tang, ready to burst out laughing. "Their long legs," the businessman continued, "are therefore beautiful and sexy. The girls of Chongqing are full of personality, full of charm and warm-hearted like fire."

Liu Tang looked at the two girls seated next to him and thought about what the businessman had just said. He wondered where they were from. Liu Tang knew that the magic hour was fast approaching and that soon he would have to decide on how to re-imagine his life. Westerners in his position would probably now be asking their God for help. *Do we need God?* he asked himself.

"Almost all Shanghai women think that they are the women of women," one of them began arguing again. "They love fashion, perfumes, and cosmetics just like they love their own bodies. Shanghai is a stylish city, destined to create a different temperament of beauties. We can't help but be attracted to their pure and beautiful appearance with their big, beautiful eyes."

Liu Tang couldn't listen anymore to the two men and their idiotic conversation on the beauty of Chinese women. He was now feeling extremely anxious. It was as though it finally hit home that his life was in jeopardy. He didn't want to wait anymore to see what was going to happen. He was repulsed now by the taste of his cigarette, and the whiskey wasn't getting him anywhere either. Clearly, he needed to act now. Liu Tang settled his bill with the bartender and was ready to head for the elevators when he spotted Cloud 9 souvenir postcards placed on a table by the hostess. As an afterthought, he took one of the postcards and addressed it to the American. Then he paused for a moment, looked at the hostess as though searching for inspiration, and began writing his brief message.

"He stands leaning against the glass wall, alone, looking out to the river toward thousands of ships passing by, but none is the one he is waiting for. Greetings from the Street of Eternal Happiness."

He smiled at the hostess when he had finished writing the note, gave her an excessively large tip, and asked her if she wouldn't mind putting postage on the postcard that had a destination for America. "For a friend," he told her, smiling. She, naturally, agreed to mail the postcard for him. He thanked her, and then promptly made his way to the elevator. He needed his passport now.

CHAPTER TWENTY-THREE

THICK, fluffy clouds concealed the moon as Liu Tang made his way by foot toward his neighborhood. As he approached the intersection that gave him the best view of his apartment, he realized that he didn't have a plan on how to deal with the chengguan if he ran into them. The truck that had been stationary earlier in front of his address was no longer there. Perhaps he had not been their target after all. Of course, he couldn't be certain that the goon squad wasn't lurking in the shadows somewhere waiting in ambush for him, but it would have to be a chance that he would have to take. If he didn't make his move now, tomorrow could certainly be too late.

But Liu Tang still waited by the intersection, unbelieving and yet knowing that something was wrong. His heart rate had increased significantly. The adrenaline was pushing Liu Tang's body to its limits; it was also changing his perception of time. Everything seemed to move more slowly. He still felt thoroughly dispirited and weak in resolve as well as in his body. But then the image of Mo Yan came into his mind, that despicable man that he hated so much. Just the thought of the man now moved him into action. Immediately he became angry again, and he no longer cared what would happen to him if he were to be caught. He hoped that he had seriously hurt the wretched man and his corporation. For now, it looked as though he had hurt the man to the tune of twenty-two million USD, and if the authorities were not on the take, Mo Yan would no longer be able to operate going forward.

He was now less than twenty paces away, and still there was no sign of the chengguan anywhere. Perhaps he had not been their target after all. But maybe they were waiting for him inside. He would know soon enough; there was no going back. He waited a moment again, listening for sounds, before inserting the brass key into the lock. Still there was nothing, nothing discernible to him, nothing out of the ordinary. So, he finally inserted the key, turned the lock, and pushed gradually the door open. Then he waited by the threshold for something to happen, but nothing did. He closed the door behind him and moved on inside in total darkness. He was not about to turn on the lights. He stopped momentarily again to listen for sounds, to smell for any unusual odors. But there was nothing to suggest that there had been any intruders. Was he really going to be safe, he wondered?

From the living room sofa, someone lit a match and brought it to a cigarette that Liu Tang couldn't see in the darkness. Then he saw the bright orange glow of the cigarette tip as the smoker began to inhale. The pungent odor of the slow-burning tobacco gave Liu Tang a chill. Double Happiness was what was most commonly smoked in China. It was not the brand of cigarette that the elite would smoke, certainly not someone like Mo Yan.

A low lamp light then came on, and Liu Tang was now able to see that Mo Yan was indeed the man who was smoking. The man removed the cigarette from his mouth, looked at Liu Tang as though he wanted to properly consider his worth, and nodded to the two men who had moved around him from the adjacent room.

The two heavily built men were dressed as cheng-guan guards, but they were, in fact, Mo Yan's henchmen impersonating as the notorious para-policemen. A thin man hit him a hard, professional cutting blow with the edge of the hand. There was something rather deadly about his accuracy and his lack of effort. When Liu Tang doubled over with pain, the other man punched him hard in the face. The fist landed squarely into his right temple, and he went down hard. The thin man then kicked him heavily in the ribs, and Liu Tang felt as though at least one of them had fractured. The other man lifted his heel above Liu Tang's head, but by then, Liu Tang's vision had blurred.

CHAPTER TWENTY-FOUR

MID-OCTOBER, the American received an anonymous souvenir postcard from China with a strange message on it and no return address. The postmark and the site of the venue on the card confirmed that it had been sent from Shanghai. The postcard had taken almost a month to reach him, and the message on it was quite unusual in that it was very personal in nature.

"He stands leaning against the glass wall, alone, looking out to the river toward thousands of ships passing by, but none is the one he is waiting for. Greetings from the Street of Eternal Happiness."

It made no sense at all to the American. Why had the writer taken the trouble to write him such an ambiguous note, and was it even meant for him?

It had to be related to that terrible business between

the Russians and the Corporation in Shanghai. The office in Geneva had been subpoenaed by the Chinese authorities through the Swiss courts. The Chinese government had requested the freezing of the Corporation's assets. To be more precise, the Chinese government had requested a garnishing of all assets. The legal department of the Geneva affiliate had to get involved with very complicated issues because Geneva held two twenty-five-million-dollar US Treasury bonds in the Corporation's account. But the two bonds had been used as collateral against two payments that had been made. The American knew that the payment for twenty-five million USD had been made to the Russians for the sugar shipment. But he was clueless as to what the other twenty-two million USD wire transfer payment was for, and he had no interest in knowing. He was hoping to distance himself as far as possible from the entire fiasco. It was bad enough that he had referred the account to Geneva, and he could still potentially lose his job because of all the headaches that had been caused by his referral. "God damn, Liu Tang," he cursed in anger.

The legal department was quite certain that the bank had first recourse to the assets under Swiss law. In fact, the bank could now begin proceedings against the Corporation in order to collect on its outstanding debt against the US Treasury bonds. The fact that a foreign government had initiated claims against the assets of the

Corporation, and the fact that the Corporation's status had been compromised as it had been found to be part of a criminal ring, gave the Geneva affiliate grounds to begin proceedings and to begin the process for the collection on the outstanding debt. The two US Treasury bonds would soon be sold on the market. The resulting funds would be offset against the forty-seven million USD debt owed to the bank, and any remaining difference from the netting would be sent to the Chinese government.

It had to be Liu Tang who had sent him the encrypted message. If Liu Tang knew about the illegal activity related to the Corporation, then he owed the American more than the note scribbled on the postcard. But Liu Tang had expressed high hopes for the Corporation. He had said that it was his ticket out of a bad marriage and out of an uncomfortable situation at his bank. He may well have been duped with all sorts of legitimate promises by the Board of the Corporation. If this is what had transpired, then it would make sense that Liu Tang would owe an explanation to his new American partner.

The American had forgotten about the personal account that Liu Tang had opened for him in Zurich. Supposedly, he had been given an initial sign-on bonus of fifty thousand USD by the Corporation for his efforts on opening the new account with Geneva, and for acting as intermediary agent for the Russian transactions. But the American had never received confirmation that the account had been opened, nor that the funds had been deposited. He had preferred to keep his distance from anything related to this business because of the uncertainty of the people with who he was dealing and who he had only briefly met. Who were these people really, and why would they want him involved in their activity? Something didn't make sense. Perhaps because they didn't trust each other, they had decided on finding some third party that would facilitate the activity between them. A banker from America with an affiliate in Geneva would work perfectly for them. Private banking with all of the experts in Switzerland to safeguard the transactions between the distrustful Russians and suspicious Chinese, some neutral entity to oversee the flow of funds was the perfect setup for them. The American could understand that well enough. But what had happened, what had made it all collapse so quickly? The Russians had not been implicated in anything illegal so far. It was only the Chinese Corporation that had problems.

The American recalled reading in The Financial Times of Shanghai how an anonymous informant had alerted the authorities about an illegal shipment of sugar that had been smuggled into the country by the Corporation. Could Liu Tang have been the anonymous source? That didn't make any sense at all. Disbelieving, and yet understanding that it was probably true, the American took up the postcard again and softly muttered, "Where does this leave us, Liu Tang?"

In Geneva, the American gave testimony as to how he had met Liu Tang at the banking conference in St. Petersburg. He elaborated on how they had casually shared drinks and dinners with other conference attendees. He then explained how on one of their outings Liu Tang had advised him that he worked as an agent for a corporation in Shanghai and that the corporation needed to establish an account with an overseas bank that would accommodate them with their trade-financing program.

"Is that all that you know about the Corporation?" he was asked by the Chinese government representative.

"Yes," the American responded. "It was also my understanding that the Corporation had an account with the Bank of China."

"That is accurate," responded the Chinese representative. "Is there anything else that you can remember?"

"No," said the American. And then, as an afterthought, he added, "Except that Liu Tang may have mentioned someone in the Bank of China by the name of Mo Yan."

"Mo Yan?" inquired the rep.

"Yes, I believe that was his name. You should be able

to confirm that quickly by verifying that with the bank or with Liu Tang."

"Yes, we know Mr. Mo Yan," replied the man. "He is an executive on the Board of the Bank of China. But we were not aware that he had any ties to the Corporation."

"Well, I'm not clear as to the ties," replied the American. "But he did mention Mr. Mo Yan's name. Liu Tang should be able to clarify that with you."

"Yes," replied the government official, "we would certainly do that if we could speak to Mr. Liu Tang. But, unfortunately, Mr. Liu Tang is no longer with us. He has passed away. But please, don't concern yourself with that. At any rate, please accept our sincere thanks. You have been most helpful."

"My God!" responded the American in disbelief. He was clearly devastated to hear of Liu Tang's death. "What happened to Mr. Liu Tang?"

"We are sorry, but we are not able to provide you with the details related to his death. Sometimes terrible things can happen when you get involved with the wrong people. Anyway, that is all that we are able to say on the subject. Please accept our thanks for your collaboration. We will not be pursuing anything further with you or with your bank on this matter. You may consider our government's investigation here to be at an end. Thank you."

And that was the end of it. The American had decided at the last second of the interview, in a rare moment of inspiration, to bring up Mo Yan. Mo Yan had been the cause of Liu Tang's misery. That was the least that the American could do for Liu Tang. He was especially glad that he had done it now that he had learned of Liu Tang's death. But the possibility that Liu Tang had been murdered sent a shiver through his body. Did Liu Tang anticipate that he could be in danger? Is that why he had sent the postcard?

When the American first arrived in Geneva, he had planned on taking the train to Zurich to check on the status of the account that Liu Tang had supposedly opened for him at Union Banque Privée. However, upon hearing of the man's death he got cold feet and had decided against it. He didn't want to be implicated any further on anything related to the Corporation. He would visit Zurich at another time after all of the investigations related to the Corporation had run their course. As of now, he only had Liu Tang's word that the account had been established on his behalf. He had never received any correspondence from Union Banque Privée to the effect. But that didn't surprise him because it was quite customary for private banking clients to have their account statements and transaction advice withheld until the clients paid a visit. After all, the point of private banking was to keep the relationship between the bank and the client exclusive and away from prying eyes.

The American wondered if Liu Tang had made an additional payment to his account in compensation for the transaction that had transpired with the Russians. He knew that the Russians had been paid, but there had been no further communication with regard to his compensation. The Corporation had been seized by the Chinese government and there would be no further transactions. It was just as well. The initial fifty thousand USD was an incredible amount of money to be paid for the little that he had done. It was also tax-free, as he was certain that the Corporation would not be reporting anything to the IRS. The American had never signed anything with the Corporation, nor had he signed any documents for Union Banque Privée. As of now, he could not be implicated in any way with regard to anything related to the Corporation, and he was glad for that. If his bank should ever find out that he had been working for the Corporation, he would certainly lose his job.

CHAPTER TWENTY-FIVE

STRAVINSKY WAS one of the American's favorite composers, and Nadya knew it. That was why she had called him, to give him the news that they were about to put in their little theater a new production of Stravinsky's *The Fairy's Kiss*. But the news about Liu Tang's death had been so terrible that there was no way that she could begin to talk to him about it.

Nadya had to admit that the American banker had fascinated her. She had not expected that he would be so cultured. It was refreshing to hear him give his honest and intelligent perspectives about what most interested her too. The man could genuinely appreciate the architectural beauty of a historical landmark, the divine grace in an Italian sculpture, and the sublime and intellectual richness in a Stravinsky score. Nadya would have to call him back at another time, because she really wanted to know what he had to say about Stravinsky's work, about *The Fairy's Kiss*.

Stravinsky had said in his old age that he tried to capture in his music the lost beauty of the fairy-tale world that he had known as a child. *The Fairy's Kiss* and *The Nightingale* were two works of Stravinsky's that Nadya knew were based on fairy tales by Hans Christian Andersen. *The Nightingale* was a tale about a Chinese Emperor who preferred the tinkling of a bejeweled mechanical bird to the song of a real nightingale. Nadya wanted to have the little theater produce the work because she thought that it would be a great deal of fun to create the exotic Asian scenery and costumes. But for budgetary reasons they decided that for now, they would go along with her second choice, which was *The Fairy's Kiss*. For the production, they could recycle some of the costumes that they already had in stock. This would save time and money. The Nightingale would be produced at a later date.

Mikhail and Victor were surprised to hear that the American had not made any sexual advances on her.

"Maybe he's queer," Mikhail had said, jokingly.

"Maybe he just likes prostitutes because there is something wrong with him," Victor added.

Nadya didn't volunteer anything. She didn't know what to say. The American was almost twice her age.

Even after heavy drinking, he had not made any sexual advances to her, and she respected that. *He is of the old school*, she thought. Most men were not like that, especially bankers who thought that everything was available for a price. And the younger men just wanted to screw anything in sight. She would have allowed the American to have her. He had big, dark, penetrating eyes. They were soulful eyes. But even after all that time they had spent together, she still had no clue what it was that he was after. He never complained about family life, which was the typical argument men gave when they tried to justify being unfaithful to their wives. He didn't really give anything away that was personal in nature. He never asked for anything either. Maybe he was a goddamned spy. *Who can know?* She laughed out loud as she thought about it. *What does a man like that want?*

"Victor, do you know that Liu Tang is dead?"

"What? No, I can't believe it. How do you know? Did the American tell you?"

"Yes," Nadya responded.

"How does he know? I must say that I'm not surprised. I tried calling him at his office and got no response. Nobody could tell me where he was nor tell me how I could find him."

"The American found out from a Chinese government agent who spoke to him in Geneva. Apparently, the Corporation that Liu Tang worked for was involved in criminal activity. The government agents were in Geneva to seize the Corporation's assets and to find out everything they could about the origins of the account. During their interview, when the American brought up his name, that was when they told him that Liu Tang was dead. They implied that he had been murdered, but weren't willing to give away much on the topic."

"Wow, Victor," said Mikhail to his business associate with contempt. "Do you see how close we were to being screwed by those fucking Chinese? Thank God that we had that Letter of Credit in place with the American's bank. That is the only way that you can deal with these people. We might have been screwed out of our money. That fucking Liu Tang," he added in anger.

"But Liu Tang was more than likely killed by the criminals behind the Corporation. Why be angry with him," protested Nadya in Liu Tang's defense.

"Maybe you're right, Nadya. Perhaps Liu Tang is, as you suggest, innocent. But if he was so stupid that he didn't know who he was dealing with, then it was right that he should die. My God, because of the man's ignorance we were put in jeopardy. We could have lost an incredible sum of money. The man was an incompetent and he is better off dead." Nadya knew that Mikhail and Victor were part of a syndicate, but she had never suspected that they were really ruthless. She was horrified by what Mikhail had just said and visibly shaken.

"Nadya, did you ever get an opportunity to study Darwinism at your university?" Victor added, smiling at her. "Darwin had a theory about why certain species survived and why others became extinct. It's all about the survival of the fittest."

"That's right," Mikhail added. "The capitalists have a similar application to the theory in the business world. They refer to it as economic Darwinism. It's the same concept, the survival of the fittest. Only the strong can survive." He looked at her and laughed. "Now, Nadya," he quickly added, "Victor and I have to go over some things. Could you ask our waitress to bring us another round of drinks and give us a little time?"

Nadya turned to do as he had requested, but was in total shock by the attitude of the two men. She had never witnessed their cold-hearted arguments before. It was true that they had a reputation, but she had no idea about the type of men that they really were. And they were right, of course. In order to survive in this cruel world, you had to fight hard. Eat or be eaten, people always said. These men had always been extremely generous with her. They were always giving her very pricey gifts or little envelopes with nice amounts of money. They had often told her that a woman of her beauty deserved to dress fashionably well. They also said that they wanted her to succeed with her art, and they looked at helping her as an investment that they were certain would pay off handsomely someday. In exchange, they sometimes expected Nadya to provide them with little bits of what they referred to as harmless information, such as to let them know when so-and-so would show up at the restaurant and whether he was alone or in company. And they would ask her, did so-and-so make any calls while he was at the restaurant or what time did so-and-so leave. Those were the types of questions that she answered for them. She didn't do much more for them and didn't know much about their business. She was also smart enough to know to keep her mouth shut regarding anything related to them.

Mikhail and Victor often dined at the hotel's restaurant. Sometimes they dined with prominent businessmen or with high-ranking government officials. They were clearly well-connected with the power brokers. They had the connections that would obtain travel visas for them at a moment's notice. The parties that they hosted were always well attended by the right society types, and on those occasions, they were always a lot of fun to be around. The good booze flowed freely, and everyone had plenty to eat. At the parties, Nadya had met celebrity actors and famous female tennis stars. Sometimes there were also well-known writers, and it was not uncommon for her to run into professors from her university. Nadya had been grateful that Mikhail had always remembered to include her on the list of invitees.

Nadya Ivanovna, she tried to reason with herself, *why concern yourself over the death of Liu Tang?* There was not very much that she knew about him, except that he was a banker from China and that he had been in some sort of business with Mikhail and Victor. Liu Tang had visited Russia on several occasions, and how Mikhail and Victor became acquainted with him she never knew. But she knew that some sort of an agreement had been reached between them about future transactions because on one occasion, they requested that she bring to their table a bottle of very fine champagne in order to celebrate what they hoped would the beginning of a successful partnership. That celebration had happened less than a year ago, and now Liu Tang was dead. It was very obvious to Nadya, by their initial reactions, that neither Mikhail nor Victor had anything to do with Liu Tang's death. But it had shocked her to see how little they cared about the death of their new business associate.

The American came from a different world, a new world for Nadya. It was natural for a young, educated woman like Nadya to want to see more of it, and she knew that she didn't want to see it with Mikhail or Victor, or through their eyes. She wanted a wholly fresh perspective on things, not more of what she already knew. She also didn't like being indebted to them. She expected that at some point they would want to cash in

on their so-called investment, as they had referred to
their helping her. She hoped that she would never have
to know what that meant. She needed to get away from
them before it was too late, and she was willing to risk
anything for a chance to take that plunge.

ON THE SECOND MONDAY IN JANUARY, THE AMERICAN
received another telephone call from Russia. He recognized the call as being from the hotel where Nadya
worked, so he answered it reluctantly. He didn't want
anything more to do with Mikhail, Victor, or any of the
other members of the wealthy mobster class.

But the very intelligent and resourceful Nadya had a
most beautiful face and the body to match, and being
able to chat with her again was an opportunity that he
couldn't pass on.

"Hello. Is this James?" the familiar voice asked.

"Hi Nadya, it's such a pleasure to hear your voice
again. How are you doing?" the American asked.

"Quite well, thank you. I called you the last time in
order to let you know that we were going to put on a
new Stravinsky production in our little theater. I
thought that you would like to know since you are such a
fan, and because you took such an interest in our other
productions." Her attitude toward him was very warm
this time, which was maybe because the mobsters were

not around. She seemed to acknowledge that they were a team.

"Oh, that's wonderful!" the American responded. "But I have a feeling that your little theater group must also be huge fans of the composer since this will now be your third attempt with his work."

"Yes, that and the fact that his ballet scores are just the right length for our audience. The storylines are also simple to follow, and there are very few characters that appear. All of these factors make for perfect productions."

"Yes, I can see that. And the music is not bad either."

"Yes, best of all is the music," she quickly agreed. "He still sounds so modern and so relevant for today's audience. He is the perfect composer for our type of theater."

The American couldn't help but love this woman, and it was obvious that it was not just because of her incredible looks.

"What work will your theater be producing?" he asked.

"*The Fairy's Kiss*," she quickly answered.

"*The Fairy's Kiss*, of course," he said. "It's the perfect choice."

"Why don't you come back to St. Petersburg so that we can go over everything together? I want to show you the wonderful puppets that they have already made and the remarkable scenery."

"Your enthusiasm is very catching. I'm jealous that I am not part of the production team."

"Then come to St. Petersburg and I shall make you my personal assistant," she said, laughing. "But don't expect to get paid," she quickly added. "We have no funds to spare."

"I would love to be your assistant, but I'm sorry to have to say that you won't get much out of me."

"Ah, you see, you are already speaking like a true Russian. You don't want to do any work, and I can perfectly understand that since there is no pay involved. You will fit right in here in Russia," and she began to laugh hard after having said it. "We work for very little pay," she then added and began laughing again.

"Nadya, you misunderstood me. I will be happy to be your assistant for nothing. It would really please me. But I have no talent whatsoever. So, I just wanted to warn you."

"No problem. You will get paid nothing and you will be good for nothing. As I said, you will fit right in here," and with that, she began laughing uncontrollably. "So, when will I see you again? I think we get along quite well, and you really make me laugh. You help me to forget all of my problems."

"A beauty like you?" he said. "What problems can you

possibly have? You have all those rich boyfriends around to protect you and to take care of you."

"You are wrong," she quickly objected. "They are not my boyfriends, and I don't want to have anything to do with them." There was a momentary silence at both ends when she said this.

"I can't get to St. Petersburg anytime soon," he said. "You know that there are entry visa requirements and all of those bureaucratic complications. But I'm planning on a trip to Geneva soon. Do you think that you can meet me there?" He didn't want to say that he was actually going to Zurich to check on the status of the account that had been supposedly opened for him. He didn't want to volunteer any information related to that in case Mikhail or Victor were listening.

"Hmm" was what she uttered in response. "I wish that it was that easy for me. The only way to quickly get a visa would be by asking Mikhail or Victor for assistance. I know that they have the connections and can probably obtain one for me, but I don't want to tell them that I want the visa because I want to meet you. These men can sometimes be very jealous. I will have to give it some thought. Do you already know when you will be going?"

"No, there is nothing definite yet. I can wait a while to see if you can work something out. I really would love to see you again," he sincerely added.

"Good, then I will see what I can do and get back to you. I promise to let you know soon."

"Sounds like a plan," he said. "I'll keep my fingers crossed."

"Your fingers crossed?" she asked.

"That means for luck," he explained.

"Ah. In Russia, we say, 'Ya budu za tebya derjat kulaki,' which means 'I will hold my little fist for you.' This is also meant for luck. Thank you, then. I will call you soon either way."

"Great. I look forward to it."

"Me too," she said. "Goodbye."

"Bye, Nadya."

The American was quite surprised by Nadya's interest in wanting to continue the friendship. Normally, when he made new acquaintances on overseas business trips, the relationships would typically fizzle out when the trip came to an end. The business cards exchanged would be used primarily to prepare expense reports, but rarely would they be used for follow-up calls unless there was a genuine business need. The vendors at the conferences were the exceptions. They were the only ones that followed up on every business card that came into their hands, and that was because they did have a vested interest in selling their products and services. But rarely would a call be made when there was no business interest to be gained.

But Nadya wasn't a business acquaintance. She was a byproduct of the conference. Intimate relationships that developed during a conference were a different case altogether. Sometimes correspondences were exchanged between the individuals that persisted for the first few weeks after a conference. These exchanges were sometimes made in response to promises that had been made during those brief periods of intimacy. But these also gradually petered out after a short interval, when it became obvious to both that there was little to be gained by continuing the long-distance dialogue. That was the primary reason why these relationships also usually came to a quick end. With time, the importance of the relationship would come to be redefined to what it really had been, a meaningless fling.

But why Nadya had now showed so much interest in wanting to meet him was something that he couldn't quite understand. If her only interest was to exchange ideas with him on the new marionette production, well, they could easily do that over the internet. He was significantly older than she was, so he did not have any romantic illusions, though it was certainly fun to fantasize. Nadya possessed those refined good looks and that sensual promise that would stir any man's emotions. It would be hard to refuse her anything.

Nadya had told him that she had tried her hand at sculpting a wooden puppet once. She had first sculpted the wood into a puppet's head. Then she proceeded to sculpt the entire puppet, sanding him and painting him beautifully with oil paint. Finally, she was taught how to make the eyes blink and the mouth move. "It was funny," she said, "I started making him with one image in mind, but then he gradually transformed into something else. You just have to go with it and see what comes out of the process." Nadya had been very proud of her first creation. "You know," she confided, "the puppet master told me that in his experience, the best puppets made were those that worked themselves out. If you forced them to be something, they usually didn't turn out as well. That's the secret to making a good puppet."

You just have to go with it, and let things work out, the American repeated to himself. Nadya, you are an enchantress! I am confused by you. I can't resist you. These things were whirling through the American's mind on the day that Nadya called. It was going to be another sleepless night.

CHAPTER TWENTY-SIX

ON THE FOLLOWING MONDAY, the American received another call from St. Petersburg. He waited until the fourth ring before picking up the receiver.

"Hello, is this James?" He had expected to hear Nadya's voice, but it was Mikhail on the line.

"Hello. Mikhail?" the American asked.

"Correct, my friend," responded the Russian. How are you doing? Is everything going well?"

"Yes. Everything is fine. And how goes everything with you, Mikhail?"

"Everything is OK with me too. Listen," the Russian began, "I was talking to Victor and we were both thinking that it was unfortunate with what happened on your first transaction with this goddamned Chinese corporation. It was very unfortunate, you know."

"Hey, Mikhail, things happen. Luckily we were not injured by it."

"That is correct, my friend," said Mikhail. "And we all made our money. So, you see, as long as we keep to the very strict banking terms and conditions, we will always be OK."

"Yes," the American responded, "except for poor Liu Tang."

"Correct, but that was not our problem and not our fault. We had nothing to do with the Corporation or anything else on that side of the world."

"Yes, you're absolutely right," said the American, not wanting to get into a discussion about it.

"That's right, my friend. The world is a tough place, and you have to watch out for yourself at all times. But that doesn't mean that you need to shy away from business. It just means that you need to know what you are doing and always be on your guard. There are plenty of opportunities out there."

"Absolutely, Mikhail," the American assented.

"Good, that is what I was hoping you would say. I can see that you and your bank know exactly what you are doing. That is critical when you are dealing with these goddamned foreign markets. Expertise! If you have expertise, you can make money."

The American didn't respond to this last comment.

He was waiting to see where the Russian was going to take the conversation.

"Look," began Mikhail again, "we want you to visit us in St. Petersburg again. We like you, and we think that we can do more business together. There are plenty of other Chinese firms that want to do business with us. China is the future, you know. There is a great deal of money to be made with the Chinese. You shouldn't get cold feet." The Russian waited to see how the American was going to react before continuing.

"Well, Mikhail, I work for a bank, and it's the credit risk group that determines whether or not they still have an appetite for the market. The initial transaction left our Geneva affiliate with a rather sour taste."

"Yes, I understand. But the Chinese market is huge, and you shouldn't close yourself off to its potential. After all, we are in the business to make money. You just have to be careful and take all the precautions to make sure that you are covered. Keep in mind that if you don't go in someone else will."

"Yes, I understand."

"Good. Listen, why don't you come to visit us? We would like to discuss with you some interesting possibilities in China. Even if you can't commit, at least come to hear what we have to say, and what we think will be a good possibility for us and your bank. Of course, you can expect proper compensation for helping to close every transaction. What do you say?"

"Let me think about it."

"Sure. Why don't you do that? Let me know if you are interested."

"Ok, I'll let you know."

There was no reference made to Nadya in the conversation, and that pleased the American. The more entangled things became, the less likely that he would be willing to participate. If Nadya, Mikhail, and Victor worked as a unit, then he didn't want any part of it. For now, he had only Nadya's word that she didn't have anything to do with them. But he wasn't certain that that was the case, and he wasn't going to take any chances. Everyone talked about making money, but he hadn't seen any of it yet. It was time to take a trip to Zurich to see if he had been paid what he had been promised.

THE FIRST THING THAT HE NOTICED ABOUT HER WAS how she was dressed. She had on a washed-out Levi's jacket with sequins and a tight, black, short skirt. Her face was an oval, and her hair was jet-black and clipped short with a sheen that invited touching. She wore a little rouge on her otherwise pale skin, and she had on the same color pigment on her full seductive lips. She was surprisingly tall for an Asian and somewhat flat-chested. Liu Tang would have liked her.

He had opened the door for her almost naked, except for the expertly pressed light blue buttoned-down Polo shirt that he was still wearing. She smiled at him as she entered the luxurious hotel room. She scanned around to make sure that he was all alone, and then she pirouetted for him to make sure that what he saw was what he wanted. He had been very clear on the phone with the agency, emphasizing that if she were not pretty he would not be accepting her services. But she was very pretty, and she knew it. After noting his approval, she extended her hand out to him, waiting for payment, wanting to settle immediately the financial side of the transaction. He quickly handed her the money without saying a word, and she silently counted it in front of him before putting it away in her oversized black leather purse. Neither of them had spoken a word. He was very pleased with the girl, and she seemed to also be in approval of her client.

The room was dark, except for the light that had filtered in from the bathroom. Soft romantic lighting, he remembered thinking, to help put you in the mood. She walked toward the light and on her way noticed that he had an opened bottle of wine on the desk that was already half-finished. She entered the bathroom and closed the door behind her, and he sat waiting on the edge of the bed in the semi-dark room.

When she came out of the bathroom she was still dressed. She looked at him and smiled again as she began to remove her clothing, placing them carefully on the elegant Gibson chair that was near the bed. The last things that he noticed her removing were the leopard-print panties and matching bra. After removing these, she walked over to him and began unbuttoning his shirt. He stopped her for a moment to kiss her hands, which made her laugh. She brought her hands back down to continue unbuttoning his shirt, and when she had finished, she was happy to see that he already had a full erection.

As she removed his shirt, he bent down to kiss her flat stomach, lots of tender little kisses on her abdomen. She stopped him for a moment so that she could lie on the bed. Her legs were parted and slightly raised so that he could easily move into the position that he evidently wanted. He held firmly onto her backside so that he could rub himself firmly against her, and after a while, she stopped him. He could tell that she had orgasmed.

Afterward, they drank some of the fine Bordeaux wine that was on the desk from the same glass, as if they had been longtime intimate lovers. The setting couldn't have been more romantic, and he didn't even know her name.

Finally, she began to dress in the same slow methodical way as when she had first disrobed. He watched her from the bed as she readied herself to leave, picking up her purse. She then came over to the bed, bent down, and kissed him on the cheek, and promptly left. They had not said a word to each other at any time. The transaction was complete. He had felt the release of bodily tension. He now could sleep soundly tonight.

AFTER THE ESCORT HAD GONE HE SHOWERED, DRESSED, gathered his belongings, and exited the hotel room. In the lobby, he went straight to the bar for one last nightcap.

"Extra dry vodka martini, shaken and not stirred, with three olives."

"Excellent, Mr. Bond," said the waitress, smiling. "Any special brand of vodka?"

"I want something Russian," he responded.

"How about Stolichnaya," she offered.

"That's not Russian, but it'll do," he said.

The American didn't have any problems having an occasional drink alone at a fancy bar or a gourmet meal alone at an elegant restaurant. As far as he was concerned, he earned it and deserved it, and he didn't necessarily need company to enjoy himself. He never felt lonely when he was alone.

"Here you are sir," said the freckled-faced barmaid. She had perfect, gleaming, straight white teeth and sported that lovely ponytail that kept her hair in place and that he always found so sexy.

After finishing his drink, he paid his bill and left the hotel. It was time to go home.

CHAPTER TWENTY-SEVEN

In a well-run business, there is always one man who is the office tyrant. Mikhail Potanin was confident, observant, prying, and meticulous. He was the one man whose authority extended into the private and personal habits of the men and women of his organization. And he was a strong disciplinarian and indifferent to opinion. He was also a watchdog over even the minutest of things and reduced disruptive influences by providing his team with a common target.

"Blind chance has ruled a man's life in this country of ours for many years," Mikhail said. "Fear by night and a feverish effort by day to pretend enthusiasm for a system of lies were what we had in the past. Solzhenitsyn described it beautifully once when he said that any adult inhabitant of this country, from a collective farmer up to a member of the Politburo, always knew that it would take only one careless word or gesture and he would be banished, never to be seen or heard from again. And much has been written about the absurdly minor infractions for which individuals were sentenced to ten years in labor camps, which was for all practical purposes as good as a death sentence. But all that has changed. You were here recently and you had an opportunity to see firsthand how things are improving. For God's sake, in the most sacred area of Moscow's Christ the Savior Cathedral, we had the Russian female punk rock group Pussy Riot performing their controversial punk rock prayer calling for Putin to be chased away! Everything has now changed, and money is all that matters."

"My friend," Mo Yan responded, with a grin, "the system of forced labor camps based on the Soviet gulags was instituted throughout China soon after the communists came to power in 1949. The justification for their implementation was the remolding of bad elements into fine socialist workers. And, unfortunately for us in China, the use of compulsory labor as a means of reform and re-education, both within and outside the regular prison system, remains very much in place. I totally agree with you when you say that money is indeed all that matters, so it should not be surprising for you to hear that the Chinese government uses these vast pools of free labor to make a great deal of it. China's prisons produce everything from green tea to coal, paperclips to footballs, and medical gloves to high-grade electronic equipment. China is now home to the world's largest slave labor camp, and America is their number one customer. China's Laogai, the system of forced labor camps, has become as notorious as Stalin's Gulag."

"So, I guess what you are saying, Mo Yan, is that things have not politically degenerated to the extent that they have in Russia."

"Quite so," Mo Yan confirmed. "But that is not to say that we have not seen tremendous changes taking place in China for those that understand the system and that are politically well connected. There are tremendous amounts of foreign currency entering China today. I believe that China now has the second-largest number of billionaires in the world. Recent statistics show that there are currently more than a hundred billionaires in our country, and nine out of ten are self-made. To be sure, many of those self-made billionaires did not make their money honestly. Money is intertwined with polit- ical power, so it is not surprising then to find that Beijing and Shanghai have the highest number of billion- aires in the country."

"It sounds like everything is going good for you

then," Mikhail said. "So, why are you here? Why did you want to see me?"

"Mikhail, like in your country, you can never rely on the stability of the political system. With that uncertainty always looming, it is necessary to take precautions. One of the serious problems that the government faces is the flight of capital, and it is easy to understand why."

"Mo Yan, Russia has the largest number of billionaires in the world, and the problems with capital flight in our country have been well documented. But, as I said, what can I do for you?"

"Liu Tang apparently established a relationship with a banker in America who opened an account in Geneva. My understanding is that they were the bank that paid you for a transaction in goods that were shipped from Cuba. I would like very much to speak to the banker about the possibility of establishing another relationship with the bank."

"And Liu Tang is no longer available to assist you with this because he is dead?" said Mikhail, wanting to see how the man was going to react.

"That is, unfortunately, quite correct," Mo Yan responded in a matter-of-fact manner, not betraying any emotion whatsoever. "He seemed to have been mixed up with something illegal, and it cost him his life."

"That shocked us when we heard about it. Liu Tang

was here for a banking conference several months ago, and he seemed to be quite an honest guy. It surprises me to hear that he was involved with something illegal," said Mikhail.

"Well, that is what I was told. I don't really know much more than that."

"I see," responded Mikhail, not really believing Mo Yan's story.

"I was hoping that you would provide me the contact information for the American. I have associates in a firm that could be interested in establishing an account with his bank. The consensus seems to be that he was quite efficient in moving along the opening of accounts with his Geneva office. We would very much like to meet with him."

"I'll see what I can do, Mo Yan," was the Russian's response. "Let me see if I still have the American's card in my office, and I will get back to you."

"Excellent! Please, here is where you can reach me."

"We'll be talking, my friend."

"I DON'T TRUST THAT CHINAMAN," MIKHAIL TOLD Victor after Mo Yan had taken his leave. Victor had been silent throughout the meeting. "Did you notice how he didn't say much about Liu Tang? He didn't say anything about the man except that he may have been involved with some illegal activity that may have caused his death."

"Yes, Mikhail," Victor agreed. "Why would Mo Yan want to have any references to any of Liu Tang's business contacts if he knew Liu Tang to be dealing in something illegal? You would expect that someone would want to steer clear of anything related to any of that if Liu Tang was as corrupt as he believes."

"Obviously, the answer is that Mo Yan is just as corrupt. All of these fucking Chinese businessmen are crooked. That is how they made their fucking millions. You heard him admit as much." After a moment's pause, he added, "The man must be politically well connected."

"Yes," Victor added. "He probably wants to have some of his capital fly out of China too. Maybe that is why he is looking for the American."

"You could be correct, Victor. I wonder how he knew where to find us. How did he know we were going to be in the hotel restaurant tonight? And how the fuck did he know that we knew the American?"

"Liu Tang must have told him about us or told someone else who knows Mo Yan."

"Yes, that may well be the case, Victor. But I don't trust him. I'll call the American to see what he thinks and if he wants me to give this Mo Yan his number. I don't want to cause any trouble for the American. You never know, we may need to work with him again."

. . .

THE AMERICAN LEFT HIS HOUSE UNUSUALLY EARLY that morning. He had a significant workload to get off his hands before leaving for Switzerland. The morning express bus had been unusually late and was very crowded. He was feeling impatient and restless but didn't want to admit that it was because he didn't know what to expect in Zurich. For Christ's sake, Liu Tang had lost his life for some inexplicable reason related to this. There was no need to involve anyone else in this business.

The bus rumbled on past the old port of Miami and then finally turned toward Brickell Avenue. It had taken him an hour and a half to finally reach his office. At Coral Way, he got off and walked the two short blocks to his office.

The American slumped into his chair with a thud and laid his forehead on the desk just as his phone began to ring.

"Hello there," a woman's voice said without introduction. "I'm sorry I've been late in getting back to you." It was Nadya on the line. It took him a few moments before he finally replied.

"I've been working myself to death," he said, in a drier tone of voice than he had intended. Nadya laughed in response.

"You must have a pretty tough job," she said. This time the silence was longer at his end of the line. "I'm calling to let you know that I was able to get a travel visa, and I am free to leave at any time." Christ, he thought, he couldn't believe that this was really happening. For a moment he didn't know how to respond. What do you want from me, he wanted to ask her but didn't.

"That's great because I really want to see you," he heard himself respond. Was it really worth the effort to see her again?

She got up and restlessly paced around the hotel's kitchen with the phone pressed to her ear. She was staring out into the dusk again when she noticed that Mikhail and Victor were walking toward the restaurant from the other side of the street.

"Listen, I have to go. May I call you later tonight?"

"Yes, of course. By the way, I will be flying to Switzerland tomorrow."

"I'll call you later," she said and quickly terminated the call.

The American felt ill at ease but decided that he would continue the conversation with her later to see where it would take them.

.   .   .

Not more than twenty minutes later the phone was ringing again, and from the display, he knew that the call was from St. Petersburg.

"Hello. Is this James?" came from Nadya. "How are you doing?" She was acting as though she had not recently spoken to him. He would play along.

"Hi, Nadya. Yes, this is James." The American looked at his watch, which had a white face with black hands and black numbers. He had purchased it because it resembled the face of the famous clock in Grand Central Station. The Terminal Clock, as it was famously referred to, was a popular meeting place for the public. "How is it going?" he said, anxious to get to the heart of the matter.

"Just fine," she quickly answered. "Listen, Mikhail has just arrived, and he has asked me to call you. Let me put him on the line." That explained everything. That was why she had abruptly disconnected the last time that she called, and why she had been so cautious in her greeting.

"Hello, James," the Russian said with his raspy voice. "How are you?"

"Fine, just fine!" answered the American.

"That's great. Listen, James, I'm calling you because there is a wealthy Chinese businessman who knew Liu Tang who has asked me to pass along your contact information. I think he is interested in doing business with your bank. I thought I would let you know before giving him your details so that you could prepare yourself. You know, it could be another opportunity to make some money, just like I told you before."

"Yeah, thank you, Mikhail. Did he say who he was and where he was calling from?"

"He was calling from Shanghai. He said his name was Mo Yan."

"Did you say Mo Yan from Shanghai?" asked the American in disbelief.

"That's right, my friend."

The American took a moment before deciding on how to respond. "Mikhail, Liu Tang told me that the man was a bastard. He apparently is a big executive at The Bank of China in Shanghai where Liu Tang worked. Liu Tang admitted to me one night that the man was screwing his wife. He hated the man."

Mikhail whistled and laughed in disbelief when he heard this. "Son of a bitch!" the Russian said. "You know, I knew that there was something strange about the man when I spoke to him. Son of a bitch! These fucking Chinese are real shits! I'll take their money, but I don't trust them."

"Mikhail, please don't give my number to the man. I just have a bad feeling about him even though I have never met him or spoken to him. According to Liu Tang, the man had made life hell for him at home and at work. Liu Tang was planning to leave his wife and the bank as things became financially viable from the income he was earning from the Corporation. It's the same Corporation that bought your sugar."

"Yeah, right," Mikhail said. "Thank God that I was paid on that shipment. I could have lost a great deal of money on that transaction. The government could have confiscated the goods and frozen the Corporation's assets. That was why I was closely following the money issue with you. Twenty-five million dollars is a lot of money, and you never can trust these goddamn Chinese. There is too much corruption all over the place. Now, do you see why we wanted to set up the Letter of Credit with your bank in Geneva?"

"Absolutely, I understand. But if there was something shaky about the Corporation, you should have told me. We would not have taken on the risk for the fee."

"Well, I didn't know that they were a shaky firm. I'm sure your bank did due diligence and noticed that the Board Members were all very reputable and wealthy businessmen. But you never know who you are dealing with in that country. It is as corrupt as Russia." They both laughed at this last comment. "Anyway, don't worry about it. I won't give Mo Yan any of your details."

"Thank you, Mikhail."

"But this has nothing to do with the other transactions that I previously mentioned to you. I think that there are all sorts of possibilities with China. You just have to be cautious and know what you are doing. I think that we can be a good team," Mikhail added. "We just won't deal with that bastard Mo Yan. Please let me know when you are ready to work with me and don't be afraid."

"Don't worry, I'm not afraid. Anyway, the ultimate decision is not mine. I have to make a brief trip soon. As soon as I get back I'll get in contact with you through Nadya, at the hotel."

"Yes, please do that. We can't let opportunities pass by. OK, thank you."

"Thank you, Mikhail, and goodbye."

Mo Yan, thought the American. What the hell was he after, and why did he want to get in touch with me? "No dice," he said to himself. "Nothing doing, Mo Yan," he continued. "There is not even a slim chance, no fucking way."

IT WAS VERY APPARENT THAT NADYA HAD NOT BEEN involved with Mikhail in any way with regard to her plans to travel, and the American could certainly understand why. But he was leaving for Switzerland tomorrow, and Nadya had not been able to discuss what her intentions were or whether she would be able to meet him at such short notice. He considered calling her but refrained from doing so because he didn't want in any way to jeopardize anything for her. He would have to wait to see if she would call him again later that night.

This was all very fascinating stuff. It had all of the dramatic elements of a suspenseful Hollywood movie. The banker was taking a trip to Switzerland in order to get his hands on at least fifty thousand dollars that had been deposited into a secret private bank account opened with him as beneficiary by a man who had been recently murdered. Nadya was the beautiful Russian heroine who was presumably trying to escape from the grips of the mob. Mo Yan was the mysterious Asian mogul lurking in the shadows, who was trying to contact him, but only God knew why. The Russian mobsters were courting him with promises for bigger financial payoffs if he would enter into business with them, but they were dangerous men and could not be trusted. Was Liu Tang murdered before he was able to wire any of the funds?

There was always the possibility that Liu Tang had not been murdered. Maybe Liu Tang realized that the Corporation was about to be seized by the Chinese government and decided to take off with whatever money he had access to before the funds were frozen. The American didn't really know what Liu Tang was capable of, so he shouldn't be shocked if he were to find out that Liu Tang had taken off with his money. The rumors were that Liu Tang had been part of the team that committed illegal activity for the Corporation, but there was no way for the American to confirm if anything had really happened to him. Tomorrow he would be flying to Switzerland, and the day after he would pay a visit to the bank in Zurich. After that, he would know where he stood.

CHAPTER TWENTY-EIGHT

THE AMERICAN'S flight was booked from Miami to Madrid, and then on to Geneva. He didn't really need to go to Geneva since the private bank was in Zurich, but it was a good cover.

AFTER A FEW VODKA MARTINIS AT THE BAR OF THE Woodrow Wilson hotel in Geneva that evening, followed by a fine Lebanese meal in the hotel's small restaurant, he was ready for an early turn-in. Early the next morning he would board the train that would take him to Zurich.

. . .

THE NEXT MORNING IN ZURICH, AT THE PRECISE SWISS time of 10:00 am, the American entered a small four-story building on a quiet side street that bore a very small sign indicating that it was Union Banque Privée. The American was escorted to the receptionist's office by a security guard where he was asked by the very well-dressed woman in her early thirties how she could be of service. The woman had addressed him in German.

"Do you speak English?" the American asked.

"Of course," she said. "How may I help you?"

"Yes," began the American, feeling a little humbled by the attention that he was being given for the very small account that he hoped was there in his favor. He knew that the private bank accounts usually had minimum balances of five million US dollars. He would probably be asked to close the account or to forward additional funds if he had planned to keep the account active. The only concessions made for keeping small accounts were when they were linked to a family of accounts that had significant sums of money. At least that was the policy for the accounts that were kept in the private banking offices where he worked, and that was also the policy with the Geneva affiliate office. Perhaps his account had been tied to a series of accounts that the Chinese members of the Corporation kept at Union Banque Privée. But if that were the case, then the fact that the Corporation had been seized by the Chinese government didn't bode well for him. It may even be the case that his account had been seized by the Chinese government. At any rate, he would know soon enough.

"Yes," he began again. "I'm here to access my account."

"Very good," she responded. "If you wouldn't mind, could you please tell me who your private banker is?"

"I'm afraid that I don't know that," he said.

"Very well, no problem," she went on. "Could you please tell me your account number and name? With that information, I should be able to assist you," she said. Then she took a moment to reappraise his appearance, curious as to who he was and how much he was worth. He was wearing a typical single-breasted navy suit with a light blue Polo shirt and a pink and blue striped tie. Nothing extravagant, she thought, nothing exceptional. But in today's world, you couldn't really tell by appearance. She watched him while he fumbled through his weather-beaten black leather wallet for the information that she had requested.

"Here you are," he said, producing a small sheet of paper with the account number 43111999 written on it, along with the reference account name P.S. Financier. In private bank accounts in Switzerland, it was customary not to have the proper name of the client appearing as the name on the account. The papers in the client files would disclose the real name of the individual. This secrecy and confidentiality kept client names from appearing anywhere in electronic records. With the creative account names, there was virtually no chance of anyone being able to extract the client's information through hacking or any other social engineering scams that went on through the internet.

"Very good," she said. "Give me a moment to retrieve your files. I'll be right back."

His hands were sweating, and he was feeling nervous. *Fucking Liu Tang, what have you gotten me into? May you rest in peace!*

Several minutes later the woman arrived with a thin file in her hands.

"Right," she said. "Let's have a look then. Can you please provide me with some personal identification?" He gave her his American passport. She glanced at it and looked at his face. "Here you are," she said, after verifying his credentials and the balance in his account. "This includes the most recent deposit into your account. Your confirmations and transaction advice are included. Please take a look and let me know if there is anything else that I can do for you. May I get you an espresso or some water?"

"An espresso would be nice."

"Great, I'll let you look over the files while I get that for you."

The American politely took the folder from her and opened it to the account statement once she had left his side. He looked at the statement, noted that there were three transfers made to his account on three different occasions, and glanced across the page to look at the amounts. The first transaction was for the agreed fifty thousand dollars and had the reference: Initial sign-on bonus. The second transaction was a deposit of twenty-five thousand dollars and had the reference: First transaction commission. The third transaction was a deposit of twenty-two million dollars and had the reference: From the Street of Eternal Happiness. The total value in the account was 22,075,000 dollars!

The last deposit had been tainted with blood, Liu Tang's blood! The reference to the Street of Eternal Happiness indicated that it had been he who had instructed the transfer of funds. There were lots of loose ends here, and the American didn't have much to go on. He also knew that the last thing that he needed to do was to draw attention to himself or the money. The money had been sitting idly in the account for months, and that was a favorable sign. When the Chinese government seized the account in Geneva they were content to confiscate whatever money was held in deposit there. They probably assumed that any money that had been transferred out of the account could probably not be traced. The secrecy laws in Switzerland made it difficult to follow cash flows. It was also fortunate that the account had not been opened in his name. It was very unlikely that the account could ever be traced back to him.

Beate Jung, that was the name of the woman that was attending him. When she returned, she carried a silver serving tray with an espresso coffee that was served in a fine bone china demitasse. When she noticed that he had a perplexed expression, she asked him if everything was in order.

"Yes, everything is in order." He then took a sip of the coffee and didn't know what he should do next.

"Will you be able to be my banker, Ms. Jung?" he asked her.

"Yes, most certainly, if that is what you would like. But I will need to know a few more things about you in order to know how best to look after your needs."

"I understand," he responded. "You would like me to complete a client profile, and things of that nature?"

"Yes, that's right," she confirmed, quite pleased to see that she was dealing with someone that understood the business. "Could you begin by telling me what type of business it is that you do?"

"I'm a banker," he said.

"Ah? Then why are you with us, if I may ask?"

"Confidentiality, Ms. Jung. Like everyone else who has an account in Switzerland."

She studied him for a moment, waiting to see if he would be elaborating on it.

"I live and work in the United States, but this is my personal play money that is my little secret. No one knows about it, and no one needs to know about it." He stopped at that and didn't think that he needed to volunteer anything more. "For your eyes only, Ms. Jung."

Beate Jung looked at him and didn't know what to say. *Quite an interesting man*, she thought. That was a large sum of money to play with. He was probably married and wanted to keep the money away from his wife.

"Would you like to establish a beneficiary for the account, in case something should happen to you?"

"To be perfectly frank with you, I just got into Zurich and am extremely tired. I still haven't booked into a hotel, and I don't even know what my next plans are. Do you think that you can assist me with the hotel?"

"Of course! How about the Bauer Au Lac hotel?" she asked.

"I leave it up to you. I don't know Zurich."

"Give me a moment and I will come back with the reservation," she said, quite pleased with taking on the task for her wealthy new client. Imagine, a twenty-two-million-dollar account falling on her lap. That should get her a nice bonus at the end of the year. When she returned with the reservation, she asked him if there was anything else that she could do to assist him.

"Yes, I would like to have a charge card and an ATM card to draw against my account. How long do you think that it will take?"

"Because you are an American, I can have an American Express Centurion card available for you in forty-eight hours. I can also have our bank debit card with ATM access made for you immediately. I hope that is suitable for you."

"That is perfect! Do you know if the hotel has a spa? I really want to have a massage and martinis before dinner."

"They most definitely will be able to accommodate you with all of that."

"Excellent. Now, I know how tiresome some clients can be. But, if you are available, I would certainly love to have some more of your company today. We can get to know ourselves a little better. I'm sure that you will want to do your due diligence on me, for compliance reasons. And I certainly want to know who it is that I am leaving my money with. How do martinis at 6:00 and dinner at 7:00 sound?"

What a character, she thought. Who is this American? It may not be a bad idea to know who he is if his account is to be mine. I would hate to be involved with an account that could be tainted illegally in any way. She considered his offer, also taking into account that the hotel's restaurant was Michelin rated.

"Sure, why not?" she agreed. "I'll meet you at the bar at 6:00 pm then." After having agreed, she walked him to the taxi stand outside and gave the driver instructions. An interesting man, she thought, with a nice bottom line on his bank account. She was glad that she had accepted his invitation.

AFTER THE AMERICAN ENTERED HIS HOTEL ROOM, HE looked at his face in the mirror and grinned, happy and relieved. It had been quite a morning. "Good," he said to himself, pleased with his interview. A few moments later he picked up the telephone receiver and dialed the number in St. Petersburg.

"Hi, Nadya, how are you?"

"James?" she asked, quite surprised to hear his voice.

"That's correct."

"The telephone shows that you are calling from Europe. Are you in Europe?"

"Yes, I flew into Switzerland yesterday." He wondered how he was going to phrase his next sentence to her. "Will you be able to join me? You mentioned that you were able to get an exit visa and that you would get back to me. But then you called back and put Mikhail on the phone, and I didn't hear anything else from you."

"Yes, I'm sorry about that. I had to get off the phone when I called because they were just entering the restaurant. Then they had me call you because they needed to urgently speak to you about something. Ugh! And now you are already in Switzerland."

"Yes," he confirmed. "Will you be able to join me? I really would love to see you again."

"I still have to work things out. I'll let you know."

"Ok. I understand," he said. "You can reach me at this number for the next couple of days. Let me know if there is anything that I can do to help. Of course, I want to pay for your ticket. Just let me know."

"I will. I promise," she said. "Goodbye!"

He was disappointed with the call, but he was not at all surprised. Dealing with the bureaucracy in Russia had to be a major ordeal for the citizens. There was nothing that he would be able to do for her now, and that's what was most disappointing.

At five minutes before six, he made his way to the hotel bar to meet his personal banker. Precisely at six she arrived accompanied by a tall executive type dressed in a very conservative dark suit, white shirt, and wearing a very elegant tie with animal prints on it. As Beate and the man approached, the American was able to decipher that the animal prints on the tie were giraffes. Beate had changed her attire. She looked stunning in a designer two-piece navy-blue suit that she wore over a blouse made of white silk fabric. Completing her elegant attire, Beate sported a luxurious vintage scarf that looked wonderfully soft and gently worn.

"Hello," Beate began. "I hope that you don't mind that I have brought along a senior member from our wealth management group. This is Tim Anderson, and he is also an American."

"Hello," said the senior executive, extending out his hand. "Yes, I hope you don't mind me barging in on you like this, but when Beate mentioned to me that she was meeting you tonight, I thought that it would be a great opportunity to meet you and to let you know about some of the services and products that we can make available to you." From his speech, the American could tell that Tim Anderson was an ex-New Yorker.

"Not at all, I'm glad that you were able to take the time to join us. I don't know anyone here, and that was why I asked Beate if she had a little free time this evening." The American shook Anderson's extended hand and then shook Beate's as well, while simultaneously kissing her on her cheek.

"Great," said Anderson. "What shall we drink? I'm ready for a nice dry martini," he told the young Swiss waitress that was attending them, "with three olives."

"What kind of vodka do you have?" he quickly asked her. "Grey Goose?"

"Yes, we have Grey Goose."

"Perfect!"

The American looked at his compatriot and couldn't help but smile at the very casual approach that the man had toward everyone and everything. He quickly put everyone at ease. The American waited until Beate gave her order to the waitress before also ordering a dry vodka martini.

"Make mine with Russian vodka, if you don't mind," he instructed the waitress. "What type of Russian vodka do you have?" he inquired.

"I'm certain that we have Russian Standard, and that is all that I can quickly recall right now," the young woman said.

"That's fine," the American responded.

"So," Anderson began, now that the drinks had been ordered. "How long will you be staying in Zurich?"

"Not long. Just long enough so that Beate can obtain my credit cards."

"Oh, that reminds me," Beate quickly interrupted him and began pulling a white envelope out of her cranberry-colored leather handbag. "I was already able to obtain your ATM debit card from our bank, as promised."

"That's great," said the American, pleased to at least have that in his hands.

"I'm still waiting on the American Express Centurion card, but that will take forty-eight hours."

"Oh, the ATM card will do for now."

"You like that?" said Anderson. "And that is why I'm here now. We would like to show you the types of services and products that are available to our best clients. Our wealth management team will be able to put together for you all sorts of information to help you decide on what investments to make and what opportunities are available."

Anderson was ready to make his aggressive pitch just as the waitress arrived with the drinks.

"To be frank with you, Tim, for now, I am not interested in doing much with my money. I only desire to invest in US Treasury Bills, with a rotation of 30, 60, 90 days, and nothing beyond that. Twenty million in total should be invested. Keep the rest of the funds in cash."

Tim Anderson looked at the American in disbelief. "I think that we can do a lot better than US Treasury Bills," he finally said. "Why don't you give us a little time to come up with a proposal for you? Take a few moments to complete your profile, and we will see what we can do."

"I'll fill out the profile, as I know that is a document that is required from private banking clients. Then, I'll look over what you come up with. But my initial invest-ments should be as I have indicated."

"Yeah, no problem," Anderson said. "You are under no obligation whatsoever. We just want to do the best that we can for you so that you will stay with us. We don't want you later taking your money because your return on investments was low." Beate never said a word during the exchange. It was clear that Anderson was running the show.

"What part of the States do you come from?" he finally asked Anderson after taking a sip of his martini.

"New Jersey," Anderson responded. "I worked on Wall Street for over thirty years."

"Me too," said the American. "I'm originally from Park Slope, Brooklyn. But when I got married we moved to Ridgewood, New Jersey."

"Yep, I know it. It's in North Bergen County."

"That's right. Do you miss the States?"

"I go back and forth often, so I'm pretty much in touch. I still have my house there. I was ready for a change, so when I was offered a pretty good opportunity with UBP I decided to take it."

"Do you have any children?"

"Oh, yeah," Anderson said. "I have a daughter studying at Rutgers University and a son working at Credit Suisse in New York."

"Nice," came from the American.

"Yep. How about if we move on to the restaurant? Beate says that it is Michelin rated. Right, Beate?"

"Yes. It's very good," she confirmed.

Once they were seated in the dining room, Anderson immediately took the wine list and asked if everyone was going to have wine with dinner. When the waitress appeared, however, Anderson said that he needed another martini and a little more time to study the wine list. So, they all ordered another round of drinks.

There was something about Anderson that was quite relaxing. Maybe it was the nervous way that he acted that charmed everyone. Beate had been right to bring him along. He kept the conversation going in the right direction. He also drew all of the attention. The American had noticed Beate's elegant femininity, but with Anderson around, there was no possibility of acting on it.

When the wine was finally opened and served, Anderson began his direct questioning again about prospects.

"Besides your private account with us, do you see any other possibilities where we can participate in business ventures with you?" This question took the American by surprise. He had not even entertained that possibility. But now that it had been presented to him, he quickly realized that this could be an excellent option for the Russian–Chinese transactions. He wasn't comfortable with the relationship for his bank because he didn't trust any of the participants. But with Tim Anderson and UBP, he could offer Mikhail and the Chinese an intermediary bank in Switzerland as an alternative.

"You know," the American began, "I had been so caught up with my account that it had not even dawned on me that UBP could play a part in a new business that I have recently participated in. Do you offer letters of credit and trade-finance products?"

"Sure," Anderson quickly answered, all ears now. "Why, what do you have in mind?"

The American then proceeded to give a general explanation of the import–export types of transactions that the Russians and Chinese businessmen were eager to grow, with a Swiss bank acting as intermediary. Anderson showed a keen interest in what the American was proposing, and he agreed that there could be an excellent opportunity there for them. But he also admitted that they did not have much by way of private banking clients in those markets.

"That would be new business for us, and we would be extremely interested," Anderson finally said, very excitedly. "How can we proceed with this?"

"Tim, I don't know you or Beate, so I want to give you a little warning that these are not easy clients. In fact, these are very powerful men in their respective countries."

"Yeah, so what are you saying?"

"I'm saying exactly what I said. These are very powerful men who deal in large amounts of money and won't stand for any excuses if things go wrong."

Anderson looked at the American for a few moments and reflected on what had just been implied. Beate was now looking at the American with a new perspective.

"Well, we will have to talk again. How long are you staying in Zurich?"

"No more than a couple of days. Just let me know if you are interested. But keep in mind what I have said."

"Yep, thanks for letting us know. Don't worry about your money. I will put our most senior person on it."

"No, Tim. I want it to be clear that my account is to be handled by Beate."

"Oh, no problem. I was just going to put a real senior person on your account. But if you like Beate, we can definitely keep her on it."

"That will work best for me right now." Beate smiled at him as he said it.

The fashionable part of the restaurant was beside the hotel gardens, but Anderson had chosen a table in one of the mirrored alcoves at the back of the large room. As they glossed over the double folio menu, Anderson asked for the sommelier and promptly ordered a bottle of Taittinger brut, stating that the occasion called for a bottle of the fine bubbly.

"A bottle of the Blanc de Blanc Brut, 1996, if you don't mind," he told the sommelier. Then, when the waiter came over he said, "We'd like to start with the caviar. Beate, what would you like?'

"Grilled calf kidneys in port wine with the soufflé potatoes sounds delightfully decadent to me if we are celebrating," Beate responded.

"Excellent choice, Madame," said the waiter.

"The tournedos, medium rare, with sauce Béarnaise and artichoke hearts," put in the American.

"Thank you," said the waiter. "And for Monsieur?" he asked Anderson.

"I'll have the Dover sole with the avocado pear and a little oil and balsamic vinegar dressing."

"Very good," confirmed the waiter.

WHEN THE EXTRAVAGANT MEAL HAD ENDED, EVERYONE settled for the twenty-year port and the stilton cheese.

"So," the American began, "that was a remarkable meal! Definitely Michelin star worthy. Thank you also for taking the time in your busy schedules to speak to me."

"It was our pleasure," Anderson replied. And then he added, "We will be in touch. I'll call you here at the hotel tomorrow if we decide to explore the Russian–Chinese possibility. But to be perfectly frank, I don't see any reason why not to move forward on it. Anyway, we will talk again either way."

"Yes, it was very nice getting to know you," Beate added, quite pleased to have landed the new account.

"Thank you. I'll be looking forward to your call." He then gave Beate a goodbye kiss and a wink as well. And then the UBP bankers were gone, quite satisfied.

CHAPTER TWENTY-NINE

"Everything all right?" the American asked as he watched Anderson beginning to drink his second scotch whiskey.

"I wish that we could get a nice dry martini on this flight," he responded, disappointed with the miniature bottles that the stewardess had placed before him. "You know what I mean?"

"Yes, I do. But if they had a legitimate bar on the flight, that could lead to other problems."

"Yeah, you're probably right," Anderson conceded. "Some of these guys look like they'd be all over the stewardesses." He chuckled.

"Yes, you can't trust anyone after a few drinks," agreed the American.

"Well, we should be able to get some decent martinis

in St. Petersburg. I mean, if there is one place that should have excellent vodka, I would guess that's where it would be."

"Don't worry, you won't be disappointed."

"IF YOU ARE AFRAID OF WOLVES, DON'T GO INTO THE woods," Stalin had once famously remarked. The American thought about that as he tried to understand why he had decided to take the flight with Anderson. The truth of the matter was that Liu Tang was dead. It was also true that the Russian oligarchs were notoriously ruthless. And that was why he was now seriously undertaking a reality check.

"Surrender is a beautiful word. When we surrender ourselves, we expand to limitless possibilities," was what his very attractive college professor had said many years ago to her social psychology class. "Our dark side is instructive. It is not to be feared, but to be loved for what it is. Surrender yourselves, and when you do so you will find an expanse so rich that you will be liberated to receive the very things that you were striving for." Now, years later, the American had done just that. He had surrendered himself as she had suggested, except that now he was realizing that in the deepest recesses of his mind, he was finding that doing so was not as liberating as she had claimed that it would be.

Then there was the matter of the money. Twenty-two million dollars were sitting in a Swiss account in his name. That amount of money was very unsettling. It made all the sense in the world to consider Mo Yan as an adversary since he was the most likely man to be in pursuit of the money. He was a senior executive at the Bank of China in Shanghai where the Corporation had their account, and he had been directly tied to Liu Tang. Liu Tang may well have exacted some sort of last-minute revenge on Mo Yan for what he had done to him. Extracting twenty-two million dollars would have been a very painful financial retaliation if Mo Yan's money had been tied to the Corporation, and it would have been motive enough to kill Liu Tang.

ANDERSON AND THE AMERICAN HAD CALLED MIKHAIL to see if the Russian would be interested in having his transactions go through UBP. The American did not want to have any direct dealings with the Russians or the Chinese, but Anderson had an appetite for risk. Mikhail arranged for entry visas for the two men so that they could entertain the possibilities in person. Anderson was delighted with the speed of the arrangement, and the American agreed to assist with the introductions, reluctantly. The only promising part of the quick visit was that he would be able to see Nadya again.

Before the plane landed, the American told Anderson that he remembered having met him once years ago at a banking conference.

"Oh, what conference?" asked Anderson.

"It was a SIFMA conference."

"Oh, yeah," said Anderson. "I remember attending quite a few of those. Which one did you attend?" he asked.

"The ones in Florida," came from the American.

"Right!" Anderson said, and then he started to recall those conferences that he had attended. "Yeah, there were several in Miami and Boca Raton."

"That's right," confirmed the American. "But I believe that it was the one in the Turnberry Isle Hotel in Aventura."

"Oh, yea," he remembered. "I did attend one there as well. Hmm, I can't say that I can recall having met you. But, you know, there are so many attendees in those events."

"That's right," the American agreed. "It also goes back quite a few years."

"I'll say," said Anderson.

"I think you were working for a global custodian then?"

"That's right."

The American had searched Anderson's name on the internet before meeting him at the airport. That was how he had known that Anderson had worked for a global clearinghouse. The American thought that it would be far wiser to admit to the Russians how he had met Anderson through banking conferences, should the topic come up, rather than to mention any information related to the private bank account that the American had at UBP. There was no way that he wanted anyone to know about his twenty-two million dollars. He also didn't want Anderson to bring about any discussions and doubts about how he had acquired his money. Anderson, as a senior private banker, would know not to reveal any information about his client's account. But the American needed to have some other legitimate pretext for the Russians as to how their relationship had come about, and that would help to explain how they knew each other. He didn't want to leave the Russians with any doubts.

The American said that he had recalled meeting Anderson, but it wasn't true. However, talking about the conferences brought back memories of the events and solidified the experience between the two men so that Anderson was left certain that it was likely true that the two men had previously met. That was all that the American had hoped to accomplish by bringing up the topic before meeting with the Russians. Subterfuge was the only means of defense that he had against the rich and dangerous. As the plane began to descend onto St.

Petersburg, the American looked out of the window and saw a band of clouds that stretched across the horizon.

THE TWO AMERICANS SAT AT A PAVEMENT TABLE IN the hotel's café drinking vodka martinis as they waited for the two Russian businessmen to arrive. There was a couple at the adjacent table conversing in German and drinking espressos. Anderson had his back to them, so he couldn't admire for a second time the woman's lovely black eyes or the small nipples that were clearly visible through the transparent gauze of her blouse. But that was fine with Anderson because he didn't want any distractions now, as he was planning his strategy for the meeting. The American was sketching on his pad different versions of the woman's dark eyes next to images of wolves with yellow eyes. They were Stalin's wolves.

As the two men began drinking their second martinis, Anderson became stupefied when his American colleague suddenly and inexplicably began laughing.

"What's up?" Anderson asked. "Why the hell are you now laughing?"

"I was just remembering something that I once read about Stalin," the American explained. "In 1927, Stalin sought medical help for his insomnia and severe anxiety disorder. After a thorough diagnosis, his doctors had unwittingly informed him that he had typical clinical paranoia and recommended medical treatment. When Stalin heard what the doctors had to say he became extremely angry and he summoned his secret service agents."

"Yeah," said Anderson. "Why is that funny?"

"The next day the chief psychiatrist and his assistants were found dead from poisoning."

"Wow, a real man!" said Anderson, now also laughing.

"In addition," continued the American, "so that the doctors' diagnosis about his mental condition wouldn't become public, he ordered the executions of intellectuals, which resulted in the murders of hundreds of thousands of doctors, professors, writers, and others."

"Jesus!" said Anderson. "Maybe that relieved some of the tension that he was having. Was he able to get some good sleep after that?" asked Anderson, now laughing hard.

"I guess so," the other replied. "He never complained anymore about any disorders after that."

"Who was he going to complain to?" Anderson asked, still laughing. "He wiped them all out." Then the two men continued their boisterous laughter just as Victor, Mikhail, and Nadya were entering the restaurant.

. . .

"Gentlemen," said Victor, as he extended his hand to them, smiling. "I'm glad to see that you are enjoying yourselves." The two bankers immediately got to their feet to extend their hands to the Russians. The two Russian men were wearing dark business suits, white shirts, and very dark ties. Nadya was dressed in a beige scarf, brown sweater, black leather trousers, and black leather booties. Anderson shook her hand, and the American kissed both of her cheeks. Looking at her now, the American no longer had any doubts as to why he had decided to return to St. Petersburg. Nadya's looks would compare favorably against any of the top models seen in fashion magazines.

But there was infinitely more to Nadya than just her very pretty face and beautiful body. When he looked into Nadya's eyes, it seemed as though he were looking directly into that unique phenomenon referred to as the Russian Soul, which was the result of an amalgamation of different religions and cultural backgrounds that had overtime reached its completeness within her. There was also this remarkable femininity about her that was difficult to explain. The American was totally enraptured by her.

"Gentlemen," Nadya addressed the two visiting bankers, "I just wanted to say hello." Then directing her gaze at the American, she said, "It's good seeing you again."

"For me too," he quickly responded. "I hope that you will have a little time while I'm here so that you can fill me in on the new production that you are working on for your theater. There is nothing quite like it in our country."

"Of course," she said. "It will be my pleasure. I'm so glad that you are interested. Well then," she was addressing them all now, "I'll leave you to your business. Goodbye."

"Nadya is a remarkable young woman," Mikhail said after she had left them. "She is an excellent student at the State University of St. Petersburg, part-time hostess of the restaurant in this hotel, and a member of the artistic staff of the Demmeni Marionette Theater. She is very special, and we just love her."

"Wow," said Anderson, "and quite a beauty!" They all shook their heads in appreciation as she left them.

"So, gentlemen, welcome to St. Petersburg and thank you for coming. I suggest that we move on to my office where we can discuss business with a little more privacy. Shall we?" And with that, the two bankers and Victor followed Mikhail to his Mercedes where there was a chauffeur ready to drive them to their destination.

AT MIKHAIL'S OFFICE, THE TWO RUSSIANS deliberated at length in a very convincing fashion on the types of legitimate businesses that they were engaged in. Mikhail began by explaining how the three major grain-producing countries of the former Soviet Union, i.e., Russia, Ukraine, and Kazakhstan, had become a large grain exporting region.

"In the late Soviet period," Mikhail elaborated, "the Soviet Union was a large grain importer. But after the breakup in December 1991, the successor countries began their transition from centrally planned to market economies. During the 1990s, the grain imports of these three major grain-producing countries largely ended, and these countries collectively became a small net grain exporter. Today these three countries have become major grain exporters, contributing 14 percent of total world grain exports and 21 percent of world exports of wheat." At this point, Victor presented posters with graphs depicting how the region compared to the rest of the world in the production of grains.

Anderson interrupted the presentation to ask Mikhail if that was a bottle of Glenmorangie that he had spotted on the table by the window.

"I wouldn't mind pouring a dram at this point, Mikhail. I think that it would help to ease us into your very thorough presentation."

Mikhail grinned at Anderson when he heard this. Then he said, "Yes, by all means. That is why I keep it there. I should have offered before beginning the presentation. Please, gentlemen, help yourselves. I'll also have my secretary bring us a bowl of nuts and some olives if you think that it will help with the concentration." Having said this, Mikhail was the first to pour three fingers of the scotch into a tumbler. After everyone had helped themselves to drinks, Mikhail was ready to resume his deliberation.

"You know," Mikhail began again, "many of the former Soviet foreign trade corporations limited their trade efforts to Eastern Europe and China, establishing companies in these countries and setting up joint stock companies on very favorable terms." Mikhail then went on talking about emerging market countries with creditable balances of trade. There were explanations on the exportation of cocoa beans, coffee, and timber as well as many other types of commodities that were moved from river deltas to mega ocean freighters and that finally ended up in China.

"My friends," he finally concluded, "we have the importers and the exporters. What we are looking for is intermediary banks that will assist us with the letters of credit. We have a list of corporations in China that would like to establish accounts with foreign banks and that are very interested in doing business with us. Hopefully, you will be able to visit some of these clients and help them to establish accounts with your banks. I can assure you that you will be personally well compensated for your time and effort. Your banks will also earn competitive commissions from these clients for every one of their transactions. After all, risk has to be properly compensated."

"This is really quite interesting, Mikhail," said Anderson. "We at UBP will certainly want to take a closer look at this."

"There is a great deal of money to be made, Mr. Anderson. You just have to make certain that you do your homework with these Chinese corporations. Your American friend here had the unfortunate luck of establishing an account with a corporation that was being investigated by the Chinese government. Fortunately, neither his bank nor our firm lost any money."

"That's right," confirmed the American. "Even though our affiliate in Geneva did a thorough check on the Corporation, we had no idea that they had been involved with schemes of capital flight and that they were under investigation by the Chinese government. Fortunately, as Mikhail states, neither our affiliate nor Mikhail's firm lost any money. But there are definite risks in this market: country risk, operational risks, and reputational risks."

"Most definitely," Mikhail reiterated. "You have to be aware of this, and you must have a very definite expertise. Otherwise, you can lose a great deal of money. But you can also stand to make a great deal of money if you know what you are doing. And I'm talking about personal money, as well as whatever your institutions stand to make."

"I can provide each of you with a list of our contacts in China," said Victor. "Then you can decide which ones are the ones that you would like to pursue. Just let us know."

"Remember," Mikhail added, "that we are in this together. We have a vested interest in this along with you. We are relying on you to make the payments to us after we have satisfied the terms of any letters of credit agreements that we enter into with these Chinese companies. However, keep in mind that any delays in processing or inefficiencies at your end could result in a loss to us, and we will not take that lightly. That is why we are looking for experts here. The Chinese are very clever, and who knows if the government's actions are perhaps motivated by the political actions that have occurred against their fellow businessmen in our country. I don't really know and I don't really care. I just want to be certain that I am paid for the goods that I deliver. It's as simple as that."

"Ok," said Anderson. "I perfectly understand. I will have a powwow with my team as soon as I return to Zurich, and we will have a look at your client list to see what we can do."

"Great. That is all that we can ask for," said Mikhail.

"And now gentlemen, my chauffeur is ready to take you back to your hotel." They all shook hands, and then the secretary came in with gifts for the two bankers. The gifts were lovely Hermes ties. "Please, gentlemen, have your decisions for me as soon as possible. The merchandise is ready to be shipped."

"We will," the bankers promised. The American assured Mikhail that he would be providing the list of clients to his Geneva office. "My team may be a little shy with this Asian market business after their recent experience with the Corporation. But they also recognize the huge potential that exists there, and I don't think that they will want to be left out."

"Excellent," said Mikhail, "I'm glad to hear that. Goodbye then, my friends. Hopefully, we will be in contact soon."

The American had an ulterior motive for giving the Russians a positive spin on the business that they were proposing, and that had to do with Nadya. The American no longer needed money, so there was no financial consideration to motivate him with regard to making him want to deal with the Russians or the Chinese again. These were powerful and dangerous men, and that was the real risk in entering into any of their proposed transactions. Liu Tang was dead, and that was a fact. He didn't need to know why. The Russians and the Chinese were involved in illegal activities. There was smuggling and elements of money laundering with their transactions. It was apparent that the Chinese government had been carefully scrutinizing these types of wealthy businessmen in their country. The flight of capital was a legitimate problem in China. The Russian government, with Putin at the helm, was probably watching the wealthy Russian businessmen as well. These Russian oligarchs with their financial clout posed a real threat to the government. No, the American didn't want any part of it. But he hoped that Anderson would be interested so that the Russians would be satisfied and kept at a safe distance from him.

CHAPTER THIRTY

I<small>T WAS</small> cool and still in the garden by the Exiles café where the American was sitting, waiting for his favorite person in the world to arrive. It was already nine o'clock in the evening when, from a long way off, he finally spotted Nadya approaching. There was a smell of freshness in the air, the luxurious freshness of the autumn.

"I have the pleasure and virtuous consolation of seeing you in good health," the American said to Nadya with a grin on his face. It was a line that he had recalled reading in a Chekov short story. Nadya looked quite cheerful. She gazed at him unblinkingly, as if fascinated. They kissed in greeting, Russian style.

"So, here you are again in our great city. I'm quite surprised to see you here so soon again. I would not have expected it," she said, clearly pleased.

"To be frank with you, I didn't think that I would be back here so soon. Under the pretense of business, I'm back, but really only to see you."

"Oh," she said, blushing. "I thought you were here because of some new business matter with Mikhail."

"No," he said. "That is definitely not the case. I really came to see you and to hear all about your new production for the marionette theater. You sounded quite excited about that. But before you start telling me about it, let's have something to drink. What do you suggest here?"

"Ok. How about sharing some blintzes, and Russian Standard vodka martinis?" she suggested. "I think you had those martinis on the last night that you were here."

"Sounds delicious," he said. "I'm ready to begin again where I left off."

She grinned at him and then gave the orders to the waitress. "The Kulebiaka is also quite good here," she advised him.

"Kulebiaka? I've never heard of it, but I'm willing to try anything with you. So, please order it."

On his say-so, Nadya gave the order to the waitress for the additional dish.

"So," he asked Nadya after the waitress had left them, "what is Kulebiaka?"

"Is that the first thing that you are going to ask me

after not seeing me for months?" She laughed teasingly at him.

"Nadya, the way to a man's heart is through his stomach."

"Well, thank God that I am such a foodie," she retorted. "Otherwise, we would never see you here." She winked at him and patted his hand. "You will love it. You can count on me to never steer you wrong. Kulebiaka is the traditional dish that is referred to as the king of pies. The puff pastry is molded into a rectangular shape, and then it is filled with salmon and slow-cooked onions, mushrooms, rice, and other vegetables. Anton Chekov was a real Kulebiaka enthusiast. He famously instructed the chefs where he dined on how they were to prepare it. He is said to have told them, 'The Kulebiaka must make your mouth water, it must lay there before you—a shameless temptation...the butter drips like tears, and the filling is fat, juicy, rich...' It is one of my favorite dishes," she said. "But we better be careful, because eating together will make us quite fat."

"Wow," he said, amazed at how she knew about the Russian culture and cuisine. "You are a national treasure, Nadya. If you ever leave Russia, it will be a major loss to your country."

"Hmm," was her only response. The waitress came just then to place the vodka martinis before them.

When she left, they lifted their glasses to make a toast. "Bóo-deem zda-ró-vye!" she said.

"Bóo-deem zda-ró-vye!" he repeated.

"To our health!" she translated. And with that, they took their first drink together of the evening.

"As I mentioned to you over the phone, we are doing *The Fairy's Kiss*. Did you say that you were familiar with it?" she asked him.

"Only the music by Stravinsky, but I don't think I recall anything at all about the story."

She beamed with excitement as she began to tell him about the new production that they were working on at the theater.

"In the story, a mother loses her child to a Fairy's sprites during a storm. The Fairy herself appears and approaches the child with tenderness. She kisses the child on the forehead and then goes away, leaving the child alone. Country folk, passing by, find him and take him with them. And that is the end of act one. It is quite a sad story," she said.

"Sounds rather depressing," he responded. "How does it develop?"

"In the opening of the second act, it is clear that many years have passed. There is a peasant dance in progress. Among the dancers, there are a young man and his fiancée. At the end of the dance, the musicians and the crowd disperse, and so does the fiancée. The young man has been left alone. The Fairy approaches him in the guise of a gypsy woman. She takes his hand and tells him his fortune. Then she begins dancing, and, charming him, subjects him to her will. She talks to him about his romance and promises him great happiness. Captivated by her words, he begs her to lead him to his fiancée. That is where the second act ends."

Just as Nadya finished describing the second act of the ballet, the waitress arrived with the warm blintzes.

"Nadya," the American said, "please order our next round of martinis before you go on with the story. I don't want to find myself facing your Kulebiaka without a martini in hand."

"Absolutely," she agreed. Nadya then signaled to the waitress to come over and gave her the order for the drinks. She then said something else to the waitress that made her glance toward the American. Then all of a sudden, the waitress and Nadya started laughing.

"What was all that laughing about?" he asked, after the waitress left with the order.

"Oh, nothing," she answered. "I just told her to bring the martinis right away, because you needed to be ready to face the Kulebiaka. Shall I continue now with the story?"

"By all means, please go ahead."

"Ok, then. So, where was I?' Nadya sipped on her martini before continuing with the story where she had left off. "In the third act, we find the young man, guided by the Fairy, at a mill. There he finds his fiancée among her friends. The Fairy disappears. There is dancing underway, and as the act draws to a close, the girl is seen going with her friends to put on her wedding veil. The young man finds himself alone again, and that is where the third act ends."

"I have a funny feeling," the American said, "that this is not going to end well for the young man."

"Why?" she asked. "What gives you that impression?"

"These Stravinsky ballets rarely end in joyous celebrations. But let me not interrupt you. Please go on."

"Well then," she said, "now we are on the final act. The Fairy appears wearing a wedding veil, and the young man takes her for his bride assuming that it is his fiancé. He moves toward her, enraptured, and bestows on her warm passion. In the midst of his ecstasy, the Fairy throws off her veil. Dumbfounded, the young man realizes the mistake that he has made. He tries to free himself, but can't; he is defenseless against her supernatural powers. She then transports him to the land of eternal dwelling, where he is condemned to remain there forever. The scene closes with the Fairy bestowing a final kiss on him."

When Nadya finished her tale, he just looked at her for a few moments without saying a word. She patiently waited to give him a chance to take it all in. He took a sip of his martini, and then looked at her again.

"I'm really looking forward to that Kulebiaka," he finally said. But she just stared at him and waited. "That is a very creepy tale," he finally admitted.

"Yes?"

"That is a very complicated tale!"

"Yes?" She wanted more.

"A powerful and mischievous Fairy, disguised as a sexy woman, enraptures a man. She takes full possession of him with her supernatural powers and transports him to a land beyond time and place where he is condemned to remain forever. Did I give a correct synopsis of the story?"

"Yes, in essence," Nadya replied.

"The children will be sure to love it," he said laughing.

"We hope so," she said, grinning.

"That is powerful stuff."

"I agree."

"I suppose that the man was already lost once the Fairy's sprites had initially singled him out."

"Quite right," she agreed. Then they both became silent, waiting for the waitress to make her presence with the Kulebiaka.

"Goddamned fairy tales," he said. "As soon as you open the door to strangers, you have to be prepared to expect the unexpected. You may find a witch or a princess, and you can't be surprised if they are in disguise. In fairy tales, everything is possible. That, and not their morals, is the primary reason that fairy tales are still popular today."

Nadya didn't comment. She just stared at him in silence.

"I can see that choosing the right fairy tale for your little theater can be quite a complicated task," he said. "For the audience, everything begins somewhat serenely, but soon they realize that they are in the midst of a story that they don't fully understand. The fairy tale begins by giving the audience false hope. But before long, there is a rude awakening to reality, like a hard slap to the face. A character displays incorrect behavior, performs unnatural acts, and even commits a murder. There are few characters that will survive the tales, but only a few." The tale of *The Fairy's Kiss* was difficult. Liu Tang was dead. It was time to leave wonderland.

They ate the rest of their meal in relative silence. He said that fatigue from travel had finally set in. He also said that he had not been sleeping well as of late. They would have to call it an early night. After dinner, she walked him to a taxi stand. Before taking the cab, he remembered that this time, he had a gift for her. It was a small box that had been nicely gift-wrapped in candy cane-striped paper. "A little present for you," he said. "It is a small token for all the time that you have spent with me, for showing me so much of your lovely self, and for sharing with me so much of your art."

"No, please, it is not necessary," she said. "It was my pleasure too. I really loved showing you my city."

"Well, thank you," he said.

"But you are not leaving Russia yet?" she asked with a surprised look. "I have a little surprise for you too."

"What surprise do you have for me?" he asked, not clear as to what she was referring to.

"Well, I'm not supposed to tell you, but a friend of Liu Tang's is in town. He has asked me where you are staying, and I know that he very much wants to meet you to say hello."

This was totally unexpected for the American. "What friend?" he asked.

"I believe that his name is Mo Yan. He didn't want me to tell you anything because it was going to be a surprise. He said that he will be visiting you at the hotel."

"Nadya, keep away from Mo Yan. He was not Liu Tang's friend. He was having an affair with his wife. He humiliated Liu Tang at the workplace. He was Liu Tang's superior at the bank, where both men worked. Liu Tang despised the man, and Liu Tang was murdered. Mo Yan is no friend of mine. I have never met the man, and I have no intention of doing so."

"Oh, I'm so sorry," she said. "I didn't know."

"It's ok. Thank you for telling me. But how come he asked you about me? How did he know that we knew each other?"

"He was at the restaurant with Mikhail and Victor. When I placed the call to you. I didn't know why he asked me earlier today for your information when he could have easily obtained it from them. It didn't make much sense, but I was glad to help because he said that he was your friend. I'm so sorry."

"Nadya, don't trouble yourself about it. It's better not to get involved with these types of men."

"Yes, of course."

"The gift-wrapped box that I have just given you contains fifty thousand dollars. It is my gift for you."

Nadya glanced nervously sideways, totally over-whelmed by what he had just told her. She could not believe her ears. She felt faint with reaction. She blushed to the roots of her hair and then turned pale. "I am deeply grateful," she stammered in a weak voice.

"You have really impressed me, and I want to help you."

"My God," she said, still visibly shaken.

He leaned forward and said, "Please don't tell anyone about the money. I don't want anyone to know."

"No. Don't worry," she quickly responded. "I don't want anyone to know either," she said, almost in tears.

"Nadya, I'm going straight to the airport now. I have to leave immediately."

"I will go with you," she said.

"It's not necessary," he argued.

"I will help you at the airport. Do you already have your airline ticket?"

"No, I don't. I just have my passport, and nothing else that I care to take."

"My God," she said again, still visibly shaken. She hugged him then and kissed him on the cheek. "Let's go right away, please."

"Ok, but I don't think that you have to come with me."

"Please, allow me. I want to," she insisted and kissed him. "There are hourly regular flights to Moscow from St. Petersburg, and from there you will be able to connect to most major cities."

"Fine," he said. He was also feeling a little nervous now, and he was glad for her company.

This was happening very quickly and it was very unsettling. He felt as though he were in a chase dream trying to flee instinctively from something that he could sense was threatening him. You could run and hide, he thought, or you can try to outwit your foe. But he knew that the distance or gap between himself and his pursuer was shortening. Was he imagining all of this? No, Mo Yan was not an imaginary figure. He was very real, powerful, and in definite pursuit. The American was tense.

The first ten minutes in the cab seemed to take forever. It was like being in a dream where your legs don't work properly, as you attempt to run away from what you fear. It was depressing for him to believe that the situation was so overwhelming that he couldn't even face it.

No. It was better to learn the truth, no matter how harsh and cruel it could be. It was better to know the truth than to blindly live in false illusions. Quite shaken, he now decided that what he wanted was another martini.

"I've changed my mind," he told her. "I want to go back to the hotel. Please tell the driver to take me back to the hotel."

"Are you sure?" Nadya asked, extremely surprised. He looked at her and thought for a moment. He loved the way she wore her hair, highly styled yet natural-looking.

"Yes, I think so," he said. The perplexed Nadya kept his gaze, but he gave her a reassuring look. Now that he had made his decision, he was suddenly feeling little spasms of sexual interest for her again. He noticed the glow of perspiration on her brow and the contour-hugging tightness of the blouse that she was wearing. After Nadya gave the cab driver the new instructions, the American quietly whispered some nonsense into her ear. It tickled her as he said it, and she began laughing. Crazy stupid lovers, the cab driver thought as he now redirected his vehicle toward the hotel.

Once they arrived at the hotel, they went straight to the bar where they ordered a round of Russian vodka martinis.

"You know," he said, "I only like them when they have three olives."

"Yes, I've noticed. I like them with olives too," she responded. Then she kissed him squarely on the lips. It was the first time that their lips had actually touched as lovers. "I still can't believe that you have given me all of this money. Are you sure?" she asked.

"Nadya, I know that you won't believe this, but giving you that money makes me extremely happy. I have never met anyone like you!"

She didn't know how to respond to him. "Thank you," was all that she could come up with. Her eyes were swelling with tears again. "This will make a big difference in my life."

"Good, I hope so," he responded.

"I have to admit that I really don't understand anything. I don't know why you have given me this money, and now I don't know why you have changed your mind about leaving Russia just as we were on our way to the airport."

"Nadya, I told you, giving you the money excites me.

I think you are really special, and I want you to do whatever you want to be happy. You deserve it. And as for coming back," he took a moment to think how he would respond to her before finally saying, "I just needed to have another martini with you. Is that so difficult for you to imagine?"

"You make no sense to me," she said. "But I don't care. I love spending time with you because you are so different." She smiled but was thoroughly confused by everything that was happening.

"I'm like one of your puppets moving right along, letting life carry me along. I have no idea what it all means, and I don't need to know right now."

"You are so clever," she countered, and kissed him again on the lips, hard this time. Then she kissed him again with slightly opened lips, and then he felt her tongue slowly stimulating his lips and entering his mouth. She pulled back then and smiled.

"This is the hotel where you work. Maybe this is not such a good idea in front of the people that you work with. Can you ask the receptionist to book a second room in your name, but to charge it to my credit card? Then we can have some privacy, and not have to worry about someone like Mo Yan paying us a surprise visit."

"That is an excellent idea," she said, and left him to make the arrangements with the receptionist."

While Nadya was gone, the American decided to go

back to his original room to retrieve the items that he had left behind. He wanted to have a change of clothing. He could shower later in the other hotel room, but he needed his things.

The American looked around the bar, before making his move. It was quite crowded, but there were no Asians anywhere and certainly no Mo Yan. He didn't have a weapon on him, and this made him a bit nervous because he didn't know what Mo Yan was capable of doing. Then he spotted a serrated knife that the bartender used to cut lemons with and pocketed it. The American moved quickly out of the bar and down the lobby toward the banks of elevators. The effects of the dry martini were already wearing off now that he was alone and possibly confronting danger. The elevator doors slid open with the familiar ping sound echoing, and he entered alone pressing the button to the fourth floor.

The passageway on his floor was silent, desolate. He opened the door to his room and stepped through into the darkness. He felt for the light on the wall and was just about to turn it on when he noticed the pungent odor of a cigarette. Then in the darkness, he saw the bright orange glow of the tip of the cigarette.

"At last," said a husky voice with a thick Asian accent. The American flicked on the light switch and saw the stocky middle-aged, balding Asian man in a dark blue pinstriped suit seated on his bed. While he was casually smoking his cigarette, he was quick to show the American that he was holding an automatic gun in his right hand.

"What's going on?" asked the American. "Who are you?"

"I think you know who I am," was the man's response. "I don't have much time to waste on you," he quickly added. "I want my money."

"I think you have made a mistake," the American replied.

"Please, don't waste my time," Mo Yan reiterated. "Liu Tang confessed to everything before he died. It was an unnecessarily painful death, I may add. So, please, no bullshit!" He aimed his automatic pistol at the American's leg and was about to pull the trigger, just to show that he had no compunction about carrying through with his threats. But in that split second of hesitation, the nervous American threw the bartender's knife at Mo Yan and caught him squarely in the left eye. It seemed initially that Mo Yan was more in shock than in pain by the American's action. He had dropped his pistol as the knife had penetrated, and then realizing that his life was in danger, he instinctively reacted with jerky motions trying to find the gun that he had dropped on the floor while also trying to grasp the knife that had pierced his eye. But in his pathetic condition, it was clear that for now, he couldn't accomplish either. The American was at first frozen by what his survival instincts had accomplished. But the fascination quickly turned to immediate action when he saw that Mo Yan began to search for his weapon. The American took the heavy glass ashtray that Mo Yan had been using for his cigarettes and smashed it hard into the protruding end of the knife that was in Mo Yan's eye. As the knife penetrated Mo Yan's skull, the American knew immediately that this final blow had been fatal. Mo Yan lay collapsed on his back on the American's bed.

The American looked on at Mo Yan's body and couldn't believe that in a matter of moments he had taken the man's life, a man who he didn't even know. As he stared at the body, he was surprised to notice that there was very little blood anywhere. There had only been a slight trickle, like a tear, on the man's face. The puncture to the eye seemed to have produced only internal hemorrhaging for now.

"Now what," he whispered to himself, uncertain as to how this would all end. Maybe thirty years in a Siberian prison if he were lucky. He didn't know if Russia had the death penalty. He looked at Mo Yan's body again and considered his options. Then he began pulling the heavy man by his legs toward the window. "What the fuck," he said out loud to himself as he was struggling with the dead man's weight. Then he shut the lights, opened the window, and in total darkness began to lift the man's body over the edge. It would be a four-story drop, but the American didn't hesitate. He pushed Mo Yan out the window without much thought, and quickly closed the window and the curtains. "Amazing, no blood," he nervously said to himself. Then he washed his face and hands, picked up the gun that Mo Yan had dropped, and headed on out to the elevators for the lobby.

Once he had reached the lobby the American headed straight for the men's lavatory, where he wiped the gun clean and dropped it into the garbage bin. He then looked into the mirror and confirmed that there was no blood anywhere on him.

It seemed like an eternity had passed by since he had last left the hotel's lobby bar, but only twenty-three minutes had elapsed.

The bar was very crowded now with the wealthy habitués, but Nadya was nowhere to be seen. The American ordered another martini with the three olives and took a long hard swallow. Two men with their backs to him were conversing in English, but by their accents, he could tell that it was not their native tongue.

The American finally spotted Nadya entering the crowded bar. He could see that she was on her tiptoes trying to find him. He raised his arm to attract her attention, and she smiled in acknowledgment.

"Gentlemen," he said to the two bankers standing

next to him, "I'm afraid that I must take my leave. There is a beautiful Russian princess who is waiting for me." The two stupefied bankers looked at him and then directed their view to the woman that the American had been signaling to. They then congratulated him in admiration of his good fortune. The American shook their hands and then realized that one of the men was the Dutchman from the conference. The American drew close to the Dutchman, and in a barely perceptible voice asked if he had received his golden baptism from the Asian banker at the conference.

"No such luck," responded the tall man, finally recognizing him. The American raised an eyebrow, displayed a grin, and took his leave of the men.

"Happy hunting," shouted the Dutchman after him, laughing loudly.

CHAPTER THIRTY-ONE

"So," he said to Nadya when he finally reached her. "You certainly took a long time," he said, mildly complaining, a little glossy-eyed now.

"Yes, I'm so sorry about that. But I was able to get for us the loveliest room in the hotel from the receptionist. It is on the top floor, so we will have an excellent view of St. Petersburg. They will also deliver to us a bottle of French champagne and blinis with caviar! Now, then, you can't complain. I believe that I have done quite well for us," she said, in a very cheery mood.

"You most certainly have. My only complaint is that you were away from me for so long. Luckily, I met a banker that was here last summer for the conference. It seems that he is here for business. The import–export business seems to be thriving in Russia."

"Well, I'm glad that you were able to meet an old friend," she said. "I was also delayed because the police were at the receptionist's counter. It seems that a businessman was attacked by Romanian gypsies. They stabbed him in the eye and brutally smashed his skull on the pavement. The police think it was gypsies because they saw them running away when they arrived. His watch and wallet were missing. Without these, it will be difficult to identify him because the police are fairly certain that the man is a foreigner. The brutality of the incident also makes the police think that it could also have been perpetrated by mobsters. The gypsies are not typically so brutal. At any rate, they have agreed to say that the body was found elsewhere, so as not to have the incident affect the reputation of the prestigious hotel in any way."

The American couldn't believe what he was hearing. He had been preparing for the worst, but it seemed that people were being paid off so that the murder would not be associated with the hotel in any way.

"Is the room ready?" he asked.

"How many martinis have you had?" She noticed that he had a dreamy look about him.

"Snegurochka, that was all that I could do to keep busy without you," he said, apologetically.

"Snegurochka?" she repeated, astonished that he had remembered that. "I have a little surprise for you." She then pulled out from her purse a small, gift-wrapped box and gave it to him.

"I'll open it in the room if you don't mind," he said and gently kissed her on the cheek.

The champagne and blinis were already there in the room when they entered. She had been right. The views of St. Petersburg from the top floor of the hotel were spectacular. Their room was small, but it was elegantly furnished with the finest mahogany woods and had parquet floors. They sat by the butler's table, and he uncorked the champagne while she prepared the blinis with caviar.

"This is authentic crème fraiche for the blinis," she said. "And the caviar is the classic Beluga. What more can we ask for?"

"Yes. And I've noticed that the champagne is a lovely bottle of Dom Perignon!" He filled the two stems and gave her one, and she gave him a blini topped with a dollop of crème fraiche and caviar. They ate first the blinis and then sipped the champagne. She then kissed him gently on his lips. The gift that had been carefully wrapped in colorful tissue paper was an extremely beautiful Matryoshka nesting doll.

"That was hand-painted in Sergiev Posad," she told him. "Sergiev Posad was the place where the first nesting doll was made in Russia. In 1340, the monk Sergius founded a small temple in the midst of a thick forest about forty-five miles outside of Moscow. In time, it was developed into the biggest monastery of Russia."

"It is really beautiful," he said and really meant it. "It is an amazing gift. You are such an angel!"

"When I was a young girl an old woman once explained to me her interpretation of the meaning behind the Matryoshka dolls. When the Matryoshka is totally opened and you finally arrive at the last one, you notice the unmistakable link of that one to the initial Mother precursor, so that the last one is clearly a descendant of the original and is traceable as would be in a family tree. This Matryoshka nesting doll in its totality, according to the explanation as I understood it, is the symbol of the Russian woman's soul. Matryoshka, she said, represents to us the unending process of discovery in the beauty of Russian women. The mechanics of a Russian woman's beauty lies in her ability to understand as she grows. This becomes evident when you see her moving through the different stages in life, cherishing every moment of her life experiences. Someone once concluded that there are brilliant adaptive mechanisms that provide us with stability, always returning us to our previous position no matter how topsy-turvy our lives become. To understand this is to understand the wholeness of the unity that binds us through family, culture, religion, and folk traditions."

"Snegurochka," he teased again. "You are a remarkable woman. Thank you for the lovely gift!"

This man had given her an unbelievable gift of fifty-thousand dollars for no better reason than that he valued her company. He was now listening to her story about the complicated onion layers that defined the Russian woman. But this man was more complicated than any Russian woman that she had ever met. She sat on his lap and kissed him, and kissed him again because of what he had done for her. This man was the ticket to a better life.

The American felt helpless, hopeless. He was being transported by her kisses to a place where there was no reason, like the Fairy transported her captive in Stravinsky's masterpiece. He was dumbfounded, enraptured, defenseless, and overpowered by her supernatural power over him. Her warm passionate kisses had him on his knees. He was now totally submissive to her, and all that he could think about was how much he wanted to please her. Then he began ceaselessly laughing, and she laughed too.

Inside the Matryoshka doll, there was a lovely little girl that had been taken by the state, and the state had turned her into a weapon.

· · ·

"QUAE ERAT OMNINO FRUENDUM," HE SAID, AND laughed again, probably because he knew that what he had just said in Latin sounded rather awkward. "Or maybe it's esset penitus consumantur." She was to be enjoyed entirely, he said, and laughed and laughed again, uncontrollably. He believed in fairy tales, and Mo Yan was dead.

That night, there was skillful lovemaking on her part, and he worked hard to give her as much pleasure as he received, because he really needed to do it, to please her as much as possible. The scenes couldn't have been steamier, nothing had been held back. Their lovemaking had left them totally exhausted, totally drained of all energy. They even fell asleep locked in each other's arms. Tomorrow they could try to sort themselves out.

Made in the USA
Middletown, DE
28 December 2021

57199914R00279